AF010571

Ixora Mara,
SOURHOUSE

Ixora Mara, SOURHOUSE

Abigail Persaud Cheddie

HANSIB

First published in 2024 by Hansib Publications
76 High Street, Hertford, SG14 3TA, United Kingdom

info@hansibpublications.com
www.hansibpublications.com

Copyright © Abigail Persaud Cheddie, 2024

Abigail Persaud Cheddie asserts the moral right to be identified as the author of this work.

Front cover illustration, *Suzie's House*, by D. Persaud

ISBN 978-1-0686993-0-6
ISBN 978-1-0686993-1-3 (Kindle)
ISBN 978-1-0686993-2-0 (ePub)

A CIP catalogue record for this book is available from the British Library

This is a work of fiction. Unless otherwise indicated, all the names, characters, organisations, places, events and incidents in this book are either the product of the author's imagination or used in a fictitious manner. Any resemblance to actual persons, living or dead, or actual events, is purely coincidental.

All rights reserved. No part of this publication may be reproduced, stored in a retrieval system, or transmitted, in any form or by any means, electronic, mechanical, photocopying, recording or otherwise, without the prior permission of the author.

Produced and printed in Great Britain

Founded in London in 1970, Hansib Publications has played a crucial role in documenting the Caribbean experience and bringing Caribbean perspectives to a wider audience. It is renowned for its extensive catalogue of Caribbean fiction and non-fiction, spanning a diverse range of genres, including historical novels, biographies, poetry anthologies, political commentaries and social narratives. It has also made significant contributions to Caribbean scholarship by publishing insightful works on history, culture, politics and social issues.

Today, Hansib Publications remains a significant force in the world of Caribbean publishing and continues to publish books that reflect the vibrant diversity of the Caribbean region and the global Caribbean diaspora. Its legacy of promoting Caribbean voices and perspectives has made it an invaluable resource for those seeking to understand and appreciate the rich cultural heritage of the Caribbean.

For
Ma and Pa,
June, Nick, Sebo,
Pete, Fif,
Mir, Mel, Lil, Yel
and Val

Contents

1. What Suzie Said 9
2. You are Ixora Mara, Not an Egg 20
3. What's the Point of Being in Charge? 32
4. Inside Suzie's Empty House 46
5. The Long Arm of the Miaplambo 60
6. The Marvellous Mermaid 77
7. The Dunce 86
8. A Library is a Cocoon 96
9. Boot Heels on an Ant 106
10. After the Fight and the Fire 122
11. Fractures 133
12. Crisp White Collars 145
13. Proud Harro Harry and Sons – Tailors 152
14. The Missing Diamond 165
15. An Ounce of Justice 179
16. Electric Love 192
17. Ixora Mara, Heiress 205

18. Thou Shalt Not Swap Thy Shoes	217
19. Bougainvillea spectabilis	231
20. Song of the Metropolis	249
21. In the Empty House Again	258
22. Tell Me Telmond, Should I Go?	271
23. A Hundred Empty Houses	283
24. The Ghosts of the Empty Houses	293
25. The Neighbourhood Hero	305
26. Suzie	312
27. Cousin Kim Kisses Local Soil	325
28. The Disappearance of the BN Trislander and Samuel A. Reid, Jr.	333
29. Boarding the Boeing 737	341
30. Bloom	346

1

What Suzie Said

I didn't want to be the sour one. But Ivy said that every village must have its own picklepuss and that I was Peaside Pasture's because I was better at being sour than anyone else in the village, especially now that old Mr Crapaud – Peaside's former Resident Sourpuss – had gone away on a plane. It was a role which some other child might have relished, if only for the exaggerated games such a part would allow. Not I. If Ivy thought I was going to fill the vacancy, she was wrong. I was going to be like Peaside's snazziest soaring star point kite, not some old lime. She'd see. Everybody in the street would see. Everyone in Peaside Primary would see. Everyone in the country and in the whole world, would see.

But, the lime had already come to me.

The first time it appeared in my body was when Suzie said she'd come to my birthday party but didn't. That day, the lime burned into my stomach. Then it spun and split, shooting juice through my chest and oesophagus and up into my sinuses.

After that, Peaside's vendors swivelled their heads from me to Ivy and back to me, pointed at me and asked Mam,

"How come dat one so sour?" They made such a regular joke of it that Mam started telling them to mind their own sour business, please and thank you.

"How you mean they own business sour?" Ivy asked one day.

We were in the kitchen emptying baskets, my hands itching from the eddo the vendor had chopped in half and begrudgingly added to the scale to top out the three pounds.

"'Cause everybody sour 'bout something," Mam said, "Don't let dem fool you. Sour in they heart. Or in they brains. Or sour down to they lil toe."

I let an eddo roll back into the basket and looked at Mam's little toe. I wondered if her nails would glow neon green if *her* sour ever reached her toes. If your lime juice pulsed through your whole body so that it reached your toes, I surmised, that would be the end of you. For then, all you'd ever be was a big old lime, a Resident Sourpuss. So I resolved to keep my sour thereabouts my stomach and above.

"Oi, pass dat eddo," Ivy said, elbowing me.

I passed the eddo. Ivy handed it to Mam. Mam stacked it in a bowl on top of the rest and continued her tirade.

"You got to be dead not to have something to be sour about," she said, "And even then you gon probably still be sour 'cause maybe Saint Peter not lettin' you in."

"Letting you in where?" asked Ivy.

"Laurie, what you telling the girls?" said Pap, grinning and getting into the conversation, and ponging the hammer on his thumb. "Ow, ow," he said, flicking his hand back and forth.

I watched Pap's fingernail and imagined its burning pain. I imagined it must feel just like the prickles in my chest when the lime juice started spreading about in my body. The day Suzie said she would come but didn't.

Ixora Mara, Sourhouse

* * *

"Any four or five ah dem could come," Mam said the week before our birthday. "You," she pointed at Ivy, "could bring four or five friends, and you," she pointed at me "could bring four or five."

So Ivy invited eight friends. Eight.

Who cares, I thought, there was only Suzie to be invited. So I snatched my skipping rope, skipped barefoot across the street to Suzie's house, told her about my party, asked would she come please and she said yes thanks she'd come.

"I gon bring you a gift," she said from her side of the gate.

I was swinging the rope round and round, and the balls of my bare feet bounced on Suzie's smooth scrubbed bridge. "True?"

"True," she said.

I stopped skipping and tootled over to the gate. Suzie smelled like lemony cream biscuits.

"What's the gift?" I asked, my heart starting up a racket.

She drew closer to the gap between the two paling staves and raised her forefinger to her lips. "Shh. Gifts supposed to be secret. Mammy gon carry me shop so I could pick it out and wrap it up."

"Oh," I said, feigning just the right amount of nonchalance and smoothing out the skipping rope. "Well, awright then," I said, "Eleven o'clock, you hear? Remember to don't forget."

I started hopping again, thinking about Suzie wrapping shiny paper over something.

"I not gon forget." She crossed her heart.

"Mam said come in time for lunch."

Food was a burden to Suzie. So in haste, I added "And ice cream."

"Yellow one?" she asked, sticking her nose between the staves. I nodded vigorously.

She grinned, and the setting sunlight bounced off the red crystal heart-shaped pendant swaying about the neckline of her sunflower print t-shirt.

I turned around and skipped home.

From Suzie's side of the street, I studied our long low veranda which Pap would soon decorate with the streamers he was hiding in the brown paper bag behind the yam crate. He'd gone to Georgetown and returned with a bag of things that he sprawled on the kitchen table to show Mam. Ivy and I took turns spying at the things through the crack in our bedroom wall. When we rested our eyes close to the wall and stayed steady at the precise angle, we could catch glimpses of the kitchen table. Eventually, we pooled what we'd seen. Pap had bought party games and red and yellow paper streamers, green paper plates, blue paper cups and a multi-coloured glittery banner that said Happy Birthday.

He didn't know about colour schemes then, Pap. Besides, it was the early nineties in Peaside Pasture. Nobody bothered about colour schemes. Everyone knows about them now though, colour schemes and décor themes, what with all the tasteful sophisticated ones hammered all over the internet – spring palettes, fall visions, winter wonderlands and whatnot. But I've had over twenty birthdays since then and Pap still goes on making the house shamelessly kaleidoscopic every birthday's eve. Even though he has an iPad now that Ivy's brought him from abroad and even though he knows better because he can just type things into a search bar and get all the answers.

Yes, Pap would decorate the whole veranda, I thought, while I skipped on our bridge and counted my rope rotations. I was almost up to a hundred rotations.

I looked back to see if Suzie was still peering through the staves but she had vanished. When she arrives on my bridge on my birthday, I thought, she'll gasp at the streamers tacked around the veranda.

I spun the rope faster over my head. Eighty-seven, eighty-eight, eighty-nine, I counted.

I imagined pinning the cloth tail, which Ganee Gwenny had stitched with dress scraps, to the pink disproportionate donkey which Pappo Harro had drawn in chalk on the ply board by the gate. We'd pin the tail. We'd sip fizzy drinks. We'd play chequers and Suzie'd be mesmerised by the yellow marbles as always.

My feet tangled in the rope. Just when I was up to ninety-seven rotations too. I sucked my teeth, flung the rope over my head and started afresh. One, two ... six, seven.

Mam would light the seven candles on the cake, and Ivy and I would blow them out together and make separate wishes. Suzie would stand beside me and Ivy's eight friends beside her, while Uncle Warbin fiddled with his instant Polaroid camera that somebody from 'merica had left for him because they had two, and he'd say, "Smile big. Smile with teeth."

Again, I tripped over the rope.

Our city cousins Lennard and Annie-Lou would come and Uncle Raffie would be forced to dilly-dally, waiting to drive them home, and Mam would wrap a huge slice of cake for Uncle Raffie's wife who usually sent two presents when everyone else brought one, but who'd said oh goodness gracious that she was allergic to the countryside and the smell of cow dung. Never mind we had no cows.

I skipped faster and jumped higher, getting close to the hearty sky.

Mam would wrap parcels of cake too for Junior's mother and his grampappy, and fill her best bowls to the brim with curry and rice. Then she'd tie everything into a bundle and settle it on Junior's head while he held it steady with his elbows sticking out as he waddled down the back street where they had no electricity and where he could stub his toe on bricks and send the food pitching into a pothole, as had happened once or twice. Junior's mother might send us a gift too. Even Small Spokes, the toddler who lived down the street and who Mam babysat on the half days that his mother went to work, he too would come. After all, it was the babysitting money, the small change, which Mam saved for months that had bought all the party things.

Yes, all of that would happen when my birthday came.

I stopped swinging the rope, stood on tippy toes and filled my lungs with sky.

The sun had set and across the street, neighbours flicked the lights on in their houses. Suzie was already at her bedroom window flashing her torchlight, outlining a smiley face on the glass with the light beam. Hers was the only glass window in her house. She shaped a circle clockwise, then added two quick flashes for the eyes and a curve from left to right for the mouth. I hurried inside to borrow Pap's torch so I could reply with my own light-up smiley face.

"Come here lemme see if dis dress fit you," Mam called.

She had stuffed Ivy in a dress with frills and was wrestling with the zipper.

"Jus' now," I said, looking under the kitchen sink for Pap's torchlight.

"Come now."

"Mam, I jus' have to flash Suzie a —"

"Now."

She passed a dress over my head and yanked the zipper but it wouldn't go.

"Psst," Ivy said. "Oi psst. You look like a yard fowl with two skinny foot an' a small head an' a stuffy middle," she whispered so that Mam who had gone off to bring more dresses couldn't hear.

I sucked my teeth. "Is you's a yard fowl," I said, looking to make a dash for the torch light again.

"Nope. You."

"You."

"You."

I made a beeline for the kitchen sink, grabbed the torch, ran to the veranda and drew my lighted smiley face on the wall. Then Suzie lit up her window again with another smiley face. Then I drew another. Then she again. Then I.

"Stop wastin' yuh father torch light batteries and come try on dis dress girl," Mam shouted into the veranda.

She tugged the pink polka dotted dressy church frocks down our shoulders.

"Oh thank the good Lord," she said when she saw that they fit just barely. "Thanks thee good Lord."

We stood shoulder to shoulder, Ivy and me, looking into the floor length mirror on the living room wall. The pink polka dots transformed us from the heavy umber of our school uniforms. The polka dots looked like the polished ladies in our story book called *Little Sally Hallie Goes to High Tea*. I lifted my chin, wondering if Mam or Ganee Gwenny had pink pearl necklaces like Sally Hallie's to lend us. Ivy went nearer to the mirror and held out the wide A-lined skirt and twirled.

"Stop twirling before you tear dat dress," Mam said, then she yanked the dresses off and went to set up the ironing board.

I followed her.

"Mam, you got any pink pearls?"

"For what?"

"Like a necklace."

"And where I gon get dat from?" She jabbed the iron at a stubborn collar.

"Your jewel box," I said.

Mam rolled her eyes and smashed some pleats flat.

But still, I wanted Suzie to see me in a pretty necklace. She had several. Like the silver one with the red heart pendant which she wore just to stand by her gate. In her necklaces she reigned like the head of fairy security, guarding the entrance to her universe across the purpleheart bridge. So before I went to bed, I sneaked up to Mam's vanity and lifted the large lid of her precious wooden jewellery box that Pap had made for her with his own hands. It was empty except for a little pale green butterfly pendant, a tiny emerald green turtle brooch and a pair of love knot gold earrings. No pink pearls. No other anything.

I crawled into bed and thought about how I could get some kind of a necklace.

And then, an idea floated to me through the window.

I would string ixora flowers together with a needle and thread just like Mam showed us one time, and I'd make Ivy and me a pair of floral necklaces.

For the next few days I strung flowers in different patterns until the garlands came together at the right arrangement.

And finally, when our birthday's eve rolled in, Pap hustled about. He raked grass. He followed Mam's instructions on how to set the jello but he almost did it wrong, so Mam clenched her jaw and set it herself. He arranged the mismatched chairs and stools. He livened up the streamers.

"Look here," he said, holding one end of a red streamer and one end of a yellow streamer and gluing them perpendicular to each other. "Looka dis." He folded the red strip down, then the yellow across. Then he folded the red up and the yellow across again, but the opposite way this time. Several times he repeated the criss-crossings. Down, across, then up, and across the other way. "Keep folding like so," he said, carefully handing over the finished bit to me. When I came to the ends of the strips, he glued them together. Then he gripped that glued end and gave me the beginning end of the entire folded strip.

"Now hold it and walk backwards," he said.

As I stepped back, the two streamers, now interlocking, expanded like an accordion stretching several feet between us.

"Whoa looka dat!" Ivy shrieked behind me where she was supposed to be helping Ganee Gwenny press down the ends of cheese rolls with a fork but where she was running her mouth off like a motor.

Every day she gabbered about the people she'd invited. Every single day, round and round like a rotating windmill. She jibber-jabbered about Anahita and Kathi and Lotte and Imani and Adalia and Basmati and Jia. And No-Jo too. But he was coming only because he was bringing his new bat and ball so we could have cricket. And because he, No-Jo, whose real name was Tainojo, was Junior's cousin and Junior had asked for No-Jo to come. Every, single, day, and night, like a windmill, the whole house obliged to hear about Anahita this, Kathi that, Lotte so and so, Imani's clever dog that was good enough for a circus, Adalia's kitten that bit strangers like a dog, Basmati's magnificent inherited bangles and Jia's unstoppable tricycle with the bell that rang like half a dozen bangles clink-a-dinking together.

"Ohh looka dat!" Ivy said again, tugging at Ganee and pointing at the streamer accordion.

Pap grinned and handed me several rolls of crepe paper. "Try then, accordionise these," he said.

By afternoon, my fingers were crampy and gluey. When the streamers were ready, Pap tacked them in bellied curves around the veranda's ceiling.

"Now blow these." He handed me and Ivy some balloons and showed us how.

It was not as easy as it looked. I had to thoroughly empty my lungs just for one balloon to live a lifespan. Sometimes I got lightheaded. Still, I forged ahead, for tomorrow would come and I would tell Suzie everything. How I had perfected the judgment in giving balloons the right amount of air. Too much would make the balloon either explode and sting your face, or prevent you from knotting it so that it flew out of your hand, kazooing and deflating. Too little would make it smaller than the one before, then they'd be mismatched and ruin the symmetry of things.

I was evaluating my most recent balloon when Suzie appeared at her glass window.

"Suzie!" I shouted across, "Look here." I waved one red and one yellow balloon.

She burst into grin and waved with both arms, and cupping her palms to her mouth, she shouted, "Yaay-hey," into the air.

"Yaay-hey Sue-zaay," I shouted back.

My feet tingled to skip across the street onto her purpleheart bridge so I could gift her a balloon and explain the important principles I'd discovered. But no, I thought, trying to shush the drumming in my chest. I'll save everything up for tomorrow and she could have two balloons then – one that I'd already blown and one to blow herself, so she could understand the technicality of the thing.

"Tomorrow?" I shouted across.

"Tomorrow," she sang into the universe.

That night Suzie's house went to bed early. All the lights went out and her flashlight faces failed to flicker. Maybe Suzie was sleeping early for my party. Mam had told us too to bed early if we wanted to have enough energy for tomorrow.

So on the night that I was six years and three hundred and sixty-four days old, Pap helped me roll down the mosquito net and waited for me to finish saying my prayers before he turned out the light.

"Nighto Ixie Pixie," he said.

"Nighto Pap-Pap." I pulled the sheet to my chin and waited to turn seven.

In the kitchen while Mam iced the cake, Madam Ivy's mouth was still windmilling.

2

You are Ixora Mara, Not an Egg

When the kitchen clock chimed five on my birthday morning, I rolled the bed covers into a ball and stood up to see if I had grown. Then holding my breath, I tiptoed in the dark to the bedroom window, eased the bolt up, minding its squeaking so as not to wake Ivy, gently pushed open half of the wooden window and looked for the outline of Suzie's very square house. I wondered when she'd rise and get dressed for my party.

Except for the cock-a-doodle-doos and the silhouette of two cane cutters hurrying along carrying lunch pails, the world lay still. So I pulled the window in, climbed back in bed and waited for my birthday. But I fell asleep again and awoke to the sizzling of sausages and eggs and Pap flinging open windows and singing, "Woo! Ixie Pixie! Ivy Jivey! Birdday time! Wake up! Ooodle-doodleey-ooo." He went out again and returned with Mam, the two of them bearing a shiny package the size of three yam crates.

I crawled over the bed, poking Ivy in the ribs as I went. "Iveey wake up, look."

Ivy wobbled over.

"Is what? Is what?" she croaked, tugging at the bow and peeling off the wrapping.

It was a house! A wooden house that Pap had built! The roof could lift off and the door and windows were large enough to stick our hands through and arrange the accessories.

"Happidy bwirday," Pap said and squished us to his tummy.

Mam set her arms akimbo and smiled.

"You can paint it any colours you like," said Pap.

"Looka dis," said Ivy, lifting and replacing the whole floor.

"Why it coming out like so?" I asked, peering at the second flooring underneath the detachable floor.

"So it could work like a trapdoor. Like in mystery stories, you know? You could call it a trapfloor," Pap explained. He seemed pleased with himself.

But I didn't know much about trapdoors or floors yet, about how they could lock things away, hide them, create the illusion that what you saw was the whole house.

"Alright," said Mam, drawing us away from the house, "come help me get out your breakfast. Y'all turn seven now, is time enough. I been making my own since I was four."

She handed Ivy a butter knife and bread and let me brew the tea while she finished decorating the cake, first drawing a seven, then beneath it, writing Ixora and Ivy.

"How come you always write Ixie first?" Ivy said, breaking off and eating an icing leaf.

Mam smacked her hand. "Jus' 'cus she born first. Stop dat."

"Naa-naa-na-boo-boo, Iii borrn firrst," I said.

"So?" Ivy said. She broke another leaf and crammed it in her mouth.

Mam smacked her hand again.

"So!" I said and dropped a wet teabag on her head.

"So?" Ivy said, and wearing the teabag like a crown, she put on a show with the green icing stuck to her teeth.

"Yuck. Close it!"

But she opened her mouth wider like Pollard. Pollard was Uncle Warbin's sakiwinki monkey. We used to feed him sour fig bananas and he used to jeer at us and sit on our shoulders while we strolled around the village so that children could come up and shake his hand, which he'd oblige if he was in the mood. But that was before he was stolen.

"Uck," I said. "You look like Pollard eating green peas."

"And you look like —"

"Shush," Mam snapped. "Since you old enough to argue, you old enough to bathe and dress yuhself. Gwan."

So we scrubbed and rinsed and shoved each other into the pink polka dot dresses and presented ourselves to Mam.

"Not bad," she said, sounding pleased for a change.

Then she grabbed the jumbo toothed comb and started yanking the knots out of Ivy's hair and while they tussled over the hair and Ivy alternated between "ouch" and "oww" until her hair was up in a puffy ballerina bun, I and my pink polka dots and frills sidled to the veranda.

It was drizzling.

What a harrowing thought, I thought — only I didn't actually use the word harrowing in my mind — I didn't know the word harrowing then, but I did conjure up the feeling of what harrowing meant — what a harrowing thought, to think that it might rain and everyone had to cram in the old kitchen and living room where Mam and Ganee Gwenny needed to get about to serve lunch. They might trip over us, and then the chowmein and cook-up rice would pitch about in the air and fly into our hair and board games. Harrowing. But no matter. Suzie and I could fit behind Pappo Harro's rocking chair and play the chequers there.

"It's drizzling Mam," I said, but only because I thought I should be magnanimous and warn everyone. Not because the rain had anything to do with me. I adjusted my dress frills.

"The rain might go 'way man. Come here." She started combing knots out of my hair.

"Ouuch."

"Girl, stop wriggling."

Pap appeared with an arrangement of ixora flowers and ivy leaves set in a crystal vase. "And now, presenting – Igzzora," he gestured towards the red flowers, "annd Ivee." He flourished his hands at the green cascading leaves, then paused. "Get it?" he said. "Ixxzoh –"

"Pap, we get it, we get it, we know," Ivy said before Pap could prolong his ritual theatrics.

I laughed and Pap rolled his eyes, shook his head at his philistine offspring and sailed off to display the vase near to the cake on the veranda. On his way back through the living room he carefully transported our ixora garlands that I'd rested on the birthday table. Mam loosened her grip on my hair so we could put them on. Ivy and I looked in the floor length mirror. We were just like Sally Hallie at high tea. We were two, and darker with fluffy hair, but definitely just like Sally Hallie.

I swirled the polka dots around me and admired my flower necklace.

Suddenly it struck me, Suzie would need one too, a flower necklace. I hadn't thought to make her one. My heart started up bouncing on the bridge of my chest. I didn't want Suzie to feel left out. I contemplated dashing outside and gathering more flowers. But I couldn't. People were almost here. Suzie was almost here. When could I ... tomorrow, tomorrow I'd make one for her, for sure. I'd tell her. I'd tell her, first thing, as soon as she came through the gate.

Mam took hold of my hair again while Ivy went to see who was shaking the gate.

"Come in," she said to someone out there, "Just push dat gate. Pussh. Oh, thanks. Look Mam, Junior bring we a gift. We could open it?"

"If you want."

"Lemme see," I said and wriggled from Mam's grip.

It was a five by four inch superbly thin colouring book with a packet of four crayons.

"Ooo, thanks Junior," I said.

Someone else rattled the rickety gate and Ivy started shouting again, "Oi, No-Jo push. No, push. Not pull! Noo man pusssh it I said!" She and Junior went down to help.

"What a dunce, boy," I said, "he dunno what's push and what's pull?"

"Don't lemme hear you callin' nobody dunce again," Mam said and shoved a hair pin into my precarious ballerina bun.

I was losing patience watching Mam in the mirror as she tussled with the gravity-defying bun. Junior had come. No-Jo was out there. Others were coming in. Suzie must be out there too. She must have brought me a new skipping rope under the shiny wrapping. The rope I had was fraying and one of the handles was broken and she knew that. Or maybe it was just socks. Most children's mothers sent socks. But that didn't matter. Socks were fine and functional, as Mam would say. Socks are fine and functional.

"Hurry Mam," I pleaded, as she added hairdressing cream until my head shone from forehead to crown. "Mam, hurry."

By lunch hour almost everyone had come. Even Uncle Raffie arrived on time with Lennard and Annie-Lou. Everyone scarfed down their lunch and hustled to the games. Junior and No-Jo managed the cricket. They had Small Spokes fielding the ball, running up and down like a puppy playing fetch. And Ivy and Anahita, Kathi, Lotte, Imani, Adalia, Basmati and Jia, whichever they were – it didn't always matter as they looked and ran about the same anyway — they carried on with their random games, screeching like parrots. But that was no business of mine. I stayed on the veranda while the parrots screeched below and I fixed my eyes up at Suzie's stairs.

She was being maddeningly slow today. Maddeningly, such a nice word, I thought. Maad-en-ing-ly. Maad-in-eng-lee. I'd heard a teacher on the top floor at school saying that word.

Lunch hour flowed by and Ganee Gwenny and Pappo Harro glided about with silver trays serving the jello and the quarter pint ice cream in rainbow bowls.

"Don't share away Suzie ice cream," I said, looking across the street. "Keep a yellow one for her, or peach."

I went and leaned by our open gate. The broiling sun burned down on my ballerina bun and through my pink polka dots. But the drizzle was starting up again.

Pap had arranged a tug-o-war and both teams were shrieking.

"Oh ho ho, haa ha hoo," one of the little parrots laughed.

"Ixie! Ixie! Get in! Get in now!" Junior called. "Pull! Hold on! Pull! Kick off yuh shoes and pull-aaah!!!"

I got in and pulled my hardest. The other team dragged us forward. But we pulled back hard. Forward and backward I went until I lost sensation of whether I was pulling or being pulled. Finally, we lost.

"I told you get in and pull!" Junior said. Sweat shone and dripped all over his forehead and nose.

"I did get in and pull! You didn't see?" I said. "I *was* pulling!"

He ignored me.

"Well if Suzie did reach, we woulda win," I told him. "Is not my fault."

He walked away towards No-Jo and Small Spokes and picked up the cricket bat again.

I sucked my teeth. "Well when Suzie come we could pull again and see if we win," I said to his receding back.

The rain was coming down a little more now.

I watched the rain and folded my arms and braced against the gate. A lime green minibus appeared and ambled along in the potholes.

It stopped in front of Suzie's house and stayed there a while.

Suzie has visitors, I thought, as somebody handed me the donkey's tail, tied a blindfold across my eyes, spun me around twice and hollered 'Pin!'

I pinned. Laughter roared. I lifted the blindfold and saw the pink donkey's forehead wearing the tail and one of Ivy's friends holding her stomach and laughing so hard that no sound came out her mouth.

"Donkey forehead, donkey forehead," the others chanted at me.

I handed over the blindfold, begrudged them the smile they expected and went to the gate again.

A man came out of Suzie's house. He carried two blue-green bags. He loaded them in the back of his bus. He went indoors again and emerged with two more blue-green bags. Suzie's mother appeared carrying another blue-green bag. She was wearing dark glasses. She had never worn dark glasses before. Besides, it was cloudy now so she didn't need the dark glasses. And she was wearing boots that came high up above her ankles. Like long rain boots but fancy, with big silver buckles. She had stuck her pants in the boots. She was holding Suzie's hand and Suzie had a yellow pony-shaped purse slung from her right shoulder to her left hip. Suzie's mother opened an umbrella, sheltered Suzie from the drizzle and they walked to the bus. Suzie got in and sat in the back. Her five gravity-defying braided knots with colourful bubbles bobbed above the back seat. I walked out on to our bridge. Suzie's father came out wheeling two suitcases and the first man hoisted the suitcases into the back of the bus. Then the man went inside and wheeled out two more suitcases. Finally Suzie's father appeared with one more suitcase, latched the gate, hauled the suitcase and himself in the bus and pulled the bus door shut.

I stepped into the street. I was still barefoot from the tug of war and now that the drizzle was coming down harder the dust started sticking to my feet.

The minibus drove to the end of the street and turned around. It ambled through the potholes slower than the pace it had come and passed my house.

The back of Suzie's head grew smaller and blurrier and the rain came down some more.

I studied the raindrops. They plummeted into puddles and grew into slow wide circles like hope. Then the drops multiplied, the circles rippling faster and smaller in breathless anticipation, until the puddles bore infinite ripples swimming far away inside of them.

When the bus was gone for good, I tried to dust my toes off on each other.

Someone ran out, hugged my right shoulder and steered me inside.

The pink polka dot dress was cold on my back and dripping everywhere. I kept dusting my feet off, one on top the other and Pap kept hugging my shoulder.

"Laura," Pap called into the house.

A peal of thunder came and the little parrots squawked and flew around the veranda. "Donkey belly, donkey belly," they screamed at some unfortunate soul.

"Laurie," Pap raised his voice. He pressed my wet bun a little to squeeze the rain out. "Lauro," he shouted.

Finally, Mam came out.

The rain pelted about on the aluminium roof so it was hard to hear what anyone said.

"What happen?" she asked, eyeballing the wet polka dots sticking to my body and the mud I was trying to dust off my feet. "What happen?" she asked again.

Pap cleared his throat.

"Let's go wash these feet eh Ixie Pixie," he said and hoisted me up so robustly that my ixora necklace caught on the empty silver platter he was carrying, and burst.

Over Pap's shoulder, I saw the parrots watching me being hoisted away.

"Mai," Pap stopped in the doorway and called for Ganee Gwenny. "Mai!"

Ganee came out wiping her hands on a towel.

"Let's help Ixie wash these feet eh," said Pap.

"What happen to the little feet? Come."

She led me to the living room and soaked and soaped and rinsed my feet as Mam and Pap's voices in the veranda rose and fell in muted tones. Then she dried my feet with a fluffy pink towel that had a cat embroidered on it. I studied the cat's triangular ears and wondered why humans didn't have triangular ears too.

"Now where these little feet been about walkin'?" Ganee asked.

I didn't answer.

She pulled the dripping pink polka dot dress over my soggy ballerina bun. Then she released the hundred hair pins from my head, let the bun down, parted my hair in the middle and sapped the two clumps. After that day, no matter how much I tried to train my hair any other way, it returned to the middle split.

While Ganee disappeared in search of clothes, I drew close to the floor length mirror and studied the girl in her bare skin, with her hair crying on the floorboards. She was not Sally Hallie at high tea.

Then the first tear came. Then the second and dozens more.

Ganee returned with a t-shirt and denim pants. She saw me sobbing at my reflection and dropped the clothes. With some difficulty, she lifted me to her stomach, patted my back and walked up and down the room saying "Shh, shh, shh, done, done, done," which made me cry more.

"Wat she cryin' about dat for?" Pappo Harro came in and said. Someone outside must have told him what had happened.

"Let her cry," snapped Ganee.

"Wat we raising really? Eggs? That crack and cry for every lil ting?"

"You see any egg here?"

Pappo Harro left the room.

Ganee dressed me in the t-shirt and pants. I looked at her in the mirror trying to pat flat the angry little curls springing out from around my forehead now that they'd gotten wet. Then she stooped with some effort and looked me in the eye. With my eyes, I traced the round rims of her spectacles.

"Never mind Pappo," she said, as if she owned the knowledge of who to mind and who not to mind, "You are Ixora Mara, not an egg." Then raising herself up with some quiet grunting she added briskly, "Gwan, they waitin' fuh you stick the cake."

I went to the veranda and watched Ivy and her leagues still screeching and flying. The rain had stopped.

Across the street, Suzie's square house stayed still and empty.

After the candles were blown, someone served cake. They sat me on the long low veranda floor among Anahita and Kathi and the whole screeching flock. We braced against the veranda wall and faced Suzie's house. I ate a spoonful of the cool green icing atop the pink sponge cake and kept my eyes on Suzie's house. And as a restless stillness fell upon the house that damp afternoon, the cool icing in my stomach started churning in a burning rotation, a sensation like a spin-bowled lime settling in, and spinning in one spot. The spinning intensified until the lime split in two and began squeezing its juice up into my chest, into my lungs and throat and spreading up into my mouth, behind my nose, in my ear canals, towards my temples and finally into my brain.

I shook my head a little to try and get the sour out of my brain but it wouldn't go. I tilted my head first to the left, then to the right to see if the sourness would leak out my ears, but it didn't. I wrinkled my nose and jammed my palm flat against it and rubbed hard up and down. That didn't work either. Junior and a few of Ivy's friends were staring at me, so I decided I'd try again later. The other children were watching Pap take down and distribute the balloons and streamers over which I'd spent the last hours of my sixth year labouring.

No-Jo and Junior popped their balloons with the sharp tipped pencils generously provided by their ringleader Miss Ivy. The girls decked Ivy with my crepe paper chains and curtseyed before her. "Yes your highness," they giggled, "Right away your highness. Here's your tea your highness." Small Spokes' mother came for him and he left with his brown paper bag of cake and sweets and his balloons tied around his waist because he was too small to hold everything. Uncle Raffie said he had a meeting and he hustled Lennard and Annie-Lou into the car.

"Bye," they said, walking out like sloths and looking back at the other children.

Someone had set up the marbles for the chequers but nobody had played with them. I put the marbles back in the box, yellow ones first. Then I dusted my feet, sole on top of instep, instep beneath sole, and retired to my bedroom. I pulled up the trapfloor of our doll's house and rested the chequers board and the marbles there for Suzie when she came back.

Then I looked out the window.

The sun was setting on Suzie's glass window. Her house seemed larger now. Wide. High. I studied it until the house loomed larger still in shadows. Night fell and hundreds of stars came out but I fixed my mind on the house. I meditated like an ant on a blade of grass, a blade bending, bending towards Suzie's house, that shadowy square universe.

3

What's the Point of Being in Charge?

Ivy and Junior paid me no mind whenever Mam deputised me. They heard people in Peaside Pasture saying that I was a sourpuss, so they parroted this and proclaimed me a no-fun scowl-face. That was the manner of things in Peaside. Once an idea got going, it could become a monster under your trapfloor or your bed, inside your photo frames, above your house, beside your head.

Junior, for one, was always up in trees ignoring me, doing gymnastics and getting a bird's eye view of things.

"Junior, get down," I demanded, and Small Spokes echoed, "Juniyorrr giddung."

Small Spokes was the only one in all of Peaside who did pay me any mind. He lived with his anxiety-ridden mother – or so Mam described her, and his hunched back grandmother. When his mother went to work, Spokes got passed around from hand to hand and yard to yard, until one day when everybody and nobody was watching him, he fell into a trench and nearly drowned. Someone said a fisherman scooped Spokes out of the trench, set him on the street and went about his business while Spokes walked around sunning himself out and humming a song about a baby whale in the sea. After that, Spokes' mother said that trusting anyone in Peaside to do anything with regularity was like trusting the weather, so she started paying Mam a small change to properly babysit Spokes.

On the days Mam was babysitting, Spokes wanted to come outside and watch us play and Mam would allow him, but she warned me to keep him beside me.

"Don't let him outta your sight," she said. She stabbed the air with her finger and pointed at Spokes when she said 'him' and pointed at me when she said 'your.'

"Yes Mam."

"Don't let him near the trench."

"Yes Mam."

"And you in charge today."

Tough chance getting Ivy and Junior to listen, I thought, as I stood under the tree shouting up at Junior. Small Spokes' little toddler eyes gleamed at Junior swinging about up there.

"Junior, I talking to you," I shouted again.

Junior gripped a branch of his mango tree and swung hard reaching for the other nearby tree. But he wasn't Tarzan and I'd just begun to imagine the trouble I'd be in if he broke his spine today when he swung right back like a pendulum and hung on for his life.

He grunted, "Oh-lala-lala."

Small Spokes giggled. "La la," he said, running to Junior's tree trunk and hooking one foot around it.

"No, no, no, Spokes," I said.

He came back, stood beside me and started singing, "Ponnng ponng pong."

Next door at our new house, Pap was hammering something.

"Junior! You not a bird! Get down now!"

"Juniiyorr, giddung neeow," said my echo.

But Junior stayed up. Didn't come down till the sun set.

When he was not in trees, or falling out of them, Junior, Ivy and I either played next door at our new quarter-finished house while Pap and Uncle Warbin sawed and planed and ponged. Or we stayed in our yard and pushed each other on the tyre swing tied onto the mango tree. Often, we ran the length of the land from the front gate to the back paling staves, pretending to run long-distance in the Olympics, our own version which Ivy and Junior called The Limepicks, a name which made my ears tickle.

Junior usually won The Limepicks and when he came first, he hopped on the rock by the cherry tree and waited for his invisible gold medal. Whoever finished last — usually me — had to stand on tippy toes and hold out the medal while he tilted his shoulders to claim it. Then he waved left and right and bowed and bowed and pumped his fists in the air while Ivy applauded and whoo-hooed.

What a couple of empty barrels, I'd think, while my cheeks prickled.

It was a burning shame to be left behind, running the fastest fast I could, pushing my eager torso, willing my fighting feet, flying until I felt my heart would burst through my ears, knowing that I'd still come last. So I'd go and stand beside Pappo Harro and he'd give me some of his mauby to sip. As the mauby stung my throat, I'd think about how long Suzie was taking to come home and how if she were here, I wouldn't be stuck earning last place in these stupid sweaty Limepicks with those two unbearable garden gnomes.

"Come Ix," Pappo said one day, when I'd lost five races at The Limepicks and was trailing behind him trying hard to get the prickling off my face. "Open yuh palms out so," he said and handed me a robust plant with leaves as broad as my palms. "Plant it," he said, digging a hole.

"Like so?" I asked.

"Cover dem roots."

Ixora Mara, Sourhouse

I knelt and I rooted my plant.

"Good, now gwan an' bring de watering can," he said, helping me pat the earth.

I dusted the grit from my knees and went to the trench. But the can was so heavy that I had to half-empty it again before I could budge it off the ground.

"Good, good, dat do," Pappo said, as I made it rain down on my plant.

Next day, there were two watering cans side by side on Pappo's tool bench.

"Pappo, these for me and Ivy?"

"Mmm," he grunted, "Gwan an' water yuh plant now."

So every morning before school I watered my plant and by the end of the school term it had a bud, and on the morning of the last day of the school term, an ixora-red hibiscus bloomed. I showed Junior. After that, he came every day during the Easter holidays, to see the watering of the hibiscus. If he was late, I waited for him. One day I let him water it and when for once he minded me and took the job solemnly, I thought of him as Junior, confederate, hibiscus tree waterer, friend forever.

But the chances of having a friend forever are less than winning the lottery or inventing something or understanding quantum physics.

One day, Junior and Ivy knocked down some gooseberries with a stick and I gathered them up in the skirt of my dress and rinsed them with water from Pappo's rain water barrel. Then we dipped the gooseberries in salt and sat around eating. I was just trying to decide if the salt was amplifying or muting the sourness of the gooseberries when Small Spokes appeared by the backdoor and Mam signalled me to watch him.

"This salt need some pepper," Ivy said.

Then she sneaked into the kitchen through the back door, pocketed some wiri wiri peppers and a knife, and returned with the knife point sticking out of her pocket.

I sighed. Here I was in charge today again and they weren't going to mind anything I said. It couldn't end well.

"Leh we just ask Mam to cut half a pepper for us," I said. Then exercising my authority, I raised my voice, "Go put dat knife back. Mam gon vex."

"Look, when I cut dis pepper, you mix it with the salt," Ivy said, taking six large peppers from her pocket.

"Ivy, dat's too much."

"When I cut, you mix," she ignored me and said to Junior. She pressed the knife point down on a fat red pepper.

"Put the rest back then," I said.

She sucked her teeth.

"Well I going and tell Mam."

"Yes, no-guts Sour Patch you go," said she, cutting more pepper and mixing it into the salt.

Small Spokes was watching us and coming closer to the bowl with the peppered salt.

"Don't put more then," I said, trying to snatch the last two peppers from her.

But she held them in the air and bolted. I lurched at her sleeve and missed. I looked around for Small Spokes, and satisfied that he was a far distance from the trench and away from the knife, I chased after Ivy.

"Junior, help me get dem peppers," I cried.

But Junior, confederate, hibiscus waterer, friend forever, daily winner of The Limepicks, would not budge, would not open his mouth.

"Gimme," I said and grabbed Ivy by the shirt but she tiptoed and wiggled, ran and twisted.

"Just give it and I won't tell," I shouted. "Junior! Junior, come help me."

I lunged at Ivy and missed again. She laughed and sped towards the back fence. I too sped up my legs but what's the use of a basset hound chasing a greyhound? Still, I nearly caught up with her but I tripped on something, might have been my own feet I don't know, and I fell. And there I was on the ground when I saw it.

Small Spokes. Dipping his dirty little fingers in the peppered salt.

"Small Spokes! You stop that!" I dashed to him.

He chewed a full mouthful.

"Stop that. Spit it out. It gon burn you. You gon choke. Spit it! Spit it out now! Spokes! I said spit!"

But apparently Spokes thought that spit meant swallow, so he, brilliant tyke, swallowed all the peppered salt he had crammed into his mouth.

He paused and looked up at me. Five, ten seconds went. Then he let out a howl fit to rattle the coconuts down from their trees.

"Bring him some water quick!" I shouted, running towards the back door to bring it myself. "Bring him! Bring him here!" I shouted over my shoulders.

I fumbled around for an enamel cup, poured some water, wetting the floor and ran out again.

Spokes was still standing under the whitey tree howling while the two garden gnomes watched.

The closer I got with the cup the louder he bawled. Everything was dripping. His nose. His mouth. His eyes dripped. His fists were clenched. How he bawled. How he turned red. I'd never seen a red child before.

"Drink dis. Drink it Spokes! Drink it quick. It gon stop the burning," I said, telling the tot lies. He'd have to drink and gargle a whole gallon of water before the burning stopped. He wouldn't drink it. He kept bawling, bawling into the stratosphere.

By now Mam was flying out the back door and running towards Spokes.

"What happen?"

"Spokes ate a whole set salt and pepper," I said.

"Arite arite," Mam said and scooped up Spokes and soothed him. She yanked the enamel cup from me and walked to the house with Spokes still crying and choking and struggling to breathe. Before she disappeared, I saw she'd coaxed Spokes to sip the water.

I didn't follow Mam and Spokes indoors. My feet wouldn't budge. And the more time passed, the less my feet cooperated. Half an hour went. I watched the back door and worried.

Finally, Mam pushed the door and beckoned.

Junior, confederate, friend, brave boy, bless his heart, chucked his rubber slippers on and disappeared through the front gate and down the back street.

I watched his receding back and thought, I'm never going to talk to you again, Junior. Not in twenty-thousand-million years.

"I didn't do it Mam," I said, as soon as I got in the house. "Mam is Ivy, she —"

"Didn't I tell *you* to watch him?"

"Yes but she —"

"And were you watching him when he ate all dat salt and pepper?"

"No 'cus Ivy —"

"Y'all tink watching people children is some kinda joke?"

"No Mam, I was watching him all the time. Is Ivy br —"

"Both of you siddong at dat table and get your story together by the time I get back."

She went to the living room to look in on Spokes napping beside Ganee. Ivy looked at me, pulled out a chair and sat seemingly unperturbed. An urge swept over me to kick the chair from under her but that would only get me into more trouble. Mam returned and delivered her lecture on responsibility and sensibleness. When she was done, the first quiet tear came and then dozens more. Tears. Clouding up my eyeballs. Stuffing up my nose. Blocking up my head. So I went to bed.

Ivy returned outdoors to ride our bicycle.

She was still cycling out there when Pap came home from work.

Our bed was under the window and I heard their muffled voices.

Pap was laughing and saying, "Arite there Ivy Jivey, take it easy" and she was windmilling her mouth away, without conscience for her deeds.

I sat up on my knees and raised my head above the window sill just enough to see out.

Pap had a kite frame and a plastic bag. From the bag he revealed kite paper of severely bright colours.

"Where Ixie?" he asked.

"Inside."

"Call her."

I tumbled back into bed and pulled the cover over my head.

"Ixie. Pap say come outside. He bring a kite," said Ivy.

I didn't budge and she poked me.

"Come out," she said and went out and told Pap something.

Then his feet were coming in. There were voices in the kitchen. Mam must be reporting my deeds, I thought. I moved to the crack in the wall to see if I could hear anything but all I saw was the kitchen table with the chowki and the belna on it, which, when we visited them, Lennard and Annie-Lou's mother insisted that we call roti board and rolling pin. When she said that, Uncle Raffie would glance at the door and try to leave the room. When we told Ganee, Ganee said that Melanie had the right to call her utensils whatever she wanted and that *she*, Mrs Gwendoline Harry also had the right to call her utensils whatever she wanted.

Pap's feet came closer and I tumbled into bed again and pulled the sheet to my neck.

"Hey there Ixie Pixie."

I didn't reply.

"I got a surprise out there."

I looked at him but kept the sheet up to my neck. My eyes still felt heavy.

"Come then," he said and came around to the side of the bed, turned his back to me and stooped.

I was still a suitable size for piggy back rides but very soon I wouldn't be and I wasn't going to decline a good piggy back because of a pair of garden gnomes, so I climbed on and Pap ferried me out to the back yard.

"Look," he said, depositing me next to the kite frame.

I must not smile yet, I thought. I must keep the sour on. But my heart stirred. There never was anybody in the history of Peaside who at the sight of a kite didn't feel in the heart a stirring – a zephyr at first and then a sturdy breeze winnowing the sourness and lifting the spirit like a soaring snazzy star point kite, robustly free. Everybody's papa in Peaside made them a kite, except Junior's. His father said kite culture was pasture mentality from which anyone with a brain or a chance should absquatulate. I didn't know what that meant but it didn't matter; he didn't know what he was talking about.

Pap walked to the backyard and Ivy followed. After a while, I followed too. I wasn't going to let her stick to Pap and see things that I didn't get to see. Pap stopped at a gamma cherry bush and picked some small green things that looked like marbles. Then he squished one to show us there was a paste inside and he rubbed the gamma on the kite frame and pasted yellow kite paper on top, carefully folding in and trimming the edges. Finally when the frame was covered he asked us which colours we wanted for the star pattern on top the yellow paper.

"Red," I mumbled, trying hard to get my mouth and voice to work.

"And green!" Ivy shouted.

"Take it easy Ivy Jivey, yuh deafin' me ears." Pap grinned.

When he was done, we had an odd many-coloured star and Pap was enjoying himself. He even cut a snowflake pattern and pasted it in the middle of the star. Then he made two flaps for ears and added a twine tail.

"Done," he said, pride coming out of his cheekbones.

Pap used to have high cheekbones but now they've shrunk. When Peaside people, up in her business, asked Mam why she married Pap and left the city to come live in Peaside, she used to mutter something about cheekbones.

"Fly it now," Ivy shouted.

"Let's see if we can wait 'till Easter Sunday," Pap proposed.

"'Cause why?" Ivy stamped.

Ganee came to the door and called us in for warm pine tarts, so I started towards the house. But Ivy, arms akimbo, neck tilted a long way up at Pap, negotiated and whined.

How Peaside couldn't see she was the sour one, I did not know. Always, she was Mary Mary quite contrary. Look, even now she hadn't respect for the warm pine tarts perishing on the platter. Only a real sourpuss would be like that.

That afternoon, Ganee Gwenny's tarts filled with the freshly boiled pineapple warmed my tongue and tummy.

With the kite outdoors and the pleasantly gooey tarts indoors, today's episode of Small Spokes choking, his tongue burning, his bawling, Mam's berating given at this same table here and my old heavy sobbing seemed a lifetime ago. I munched on a tart and traced the natural swirl of the wood pattern of the table top. This particular swirl always peeped out from under my plate when we sat down to meals and I'd grown accustomed to tracing it with my left pointer finger. When Ganee'd cover the table with pretty cloths at Easter and Christmas, a panicky sensation would rise in my stomach. But I'd imagine where the swirl was under the cloth and trace above it. Then my stomach would settle down again.

Here is where we sat for years, Ivy and I, in the kitchen at the small dining table that Pappo had made. In addition to this small dining table, there was the kitchen table beside it, where roti was rolled and vegetables diced, the table of which we could catch glimpses through the crack in the wall. Pappo had built a much larger dining table too but it was out in the backyard because it couldn't fit in the house. Pappo had said to Ganee, "What yuh gon put it outside for? The birds?" And Ganee'd said, "If yuh see anywhere in this mansion here to put it, just let me know." Then Pappo went outside for the rest of the afternoon and tinkered with the old tractor behind the tool shed.

So here at the small dining table, we'd sit, Ivy in the chair facing the old wooden window and out into the street and I on the opposite side, facing the wall on which hung the pot spoons below a faded painting. I'd bite into the flaky pastries and watch the painting of a bushy haired woman in silhouette sitting in front of a house, with a door that had a large orange knob. Beneath the scene in small squiggles the artist had written *Keeper of the House*, I.M.G. I'd see the writing when I climbed up to hang the pot spoons. The artist had two out of three of my initials and often I'd think about that. Sometimes I even saw the painting in my dreams. But blurry. Like moving salt water going backwards.

We flew the kite many times.

After church on Easter Sunday we scrambled for it.

"Come take off your good shoes first," Mam shouted, "and those good dresses."

But Pap was already holding up the kite and running with it and we were running behind him in our white shoes and white socks that folded over with curly lace at the ankles. And on Easter Monday too, Pap carried us and Junior to the pasture lands. He even brought a paper bag full of sandwiches, though Mam was upset about the state of said sandwiches because Pap had cut the cucumbers in cubes instead of circles and the cubes kept falling out.

"Ow Laurs," Pap said, "is still cucumber if it round or square."

All of Peaside's households were there flying kites. I saw then that our kite paper that seemed severely bright on the ground had just the right finesse in the air against the sky of other kites. I was still sour at Junior for abandoning me with the pepper trouble and I was still trying not to talk to him. But Junior hopped about, hoisting and defending, admiring and boasting about our little kite so much that it was hard not warm up to the old traitor again. When some boys came near with their big box kite tangling up our twine, Junior said they'd better scram because we were here first. And his swagger grew after the boys stepped a few paces to the left, though I suspect they did so because they spied Pap sitting under a tree eyeing the scene over his newspaper, not because of Junior's bravado. Besides, I thought, Junior hadn't really done anything terrible during the Small Spokes debacle. He simply hadn't said or done anything at all. So I let the sour go and when I did, Easter pulsed through my veins.

And it became easier to enjoy the symphony of kites.

If you ever heard a kite sing, then you've heard nothing until you hear dozens, hundreds of kites singing in unison. Singing back to each other. Singing with each other. For each other. Beside each other. Singing with the lowest notes and highest notes. Singing melody, singing harmony. A wide song of love in the sky. Sky love. "Wow!" Junior kept saying and cracking his neck up at the sky, as we scooped spoonfuls of watermelon and lay about on the grass among familiar strangers and their watermelons and their kites calling out to heaven.

That night I dreamt about a house that had two hundred kites for a ceiling, tree trunks for walls and floor strips of wooden grass on which we all lay looking up at the roofsky of kites, enclosed by the trees, humming together. When I awoke, I wrote the dream down. But I omitted the bit about the cloud-like monster coming and peering over the house.

Next day, Junior and Ivy and I flew the kite on our street. But there wasn't enough wind. Several times the kite came down and landed in the abandoned yard and Junior volunteered to pull apart the thick grass and two paling staves and squeeze into the yard to get it. After a while, Junior panting, pointed and asked if we wanted to squeeze through the fence with him this time, rescue the kite, cool down and have a look-about-see.

I didn't say anything. That was Suzie's yard.

"Come on," he whispered, pulling the two loose paling staves apart and gesturing for us to come through.

Ivy squeezed through and stood in the empty yard.

"Get in," Junior whispered to me, "Hurry up."

I hesitated and looked back at our new house wondering if Pap would see us. He was hammering something. Pong

pong pong. I glanced up at Suzie's glass window. I looked at Junior who was gallantly holding the paling staves open. I looked at the staves, the fence, Ivy on the other side in the neglected yard. I looked back at our new house and heard the ponging. And my heart started up its old racket in my rib cage, on the wooden bridge of my chest.

"Hurry up you snail, before Pap see we. You ain't got no guts?" Ivy whisper-shouted and ran towards the empty house.

"What if Pap ketch us?" I asked, knowing that neither of them was going to heed anything I said, even though I was in charge again that day.

"They gon ketch us if you stand up there asking if they gon ketch us," Ivy said, tapping her foot.

The ponging started again.

I wondered what Suzie's room looked like now. Surely, she'd have to clean it up sharp when she came back.

I spoke up, "Is not our house. We can't go inside."

"Look," said Junior, and pointed at the kite lying on the grass inside the fence, "is like it want us to go inside. Why you tink it keep flying in there?"

I put one foot through the staves.

Junior shoved me through and followed.

4

Inside Suzie's Empty House

As soon as I stepped into Suzie's yard – once her fairy queendom, a chill swirled around my right collar bone. Then it circled the back of my neck and rolled down my backbone. I hoped Junior who was behind me hadn't seen me shiver. No good would come of this venture, I thought. I trod slowly, pressing down the waist-high grass. Things could be lurking there in the grass, under the vines, behind the trees. It would be best not to linger. One never knows what one might find in empty places where one lingers.

"Get the kite quick and leh we go," I told Junior, and pointed to the kite under the sapodilla tree.

I studied the tree. Its bunchy branches resembled the hair of a giant in our book of fairy tales. Junior thought so too because he whisper-growled slowly into my neck, "Fee-fi-fo-fum, I'll grind your bones to –"

"Shut up Junior!" snapped Ivy, elbowing us out of the way. "Come leh we 'vestigate by the back yard," she said and disappeared round the corner of the house.

Junior followed.

"Leh we get the kite and go," I called after them, but as usual, I was talking to the wind.

I looked at the tree-giant and swallowed. If nobody was going to do what we came to do, I was going to do it and get out. So, with balled fists, I made a dash for the kite, snatched it by the tail and pelted to safety, the kite going thunk-a-thump, thunk-a-thump behind me.

But as I hustled to put one foot through the paling staves, I heard Ivy saying, "Boy is where pickle-face gone? Like she get lost in the grass?"

I let the stave fall back, feeling my face pickling-up indeed and imagining how eatables felt when people popped them into jars and heaped agonising amounts of salt and pepper on them. My ears tickled just to think about it.

"Who you calling pickle-face?" I said, sneaking up and giving her a pinch.

"Oww," she yelled and pushed me. I stumbled backwards, stepped on the kite's tail and it tore away, almost detaching from its head.

"Now look what you do," I said, looking to see how to get the tail on again.

She ignored me and flitted about among the fruit trees and the thickly layered vines. There were trees here just like in our yard – a star fruit tree, a guava tree, a golden apple tree. But these trees were not like ours. The leaves were mottled and a white mildew grew on some of the branches. Birds had pecked the guavas dry. The golden apples were a dying yellow and many had dropped to the ground. Ivy reached out to pick one.

"Don't eat it," I said.

"Why not?"

"Suppose it not good?"

"How you mean it not good?"

Suzie hadn't been there for a long time so I wondered if anything could be good.

"What if it rotten?" I asked.

"Ain't rotten, look, it just yellow." She held it up.

"Maybe it gon expire soon," I said and they both looked at me like I was a cretin. "Well maybe it toxic," I tried again, using a word I'd heard our head teacher use to describe our school toilets. I didn't know what I was saying. I was wary of something but I didn't know what.

Ivy sucked her teeth and raised the miserably ripe golden apple to her mouth.

"Pappo Harro tree got plenty nice one. Don't eat dat. It ain't gon taste good," I said, proud at last to sound a little more logical. "What if you get sick?"

She spat it out and pelted it far. I watched as the towering grass that ran along Suzie's back fence swallow up the bitten fruit.

"Leh we go upstairs and play inside," Junior said glancing around.

I looked up at the empty house. It was tall, taller than all the other houses in the street. It was the only two storey house on both sides of the street, except for our new house Pap was building. His hammer was still ponging. He only had to glance over and see us sneaking around Suzie's yard. Then he'd probably mention it to Mam. Then Mam would sit us at the kitchen table and roll out a lecture and it would be my fault again because fate had decreed I was in charge today.

"Yea, leh we go inside and see," Ivy said and she and Junior stamped down the grass blocking the path to the stairs.

I looked up at the house again. It looked down at me, frowning. I was a small ant in the grass looking up at it. My sweaty palms were dampening, almost tearing the kite paper so I clutched the kite to my chest, detaching tail and all, and turned to the loose paling staves.

"Come on scaredy weirdy," Ivy called and put her foot on the bottom step.

"No. That's the people house, we can't just go ins–"

"Shh," she said, "ain't nobody house."

"So if it right to go inside, then what you whispering for? What you —" But I was talking to the wind again. They had already tiptoe-sprinted up the stairs.

Still, for the first time, I thought about the possibility of seeing inside Suzie's house, the way she'd left it. Maybe I could find a clue as to where she'd gone and why and when she was coming back.

Junior tried the door, but it didn't budge. So he leaned over and rattled a wooden window that hung over the stairs. He shook and wiggled it until one side swung open. Then he climbed in effortlessly. Ivy, with some effort, managed to balance herself on the rail of the stairs, stretch, put her knee on the window sill and pitch herself over. She fell in with a thud. Junior giggled and snorted. Ivy sucked her teeth. They stood together on the inside looking out at me and waiting for me to come in. I told them I was sorry, that I wasn't going to fall in and break my face. I could see Ivy about to say something, probably about how I had no guts or how it might be good to break a sour face.

"Just open the door man," I said to shut her up. After a while, one grows tired of being sour and guts-less.

It appeared they hadn't thought of opening the door and were expecting me to climb through the window like some homeless village cat.

Finally, Junior opened the door.

The odour of locked up spaces hit me and my temples started throbbing. I held my breath, then let it out slowly and put one foot inside Suzie's empty house.

It had been a couple of years since Suzie left and since I'd been inside her house. Ivy and Junior had never been inside and they rushed around investigating.

I moved slowly around the open plan room, wondering if I should have left my rubber slippers at the door. They were making footprints in the dust on the peeling peach linoleum. I studied the chairs, the dining table, the aluminium oven like Mam's, the jumbo pot spoon like Ganee's ponged into the kitchen wall, the stand of ornaments with dirt in their crevices. There was a film of dust too on the wall but the paint was still shiny beneath. I could tell from where my palm prints had lifted off the dust.

Ivy and Junior went to explore one bedroom each but I went and sat on Suzie's sofa. It smelled worse than the curtains framing the three bedroom doors. It smelled of rats and bats, roaches and mould, stink bugs and abandonment. I held my breath, only breathing when I ran out of air, wondering if Suzie used to sit here and watch the black and white television.

I sat for a while watching the empty space where the television used to be and let my hand rest between the cushion and the back of the chair. Suddenly I felt something cold. I jumped. Then let out a slow hot breath and picked up the cold thing. It was Suzie's red crystal heart pendant dangling uncannily at the end of a silver chain. Alright, I thought, I'll watch over it for you Suzie, don't you worry. I'll watch over your heart with all my heart until you come back.

So I took the crystal heart and went into the room where I knew the glass window would be. Suzie's mattress was still on her bed. But there was no sheet. Cobwebs covered the things on her vanity. Cobwebs were on her broken pink watch with the Minnie Mouse on its face. Cobwebs were on her comb with her hair still on it. On her Johnson's baby powder. Her empty powder dish, lemon yellow. Her baby oil. Her shea butter for her hair. Her jewellery box with the ballerina on top. It was an exquisite box. I opened the top and looked in but it was empty except for some braided yarn friendship bracelets and a pair of the tiniest pink Barbie shoes. I pulled the cobweb off and wiped the vanity with the bottom of my shirt, which soon turned a gritty black. Mam would launch into a harangue about how I'd gotten this dirt on my white t-shirt. I had to try and remember to wash the shirt hem with some water from Pappo's barrel as soon as I got home. I wiped the ballerina. Then I put the red heart in the box and looked around the room and tried to imagine where Suzie was now. But all I could conjure was the image of Suzie standing in the middle of a new blank house with plain walls. I couldn't tell if she was lemony fresh or if she was smiling or eating ice cream. She didn't move. Didn't shrink, didn't grow, didn't know I was here in her room. She just stood on the blank.

I went to her glass window. It was dirty and I couldn't see through. I looked at my woeful shirt hem and considered whether I dared continue using it as a rag. Beneath the window stood Suzie's torch where she'd left it. I tried it but it wouldn't work. I screwed the bottom out and one of the batteries came tumbling out. The other batteries had corroded. I reached under the vanity to retrieve the battery and I felt some paper back there. It was an exercise book with crayon drawings of sunflowers and stars and two stick figures in triangles for skirts – one wearing a heart shaped pendant, the other carrying a skipping rope. I looked at the drawings for a long time, memorising them. Then I slid the empty top drawer of the vanity out and placed the book inside. The battery I returned to the torch, replaced the torch under the window and exerting some pressure on the window, I pushed it up until I could see out into the street. A gust of fresh air burst in and I stuck my nose out to breathe.

Across the street Pappo's fruit trees and flowers bloomed. I saw my own red hibiscus tree too, flaming up in the corner. Ganee was sitting on the stairs grating a coconut and Pappo was talking to her and gesturing with his arms in and out and they were laughing.

I memorised the view of the whole street, from the overgrown community garden plot at the very end, to Ole Lady Bargains's shack next to it, to our old low house with the long veranda, and then our new quarter-finished two storey house. From Suzie's vantage point, my side of the street from the community garden to Pappo and Ganee's house looked ancient and quiet, like a sad dog-eared postcard. And from our new unfinished house to the street corner looked like a turtle struggling to crawl off the end of the postcard. I didn't know that this is what Suzie saw when she looked at my side of the street.

Shame burned through my chest and I thought that maybe if Suzie didn't come back in a hurry it would be alright. She wouldn't have to see me live in the postcard house if she stayed away long enough for us to move over to our new house next door. So I started praying she'd take a little longer to come back and that Pap would hurry up building.

Ivy padded in and stood beside me and we looked through the window, saying nothing, until Junior's voice broke the silence.

We hustled to the room from which his voice was booming. There Junior was, majestic, standing on the cobwebby bed, his arms akimbo and chest puffed, wearing a black adult-sized shirt as a cape. The collar was turned up and around his head, he'd wound a smaller t-shirt, taking care to pull two points upward like animal ears.

Ivy choked with laughter and I sighed at the long script about to unravel.

Junior remaining stoic, improvised all kinds of lines. Then he went leaping off the bed and on again, round and around in a swoop, which after a while made it look like he was really flying.

"Batman can't fly you know," Ivy said.

"I *could* fly," Junior snapped, upset at his performance being critiqued.

"Fine," said Ivy, rummaging in the wood ant-smelling wardrobe and hauling on a moth-eaten blue shirt. "I be the guy you gotta fight then. You," she pointed at me, "stand-up here next to dis wardrobe and pretend yuh hands tie up behind yuh back, like so." She demonstrated.

I stood. My head was getting hot and my temples started to throb.

Ivy put her arms akimbo and said to Junior, "See here Bat-ears, you can't save the old lady now. Quicksand be eating her. Ixie, you have to do like you going under. Be the old lady."

I had no idea what to do in these stupid childish games of theirs in which I had to be the subject threatened by one of them and saved by the other, so I slumped down and studied the multi-coloured dusty scrap mat across the room, wondering if Suzie's parents used to wipe their feet there. I looked all around for any clue to Suzie's whereabouts. But clues to one's current life are hardly to be found in one's old house.

"Outta my way," Junior continued with his heroic dialogue.

He swooped down, grabbed me up by the ribs and deposited me on the scrap mat that was supposed to represent the solid ground. Ivy let out a maniacal laugh which echoed about the house and tightened my stomach. A faint feeling fell upon me, like walls slowly tilting in. The mat smelled of stinkbugs and I sneezed and coughed and couldn't stop. But those two thought it was a part of my performance and paid me no mind. I could die and they wouldn't notice, I thought.

"Leh we go," I said, my voice struggling to push back at the slowly tilting walls.

But they refused and went rummaging for more costumes, so I grabbed the kite and went without them, trembling to have to make my way out alone past the watching tree-giant and the hungry gobbling grass, but determined to leave. There was nothing to learn here, except that Suzie's empty house could be the end of me. So I dashed down the stairs, making a beeline for the paling staves. But the kite tail caught on something and yanked me backwards. And I went skidding down the steps, hitting my backbone and elbows on the way down.

The next day Junior came with another idea, a better one he declared. "Since Ixie didn't have the guts to play TV, we could play our own thing," he said.

"What?" I snapped.

My backbone hurt and my elbows were still sore and crusty from where Mam had put the iodine. "What happen to you girl?" she'd said, when inevitably she saw the grazed and bleeding elbows. And I had to say that I fell. "Fell where?" she asked and I mumbled "outdoors," quite truthfully, to which she followed up with "And how?" I boxed my brains. "Running," I said, still truthfully. Please Lord, I prayed, don't let her ask me running where and why, and I kept quiet about my backbone too.

Junior outlined his scheme. "It could be," he paused, thinking, "it could be like a anything kinda house."

"How it works?" asked Ivy, Junior's comrade-in-arms. Even if Junior woke up one day and said that we must go find a monster and fight him, Ivy would agree and ask where the monster lived and ought we to make an appointment. Neither of them was sensible, I thought, as I watched them gearing up for this new hare-brained gallivant.

Junior continued explaining, "You go inside the house and make it anyting you want."

"What kinda things?" Ivy asked.

"Like anyting. You go in, you point. Then it gon turn into the place or thing you say."

"Like a palace?" I asked, "Or a circus?"

"Yea," he said, sure of himself. "Anything, anywhere."

So we squeezed through the loose paling staves again. We had hooked the door from the outside, jamming a piece of branch between the rusty hasp and staple.

As soon as we stepped in, Ivy pointed at the opposite wall.

"Cinema," she said, directing us to sit on Suzie's peach linoleum and pretend to eat popcorn and watch an American film. After the pretend movie was over, she said it was my turn.

I cleared my throat and tried but nothing came.

"Wait, wait. Me again," said Ivy and stood up. She pointed to a corner and said "Boop!" like she had a magic wand.

She said she was graduating from a foreign university and that she was wearing her hair straight with a black cap and gown like our cousin Kim was wearing in the photo she had sent us in the mail. Kim was Pap's niece, his brother Goodwin's daughter. They lived abroad and we had never met them but we knew them from pictures. Kim's mother was a pink-skinned smiling woman and under that graduation cap of hers, Kim had hair like her mother, hair immensely straight and smooth. Immensely. Ganee had five photos of Kim on the living room wall. One, with Kim as a baby, one as a toddler, one as a child, one as a taller child, and one as a young teenager, in the cap and gown, with the immensely smooth straight hair. Cousin Kim. Kimberly. A forward, popular name from another place. A clean television action kind of name. Not any kind of flora and fauna of the landscape kind of nonsense name. Ganee had photos of Kim and of her own three boys too – our Pap Michael, and her second boy Goodwin and her third boy Raphael, our uncle Raffie from Georgetown. Once, Ganee had a girl baby too but she was stillborn. They say when Pap met Mam, it was like Ganee Gwenny got a daughter back, and she put photos of Mam all around her house too, next to the photos of her three boys and the photos of Kim, of course. Ivy walked around pretending she was wearing high heels like Cousin Kim and giving a speech in a big hall and said that she was the "valictoran."

"What's a Victorian?" asked Junior.

"Not a Victorian, dummy. Dat's like dem old time people wit big dresses. A valictoran, like the person who get first in class," Ivy explained.

Then she pretended to read a speech from behind a podium and made us applaud twice.

"Now you," said Junior when Ivy was done with her scene.

"I, um, boop, uh —" I tried to imagine something impressive too, something grand and far away, but could think of nothing. All I managed to conjure up were three houses in a neat row, in which Ivy, Junior and I leaned far out of our own windows and waved at each other. But that would be a damp performance and the two of them would give me incredulous looks and criticise my dull brain and be most unwilling to enact such an empty mime. So I patted my sore elbows and swallowed my words.

Ivy sucked her teeth and declared, "You next Junior 'cus like cat got her tongue."

"Well, boop," he said and pointed at a corner. "A field with a plane," he said. "I flying."

And he took us into the sky. Ivy and I looked down and he told us about the kinds of trees we were seeing below and the rivers.

"Look the Demerara river," he said.

And we craned our necks and tried to see it.

"I want go in a real plane," Ivy said after a while.

"Mee too," said Junior.

After a while I said, "Me too." But only because everybody else was saying it and I didn't want to sound stupid.

Junior swayed and swung to the side as if he were swerving the plane in a storm but he fell over and hooked himself on a curtain and it came tumbling on his head. Ivy choked with laughter. But I worried.

"You breaking up the people house," I whispered.

"Is nobody house, nobody want it no more," Junior said struggling to get out of the curtain and sneezing like a cat. Ivy rolled around on the peach linoleum and laughed.

"How you mean?" I asked.

This was Suzie's house. We shouldn't be playing in it like it was some oversized doll's house.

"They ain't comin' back. They don't want it," Ivy said.

A marabunta buzzed around us and made its way to the nest hanging in the rafter beneath the aluminium roof.

"How you know they ain't?" I asked.

The old limey sensation was returning and pulsing in my temples and I feared the lime juice would squeeze from my eyes. I rubbed my eyes shut.

Was Suzie really never coming back? Why didn't she want her house? There was nothing wrong with it. Sure it smelled and rotted but that was only because she wasn't here.

"Well is your turn," Junior said to me. "Do your boop."

I tried my imagination again, but it was still broken. All I could see was a chain wheel and sprocket in my brain and someone pedalling far far away. But though the chain moved around and around, the bike stayed in the same place forever.

"I goin' home," I said, rubbing my eyes.

They looked at me and I thought they seemed a little deflated and I was pleased to have an effect on them. But it must've been my sour eyes blurring my vision because the next weekend they said they were going into the empty house again, even if I wasn't.

"Suit ya-selves," I said, practicing to stand my ground.

I was under a tree in our new yard while Pap and Uncle Warbin sawed wood.

"Come on man," Junior said to me.

"So what we gon do wit Small Spokes?" I asked, looking around for a tangible excuse.

Small Spokes was going to pre-school these days and was only with us on Saturdays. He was sitting under the tree, imitating me and scratching in an art book.

"Bring he," Ivy said.

"I not bringing he over there to get sting by no 'bunta."

"Carry he inside to Mam then."

I concentrated on my sketch pad, shading in the petal of a sunflower.

"So what you gon do wit he then?" Ivy harped, trying to get me to come.

"Nothing. I staying here with he," I said, making my voice high, mighty and sensible. "I not getting he in trouble again 'cause of y'all two."

"Suit your sour self," she said, and she and Junior ran out the gate.

An emptiness washed over me as I watched their receding backs but I carried on helping Spokes with his shapes and letters and he learned fast, his little grubby fingers tracing and colouring and scratching everything I outlined for him. Small Spokes, the only loyal friend I had left in all the world, I thought.

But the two garden gnomes returned in ten minutes, though it may as well have been a century. They came and sat under the tree. I ignored them and kept writing things down for Spokes who was rolling on his tummy and gurgling. It must have been dull playing in the empty house without me after all, I thought, marvelling at my own importance. They were going to learn their lesson once and for all because I wasn't going to play with them ever again if they kept going into the empty house. I certainly didn't have to pay a couple of garden gnomes any mind. For company, I had Small Spokes and didn't need them. They'd see.

But the next Saturday while they took turns pushing each other in a wheel barrow and I waited for Spokes, he didn't show up. It was excruciating sitting waiting under a tree, pretending I didn't want to be wheeled in a barrow. So I went indoors.

"Mam where's Spokes?"

"Spokes and his mother going to America next month," Mam said, as if she were saying Spokes and his Mammy are going to the shop for bread.

"America?"

"Yes. There goes the small change."

We looked at each other.

"Well, we just gon have to sell plantain chips or plant more wiri wiri pepper," she said, then she picked up a frying pan and mumbled, "least this time Spokes not gon be here to eat it."

"Oh," I said, dusting off my feet a little, sole upon instep.

Even a small boy with a name sounding like a miniature bicycle wheel could go to big places you saw on TV. Even a small boy who barely knew his shapes and letters didn't need me anymore to teach him any.

There was a glass mug of lime juice on the dining table. I averted my eyes. But it was still as if I'd glugged the whole mug and the juice was spiking my palate.

I went out under the tree again and conjured up half a dozen new friends to sit with me.

"How do you do Theophilus Ballafarious," I said to one of them.

"And how do you do?" replied he.

5

The Long Arm of the Miaplambo

Now that the steady small change from babysitting Small Spokes was gone, Mam erupted in a frenzy about other sources of income. She massaged the tops of her eyebrows as Ivy and I grew out of our shoes and clothes faster than our house next door could go up.

"When it gon done?" Mam said, one morning, looking over at our new unwalled, windowless, doorless house.

Then she sighed and bustled about. She hustled all day at the stove, sweating and grumbling. Then that afternoon, she hauled the small dining table and set it in the street in front our gate. She ferried bowlfuls of delicacies — plantain chips, mithai, channa, pholourie, jalebi — and thunked them down on the table.

I stood in a corner observing and offering no help.

"Bring some paper and a big marker," she said.

I brought them.

"What you been doin' so long? Come here and write the signs. Write C-h-a-n-n-a, dollar sign, sixty."

I wrote it.

"Write neater," she said, rolling out a piece of adhesive tape and sticking the sign to the side of the table. "Now write plantain chips, sixty and a hundred."

'Plantin chip 60 and 100', I scrawled.

She grumbled, snatched the marker from me and scribbled at the bottom of the paper 'Plantain Chips $60 & $100'.

"Now copy that bigger and neater," she said and I hustled to copy the sign, obsessing over the ampersand.

Ivy cycled out and hovered over the chips, "I could have any?"

"No," Mam said. "Jus' cycle up the street and see if you find customers yea."

So Ivy went pedalling past our unfinished house.

"Uncle Warbin," she called. Uncle Warbin was up high in our two storey house frame, measuring something. She asked, "Ya want buy chips or anything?"

He grinned and shook his head no.

She pedalled down to the back street and returned with Junior, he pedalling and she riding on the handle bar, her feet sticking out.

"There," Ivy said to Junior with a flourish, "You want buy anything?"

His eyes darted from this dish to that, but he swallowed and said, "Naa."

"Well then you can just walk back home by yourself," Ivy said, grabbing the bicycle, and looking in the air now that she had exhausted the only two potential customers on her list.

"Go and ask Ole Lady Bargains then," I said.

"For what? So she could holler at me and try get everything half price?" Ivy sucked her teeth.

Ivy was rude but right. Ole Lady Bargains bargained for everything but nobody could bargain with her for anything, least of all her pricey shrimp. And if it was on a day that her hearing was poor, we had to keep adjusting our voices a few decibels until she stopped hollering 'Eh what?' If it was on a day that she did hear well enough, she'd ask why we were shouting and if we thought she was deaf. She was Ganee Gwenny's friend and one time when Ganee was in the rocking chair sewing the holes in our socks, she pushed her spectacles up her nose, beckoned to us and whispered that if we made fun of old people's ailments and idiosyncrasies, our day would come when youngsters made fun of us. So I asked Pap to spell 'idiosyncrasies' and 'ailments' and looked them up in the big Oxford dictionary. Then I stopped imitating Ole Lady Bargains and saying 'Eh, what?'

Ailments and idiosyncrasies. Idiosyncrasies and ailments. The words floated around in my head. Idiosyncrasies – such a nice sounding word, I thought, as Ivy pedalled off again with Junior running beside her.

Mam went indoors leaving me to call her if customers came.

So I manned the stall and looked over at Suzie's house. How very square it was. When I grew up I didn't want any boxy square house, I thought. I wanted curves, turrets and spirals, sentinels and gardeners. I thought too that Suzie and her mother would've come to buy Mam's snacks. Then at least the cookie tin would have some money and Mam wouldn't look as wild.

I studied the tilt of the coconut trees behind Suzie's house and the soft motion of the birds returning home. The hammering had stopped, the street was empty and there was just me and the slow breeze and the price tags fluttering lightly. The afternoon reminded me of a poem Miss Pam was teaching us and I was just settling into the perfect quiet of my own live poem-scene and almost dropping off to sleep when Ivy's bicycle bell pealed urgently.

"Customer, customer," she yelled.

"Who?"

"Small Spokes Grammy. Say she want a bag channa and two bags jalebi." Ivy held up a roll of twenty dollar notes.

"Don't she have diabetes?"

Ivy shrugged and I went to summon Mam.

"Customer number one," Mam said, smiling and resting the bills in the tin.

Up the street a truck stopped and eight cane cutters got out and started walking home in a group. Mam and I watched as Ivy cycled up to them and gestured at our stand. Then the whole group of cane cutters nodded, did an about-turn and came towards our stand.

"Little entrepreneur," Mam chuckled, getting her spoons and wax paper ready.

In ten minutes everything was sold out and the cane cutters turned back up the street gobbling things as they went. Only one of them, a young man, wrapped everything with his tidy slim delicate hands and stored the packages in his sack.

At the dinner table, everyone said how Ivy was the latest family entrepreneur.

"Aunty-manure," Ivy whispered, re-packaging the word and making me laugh my tea through my nose.

Mam frowned, got up and brought me a rag. Then she listed her sales menu for the next day, her notepad saying – cassava balls, egg balls, cassava pone and fudge.

Next afternoon, a little earlier this time, I helped Mam haul the small dining table and drape a neon pink plastic over it. Then we loaded the warm snacks and peppery condiments in the wheel barrow and transported them to the stand.

"Where your paper and big marker?" Mam asked.

In time, I became adroit at making price signs with bold lettering and snazzy backgrounds. And I could do reasonably realistic illustrations of the snacks for those who couldn't read. I thought with satisfaction, if I were a customer, I'd come just to see the signs.

The cane cutters came often, holding out their lumbering smelly lunch bowls for the snacks with the big dollops of spicy mango sour on top. Only the thin young cane cutter with the skinny delicate fingers and the moustache so light you could barely see it, asked for everything to be wrapped in wax paper which he folded over and rested in his sack. He had the kind of face and stick slim shape that could get a small part on TV in a Cowboy movie, as a porter standing beside a train. They'd call him Jack or Bob or something like that, and he'd say "Aye sir" and hoist about valises with his long thin hands.

Some afternoons, other neighbours, including the window-peeping gossipy one, eagerly carted off the snacks. Even Old Lady Bargains appeared, demanding a taste of everything before settling on what she wanted. Then she shuffled home, her egg basket stacked up with sugar cake and fudge. And while Mam waited for customers, Ivy and Junior and I played in our new unfinished house while Pap and Uncle Warbin worked.

Uncle Warbin wasn't our biological uncle. But he was uncle-ish, told proper stories and made us feel more sensible than did our two uncles – Uncle Raffie, who treated Ivy and me like double vision and only patted our heads, said "Hello twins" and kept asking which of us was who, and Uncle 'Winnie' Goodwin – who when he called from oversees enunciated every single word with caution and said things like, "Well haii there and how haave you been keepingg," like we were a pair of doofuses or bereft of the English Language. But Uncle Warbin, who was usually over for dinner and sometimes for lunch so much that Mam had said he was a sponge – which upset Pap that he asked her not to say that again, and then explained that many days he, Pap didn't have enough to pay Warbin for helping with our house so that often Warbin worked for free – this Uncle Warbin, spoke to us like we had growing brains. "Fine," Mam had said, "Sorry to say he's a sponge, but he can get his own plate and help himself for a change." Then Pap flattened his lips and went outside to work on a birdhouse. Even though birds didn't come into our garden anymore because Pappo Harro had sprayed the scarecrow's clothes with garlic water.

"Once pon a time," said Uncle Warbin, "was a man livin' pon a hill in a valley down by Timehri."

"How," asked Junior, "he could be in a valley and still on a hill?"

"You never been Timehri, boy?"

Junior shook his head.

"Well then don't ask 'till you see boy."

Warbin walked to a beam and we three followed. His parrot flew to his shoulder and said, "Squaawkk, ask, see boy. Squawk, askk, see."

"Shut up bird," Junior told it.

"Careful," Uncle Warbin said, directing us to a corner, "Go over there 'way from wood and nails. And don't tell Putty shut up. You hurt her feelings."

"Which feelings?" Junior said.

"Now dis Timehri man was the only one who didn' sleep at night 'cus guess why?"

We shrugged.

"'Cus he know about the," Uncle Warbin paused and tiptoed closer, put his arms up and curved them like a monster's claws, then shouted out "the Miaplambo!"

"Ahhh," we screamed in unison. I grabbed Junior's t-shirt. Ivy jumped and grabbed her head, jamming some wood that went clattering behind us. Junior trembled a little but planted his feet shoulder width apart.

"Careful down there by all dat wood I said." He showed us where to stand instead. And we moved to the side, but only by an inch because the story was freezing our legs.

Junior anchored his arms akimbo, "Dat not real!" he said, referring to this Miaplambo thing. "We never hear 'bout it."

Uncle Warbin laughed, "Oho, it not real boy?"

"What kinda ting is it then? Like a jaguar or something?" Junior said, stamping.

"But I neva see it," Uncle Warbin said, "How you can ask me? You think I ever went Miaplambo sightseeing with a Polaroid? You think is like bird-watching or monkey-catching? Dat you gon watch for it and eventually it gon come up to you and sit on a telephone wire or a branch and you gon take a picture of it and put it in the National Geographic? No ladies and sir. But –"

"You ever find Pollard?" I asked, partly because he had mentioned monkeys, but mostly because I wanted to ease up on this Miaplambo business.

"No. But one ah dese days I sure find out is who thief him. You better believe me Big Two-Step," Uncle Warbin said.

He had started calling Ivy and me the Two-Steppers in the weeks that we waited about impatiently to attend nursery school; he'd occupied our time teaching us the two-step waltz. I, he called Big Two-Step and Ivy was Lil Two-Step because she was born second. He'd showed us other dances too that he used to dance in his boyhood village.

Junior knuckled my arm so I'd shut up about Pollard. He said, "So it in Timehri then? This monster thing? But dats where all the planes go and come. By where the airport be."

Uncle Warbin continued, "The ole man from Timehri, he hear it going an' coming in the middle of the night. It go –"

"You lying you know," Junior said, keeping his fists balled.

"What good it do me to lie to you?" said Warbin. "You tink I wukking fuh de Miaplambo on commission and dats why I advertising him?"

"So what it do to people then? It bite? Sting?"

"Sometimes it carry people 'way and they can't come back. Reowrauzzz," he growled at us like a cross between a cat, a bird and a plane.

We jumped.

"Or sometimes they come back, but they don't come back the same, hooo," Uncle Warbin hooted like an owl now.

"Hoo," said Putty high-pitched, "hoo hoo."

Junior had his arms akimbo. He was disturbed I could tell, but he kept his hands on his hips and tried not to show it.

"Don't worry Junior," I whispered, "it not real."

But that night I awoke a little after midnight and lay in bed holding in my urine for a very long time. What if the Miaplambo were under the bed?

"Ivy." I elbowed her in the ribs. "Iveee."

"Hmm."

"Follow me to pee pee."

Ivy wobbled out of bed and trailed behind me, propped herself up against the doorframe and continued to sleep standing up.

"Come back," I said, when I was done.

I bounded into bed and hauled her in by the nightie. Then I pulled the sheet over my head and dusted my feet off, sole upon instep, imagining what would happen if the Miaplambo ever came after me, wondering if it had got Suzie and that's why she never came back, and trembling because I never even tried to save her, and now her crystal heart was lying in the ballerina box across the street.

"Ivy?" I whispered, wanting someone to dismiss my imaginings but she was asleep again.

The next day we waited for Junior to come with us to go confront Uncle Warbin once and for all about this thing, but Junior didn't come. My hibiscus plant was growing and blooming dozens and I wanted him to see it. But most of all I wanted to know if he was still scared of the Miaplambo. If he wasn't scared, then it couldn't be real after all. But several afternoons passed and still Junior didn't come. So I asked Mam if we could go see what was the matter with him. "Yes," she said and wrapped some dhal puri in wax paper and sent enough for Junior, his mother and his grampappy.

"Get on," said Ivy, tapping the handle bar of the bicycle.

"If you make me fall off again I gon tell Mam." I clutched the wax paper with the warm dhal puri close to my body.

"Get on blabbo-mouth."

And she pedalled fast down the back street, in, out and around potholes while I held the food and my breath and prayed to the good Lord that she wouldn't ride into the trench. I couldn't even swim. Plus I didn't like my feet getting wet for no good reason. Long ago when the ice cream truck used to come down the street, Suzie and I would take our cones and sit on her bridge and hang our feet over into the trench and drop pieces of cone wafer in the water for the fish. But that was long ago and I didn't like my feet getting wet anymore. Especially if they were wet and dust got stuck to them.

Junior was at home fetching water in a bucket and pouring it into a barrel.

"You gotta full up dis barrel, Junior, then you could come and play?" I asked.

He nodded. "Dat one too," he said, pointing at another barrel. His mouth was turned down and he didn't look at us.

"We can help you," I offered.

He gave us two buckets and we fetched water from the pond to the barrels lined up at the back of the yard, spilling much of it halfway through and wetting our skirts and feet.

I asked him when he was coming so we could investigate the Miaplambo situation and he said that first he had to feed the chickens.

"Your Papa don't feed dem no more?" Ivy asked.

"Yes but," and then there was a hiccuppy sound. "He gone 'way."

"Oh," I said. "Gone where?"

"Dunno. In a plane."

"When he comin' back then?"

"Dunno."

"Oh," I said, not knowing what else to say.

We watched him through the mesh partition of the coop as he took his precious time filling the feeders.

The next day Junior's mother showed up at our gate. Ivy and I ran to the veranda.

"Warbin!" Junior's mother yelled, "Warbin, come out."

Ivy said, "He over there," and pointed at our new house.

Junior's mother marched over. "Warbin, come out!"

Putty flew out, perched on the fence and said, "Squawk, Warbin, Warbin."

Uncle Warbin strolled out and Putty flew to his shoulder like a sentinel.

"Warbin, what kinda lyin' jumbie story you tell my boy? Meeplobee or something? What lyin' stupitness is dat?"

Uncle Warbin looked sheepish and said nothing.

"Squawk, 'pitness."

Ivy whispered, "Is the Miaplambo she talking about."

"Shh."

Junior's mother was still hollering, "Why you and dat loud mouth bird scaring my boy? If you don't stop it, you gon know wah's good for you Warbin."

Uncle Warbin stood there and shut up.

Mam peeped out and hustled over. She patted Junior's mother on the back and spoke softly. Finally, Junior's mother retreated to the back street with one final scowl at Warbin.

Later, through the crack in the wall, we saw Mam telling Pap and Uncle Warbin that in his sleep, Junior shouted out Meeplobeo or something like that.

"Warbin, you need to stop wit these stories you know. You can't give children nerves like dat," Mam said.

Uncle Warbin, bit into a chicken leg, swallowed, looked up from his plate and said, "Why I must stop a story? If is so the story go, is so it go. Is I the one giving the boy nightmares? Not so it go," he said softly, like he was addressing a nation.

And so, the story went how it went several weeks later when Pap tried to fix the pieces of the puzzle back where they belonged. But Pap in his early greying years should have known that you can't fit an old scene back when the pieces are always changing.

We stayed indoors a lot. Without Junior, there was nothing we wanted to play outdoors, except maybe ride our bicycle. Bicycle, singular. And Madam Ivy always took more than her contracted ten laps, so I'd get fed-up waiting my turn and go indoors and read. After a while, Pap seemed to think Ivy and I were too cooped up, I reading and Ivy, when she was supposed to be doing homework, secretly polishing her nails with Mam's red nail polish and wiping it off quickly when she knew people would be around. Once she got caught. She had told me to stand at the bedroom door and lookout. I did stand at the door but by the time I lifted my head from my Molly Mumpkins Mystery novel, Mam was already staring over my shoulder.

Mam rattled on at Ivy about a time and place for everything and about a little thing called deception. Ivy scowled at me between Mam's words. As for me, Mam thought I was simply standing there reading. She'd seen me reading in the kitchen in front of the sink while I was supposed to be washing wares and she'd seen me reading at breakfast and told me to put that book down and eat. She saw me hiding the Molly Mumpkins Miss Pam lent me, behind my science books and pretending to do Science homework. So she asked Pap to talk to me about it. All Pap said was, "How about we just get the science homework out of the way first eh Ixie Pixie? And the wares too." And she saw me take the books into the toilet. So I was spared the usual scolding reserved for the accomplice because Mam thought I was standing there oblivious, reading like any normal day of my recent life.

Afterwards, Ivy treated me to menacing stares and air punches. But I buried my head in Molly Mumpkins's tidily wild world. Why come out when it was a good solid world?

But Junior's absence and the stretched rubber band tension indoors made Pap plan an outing to the zoo where we could all come out into the same world again, into a common puzzle scene and fit the pieces back together. So he convinced Mam to come.

"Captain Adventure, I ain't got time for no zoo excursion," she said. "All that plantain over there gotta peel before they ripe out."

"Come na Laurs," he pleaded, "is a hundred years since you go anywhere wit me."

And he told us we could ask Junior to come if his mother said it was alright. His mother said it was alright as long as the shameless village storyteller and his good-for-nothing-parrot weren't there. But Uncle Warbin wouldn't come, even if we asked. Once he said that back in his home village they didn't put animals in zoos. When we asked why, he said 'cause that's just how the story go. So Junior came.

We caught the public bus. Ivy sat between Mam and Pap. And Junior and I sat behind them. I tried to catch his eye but he kept his head out the window. I thought about poking him in the ribs, but now that I knew about his Miaplambo nightmares I felt ashamed having glimpsed inside his head and I didn't know how to talk to him anymore. So I settled for comparing the scars and scabs on his knees to mine. His knees had more and he smelled like Dettol soap, like a Dettol soap with its head out the window.

When my scientific observation of the scabs and scars was done, I studied the back of Pap's neck and the newly greying tight little curls cropped close to his head like elbow macaroni cut with a fork in a dinner plate. I followed the grey stripes slanting down his shoulders on his white t-shirt. And I watched the middle part in Ivy's hair, wondering if this was how my scalp looked too and I was just raising my hand to my head when the bus stopped.

The zoo gate was crowded and we tried to stick together and surge through the sweaty crowd but we got separated. A towering woman and a lanky man at her side blocked my path and a faint feeling fell upon me. I wanted to call out "Pap-Pap lift me" but I couldn't risk Ivy's snickering. Besides, Pap had to be right there. His Musk cologne was still near. Suddenly the towering woman made me jump.

"Lawwd! Laura? Laura 'Smart Bones' DeFreitas? Girl!" the woman called out. "Is you? Lawd, yuh put on lil weight girl. Ah nearly didn't recognise you. But I said to myself dat gotta be you. Mike how you do? Laura stress you out mek you goin' bald?"

The lanky man beside the woman touched his own thinning hair and put his hand down.

Pap seemed amused.

"Look how dem twins grow though. You didn't get no more children? What you waitin' for?" she exclaimed, pinching Ivy's cheeks and then mine. My cheeks stung. "This one more chubby than this one," she said pointing to Ivy.

"*You* must eat your food more," she said, wagging her pointer at me. "And who dis lil boy be?"

"*This* is our friend Junior," Ivy said matching the woman's loudness, and yanking Junior, she walked off making me wish I too could raise my voice and march off grandly. But all I could do was rest my fingertips on my stinging face and only in my head did I dare say, 'lady, I wish you hadn't stung me'.

Finally, Pap said that we must be going now and for everybody to have a good afternoon.

"Who's dat?" I asked when the people were gone.

But Mam, for once, was tongue-tied.

"Well!" was all Mam could say once we were inside the zoo. "Well!"

"Who's dat Pap?"

"Somebody from your mother high school, I think," Pap said, steering us to the manatee pond.

Mam was quiet. She straightened herself more than usual and sucked in her stomach. She undid and re-did the low bun in her hair three times, once into a pony tail, then into a half-up half-down style and finally back into the chignon bun again. That was the most I'd ever seen Mam rearrange her hair at once, in public or anywhere. Mam was never rattled by anything, not even when the old zinc sheet flew off the kitchen roof in the middle of a rare high breeze. She simply clambered up on the roof in the wind and downpour, hauled up the zinc sheet, pounded it back into place and sapped up the swamp in the kitchen. When Pap and Pappo Harro came home, their eyeballs bulged at the tale of the flying zinc sheet that Ivy repeated matter-of-factly between bites of fish cake and yam.

Pap saw that Mam was rattled today and he held her shoulder and said, "Hey Laurie, how about the seesaw?"

Mam, distant and distracted perched on the seesaw. It was the first time we saw them playing like a couple of adolescent sweethearts, seesawing up, down, down, up until they came to a poised, perfect balance in mid-air, suspended, feet off the ground, at one with the universe. It could have been a puzzle scene, with all the pieces found.

Then as we three children took turns down the slide, Mam and Pap went to the swings. But when Ivy spied Pap pushing Mam on the swing she pelted across.

"Push me too Pap," she said.

And as I watched them swinging, Ivy up in the air two or three feet off the ground and Mam on the swing beside Ivy, my feet hurried down the slide and ran to them with my tummy growing warm, warmth running towards warmth, wholeness. Amen.

"Me too. Push me," I said and Mam vacated her swing and pushed me.

I looked at Ivy shrieking on my right. Sometimes both our swings flew up together. Sometimes I flew up as she dipped down. Other times I swung down and watched her swinging past and flying higher than me. It was a good scene for a puzzle box, I thought. And on the days when Ivy is a little hard to find inside the house of my chest, I still fit these puzzle pieces together. Pieces of the swings flying up and down, taking us with them like a pair of bird friends – flying, dipping, rising.

Behind us, Mam and Pap joked about a man with a macaw on a swing. Mam giggled and I marvelled at her having the capacity for delight. Pap was right after all. All we needed was to fix the old pieces back together.

But Junior, directly across us, at the top of the slide, sat frozen. He looked straight at us, his face contorted. I checked if he was looking at someone behind us. But no.

"Mam I want to come down," I said, not really wanting to come down. I didn't want to exit our puzzle scene.

But I came down and ran to Junior.

"Junior," I said, climbing the ladder to the slide, "Junior, what happen? Slide down and I gon slide too and keep you company."

But he got up, turned around and climbed down the ladder.

"What happen Junior? You want go on the swings too?" I asked.

He didn't answer.

"Take my swing then." I went behind the swing and waited to push him.

He didn't come so I sat on the swing.

"Well gimme a push then, Junior."

He pushed me steadily at first. Then faster. And my heart pitched about in my chest. I was afraid now, so as I swung towards the ground I angled my feet to slow the swing but my legs bent awkwardly and I pitched off the swing, landing on my hands and knees.

Please God, I prayed, let nobody be watching.

But before the burning of my knees and the shame of tumbling off a swing could thoroughly take hold of me, a shape rushed by.

Junior was dashing away, running past the seesaw, running past the otter cage, past the sloth cage. He was about to cover the cages of the Amazonian birds when Pap started running after him. I stayed with my knees in the dust and watched Pap's three decade old legs trying to catch up with the undefeated champion of The Limepicks who had just crossed the length of the toucan cage. Pap didn't stand a chance, I worried. Then thankfully for Pap, Junior dawdled for a while by the harpy eagle, then he ran on out the zoo gate and into traffic. And Pap with the legs of a basset hound pressed on. And I thought, this is not a scene for a puzzle box. Nobody is staying inside the frame. Pap was wrong after all.

Finally Pap caught up with Junior, plucked him out of traffic, raised him to his chest and held him up with some difficulty because Junior's legs were now so gangly. He patted Junior's back and said, "Alright there sonny?" But when Junior didn't reply, Mam said it was time to go.

Junior didn't say anything on the way home and as he flopped onto Pap's shoulder and slept, I wondered if he had a lime splitting and spreading inside him, making him sour too.

After Mam washed and cleaned my knees, I went outside to look for Junior, proud to show him my Band-Aids. I thought we could play war and I could be a wounded soldier and he and Ivy could carry me across a field to save me. I would consent to one of them holding my ankles and the other holding my arms and I would close my eyes and groan and allow them to carry me across the yard. I wished Small Spokes could see us acting out such a scene.

But when I came out, Junior was gone. Night had fallen. My hibiscus tree was asleep and the old block of darkness covered Suzie's square empty house. I thought I saw a torchlight glint on her glass window, but it was only the reflection from the headlights of a car ambling through the potholes.

I hurried inside and shut the door so I could keep everyone together, just in case the Miaplambo was lurking out there in the shadows, in the outer edges of this new puzzle, working his way in.

6

The Marvellous Mermaid

I arranged my exercise book with the Arithmetic homework and waited for Miss Pamela.

I had triple-checked my sums and was pleased with my progress in Mathematics, even though my reading habit had grown uncontrollable. Pap didn't seem to mind. He left us to our own devices, so long as we weren't breaking any bones, each other's or our own. But Mam, like a chicken hawk, glared and inspected my books until finally I made a show of labouring evenly on all the subjects. Before bedtime, she instructed me to stack my exercise books at the end of the small dining table and in the mornings, I returned them to my backpack. Sometimes, Mam set aside one or two of the books with her notations about what I needed to practise. And always, it was the Mathematics and Science books singled out. And always, I did as she directed.

But Miss Ivy, Ignorer-of-Adults, kept quoting Pap's words. That we were responsible enough to decide if our homework was worth doing and that he trusted us to make the better decision between doing it and not doing it. So she only did the homework she felt like. When Mam singled out her muddled or incomplete compositions, Ivy looked at Mam, glanced around the room, stuck the books in her bag and said nothing. And when she was made to line up in front of the class with the other slackers, she seemed delighted, for when Miss Pamela wasn't looking, Ivy pulled piggy and fish faces to entertain her giggling geese friends in the back row.

Miss Pamela resembled the star girl from the TV show *Zorro*. She shimmered about in shiny pointy nails and shiny pointy heels. I'd go home and pretend to be her. She wore crisp skirt suits of ruby red and powder blue, dandelion yellow and silver grey. Usually on Thursdays she wore the grey. And then on Fridays she burst upon the scene in blue jeans like models in advertisements. And she wore these bright tops. One with green florals, one with pink polka dots, a purple one with brown horses and another with blue anchors. I memorised them. So that when I grew up I could buy shirts like those, though not ones with pink polka dots. Pink polka dots were unfriendly little limes. But they looked alright on Miss Pam. A potato sack could look alright on Miss Pam. She was too good for this world. She never swallowed whatever needed to be said and while her lipsticked mouth brought forth smooth words against the universe of the dark chalkboard, I marvelled at her quaint earrings and necklaces framing the sensibilities of her face. I became obsessed with her voice and her hair, especially her hair. It was smooth, so smooth and flowed in a sturdy silken pony tail. Miss Pam was a mermaid, but people.

The day she greeted us smiling in front of the bedazzled handmade posters in her orderly Primary Three classroom, I went home and studied my hair in the mirror. I despaired at the frizz springing out around my temples and at the flatness of my head with the awful middle split. I squeezed my two thick braids that were as dry as a coconut's husk and I examined the bushy blob of curls fluffing out beneath my brown ribbons. And one time when Mam was pressing

Pap's shirt and stepped out the room, I ran to the iron, held one of the blobs of curls to the ironing board and pressed hard on the curls like they were tough denim jeans out of which I was trying to get the creases. Some of the hairs flattened and my heart somersaulted, but then the curls bounced up again and I had to slam the iron down and run because Mam's feet were coming back.

It was easy to learn in Miss Pam's class because she had the mermaid hair and because her patience with us could fill about ten of Ganee's large pickle and cookie and chip jars. Even the duncest pupils improved. And yes, Mam had told me not to call people dunce, but she didn't know them in our class. They were a dozen yam crates full of dunceness, so why lie about it when it was Mam herself who had taught us not to lie. She, Mam, didn't know everything.

So with Miss Pam, some of the dunces improved their handwriting. Some tried with their spelling. We the physically uncoordinated improved in Physical Education. Even Kalleecharran, who used to stand burly and sulky by the gate refusing to kick a ball even if it rolled up to the toes of his clean white sneakers, played a lazy kickball on Fridays and smiled about it. Others made an effort to read, even that old clown Ivy. Some even came five days a week, though they had no lunch. Miss Pam brought them a basket of fruits and fluffy rolls which she baked herself and which the rest of us longed for, though we had our lunch. And some, like me even graduated not only to being awarded first or second in class, but to triple-checking their Arithmetic, arranging their exercise book on their desk on Monday mornings and waiting for their red stars.

But for me, there was more. Miss Pam discovered I was writing stories. During recess I'd stay in and write on scraps of paper Ganee'd given me. One day, Miss Pam peered over my shoulders and said, "What are we writing on this fine sunny Friday?" And with a swish of her mermaidian hair, she handed me typing sheets. So I wrote more stories and hid them under the trapfloor of the doll's house that we'd never got around to painting.

Miss Pam asked what I did with the stories when I was finished and I revealed my secret. Then she put her arms akimbo, with the pointy red nails pressed against the waist of her jeans, pouted her lipsticked mouth and said, "Hiding your story won't do you any good, Ixora." I gazed at her shiny nail tips and thought of the scrawly handwritten pages under the trapfloor. Then she said I could read one of my stories on stage on graduation day. She'd ask the headteacher.

When she said that, warmth grew in my chest and spread outwards like heated guava jelly baking in a tart. Miss Pam knew me, and finally everyone in the whole school would too. They'd see I was a brain, not some sour stomach.

That morning though, when I laid out my exercise book with the sums in the middle of the desk, Miss Pamela was late. Maybe she had gone back to get an umbrella for the drizzle. Fifteen minutes passed. Maybe she was looking for a raincoat. Or changing her shoes into rain boots, and bringing her delicate heels in a plastic bag to save them from getting muddy. Some rainy days she did that.

But one hour later, my book with the sums remained in the middle of my desk.

A few times Miss Pam had taken the morning off to do business in Georgetown. So I took a Molly Mumpkins book from my bag, the one that she'd lent me last week, and I read and waited for her city business to be over.

Ivy though thought it was a good time to entertain. She planted herself in the middle of a group and showed them how to make shapes with a rubber band. Other children made paper planes and boats and launched them at each other. What idiots, I thought, disgracing Miss Pam's motto of 'Make hay while the sun shines.' They were all going to get into trouble when she comes, I thought. Littering the floor with nasty paper planes indeed!

But the day ended and Miss Pam didn't come.

"Maybe she sick," I told Ivy as we walked home.

"Leh we go and see," Ivy said and turned down the street towards Miss Pam's house.

"Mam gon quarrel." I pulled her back, dreading going somewhere we were not yet granted permission to go. "Plus, it going and rain again."

The next day, the homework sat on my desk again. And while I quadruple-checked yesterday's sums and read Molly Mumpkins, everyone played. A boy, pretending to be a Power Ranger, jumped from desk to desk and posed while his friends cheered his performance. It was a stupid, but good imitation, I admitted. Others huddled and exchanged chewing gum and jub jub candy. Some even sneaked outdoors to play cricket and no teachers noticed.

"Come leh we see if she be sick or what," said Ivy on our way home that afternoon. "We could ask Mam to bring noodle soup for her."

Beside Miss Pam's fence, two rows of fuchsia jump-and-kiss flowers bloomed and I thought if I made Miss Pam a flower crown with them she'd look like a sea princess.

Ivy shouted, "Miss Pam, Miss Pam."

A man with some cows passed behind us.

"Miss Pam?" Ivy called a few more times, while I watched the cows. "Miss Paaam!"

"You deafing me ears," I said, sucking my teeth.

"So how she gon hear me then? Miss Pam!"

A man from the house next door came out on his veranda and asked if our mammy didn't train us not to shout in public like two drunk men.

"We're looking for Miss Pam," Ivy said. "She didn't come to school today, or yesterday."

"She gone away," he said and turned to go in his house.

Everything was still except for an aeroplane passing overhead. We all looked up at it.

"Gone where?" I shouted at the man's back, thinking that if I spoke up for once in my life and showed some anger, it wouldn't be true that Miss Pam was gone.

"Gone Canada or somewhere," he shouted over his shoulder and kept walking, as if he'd said, gone to buy eddo for soup, and all were still well in the world.

"When she coming back?" I asked, getting proactive.

"She not comin' back," he said, then did an about-turn and came back to accuse, "You mean y'all school didn't tell you nothin'?"

"How do you know?" I asked indignantly, as if he were not one to know anything, especially anything about my Miss Pamela.

"Look," he said and pointed to a row of eight pots of plants in front his house, "she gimme all her crotons." He didn't look like the kind of man who would paint little pink stripes all the way around the base of plant pots. What he was saying must be true then, I thought.

"Oh," I said, holding my stomach. The limey sensation, becoming ridiculously familiar now, was stirring up in my belly. I glanced at Ivy to see if she had the lime too, if she could feel her own lime juice spreading in her body. But she seemed just the same plain old Ivy Lee Harry, no lime.

"Alright thanks," Ivy shouted at the receding back of the new owner of Miss Pam's immaculate croton pots. Then she turned me around, pushed me off the bridge and steered me home like I was a wardrobe on wheels on moving day.

For weeks, my books remained unmarked. I wondered what to do with Miss Pam's Molly Mumpkins. It wasn't mine.

I couldn't keep it. So I put it under the trapfloor of the doll's house.

The next three days at school were like recess period multiplied by infinity. You could feel your neurons shrivelling up and duncing up your brain.

Even Ivy started getting impatient with no one coming to say what was to become of us. Finally, she told one of her friends that Miss Pam had gone to Canada. The friend told someone and that someone told someone else, and eventually someone told me that someone said Miss Pam was never coming back. Then that was all anybody could talk about. Tales of North America. Things from TV. Barbies. Polly Pockets. Tickle Elmos. Crocodile Dentists. What a bunch of clowns, I thought.

I was just thinking I'd beg Pap not to send me to school anymore, when the headmistress barged in. It was improper to spread around news that wasn't ours to tell, she said. We were not *The Guyana News Stand* she said, nor were we selling tales cheap like greens at Bourda market on wholesale day. We were civilised young men and women and we were to get our books and revise and be constructive, not gossipy. Meanwhile two strong boys were to remove the blackboard partitioning our class from the one next door and we were to sit with Sir Ghanpatsingh's class and not cause trouble for which it seems we had a proclivity. Conss-truct-tive, I said in my head. Connstruckk-tive, gos-sip-ee, pro-clivv-itt-ee.

"Don't you children have better things to do? Who started this tale?" the headmistress carried on screeching so loudly that I almost pulled out my lunch towel to stuff it in my ears. But I stopped myself in time. Everyone already thought I was some sort of nutty sour cracker and I wasn't going to give them more fuel for their old motor mouths.

Nobody answered the headmistress.

"Who?" she asked again, "I want that troublemaker to come up here and read this whole chapter aloud," she said, grabbing with her smudgy chipped burgundy nails a random dog-eared book off Miss Pamela's bookshelf and thumping it on the teacher's desk. What a wicked witch, I thought, dumping Miss Pam's books around and yelling at us like it was we who were the imbeciles.

Ivy's bench scraped back. She shot up. Her mouth opened. She pointed at the headmistress.

Oh Lord, I thought. I couldn't bear to see a brawl break out in Miss Pam's class, neither did I want to wait around alone under the silk cotton tree while Ivy served detention on the top floor for mouthing off a teacher. Again. I was tired of that. And agitated by children whispering stories about that tree and muttering prayers in different languages whenever they passed it. So I stood up in what must have been a quick second because it was just in time to shut up Ivy. But it felt like I was swimming in a painful slow motion like on Pappo Harro's TV when the cowboy pulls out a gun and takes the slowest time to bring his arm up to shoot the bad guy. Or like getting pulled slowly under water and not breathing, like the time Uncle Raffie took us to a pool in Georgetown and Lennard pulled me down and I thought I was going to drown, and orphan-twin Ivy and she would get Ganee Gwenny and Pappo Harro all to herself, and the cherry buns and pine tarts too.

"Miss Moses, I will read it," I said. My voice barely came out.

"What's that girl?"

"I will read it."

She chucked the book across the desk and stomped out.

Ivy's bench screeched forward. She sat down, nostrils still flared.

I went to the head of the class and picked up the book. It had Acts and Scenes, not chapters.

"Hamlet, it says," I read to the bewildered faces enjoying the scene. And fumbling over the term 'dramatis personae,' I began.

7

The Dunce

The merge with Sir Ghanpatsingh's class was a nightmare. I had to strain my whole nervous system to hear when Sir spoke because the class was so large. The girl next to me craned her neck to see the board even though she had glasses. I called out the numbers and letters for her until I got tired and left my book open for her to copy everything. Sometimes she didn't even know she was copying my answers too until she settled down to puzzle over her page.

Ivy though sat with a group from Sir's class. They exchanged smiley face erasers back and forth as if they'd been best buddies all term. But what was I going to try and belong for? Children sat so close to me I could see their pores and the hairs on their arms. Their elbows hit mine when I tried to write, making my pencil scratch across my page so I had to keep erasing things. But it didn't matter. Sir never learned my name or looked at me. He looked only at the pupils in the front row. I didn't understand what to do for homework and didn't say so because people would think I was a dunce, the worst thing in the world that someone could be.

My terror of being a dunce plagued me for a long time, even when the new teacher came. Mr Jonathan Albert

Jeremiah Lee, he said his name was. Mr J.A.J. Lee, for short. He had wrinkles. He wore brown suits. He had a briefcase with a stack of cream folders. People said he had studied abroad. That he'd written policies. Was a distinguished son of the soil. That was how the headmistress, standing on the platform at the top of the stairs, introduced him at General Assembly, while the whole school, in rows in the yard under the peevish sun, looked up at her and the two figures flanking her sides. We were very lucky to have J.A.J. Lee at such short notice, said she. Very lucky indeed to even have him at all. We had to applaud twice, when she said that. She said, "Come boys and girls, let us have another round of hearty applause." She said the word hearty like it was a big dollop of ketchup at the side of a plate of fried potato wedges.

Then she gestured at the large sour-faced boy on her right. She said that this was Mr Lee's nephew from abroad. He was staying with his uncle for a while and we were to share our school while he shared his experiences from abroad. When she said the word abroad she flourished her open palms towards the boy like he were a great specimen in an international exhibition at which we had to marvel. All the pupils fixated on the boy standing on the platform and they clapped while the boy raised his chin about three inches and surveyed the population, his mighty round face rotating slowly clockwise, from one end of the school fence to another.

My palms wouldn't raise to applaud. I felt like I had a five pound brick in each hand weighing down my palms from raising to my bosom in applause for the specimen atop the stairs. Instead, I raised my hand to wipe the sticky sweat from my hairline. But just then the boy's eye caught mine. He saw I wasn't applauding like everyone else and his mouth curled down a little. I thought, maybe I should applaud after all, just in case I was making him feel unwelcome. But before I could put my palms together, his head rotated on to the rest of crowd.

Mam and Pap said that J.A.J. Lee was one of Guyana's scholars.

"What's a scholar exactly?" I asked.

'Skoll-ar', I said in my head. 'Skull-er'.

J.A.J. taught us quickly because we had lost weeks of class time. He was going to conquer the syllabus from cover to cover, he said. Read this and that, cover to cover, he'd say. Paper all your books in brown. Cover to cover. Complete the whole textbook by term end. Cover to cover. So Ivy and I called him Mr Cover-to-cover behind his back. At term end said he had covered the whole syllabus, cover to cover. He might have done so indeed, but he couldn't have been as smart as everyone said he was because I don't remember learning anything.

Ivy's performance on the other hand, was just the same. No better, no worse. She was as she had always been, not thrilled about school, but not allergic to it either. She explored new things to make it bearable, such as striking up a friendship with a girl called Brave Bonnie. In the mornings, she and Bonnie hid behind the big tree trunk and waited to paste signs on the backs of the boy bullies in our class. The signs usually said things like 'Kick me in the Buttocks' or 'Call me Fool' or 'Jackass Express.' They learnt these games from J.A.J.'s sullen nephew.

The Nephew was J.A.J.'s sister's boy from Brooklyn. Brave Bonnie told Ivy that The Nephew's parents were getting a divorce and that his mother had sent him here until everything nasty settled down and his father couldn't snatch him and scram. The Nephew was as large as Brave Bonnie, so she had a crush on him. She was impressed that he was from away and not from Peaside Pasture. "Eww," she'd say, looking at the skinny scab-kneed boys from Peaside. She'd sneak up to the chalkboard when no teacher was around and draw a heart. Then she wrote her name above the heart and The Nephew's name below the heart so that it read, Bonnie hearts Claude. And everyone made 'Ooo' sounds.

The Nephew brought something called a Gameboy to school and all the boys wrote their names on a list to get a chance to play with it. He made them each pay five dollars for a turn. Bonnie wrote her name too and The Nephew laughed.

"You're a girl," he said.

He and the boys sat behind the school every day and played with the gadget. But when he got tired of waiting for it, he entertained himself by showing Bonnie and Ivy how to stick rude signs on unsuspecting people.

Once they stuck one on me.

Ivy came up, patted me on the back and said, "You ready for dat Maths test eh?"

"No," I said, my heart warming because she was interested in my worries. Mathematics was a terrifying word, chilling my fingertips and burning my stomach now that Miss Pam wasn't here. So it was nice to have someone ask how I felt about things, so I could say things weren't alright. And there I was, with my heart warming and trying to forget about the test, that I didn't know I was walking through the school yard and into class with a sign on my back that said 'The Duncified Goat.'

Children chanted 'Duncified goat, duncified goat' but I didn't know they were talking about me until J.A.J. said, "Miss Harry, take that label from your tunic instantly. Your school uniform is not a joke."

I didn't talk to Ivy for days.

"Sorry sorry sorry," she said, still laughing. "Bonnie and Claude made me do it."

"I'm telling Mam."

"Come man, don't. Was just a joke."

"Y'all getting foolish? You better tell Claude stop bringing his stupid games here."

The Nephew heard his name and came over.

In his Brooklyn accent, he said "Whad a dunce who can't take a joke. Geez, you guys awfully backward down here."

"You better not call us backward. Don't call me dunce either. And stop sticking signs on people," I said and stood up. But I couldn't even look him in the eye. He was too tall.

"Or what?" he said, looking down.

"Or I'm telling Sir Lee."

Brave Bonnie came up beside The Nephew and more of his loyal soup drinkers gathered behind him.

"The last person tryin'a tell me whad-a do got a nice surprise coming to him," The Nephew said to someone behind him as Ivy shoved me out the door into the sunshine.

"I telling Mam you following bad friends," I said. "That's the terriblest boy in the whole school. I dunno what J.A.J. had to go and bring him here for. That boy not right in his brains. I telling Mam 'bout you."

But I didn't have time to tell Mam anything. The Math test was the next morning and I was afraid I was going to get a zero, so I stayed up half the night wondering what kind of job that I, as a dunce, could get if I quit school and became the one and only disgrace to the Harry name.

"Pap-Pap," I said, when he came to tuck us in and make sure we'd said our prayers.

"Hmm?"

"What you make me go to school for?"

Pap chuckled.

"To learn," he said.

"But I not learning."

"You're learning more than you know. Trust me Ixie Pixie."

I pulled the sheet over my head. Pap didn't understand school, I thought.

The next day during the test, The Nephew balled his fist and gestured a punch at me.

I ignored him. I had bigger problems. I didn't know enough answers on the test.

But The Nephew scribbled and sat up before the timer buzzed. He and all the boys in his squad winked at and thumbs-upped each other. Even Brave Bonnie finished ahead of me. If she and these dunce boys could finish before me, then it was true. I was now the official class dunce.

But something seemed wrong when J.A.J. strolled down the rows and collected the answer sheets. He glanced at them one at a time and grunted when he came to mine. I wished the school floor would lift up like a trapdoor so I could fall underneath and hide. He eyed Ivy's script but made no sounds. Then he picked up Brave Bonnie's and his eyebrows shot up. He picked up The Nephew's and his eyebrows furrowed. Pulling down his glasses, he watched The Nephew like he was peering into his soul. Then he snatched some of the boys' scripts and the furrow dug further into his brow, and J.A.J. for the first and only time sent us home a whole five minutes early. As we filed out, I looked back and saw him bury his face in his palms with his neck squishing into his collar as if a boulder were pressing on his head.

I couldn't eat my dinner that night, even though Pappo Harro had cooked something new from an old recipe concocted by his grandfather who'd come on a ship from far away somewhere, somewhere that had nothing to do with me, I thought. I put a spoonful of whatever it was in my mouth but the food came up my throat. Tomorrow everyone would know that I was a Dunce.

But the next morning J.A.J. didn't return the marked test papers like he always did.

At lunch time, I was sitting by the window with my textbook open to the chapter on simple machines – levers and things, when I heard a racket downstairs. I hung my head out the window and saw my class clamouring by the back wall. The Nephew was holding a paper and copying something from it on the wall. Ivy too was with the group. And she was pacing. So I flew down the stairs and joined the group. But I couldn't see what The Nephew was writing. The crowd grew silent when they saw me. They stepped to the sides and I walked up.

The Nephew had written a list of everyone's first names in the class. And next to each name was a number. No number was higher than eighteen. His own name was at the top and eighteen was next to it. There were some other boys' names too with eighteen next to them but their names came beneath his. Brave Bonnie's was somewhere in the middle. Ivy's was somewhere below Bonnie's. Then there were some other names. And then there was my name and some other pupils' too down at the bottommost bottom of the list. The bottom group of us had a nine written next to our names.

"What's this?" I asked the bespectacled girl who used to copy the things from my book.

"Marks for the test they say," she whispered.

"What test?"

"Yesterday, Maths."

I swallowed.

"Out of how much?"

The girl shrugged.

"Twenty," somebody whispered.

The first tear squeezed itself out. Then the second and a dozen more. I turned to go.

"Hasta la vista Duncified Goat," The Nephew said, and his squad laughed.

I swivelled in an about-turn to tell him to go wash his mouth and his mind with soap, but already he had his pointer finger shooting pow-pow at me like I was the villain in one of his video games and he was finally bringing me down to claim his top score. It felt like he was shooting at my skull right where the old lime had just showed up and lodged itself. When he pow-powed, the lime split and the juice spread through my brain, squeezed down my cheeks and into my tunic. I hustled into the building before he could come after me and witness the lime tears. I bolted up an empty corridor with my vision burning and blurry. And as I bolted, I imagined Miss Pam's croton pots with the pink bases chasing me like horses.

It was that day that I discovered the school had a kind of library. There it was, a pale brown door saying 'Library.' I knocked and turned the handle but the door wouldn't open. I wanted somewhere to get in and hide. Miss Pam had said we mustn't hide our stories. But what did she know? I tried the knob again. It wouldn't budge.

Just then, a shape flitted by, then walked backwards towards me. I thought The Nephew's come to shoot more acid into my head. But it was only the janitor. He smelled of disinfectant and something else in an undertone, something strange and not too great, something like a very expired cologne.

He stood in the corridor looking down at me, saying nothing. I felt small and sour, and contemplated dashing past him up the corridor from where I'd come. But just then, he produced a bunch of keys, opened the library door and went away.

Inside the little rectangular room were five empty bookshelves. There were two large desks in the middle of the room too, with several tall stacks of books. And I put one foot out and before I knew it I was walking around, breathing away my sour, blowing dust off the ancient books and feeling just as ignited as the time I started attending university and Junior held my hand at the campus fair.

The books were sneeze mines but I didn't care. I sneezed and dusted them with my tunic and sneezed some more, eyes and nose happily runny. I spotted some Shakespeare plays and put them in one corner. I knew about those from the stack Miss Pam had left on our class bookshelf. There were poetry collections too. So I grouped them on one shelf. Then I went prowling around for more poetry books to add to that pile. The heavier books with shorter passages and comprehension exercises I stacked on another shelf. By the time lunch was over and the janitor came back I had several categories of books at my arm's length.

The janitor stood at the door, mouth open and eyes darting around at the books I had started categorising. He closed his mouth and pulled his lips lower down, pushed his eyebrows higher up and nodded as if to say: Not-a-bad-job-indeed!

Then he smiled, with the smell of disinfectant and expired cologne bouncing off him.

And I smiled back, my sourness dissipating.

J.A.J. never returned the test papers, the ones for which The Nephew had written the alleged scores on the back of the school wall. But the next day, J.A.J. shocked us with a pop quiz, graded it and returned our papers within an hour. He was taking the marks for this new quiz instead, he said, but didn't explain why. He said it with pebbles in his voice and his cheeks pufferfishing up. The Nephew glared at his uncle like he wanted to bulldoze into the old man's stomach. And J.A.J. stared right back, grimly.

Finally, on the day that J.A.J. returned our report cards, my throat dried up.

"Miss Harry comma Ivy Lee," he said like an alphabetising machine and handed Ivy her blue booklet, "Fair performance."

Then he handed me mine, "Miss Harry comma Ixora Mara," he said and pulled his glasses down and looked at me. I hadn't done as well as my twin, he said. He was disappointed as he had expected better from me overall since my writing was exceptionally commendable, and could I ask my parents to come to the school tomorrow?

I nodded and avoided Ivy's eyes.

My neck and ears burned with shame because Ivy had done as well as she had always done and therefore that meant I had no reason to perform poorly, and because every report card day Pap towed us out on his bicycle for ice cream cones and this term I didn't deserve one.

I rubbed the tears back into my eyes, barely able to bear the dunceness creeping around in my brain. The blue report card weighed like a five pound brick in my hand. I thought of Miss Pam swimming about in flourishing figure eights in her mermaid's life, somewhere marvellous on the other side of the planet and I wondered how I could get rid of the relentless sourness flooding my brain again, mingled this time with ounces of dunceness. I wondered how I could make the sour-dunce go out of me so I could grow into as shimmering a lady as Miss Pam.

8

A Library is a Cocoon

Mr Fred, the janitor, opened the small dust box of a library every day for me. There I pottered about imagining that the cobwebs cocooned me from the machinations of The Nephew and the whole wide world that rolled themselves out at his feet and danced to his tune. With every new toy and gadget he brought, they danced. The more remote controlled cars, the more ring pops he brought, the faster they danced. Even Ivy, who hardly remembered people's wrongdoing – what about forgiveness and all that, she'd say – she too, danced on occasion to the delightful stream of comic books that The Nephew's father kept mailing in barrels. So whenever Mr Fred turned the key, I left Peaside Primary, that moribund sliver of educational practice, behind. Moribund, a sour sounding word I found in a vocabulary book in the little dust box. Murey-bunnd. There in my dust box, I descended into books, into illustrations. In a coral reef. Inside the Milky Way. Beside a mountain. In another civilisation. Inside an alabaster jar.

Soon I'd sorted the books into a system. Using the shelves as rungs, I climbed to the top and stashed the Advanced Chemistry books there, knowing that nobody in the school would want those. Most of the books had the stamp of a foreign school inside their covers. Someone somewhere must've thrown these books out and someone else thought it magnanimous to bring them down here to Peaside for poor souls to sponge up the knowledge.

One day, Mr Fred passed the library, walked backward, looked in and went away again. Then he returned, set down a bucket of clean water, laid a detergent tin and rag on a desk, bobbed his head at the items and left. I didn't know anyone else in the school who'd bother to bring an ant-of-a-pupil a cloth and bucket to aid her venture. It's like Mr Fred is a tomato or something on a big platter of lettuce, I thought, as I bit into my sandwich during lunch. That's when I decided that was exactly what I wanted to be too – the tomato on the platter of lettuce. Thus, my obsession with libraries, and tomatoes for that matter, began.

By the end of two weeks the books were in a discernible order on the shelves. In two more weeks, each section was alphabetised by author, at Mr Fred's suggestion. He said he'd seen it done like that in a movie. "Oh," I said, and repeating the alphabet in my head, I shuffled the books.

After all the books had been cleared off the two desks, Mr Fred mumbled how about we paint one of the desks and put some chairs around it like a real library. That sounded grand. So he said he'd ask the headteacher about it. But he came back with his mouth sagging.

"Headmistress say school can scrape money for one bucket paint but can't 'fford chair." He looked at the ground.

"Oh."

"We can mek dem though."

"Make them?"

"Hmm."

"But I don't know to make chairs," I said, suddenly feeling like I should have been learning to make chairs all my life. My Pap was, after all, a carpenter.

"Lil bit wood," he said, as if just having some wood could turn me into a carpenter.

He sat down to think and his disinfectant and expired cologne hit me. Ugh, I thought, trying not to wrinkle my nose and hurt his feelings.

"Well," I said, a little doubtfully, "my Pap, he's building our house with wood and maybe he could get us some."

Mr Fred was sitting at my eye level and I could see his irises expanding. I studied the red branches in the whites of his eyes. I'd never seen eyes with branches as red as those, except those times when I'd bawl about something, then look myself in the eye in the mirror.

"Aright, see what your old man seh."

I practised my speech in front of the living room mirror, reciting how Peaside children should have something to read and somewhere quiet to read it. But I knew I was Pinocchio-ing. I didn't want the library for the greater good. Those empty-headed Peaside delinquents wouldn't read a word if it wasn't coming on a test and still not even then, not even if you bribed them with sweeties. I wanted the whole library world for my own dear self. Selfish, hypocritical, trickster-ish, Pinocchio-ish is what I'm turning into, I thought, imagining the horror on Mam's face if she could see inside my head.

"Talking to yourself aay?" Pap said, on his way through the living room.

Finally, when I managed to mumble about the wood, his eyes lit up. Right away he said he could do it. He said he would help Mr Fred make the chairs. And my chest warmed at the thought of a private cocoon.

But that evening I heard him and Mam whispering.

"But dat gon cost a good small change," Mam said.

"Yes, but I gon help make dem myself."

"Last month wood already on credit. You develop amnesia or what Mike?"

I felt guilty for peering through the crack in the wall, listening to grown-ups' conversation, so I grabbed a book and rationalised that if I were standing there reading, it wouldn't be eavesdropping.

"Yes, but —" Pap tried to continue.

"Yes but why the school can't raise dem own funds. Why dem other children parents can't share the cost?" Mam was getting furious.

Pap sighed.

"When last Ixie ask for anything eh? Since J.A.J. say put her in the extra lessons class, she get so quiet. No man Laurie, we gotta do something to buy the wood," he said.

Mam sighed. "What we gon do then? When they want these chairs?"

But I didn't hear the rest for Ivy came in singing and dancing the 'Macarena,' her latest obsession, so I abandoned the crack in the wall before she ratted me out.

The next day, Mam and Pap picked breadfruit and coconuts, loaded them in crocus bags and filled baskets with fruits. Then after church, they sold them at Sunday market. During the week, Mam made mango achar and fruit juice and arranged them on the stand. And by the end of seven weeks, they announced that they'd raised almost enough money to buy wood for ten small chairs. I shrieked and hugged Pappo Harro who was walking by.

"Hmm?" he asked, making cartoon sounds in his throat.

Sudden hugs made him uncomfortable. Apart from Junior's grampappy and Ganee who drew out his laughter, Pappo didn't wear expression on his sleeves, except of course, for his disdain towards Pap, Uncles Winnie and Raffie and the rest of the whole miserable world. He didn't do hugs. That's why he and Mam got on fine, as if she were his biological daughter. "Cut from the same cloth, those two,"

Ganee'd say and point at Pappo and Mam at the dining table, each eating half a pawpaw, and saying nothing.

So as Pappo stood there, not hugging me back but not moving away either, I told him about the project.

"Almost enough? How yuh mean?"

Pap explained.

Then Pappo went into his bedroom. After the pop of a tin and some clinking sounds, he came out and handed me a few bills.

I passed them to Pap.

"Dat enough?" Pappo asked me.

"I think we gon even have more to buy a bucket of paint," Pap said, his teeth showing, his cheekbones rising to the ceiling.

And he and Pappo, Uncle Warbin and Mr Fred made quick work of the chairs and we loaded them on Junior's grampappy's donkey cart and transported them to school. And what a fuss. The children from our class and Junior's class poked their heads out of windows and hee-ed and haw-ed at the donkey. They scooted down the stairs to pet him but teachers hauled them back. A few delinquents escaped and reached the donkey and hugged him and asked what his name was. They begged for rides on him and Junior's grampappy obliged. Children on the top floor cheered at the commotion below. I looked up at them and for a moment, for setting all these things in motion, I felt like a tomato on a platter of lettuce leaves and I lifted my nose three inches for a bit of crisp fresh air.

But following me were The Nephew's eyes, like two black boot heels ready to come down on an ant.

Breaking eye contact and hoping he'd look away, I put my head down and helped Ivy carry a chair.

We put the white desk and the ten crisply white chairs surrounding it in the middle of the rectangular library. Mr

Fred repainted the door and Ganee and Ivy embroidered a sign that said Library. And Ganee even made some curtains for the four small windows.

Sometimes Mr Fred lent me books of his own. He said I could leave them on the shelves for anyone who wanted to borrow. But nobody came to the library except me. After the books had been sorted, they seemed sparse on the shelves and my classmates weren't enticed. No matter, I thought, a library was a far better world than the regular world and if those juveniles didn't know it, I wasn't going to volunteer such priceless information. I read all the books Mr Fred brought and when I was through with that set, he took those home and brought more. I read every single book in every new set he brought. He had dozens of books, it seemed. And when I wasn't reading I was writing stories again.

I created a detective. His name was Inspector Sim Art, Inspeck S'mart for short. I sketched and coloured him. He had a beret, a bright blue shirt with huge buttons and a whistle in its pocket, a big belt buckle and big shiny shoes.

Inspeck S'mart made going to Peaside Primary bearable again. I looked for material to write and spent hours in the library formulating story lines and counting clues with him. That was his thing. By the time he reached his fourth clue, he could solve the case. In *The Case of the Disappeared Breadfruit*, he'd say something like: Who stole the breadfruit? Clue number one – a few dog hairs by a post. Hmm, a dog was scratching itself there. Someone with a dog. Bam! I'm coming to get you. Clue number two – cigarette ash by the gate. A smoker. Bam! I'm coming to get you. Clue number three – no shoe prints, just barefoot prints of a man. Someone who doesn't live far. A neighbour. Bam! I'm coming to get you. Watch out! Clue number four – all the yards around here have a breadfruit tree, except that one. Oh-lala-lala.

Then I'd get excited about the conclusion and write something like: Finally, the detective inspector spied the opposite neighbour through his binoculars. The man was barefoot. He was smoking and eating fried breadfruit chips. Plus he was feeding his big brown dog Bruno a tasty chip too. 'Good day Mr Breadfruit thief,' the marvellous Inspeck S'mart said. 'Bam! I've got you. Do not cook things that don't belong to you sir.' The end. Then I'd giggle and choke at the dialogue I'd written, thinking myself thoroughly spectacular for knowing how to use indentations, quotation marks and exclamation points.

But, The Nephew was at it again. He'd come stand around in the doorway with his high and mighty squad and say, "I told you guys, she's like a mad woman cackling away in a cave."

'Cackling' was one of my least favourite words but I ignored him. I wouldn't waste another minute on a boy who lacked integrity and brain. And he lacked both, I knew. Ivy'd told me that Brave Bonnie told her that before the Math test from weeks ago, she, Bonnie saw a copy of the test, except for two questions that J.A.J. changed at the last minute. A boy from The Nephew's squad had a photocopy of the question and answer sheets and he and The Nephew sold copies for twenty dollars each, the profits of which they split, eighty-twenty, eighty for The Nephew. This is what Bonnie said, and what did she have to gain by lying and incriminating her own self? When Ivy told me, I sobbed into my pillow and Ganee came and brought me tea in a dainty floral-print teacup and matching saucer borrowed from her side cabinet of special wares for guests.

I sipped from the magical tea cup and surmised that I probably didn't rank at the bottom of the class after all as The Nephew wanted me to believe. He must've stolen J.A.J.'s list with the scores and written them on the school wall because he wanted me to think I was really a dunce. Why else? I tried to solve it like a mystery. If all The Nephew wanted was for him and his squad to pass the test or to make some money off the photocopies, then why put the writing on the wall? It must be me he was after. But why? I never did anything to anybody in my whole life. Besides there was no way to prove it, and there was nobody to prove it to. Something sour pushed my tea back up, so I swallowed and cried more.

Ganee stooped by the bed with a few groans. Through her round rimmed glasses, she looked me in the eye and said, "You are Ixora Mara and no writing on the wall can stop that."

That made me stop crying right away.

Ivy stood at the foot of the bed, listening and picking at her finger nails.

So whenever he stood in my library doorway, The Nephew, he and his henchmen, I said in my head, I am Ixora Mara and no writing on the wall can stop that. Ivy said that all The Nephew really wanted was to make friends with everybody in the whole school and because Ivy clearly didn't possess the capacity to think straight, I had to let her know that nobody could be friends with everybody. Besides, if you really wanted to be friends with somebody, I doubt that labelling them a duncified goat with a sticky sign and a low class rank was the best approach. So whether The Nephew loitered by my library doorway for distorted friendship or foeship, I told him to scram and skedaddle, expressions I picked up from Ivy's TV shows. Then I slammed the door in his face, sometimes bolting it from the inside, and I carried on reading and writing.

I often hid my Inspeck S'mart stories in a big purple hardcover Encyclopaedia of Birds and shoved the book against the wall behind the row of animal books. Someone would have to read or remove the whole row of books to even catch sight of my purple encyclopaedia. And no Peaside pupil was going to try and read a whole row of animal books, so Inspeck S'mart was always safe counting his clues back there in the gap between the wall and the row of books. I brought him out and worked on a bit of story every day during recess and lunch hour. And sometimes, when the school was swarming with extra-curricular activities like Market Day or Sports, I tried to sneak away into the library when J.A.J. was demanding that every single pupil participate in every single event. That pest. Mister Cover-to-Cover, Commander of Every-Single-Event, Ruiner of Worlds, Skull-er.

On one of these sweaty extra-curricular days, when everyone was outdoors and I was hiding out in the library struggling to write a series of clues and mocking J.A.J. in my head – Potential for better marks Miss Harry, Pohh-tenn-shall – I heard a scuffle outside. Cautiously, I cracked the door and peered out. In the corridor, The Nephew was threatening a boy half his size and wrestling a ball from him. For a second I considered coming to the boy's aid. But that would do no good, I thought. That boy had to stand up for himself. I wasn't his fairy godmother who could pop up every time he was getting beat up. Besides what if I popped up and made things worse? Or what if I popped up and got beat up myself? And for what, a ball? Mam would rage. Yes, The Nephew couldn't be allowed to carry on like this, but today it was none of my business. I pushed the door back in place, but before it could close, the door creaked and The Nephew's eyes flashed up and caught mine. I slammed the door and ran to my desk.

And a few seconds later, when the knob rattled, I looked around for a place to hide or escape, but there was none. The library really was a cocoon for better and for worse.

Surely, it was The Nephew coming to demand to know what I was going to do about what I'd just witnessed.

But it was only Mr Fred, thank the Lord. In he came, rolling his bucket, grumbling that he hadn't given the floor a good mopping in a while and could I help him stack the chairs in the corner so he could mop under the desk.

"Suppose' to call me niece, yuh know. Tell she how you nice-up dis book room. She guh glad fuh hear. But me na geh fuh call yet," he said, as he slopped the mop around.

"Why?"

"Na get time. Ah me alone. Gah fuh cook fuh meself since the Missus gone 'merica fuh babysit. Gah fuh wash wares, wash clothes," he went on.

"No, I mean why tell your niece?"

"She teach hey. Pamela."

The neon green jub jub candy I ate at break was suddenly back on my tongue, spiking the buds.

"Miss Pamela was ... is your niece?" I said, a little shocked at such easy connections existing in the world. "She was my teacher. Tell her I said hi. My full name is Ixo—"

"Write something. Me post am fuh yuh."

So one afternoon while the delinquents in the back row hustled their homework before the Lessons teacher came out, I started writing the letter behind my science book. Although I wished I hadn't, because it made the hullabaloo that followed, twice as bad.

9

Boot Heels on an Ant

Ivy and I attended the Extra Lessons given by a teacher who lived on the opposite side of the village. Since this teacher came highly recommended by J.A.J., Recommender of Extra Lessons, Stiffler of Childhood, we now spent our afternoons ticking multiple choice questions, filling in the blanks, breaking words into syllables, tracing the four natural regions and ten administrative regions of Guyana, labelling diagrams and cramming definitions for things like photosynthesis.

Three afternoons a week, we walked from school to the Lessons Yard over in Seaside Strip. Seaside Strip had large houses with tall iron fences and menacing dogs guarding gates. You couldn't tell that Seaside Strip and Peaside Pasture were the same village. Even I didn't know, until our lesson on writing formal letters.

"Pap? How we write our address?" I handed him my notebook.

He wrote it and passed the book back.

"What's Zeker-he-id?" I asked.

"Zekerheid. Zeke-er-ide," he said.

"What's dat?"

"Our village."

"How you mean?"

"Zekerheid is here where we live Ixie Pixie. Our village."

"Here?" I pointed to the floor. Pap nodded, amusement lighting up his cheekbones.

"So where the Peaside Pasture part?" I asked, looking at the address again.

Pap burst into laughter, probably at my bewildered face and my voice growing higher pitched with every exclamation.

"Dat's not the real name of the village you know," he said, still laughing.

I was accustomed to Pap laughing with me, not at me. I looked around feeling the living room floor being yanked from under me. There I was standing on a blank world.

"People jus' used to call here Peaside 'cus we farm," Pap said. "Long 'go they used to farm plenty here. Sometimes peas. People on the strip near the seawall must be ashamed of planting peas so then they jus' named themselves Seaside Strip." He laughed again.

"But why?" I asked, appalled that I didn't know the real name of my own village, even though I was practically a grown-up. Maybe The Nephew was right, I really was a dunce. Even kindergarteners knew where they lived.

Pap stopped laughing after a while. He shrugged. Then he sighed. It seemed like there was more that he was too tired to tell me.

"People find ways to distinguish themselves for all sorts of reasons Ixie. People do things to make themselves visible. Or to let it be known that they're not you, and you're not them."

He put his head down and continued sketching the floor plan he was working on for somebody's house. I didn't entirely know what he meant but I remembered what he said because I liked the sound of the word dis-ting-wish. It was a posh word, like the upturned collars of winter coats and polished shoe tips.

It was only until I grew up I could see that Zekerheid's landscape from a bird's eye view was shaped like a square one dimensional house if sketched on art paper. But it was like a house split straight down by a level brick road. In the middle of the square was the church, the Primary school – that was actually named Zekerheid Primary and not Peaside Primary after all, and the market. On the left, the ground was slightly higher than the brick road and on that side, near the sea, the streets were smooth and the little Pharmacy and Clinic, Community Centre and Lessons Yard were aligned behind neat rows of Madagascar periwinkle. On the right side of Zekerheid, the land tapered down to drain itself of excess water from the vegetable beds. On this side of the square, there were just pasturelands and about two hundred small houses with zinc roofs, including our own house.

To cross the road from Peaside to the self-proclaimed Seaside Strip, Ivy and I were told to look right, left and right again, hold each other's hand and cross with purpose.

"You two listening to me? Don't cross 'way and leave your sister," Mam commanded, speaking to both of us, though we all knew she was speaking more to Ivy than me, "You hear me? Who ah talkin' to? Dat post over there?"

I didn't like crossing over into Seaside. People stared at us. Back then I couldn't tell why, but we must've been a spectacle because we looked alike – a whole parallel two-part story to watch – walking side by side, different but same. Uncle Warbin's old Polaroids of us attest to that. Like the one taken on graduation day, with us in the same umber and white uniforms, same brown shoes and tall white football socks up to our knees, same pigtail braids sticking out at the sides of our heads. Same height, same smiles, same angle of hugging each other, just mirror opposite. In some of our other photos, even I had to peer closer to make sure which one of us was me. For the Seasiders, it must've been like seeing double.

I wish Seaside would get their own pair of twins, I'd think, as their impeccably groomed dogs growled at us through bars.

Along the way was a trench where schoolboys fished and limed, and all the children going to lessons stopped to spectate. The Nephew, whose mother's money rented one of the big houses in Seaside for him and J.A.J., he and his squad would be there too. To his delight, life was "bedder" now than being cooped up in his parents' apartment. And why wouldn't it be, now that he could roam the countryside and command his local squad of impressionable scab-kneed provincial boys hanging about to do his bidding.

On the day after The Nephew's tussle with the boy outside the library, his eyes met mine by the trench. He watched me closely as I pulled Ivy along, who for no sensible reason, wanted to peer into buckets and ask the names of fish and barter a smudgy but sizeable eraser for the chance to put worms on hooks.

"Come on. Mam don't want us dilly-dallying," I said.

I held my head up and walked past The Nephew, keeping my eyes away from his. I started reciting my new mantra in my head – I am Ixora Mara and no writing on the wall can ... but The Nephew had a monkey on his shoulder, feeding it nuts and trying to teach it tricks and it was hard for me to keep my eyes away.

"Pollard?" I said, trying to see the sakiwinki more closely.

The monkey stopped and turned a little towards my voice.

"Pollard," I said again, louder.

The monkey looked around.

The Nephew looked at me and told his squad, "See? Told you guys this one's a cracker."

"Where'd you get this monkey?" I asked.

"He's mine," The Nephew said.

"Where did you get him?"

Everyone gathered around.

"He's mine. I told you already, you deaf dunce."

"That's my Uncle Warbin's monkey. Where'd you get him?"

Ivy tugged at my sleeve and said softly, "We can't be sure. Them sakiwinkies be looking alike you know."

"No, that's Pollard," I said.

"Come to lessons," she said, conveniently only now wanting to go to class, "we can't tell if that's really Pollard. Plus it getting late."

"Pollard," I called firmly.

This time the monkey tried to escape and come to me but The Nephew held him back while Ivy pulled me forward, hauling me to classes where she went to sit in the front row. I settled into the one of the back rows, hot and flustered, still thinking about Pollard. I was going to tell Uncle Warbin and he'd go and demand Pollard. He would get him back for sure, I thought, counting my breaths and calming down.

And as everyone had their science book out hurrying to get their homework done, I stood my science textbook up for some privacy and began my letter to Miss Pam behind it. I'd tell her all about The Nephew and everything he'd done. Even about Pollard. She was the only one who'd understand.

The note pages were short and I was already on the second page when The Nephew came in and sat behind me, his sweat stinking up the back bench.

"Where's that monkey?" I asked.

"Home," said The Nephew. He handed a boy a twenty dollar note in exchange for his own exercise book.

"How'd you get Pollard?" I said, noting that he was still in the habit of cheating, this time paying off plebians to do his homework.

"He's mine. His name is Dumpy."

Dumpy? I thought, what an undignified name for a class act like Pollard.

"You stole him," I said, my slow breaths and calmness dissipating again.

"Do I look like some kinda thief, you country rat! I bought him."

"From who?"

"He's mine!" He said the word 'he's' low and growling and 'mine' high-pitched and shrieking.

Everyone in the room stopped their homework and watched.

Then The Nephew caught sight of my unfinished letter to Miss Pam, and his pupils dilated and danced all over my note paper. I had been complaining about him to Miss Pam and I hoped he hadn't seen his name. But before I could cover the paper with the textbook, he reached over and snatched it. I jumped up and tried to grab it. But he was too burly.

"Give it," I said.

"You are dearly missed," he read a line from the letter aloud. "Oh oh oh now," he sang, "A lurrve letter, oo."

"Give it." I leaped as high as I could.

"'Classes haven't been the same without you,'" he read. "Oh oh oh now."

"Oh oh oh now," my traitorous class echoed.

"Give it!"

Sour tears pricked at my eyeballs. Soon I couldn't see the sheet of paper I was trying to retrieve. And neither did I see clearly when Ivy climbed on a desk and jumped on The Nephew's back, choking him and snatching the letter. By the time I blinked the tears out, the two of them were on the floor and Ivy was sitting on his head, he looked like he was breathing dust and the lessons teacher was panting and pulling Ivy off.

"Miss Harry! Get off that boy's head!"

In the aftermath, J.A.J. whipped his nephew in both palms a dozen times with a cherry tree whip, we heard from Brave Bonnie. And Ivy, she, was scolded and sent to our room without fruit cake that evening. She didn't care. She snuck out at ten thirty that night, pried open the cake tin, sawed herself a slice, climbed back in bed, pulled the sheet over her head and ate it. And me, Pap coaxed me into finishing my letter to Miss Pam, as Mr Fred had come around for it since he was going to the post office for the school mail. But I scrapped that letter and wrote a curt new one asking Miss Pam when she'd be back and I excluded all the parts about The Nephew because it was really all her fault that he had come to Peaside with J.A.J. in the first place, and the thought of that was souring up the middle of my brain like a little ponging anvil giving me a liminoid headache.

"It's going to be all right Ixie-Pixie," Pap said. But it wasn't alright.

The next day at school, The Nephew, furious from his whipping, told Brave Bonnie to deliver a message to Ivy and me. Bonnie told Ivy if we took the path again beside the fish trench in Seaside that Claude would bet us up for good. Ivy just looked up at him from across the class like he was not even there. All night I worried whether I should tell Mam. On the other side of the bed Ivy snored with her head under the pillow. The next day, I suggested we walk the long way around to the lessons. But Ivy wouldn't.

"Walk a whole ten minutes more? For what?" She wasn't going to shift 'round her life for nothin' or nobody, she said, something she had heard on TV. "This be a free, independent, republic country, Miss Mara," she said, also things she had heard on TV, minus the sarcastic Miss Mara bit of course.

That was the attitude that got us into our first and only public fist fight for which the people of Peaside said that the sour-faced one was leading the sunshine-faced one astray.

When we passed by the trench, something smacked the back of my head. I turned around and saw a fish on the ground. Somebody had thrown a fish at me! Without missing two seconds, Ivy aimed the fish straight at The Nephew's face, plat!

The children grew silent. Watching.

Five seconds passed.

Then The Nephew advanced. Five big boys trailed him. The sakiwinki sat on his shoulder. I started falling into the sensation of being an ant again.

"How *dare* you!" said he, his Brooklyn accent cymballing in the air.

"How dare *you*?" said Ivy.

"I'm gonna tell my father!"

"Bring him then," Ivy challenged, "to defend his little fish-throwing, test-cheating whiney-baby."

"Don't forget monkey-thieving," I said, keeping an eye on Pollard, wondering if I dare steal him back.

The Nephew said, "Gedd offa my side," his accent menacing, harsh tones coming down on the words 'get off.'

Ivy said, "Anywhere I want, I walk. You not the traffic police and," she went closer to him, "nobody own this side or that side." She pointed on the ground for Seaside and into the air for Peaside. "This is the twentieth century, you know that?" she added.

He looked down at her and chucked her to the ground.

My stomach burbled. I needed the toilet.

"Stop," I said feebly.

But Ivy was up faster than she had been pushed and she pressed back against him and as to be expected, the crowd of boys right on cue, in perfect melody sang, "Fight, fight, fight."

The monkey shrieked and twirled in circles.

I tried to pull Ivy away. But the fight song was only riling her up. I could tell she wasn't going to let it go. Not today. I looked around for a sizeable referee.

One of the boys sitting hunched up beside the trench was Kalleecharran, the boy from school with the clean white sneakers who used to oblige to do his Physical Education lessons when Miss Pam was here. I thought, I know that large boy, maybe I could get him to help me. But Kalleecharran just kept sitting hunched up looking into the trench, not even taking much of an interest in the fight. I had never met a person who didn't take an interest in a fight. Absolutely useless, I thought.

"Ivy! Stop!" I pulled at her tunic.

But her head was already going full force into The Nephew's stomach.

"Ahh," he hollered and pinned her arm back.

She grabbed his collar and pulled. A button popped off. He pushed against her and she fell. She got up and the sight of blood appearing on her elbows nearly made me melt into a faint. She charged at him again.

"Fight, fight, fight," sang the choir.

"Ahh," groaned The Nephew again.

"Fight, fight, fight."

He pushed back at her with his hefty stomach. She stumbled. And taking advantage of the moment in which she stumbled, he re-doubled his efforts and pushed her again.

She fell and hit her head on a rock. And just lay there.

All the breath and blood and bone went out of me. I couldn't get my legs to work and for a long time I stood there listening to somebody's bleating goat holding the motion in the air.

Then I ran to Ivy.

Her eyes flickered but she didn't get up. A burgundy pool was forming slowly under her head by the rock. I tried lifting her head to sap up the leaking. But The Nephew was coming towards us again. I swallowed a howl. The tears swimming in my eyes felt as thick and gooey as the warm dye on my hands. I couldn't see what to do.

And then, I got up. I got up and I, flying towards The Nephew and shrieking with all the life in my body, pushed hard.

The choir grew quiet. A splash charged the air.

It was five slow seconds before my brain registered that it was I who had pushed The Nephew into the trench. My stomach churned. Torn between returning to my dying twin and saving the stranger – the re-migrant nephew of J.A.J., scholar, applause – that I'd just drowned, I froze. Good Lord, my name would be on the front page of the newspaper tomorrow – *Local Girl Loses Twin, Drowns Foreign Boy in Revenge*. Lord, my mother would never recover and my father's heart would break for good. And Ganee Gwenny and Pappo Harro would retire in shame for the downfall I'd brought upon the short working-class local legacy of the Harry name. God in heaven, what have I done, I thought.

Then I unfroze, my feet moving quickly towards the trench.

"Save him," I said to the jaw-dropped boys as I ran to look in the trench. But he didn't need saving. He was a swimmer, the trench was shallow and two boys could've easily dragged him out if they had to. But nobody had to.

He was already walking out of the water with his chest puffed out like a hero.

I ran back to Ivy who was trying to get up and wobbling. I helped her up. She placed her arm over my shoulder and I held her up by her back. I managed somehow to drag up our laden backpacks and we limped away.

I looked behind me at The Nephew, relieved I hadn't drowned him.

He stood there in a stupor, wet. His fists clenched around the sakiwinki.

Later in the school term some girls told me that a girl who was the sister of the friend of The Nephew said that he, Claude, still couldn't believe that it was the puny bookworm lunatic who had chucked him into the trench. And the girl said that Claude had promised everybody that someday that loony worm, that dunce goat, that puny ant would get what she deserved.

Our walk home was long and painful. We took ages to cross the road into Peaside. I feared a car would come and hit us because we went so slowly. Ivy's ankle was twisted too. She wasn't talking, just concentrating on walking home, her head and elbows still leaking burgundy. My vision kept blurring wet. And with her arm over my shoulder and the blood dripping down her temple and the silence, I'd just started to think that what was happening wasn't real when the cane cutter, Mam's customer, the young one who always wrapped all his snacks and put them in his sack, rushed up.

"What happen?" he asked frantically.

"A fight," I said, startled by the raspy voice coming out of my mouth.

He took Ivy's other arm and put it around his shoulder.

"Come, I gon help you walk," he said and he put his arm around her waist and hoisted her a few inches so that her feet were off the ground.

We struggled like that, but the going was faster with me on one side and him on the other side trying to lift her off the ground so she wouldn't have to use her feet, and we made our way home.

"Gimme one o' dem bags to hold," said the young man and relieved me of Ivy's heavy backpack.

Before we got to our gate, Mam was flying out the house. "What happen? What happen?"

I opened my mouth to speak but no words came out, and the young cane cutter spoke for me and explained what he'd observed about the injuries.

Mam lifted Ivy into the house, inspected her head wound and cleaned it. She felt all over Ivy's body and it seemed like only Ivy's shoulder and ankle were giving trouble. She turned to me and ran her eyes and hands over my body asking me if anything hurt.

I shook my head, no.

Then she asked Ivy if she could sit and be towed on a bicycle.

Ivy nodded, yes, but looked like she was going to faint.

Mam went outside and spoke to the young cane cutter again.

Pap wasn't home from work, and in those days there were no taxis running on our side of Zekerheid and we didn't have a car of our own. When you wanted to go into town, you had to walk half a mile right out to the road to where the public buses ran. Mam grabbed a plastic bag of money, yelled something to Ganee who didn't yet know what was happening, got out two bicycles, rolled one to the cane cutter and told me to hop on to the handle bar. Then she straddled the other bicycle, lifted Ivy on and towed her out. The young cane cutter towed me. When we got to the bus stop, Mam asked the young man if he would return the bicycles home for us.

When I looked out the bus window, I saw him riding one bike, steering it with one hand and pulling the other bike alongside him as if it were something he did every day.

Mam rushed us to the emergency ward where Ivy's head and ankle were bandaged. I, the doctor said, looked fine.

Early the next morning, Mam stood waiting outside the headmistress's office with Ivy and me. Ivy still had her bandages and was limping but she was in top spirits. Mam told us to wait outside and she went into the office. I don't know what she said in there but by midday the five boys from the squad and their parents arrived at the office. I don't know how the school identified the boys or got their parents to come right away, but Mam said that she wasn't leaving until they all assembled and she'd said her bit. J.A.J. was in the group too, with The Nephew.

Everything was swimming before me again, moving in muffled motion.

All we heard through a crack in the door was Mam warn the entire audience that under no circumstances was anyone, and she meant anyone, to lay so much as a pinkie finger on her girls ever again. The emphasis was on the words no and ever. I heard J.A.J. starting to say something about how that sounded like a threat and that it went both ways. Through the crack in the door, we heard his defence cut short. Mam must have shot him a stare because there was an uncomfortable silence. We watched each other and listened but nobody said anything else.

And nobody in the whole of Zekerheid ever laid a pinkie finger on us again.

By the next day the whole school knew some version of what had happened. The Harry twins had beat up the foreign boy. Or the foreign boy had picked a fight with the Harry twins. Or Foreign Boy had beaten both of them single-handedly. Or the quiet sour Harry twin almost drowned

Foreign Boy. Gasps all around. He got what he deserved, some girls said. These girls were willing to pay the twins good money to go fight other troublesome boys for them. Or the sun-faced Harry twin had a busted up head because of her sour twin. And she had a broken foot too. Some nasty looking cane cutter lifted her home. Somebody had seen the scene through a window. The cane cutter was in lurve ... ooo. Mike Harry's daughters were badly behaved, some parents said. Righteous Mike Harry's daughters fought in the streets like little vulgar stray dogs. After which Mam tracked down the origin of that comment, found out it came from our window-peeping gossipy neighbour up the street, and kindly thanked the offending woman not to refer to her daughters as dogs, or strays or vulgar.

Outside of the house, Mam was the single-handed goddess of war against the world.

Inside the house Mam, exhausted, only said five things to us on the matter. One, standing up for oneself was a good thing to do. Two, standing up for another, was a noble thing to do. Three, standing up in a way that was ill-thought out and dangerous was a stupid thing to do. Four, could we use more cerebral means of dealing with conflict. Five, if we ever drowned anybody or came home with exposed brains again we were going to send her to an early grave. And could we please not.

In the weeks that followed, Ivy grew popular, what with her crutch and head wound that carried five stitches where her hair had to be shaved. She wore her bald patch like a heroine, and when she could get away with it, sometimes she even put cartoon stickers like Tweety Bird on it. The girls in the class and even those in senior classes gathered around to be her friend. Some even wanted a haircut like Ivy. They called it Zee Ivy Lee. They pronounced it zee so that it could sound French and high fashion. I think one of them even tried out the haircut at the back of the school. But in those few days, my thoughts felt like deep burgundy wobbly jello in a shallow bowl and I couldn't be bothered to mind which girl had volunteered her head for Zee Ivy Lee. Whoever would be so stupid, then let them make their beds and lie on it.

I retreated into my library and brought out Inspeck S'mart-bam-I'm-coming-to-get-you. And I wrote until the ground beneath my feet felt steady again, though on a Friday afternoon, when I tucked my story in the purple *Encyclopaedia of Birds* and shoved it against the wall behind the row of animal books, I saw from the corner of my eye someone watching me in the shadow of the doorway and I jumped. When I peeped out, the person had vanished and I retreated and closed the door. But I should have done what Inspeck S'mart would do. Investigate my watcher. Track him. Spy. I should have done something, instead of nothing.

Because on Saturday morning early, Mr Fred came cycling to our house and shouting in the street, "Run come! Run come! Fi-yah! Fi-yah!"

Across the street from our school, I stood barefoot, with dust sticking to my feet, watching as smoke billowed around my cocoon. As my library burned.

Dust. Barefoot. Smoke. Choke.

My library burned to the ground.

Dust, barefoot, smoke, choke, library burning to the ground. And my own Detective Inspek S'mart inside the purple bird book with his enormous shoes and belt buckle, he too was burning. Burning to the ground. All the wood of the chairs and the window curtains and the handmade sign that said 'Library.' All the free pity-donated books. A whole world. Burning to the ground.

The headteacher's office and two classrooms burned too before the fire truck could relieve the bucket brigade.

Done. Burned. Burned to the ground.

Later, behind the school in a clump of bushes they found a box of matches.

On Monday, in the commotion of displaced children trying to redistribute evenly into other classrooms and the teachers, especially the one called Miss March, running up and down exchanging troublesome children for placid ones, I saw The Nephew looking straight at me with a smirk that flared his nostrils and reached his eyes. When I looked straight back into his eyes, I saw his pupils dancing like two sakiwinkies behind bars.

10

After the Fight and the Fire

After the fight and the fire, Pap examined Ivy's head every day and teased that her hair wasn't growing back, that she'd have a bald spot for the rest of her life like an old man.

"You and me get the same type o' head now pal," he said.

That wasn't true. Her hair was growing fast. Still, either way Ivy was unbothered. Bald spot or not, a head was a head. So Pap left her to her own devices.

But he stuck close to me. At dinner he'd nudge Mam and Mam'd clear her throat and say something like, "Eat all dat pumpkin and shrimp, Missy." On weekends, he coaxed me out of my room to ferry tools between our two houses. He went to Georgetown and bought me novels out of savings I knew he and Mam didn't have. He asked for my opinion on things like where the new kitchen cupboards should go and about installing a shower, even though he knew there was no water pressure for shower equipment in Peaside like there was in Seaside Strip. People didn't have showers here. They used a bucket and a butter bowl.

"Okay," I mumbled about the shower, knowing that we wouldn't get it to work. But Pap wasn't satisfied with me ferrying the tools uncomplainingly, and saying 'Okay Pap' and 'Yes Pap' to everything.

In the end, like he always did when he thought we needed a change of scene and some buoying up, Pap convinced Mam to ship me and Ivy off for a weekend to Uncle Raffie's in Georgetown, the only other family we had in the country. The only other family, except for Ganee's old cousins, of course, who when they saw us, barely glanced down, and continued their conversations about the price of cheese.

So we went into the city.

Aunty Melanie took us shopping down and up Regent Street until the corns on my feet bled. Aunty bought four of the same knee-length denim dungarees and four white short sleeved t-shirts on wholesale. Ivy enjoyed weaving in and out of stores. I didn't. I didn't like the crowded narrow pavements with strangers grazing me with shopping bags and walking their bellies to my face. But still, it was nice to be in the company of family, with my burning bleeding feet.

Aunty dressed us in our new outfits and sent Uncle to drive us to the photo studio. There the photographer arranged us against a blue background with clouds and said, "Say cheese and freeze or I turn you into fleas." He said it so matter-of-factly that Annie-Lou's eyebrows and nostrils went up and the horrified scorn that appeared at the corners of her mouth made Ivy and Lennard explode into bull-snorting giggles that I couldn't help but join them.

For a long time, I kept a framed copy of that photo on my shelf, next to my letter from Miss Pamela. The letter which said: Dear Ixora Harry, Congratulations on your endeavours in re-establishing the school's library. Yes, I left urgently as my application to study at college was accepted and I couldn't waste such an awesome opportunity to put down roots in this spectacular country. No, you needn't return the Molly

Mumpkins. Please find enclosed a dollar for you to buy yourself something nice. Sincerely, Pamela B.

This voice didn't sound like Miss Pam and the dollar still sits in its envelope with the letter that for a long time used to be propped up against the photo of me and Ivy, Lennard and Annie-Lou smiling cheese-freeze and looking like quadruplets. After a while, the envelope and the photo made their way under the trapfloor of the doll's house.

Later that afternoon, we quadruplets sat dangling our feet over the seawall and looked out at waves as Uncle Raffie handed out ice cream cones and patted our heads with two taps, like one would pat good little puppies after offering them a treat. He bought a cone for himself too and one for Aunty.

"Did you forget I'm on a diet," she said, and took the cone and ate it.

Then Uncle Raffie chauffeured us around the city and we looked at buildings.

Ivy said, "Whoa, what school's that? I gotta go there." She pointed at a building with three imposing turret-like structures evenly spaced across the lawns and connected by navy blue walls. There was a basketball court and volleyball net too.

"Exceptionally gifted children with top marks go there," Aunty said and ruffled Annie-Lou's silken tresses that had been twice-conditioned by one of those hard-to-pronounce separate shampoo and conditioner French products. Not the minty-smelling two-in-one Pharmacy-bought dandruff-controls Mam soaked our heads with every Saturday morning.

"Oh," said Ivy, "you been there?"

Aunty's mouth trembled.

"No," she said.

The next day was Sunday and Lennard and Annie-Lou glued their eyes to their large colour television all morning.

They handed us the remote control to choose any channel and we sat on the floor snuggled together under a blanket – Lennard and Annie-Lou on either side of me, and Ivy next to Annie-Lou, with her mouth hanging open as she clicked on show after show.

"Close your mouth Ivy," I said.

And Lennard and Annie-Lou chuckled and passed the bowl of chips side to side.

Ivy said, "Why our TV can't show so bright and nice like this?"

"Bright? Nice? In Peaside?" Aunty scoffed from where she sat polishing her nails at the end of the dining table.

Uncle Raffie cleared his throat and looked at her from behind his newspaper.

"Aren't we going to church then?" I asked. Lennard and Annie-Lou cast me fleeting puzzled glances and shoving chips in their mouths, returned their eyes to the screen.

Aunty came and stood with her pointed red nails and arms akimbo, and frowned down at me. I didn't know what I'd said wrong, so I kept my mouth shut and waited to go home.

And in the afternoon, Uncle Raffie drove us home. Lennard and Annie-Lou came for the ride too and on their return journey, peered through the back windshield and waved until we couldn't see them anymore.

"Come," said Pap, when he was done waving back, "Close your eyes." Then he led us through our new unfinished house until we came to a stop. "Open," he said.

We peered through a doorway. The walls inside this room were finished. There were two windows in the middle of the room and two desks beneath them. Then against the two side walls on opposite sides of the room were two single beds and one window above each bed.

"Mine!" Ivy shrieked and ran to the bed on the right and jumped in.

"What you say Ix Pix?" Pap was still holding my hand. My heart warmed.

"Try it out," he said, gesturing everywhere.

I glided my hand over my new lacquered desk and sank myself into my new mattress. I looked around the room feeling very important and perfectly balanced.

Pap had worked many hours on the room while we were away, but there was still more to do.

So the next day we primed the walls in white. Then Pap said we must choose which colour we each wanted for our own side of the room. Mam raised her eyebrows, pursed her lips and said that Pap should paint everything white and just get on with it.

But Pap said, "Come na Laurs, is just a little colourful activity, not the end of the world."

"*Oh?*" she said, pounding hard on the dough.

So Ivy and I spent a whole day deciding on colours.

"Red," I said.

"You can't have a red room," said Ivy.

"Just my half."

"Well what if I want green, then together red and green gon jus look like Christmas all year," she said, refusing everything I proposed. "Pink?"

"What kinda pink?" I asked.

"Bright pink."

"Bright pink and red? Ick."

"Blue then."

We went on like that for the whole day. I brought out crayons and sheets of paper and we tried various combinations. Pap looked in at the door several times, and every time I turned to watch him, he smiled and walked away.

In the end, after the teeth sucking and the arm pinching, we settled for a symmetrical paint job. On the two side walls that faced each other, we decreed two sets of three bold vertical stripes of red, yellow and blue lines running from the ceiling down to only the upper half of the walls. So there was a red stripe and then a yellow stripe and then a blue stripe and then the pattern was repeated once more. Then for the bottom half of the wall, we wanted white all the remaining way around, almost to the ground and then at the very bottom of the white we decided on a large horizontal green stripe. The middle wall would be white.

Uncle Warbin supervised the paint job, rolling painter's tape around the room and making sure we painted the stripes straight. While we painted, he played his harmonica and in the afternoons, he stayed in the new veranda asking Pap's opinions about mortgages, complaining about the price of raw material and playing folk tunes and ballads and not heading home until the moon came out.

Mam told Pap, "Mister, why you don't inform Warbin this ain't the Bureau of Consultations eh? And tell he stop bawling 'bout the economy. And to stop mekking dat noise. The girls got homework and dat mournful medley grating on people nerves. Ain't nobody died here."

"Man Lauro don't start dat again. It not even mournful."

Mam didn't like music. During music hour, she turned the radio down. She changed the TV channels from music videos to the News. She didn't attend concerts or sing in church. Just folded her arms and waited for hymns to end. But Pap could never let a good tune go to the wind. Besides, he would never tell Uncle Warbin to stop the harmonica or to go home. He and Uncle Warbin had apprenticed to learn carpentry from Crabwood Bollo who used to live deep down in the back of the pasturelands, and because of the apprenticeship, they called themselves The Carpenter Brothers.

Crabwood Bollo taught them everything he knew about carpentry and in return they worked for him for five years.

Before Crabwood Bollo died, he gave them all his tools. And Pap said that Uncle Warbin was the biggest cry-baby the day he was bequeathed the old tools. One time on a big job, a beam even slipped by accident and hit Uncle Warbin in the head and Pap rushed him to the hospital. The nurses said when Warbin woke up from his coma the first thing he intoned was, "Michael Herbert Harry next time the beam comin' for you boy. I see it." But Uncle Warbin said he didn't remember saying that. All he remembered was that Pap laughed and split his own salary in half so that he, Warbin could still have something to send home to his ailing mother in another region, while he lay up in bed with his head healing. After that, it was hard for anyone to speak ill of either Pap or Uncle Warbin in front of the other. If Pap heard someone in the village say, "Dat War-bean talk more than he wuk. And still ah have to pay he," Pap would say "Ah, Warbin is a jolly fellow," to which the villager would reply, "Jolly me backside." Or if someone said "Mike Harry bruk-uh-tuka bicycle more old than the grey hairs on he head. After all dese years, he can't even 'fford new bicycle?" Uncle Warbin would reply, "Zip your mouth and save your sense to full a small sugar jar."

That was the kind of thing Uncle Warbin knew. He could just watch someone and tell if they had enough intelligence to fill a large, medium or small sugar jar. He was a prophet too because everything he said came true.

Like when I told him where I thought Pollard was. Straight away he hopped on Pap's bicycle and went. But he came back empty-handed. It *was* Pollard, he said. He didn't have to look twice to tell. But the boy, that is, The Nephew had bought Pollard from some man over at Peaside and he didn't know who. It wasn't the boy's fault. Nothing was ever going to be The Nephew's fault, I thought, digging my thumb nail hard into the banister. Uncle Warbin said it was the thief's fault and that whoever he was wouldn't thrive for long. Sure enough, one day in the news, we read about a man in Peaside who was caught and charged for pet-napping and selling people's pets, among other stolen valuables. So everything Uncle Warbin said came true.

"Hummph," Uncle Warbin had said, pointing at the article and shaking his head, "Moon run till daylight ketchim."

And it took me a long time to puzzle out what that meant.

So Uncle Warbin, harmonica player, carpenter, prophet and painter showed us how to hold the brush and how to make the paint drip as little as possible.

On the white spaces and on the white middle wall, we drew murals.

Junior was good at drawing so we summoned him to help. His sketches of planes were almost professional. He surveyed our drawings of coconut trees with golden coconuts and the red flowers and the golden sun that bore too much of a resemblance to the coconuts. Technically the flower I was drawing wasn't correct, he said. It was too flat, had no dimension, its proportions were wrong and I was painting like a baby. Without perspective, he said.

"Shut up Junior," I said, "You turnin' into a idiot."

"Well technically he right," Ivy laughed.

"Technically he's an idiot," I said.

Also, technically, he said, his name was Sam, Samuel in fact, not Junior. His name was really Samuel Reid, the Second. Though, he thought it was an outdated concept to name anyone after their father. When he said this, his voice wobbled. And anyway, nobody was to call him Junior anymore. If we did, he wouldn't answer.

He asked if he could draw and paint an aeroplane on the wall.

"It wouldn't look good Junior ... uh, Mister Samuel Reid the Second," I said. "It would be out of place. It would need a kind of plane strip, what you call it? Like a kind of airplane road. A ..."

"A runway," he said. "I could draw one."

"But anyway, that's dangerous things from outside. It wouldn't look good inside," I said, as a sour tickle irritated my ear canals. I titled my head and shook it a bit.

Mister Samuel narrowed his eyes at me. Then he asked Ivy about the plane.

"It gon look aright," she said.

"How you supposed to get any peace with a loud plane in your bedroom eh?" I asked her.

She laughed. "How a drawing gon be loud?"

"So why you have coconut trees and hibiscus and sun inside your bedroom then? Them's things from the outside," said the indignant Sam, eager to draw his plane.

"That's different," I said, unable to think of a logical reason. Flowers and sunlight just were what they were. They weren't reverberating, obscure, or associated with the Miaplambo.

In the end, two votes to one, the plane went up and on my half of the room too. It really was a well-drawn plane though, so well-drawn in fact that it seemed not to belong on the wall with our childish bending coconut trees and one-dimensional flowers, but in an art gallery somewhere. Or in the air. For goodbyes.

There was also a well-marked runway for the plane.

"Draw somebody on the runway," I said.

"Never," said Samuel Reid, waving his brush with the arrogance of a criticised artist who knows what he's talking about, "never, walk onto a runway without being cleared to do so and never," he said the never with such pompous emphasis, "stand idly on a runway, anywhere in the world."

"Why not?" I asked.

"Unless one minds dying," he said, using words like one and minds and dying and unless, as if he were a specialist in philosophy or aeronautics or linguistics or something.

I thought about complaining to his mother about this new attitude of Sam's. But no good would come of that. She seemed to encourage it, walking with Sam's report card at every house she went to sell cow's milk in the mornings. Showing all the neighbours her boy's top marks, that weren't even that top anyway. Telling everyone that Junior was born a blessing and all he had to do was put his head out of distractions and reach for the stars so that everyone, even his own father, would see that a small boy from Peaside with no electricity could become a pilot.

"Didn't you say your father was to send you a remote control plane?" Ivy asked.

"Yes," Sam said, "for Christmas."

"Oh, and for Christmas, I be asking for a Building Set," said Ivy, without even thinking if Mam and Pap had money to buy any such thing.

"What's dat?" Sam asked.

"It got plenty parts and you have to fit them up into a building like a house or a museum or a hotel," she explained.

"Like a model building?" Sam asked.

"Yaa."

"Where Mam gon find dat from Ivy?" I asked.

"In Georgetown somewhere. See it in a store."

How presumptuous of her, I thought, for demanding outlandish things. Anyway, there was no way she was going to get it.

When the paint job was done, Ivy and I took turns exiting our new room, closing the door, opening it and coming back in. It was a wonder, taking in the whole room with the newly painted stripes and beds and desks, plural. This room was larger than the half-room we shared over at Ganee and Pappo's house.

There we shared one twin bed and one pillow. Sometimes Ganee lent us hers, pretending she didn't like pillows. But we kept returning it. And we had a low stool for a vanity, where we put our comb, hair cream, ribbons and clips. Ivy'd make my ribbons fall behind the stool when she yanked up hers to get her hair done. It happened every single school morning and I'd puff about it. And we had one short bookshelf. There we put all our story books and school textbooks and notebooks and toys, with Ivy always shoving her backpack on the shelf, so that to get to my novels, I had to keep hauling out the backpack and chucking it under the bed next to the shoes where it belonged. But she didn't want it there for the spiders to crawl in and she kept heaving it back on the shelf and blocking my stories.

Mam said that if Pap and Warbin didn't get our house done before we started high school that Ivy and I'd kill each other with our physical and personal growth. When she said that it didn't sound quite like Mam. In Peaside, one couldn't afford to kill each other with growth and development as Mam knew. Yes, the language felt more like Mam's one psychology book called *How to Raise Healthy Twins*, that she used to keep under her Bible and her extra-large Dictionary.

So Mam made one thing clear to Pap and Warbin. They were to build build build. She made them say 'Build, build, build.' So they'd come home from work, swallow a snack and then start hammering away at our house next door.

To Ivy and me, she made another thing clear. We were to study study study. Our big exam was coming up and I knew that if I failed the exam and Ivy passed, that the whole of Peaside would say that The Pickle-face finally let the sour take over her brain.

11

Fractures

"Forget about that nasty bully," Mam said, referring to The Nephew.

She looked directly at me so I fiddled with the pickle jar, giving the cucumbers a massive shake.

"He, whatever his name is, will have his bread well-buttered," Mam's tirade continued as she slammed pots into the cupboard. "You two," she pointed at us with a small frying pan, "you two got no bread if you don't study. And if –"

"Any eatables?" Pap asked grinning. He had come in to make himself and Uncle Warbin some tea and bread.

"And if," Mam side-eyed Pap and continued, "you barely study, you gon have bread, yes. But if you don't study more than enough –"

Pap, oblivious, was stirring the milk and sugar into the tea, and the spoon was going cladanks cladanks on the insides of the enamel cups. Mam side-eyed him again.

She raised her voice, "*If* you don't study *more* than enough, then you ain't gon have no butter," she finished, and hung the frying pan on a large nail.

Cling, went the frying pan against the wall.

I watched Pap spread butter onto a slice of bread and wondered what it would be like to eat the bread dry.

So we studied studied studied.

J.A.J., Scholar, Cover-to-cover, Applause, was pleased with our performance now. He kept waving our marked test papers and berating the rest of the class, telling them they were going to get into poor schools if they didn't sharpen up like the twins. Many times he wrung his nephew's ear. If I was sitting behind The Nephew, I'd get the urge to dab some fresh aloe on the traumatised ear. But then I thought of Inspeck S'mart turning to ash, his belt and boots disappearing and my mind wandered into the perished library and into the memory of The Nephew's eyes possessed with that menacing motion, those unsteady eyes that contrasted the fixed terrified sad burning red ear. Mam was right, the more I became consumed with the bully, the more I lessened my chances of butter.

So we wrote the big exam and I fixed my mind on Pap's hands holding the bread and spreading the butter, even though I suffered the alphabetical misfortune of The Nephew sitting directly behind me in the exam room and boring a hole with his eyes in the back of my head.

After the big exam, Pap built Ivy and me each a bookshelf for the new room and Mam bought new sheets and mosquito nets. Then she said it was time for a luncheon celebration. That we needed to celebrate graduating primary school in one piece. When she said that she looked at the top of Ivy's head. Also she said we could invite Junior, who she kept forgetting to call Samuel, and she would ask Junior's mother too as Junior had passed his exams for a city school as well, a bit of news which Sam's mother announced to the whole of Peaside. Mam said too that we would invite that nice cane cutter who helped bring Ivy home when she busted her scalp because we never even said a proper thank you.

Ixora Mara, Sourhouse

Ivy asked if she could bring Brave Bonnie.

"Why is her name Brave?" asked Mam.

"Her name not Brave, people just call her brave cause she don't back down from no dares."

A line of disapproval crossed Mam's brow. Then she asked me which of my friends I'd like to bring.

Without warning, the old lime appeared in my chest again. I went to the window and looked out at Suzie's house.

"Nobody," I said, while the nerves in my face pulsed and prickled.

"Oi pickle-face," said Ivy, taking a huge bite into a chicken patty and jamming me in the ribs as she passed, "just invite anybody."

So after I woke up next morning, I said maybe we could invite Mr Fred. After all, he had helped me with the library. And even though it was gone, he still brought me books. He kept them in his rucksack for weeks and when finally he picked me out from the line-up at General Assembly, he waved a new book at me and signalled if I'd ever read this one. It was like having a custom-made mobile library. Sometimes when I returned the book, he'd be trimming the hedges into interesting shapes like a cartoon cat or a hand holding a book. People said no other school on the coastal countryside had hedges like Zekerheid Primary. But the pupils of Zekerheid Primary couldn't tell what the shapes were. They laughed and said the old cuckoo was at it again, butchering up the bushes and embarrassing the school. But when I stood at just the right angle and stared at the bush long enough, I could make out what it was that Mr Fred was clipping into being. So whenever I returned the books, while his shears went in and out between the leaves, he asked me about the story and I repeated it from beginning to end just to prove I had read it thoroughly, and his eyes sparkled. They were still red as always, the eyes, but they sparkled.

"You remember that part, yes?" I'd ask often. "I told it correct?"

"Ah dunno it. But is a nice story," he'd say and then go off whistling.

So Mr Fred was invited to the luncheon in our new house that Pap and Uncle Warbin had built built built. There was only a small section of the house left to complete but they'd partition that section and the rest of the house was ready for the lunch party.

Mr Fred arrived first on his bicycle. He wore a white pleated shirt and a lime green bow tie.

"Is like he think he going to a ball at Buckingham Palace," said Ivy.

"Shut up," I said.

We'd never seen him in a bow tie, always it was the mogey dirt-brown jumpsuits. He hopped off his bike and retrieved from the carrier basket a little pot of cactus for Mam and another pot with an aloe plant for Ganee. And though he stayed in the veranda, his shoulders hunched up, talking with Pap, Pappo Harro, Junior's grampappy and Uncle Warbin who had Putty on his shoulder, and he didn't say a word to me, except to nod and say, "Miss Harry, thank you for lunch," it felt like a bird burst out of my chest and shot to the sky. It was unbelievable that someone who I, Ixora Mara, had invited came. On time. Dressed to the nines. Bearing gifts!

After Mam, gracious hostess, obligingly contributed to the discussion in the veranda – the type of spiralling discussion that went on when big men sat down to debate politics and policy, labour and economy, and the price of gas and chickenfeed – she, Ganee and Sam's mother served dhal, rice and fried vegetables and, what they demanded we say in school as, curried chicken. Not chicken curry.

Ivy, Brave Bonnie, Sam and I were still in the new veranda trying to follow the conversation on the world economics and looking out for the young cane cutter, who ended up not coming, when a car ambled through the potholes and pulled up in front of our house. Lennard and Annie-Lou leaped out and without closing the car doors ran across the bridge and up the stairs. We waited for Uncle Raffie to come out but the leg and torso that emerged were not his.

Instead, strappy sandals, a flowy melon-coloured skirt and Aunty Melanie emerged.

Ivy dropped her lollipop. Pap's jaw dropped. Pappo Harro dropped his sentence for a few seconds, then continued. Ivy and I had never seen Aunty come to Peaside.

Ivy lowered her voice and asked, "Why she come?"

Putty said, "Squawk, aye she come, aye she come."

"Putty, shh," I said.

Aunty stood in front our new house surveying it. Then without closing her car door, she followed the children. Ivy sprinted to the kitchen and shout-whispered, "Mam! Mam! Come see who come!"

Bonnie, Sam and I came indoors at the same moment that Aunty stepped through the main door and Mam stepped out of the kitchen. They came face to face. Ganee stood behind Mam and Sam's mother stood behind Ganee. And everyone stared at each other until Annie-Lou said, "We bring a new Monopoly game." And Lennard said, "Leh we go play. Where the brand new bedroom?"

As we went to show them the room, Uncle Raffie's feet shuffled spiritlessly up the stairs.

We bounced on our new spring beds and spread the Monopoly on the floor.

Sam was a little slow at catching on. Ivy and I were a little better as we'd played it when we visited the city. And Lennard and Annie-Lou were experts. But Brave Bonnie was a mess at Monopoly. She kept forgetting to give players their change. She didn't know how to calculate the correct change. Didn't know if or how to buy properties. Didn't notice when players landed on her two plots and didn't demand rent. I could see her embarrassment and tried to help her.

Lennard turned to Bonnie, "You slowing up the game man."

"Let her play," I said.

"Well she gotta play brave, not so scaredy cat-ish scaredy cat-ish," he said.

"Why your mother name you Brave then, if you scaredy to play a liddle board game," Annie-Lou taunted.

Both she and Lennard were acting more grown up and brazen than usual.

"Bonita is my real name," said our Brave Bonnie, surprisingly unnerved.

"Y'all in the country get funny names. Like how Uncle Mikey calls y'all Ixie Pixie and Ivy Jivey," Annie-Lou said. "In town and in foreign, you just have one proper name."

Lennard snickered.

I waited for some sort of defence from Ivy but she was pulling little houses from the packet.

"What about you? What's your name?" Annie-Lou asked Sam.

"Samuel Reid, Junior," he said.

"How you mean Junior?" she asked. "That's your surname, your father last name?"

"The whole thing is my father name," he said.

"Your father name Samuel Reid Junior?" she asked.

"No, his name is Samuel Reid," I said, knowing this bone of contention couldn't end well.

"Junior, means he has the same whole name as his father," explained Ivy impatiently, "Just roll the dice man. Is your turn Annie, come on."

"So why your father couldn't think of a new name to give you? Why he just give you his own old name?" Annie-Lou persisted.

"I dunno," Sam said quietly and he looked at me. I wanted to cast a fishing rod and reel the helplessness out of his pupils.

"Well when you go home must ask him," Annie-Lou said.

"He in America," said Sam.

"Oh? We going to America too. When I go I can ask him for you," Annie-Lou continued.

"Just be quiet and play Annie," I said.

Annie-Lou's maternal grandparents lived abroad and for years Aunty went on saying hasta la vista, sayonara and arrivederci, how her papers were filed. But that was all. And now, here was Annie-Lou spouting tales about going to America. First, she belittled all of our names and where we lived, then she ran her double t sounds into ds, and now she was telling lies. Occasionally, Annie-Lou could be snobbish but today was the worst.

"When he come back I gon ask him," Sam said.

"When he coming back?"

"I dunno."

"He not coming back then," Annie-Lou said matter-of-factly, "We not coming back neither."

"Well, when he send for us, me and my mother," Sam said, "I will ask h—"

"He might not," said Annie-Lou.

"Might not what?"

"Send for you."

"He will," Sam was growing angry. His voice trembled. The dice fell from his hands.

"Shush Annie," I said.

But she wouldn't shush. "He won't come back. My mother says one of her school friends go way and leave her boyfriend and marry another man in America cause he educated and handsome and rich and he treat her right too. Besides, once you go, ain't nobody comin' back to this backwater for nothin', 'cept emotional 'ratification and to empty skilletons from closets," she continued. I'd forgotten how knowledgeable and loose-lipped she was about these things and how good, like Putty, she was at parroting everything grown-ups said, without understanding what she was repeating.

That's when I saw it, a blob of thick burgundy blood trickling down her nose and dropping onto the pastel green Monopoly board.

Samuel Reid, his father's namesake, had impulsively shot a fist out at the knowledgeable little parrot, and punched her in the face.

And then, Annie-Lou's bawl shot out like an owl hoot.

All the adults flooded in and the audience made her bawl louder. She held her nose and howled. She pointed at Sam, who sat looking at the Monopoly board and grinding his teeth. For one brief second his eye caught mine and I wanted to go over and throw myself on him and cry as loudly as Annie-Lou.

"Who hit you?" Aunty Melanie was on her precious little crystal ornament, wiping and smearing her blood and snot with a melon-coloured monogrammed handkerchief.

Annie pointed at Sam again.

"How dare you hit my girl?" Aunty shouted. She looked down on Sam. "Answer me boy!"

"Don't holler pon my boy," Sam's mother came in and shouted from the back of the crowd.

Annie-Lou bawled louder.

"Ask him why he hit my daughter 'cause he seems deaf and dumb."

"Call my boy deaf and dumb again, and I cuff you yes!" said Sam's mother, rushing up to the front of the crowd and raising her fist in Aunty's face.

"Raphael," Aunty called, "Tell these country people if they talk back to me I swear to God I will –"

"Alright, alright," Pap said standing between Uncle Raffie and Aunty, "No need to swear to God and all that."

"Shut it with your self-righteous church-attending self, Mister Mike-rophone," Aunty raised her voice at Pap. "Like you alone know about God above? Like y'all is the most righteous-est people dat ever live?"

"Alright. Y'all calm down and see what happen to the child," said Mam who had now stepped between Pap and Aunty and bent down to reach out to Annie-Lou.

Aunty sucked her teeth and turned to Mam, "You keep your hard crusty hand away from my child. I thought you tell me not to tell you how to raise your girls. Well you better don't tell me what to do neither."

"You see me telling you what to do Melanie? I just seeing if her nose break. You don't always gotta be ridiculous man," Mam flared up.

Uncle Raffie put his hand to his face and rubbed his eyes into the back of his head.

Aunty looked at him, "You see why I don't come to the country eh? To this unruly backwater where every time you come is some horse show and cow sh–"

"Mela, calm down," Uncle Raffie tried a soothing tone.

Ganee cradled Annie-Lou. "Doudou," Ganee said, sapping the little pet's crocodile tears.

"Annie-Lou come here," Aunty demanded.

Uncle Raffie started to speak, "Mela –"

"You – don't – Mela me," Aunty Melanie said slowly, very slowly.

Uncle Raffie shut up. A sunbeam stretched out across the floor and dust particles floated in the light. The drop of blood had settled and spread flat on Boardwalk. Lennard inched closer to his father. Bonnie was hiding behind Ivy but from her collar bone upwards was still showing. Sam was still sitting on the ground. But now he got up slowly. He started walking out of the room.

"Come back here and apologise to Annie-Lou," Aunty said in a low voice.

Sam's mother bristled and pushed Sam behind her.

I couldn't see why Aunty was still growing this molehill into its own mountain. Annie-Lou's nose was just fine.

"I apologise," Sam said in a low voice, from behind his mother.

Annie-Lou started with the whimpering again.

Sam's mother turned to him, "And what she tell you Junior, dat make her deserve a cuff eh?"

"Come here Annie-Lou," said Aunty, ignoring the question Sam's mother asked.

"Speak up Junior," said his mother.

Aunty said, "Annie-Lou, come here, we going and never coming back."

Uncle Raffie sighed. Annie-Lou clung to Ganee, then trembling started walking to her mother.

"Speak up for yourself," Sam's mother said to Sam, "What she tell you dat make you had to cuff her?"

Sam's tears were coming now. "She said they goin' to America and not comin' back and how my daddy not comin' back neither and how he not gon send for us never," he said. He squeezed through the crowd and ran out the room.

Everyone looked at Annie-Lou hiding behind her mother's floor length melon-coloured skirt.

"Yes," said Aunty Melanie, raising her shoulders like a Victorian woman at a grand ball, "and that's why I came today. To tell y'all hasta la vista and sayonara, au revoir and arrivederci. We get through and we goin'."

The dust particles floated in the sunbeam and everyone looked at each other.

Pap looked at Uncle Raffie and Uncle Raffie rubbed his eyeballs into the back of his head. Pappo Harro looked down at Lennard. Ganee looked at Annie-Lou's feet poking out from behind the melon-coloured skirt. Mam folded her arms and looked at Aunty and Aunty looked back. For a few seconds her eyes relaxed and her bottom lip retracted. Bonnie looked at Ivy, her eyeballs bulging at our family drama. No doubt, she was going to tell half the class who would tell their parents. Then the whole of Peaside would know everything by tomorrow afternoon. Ivy looked back at Bonnie and shrugged without shame.

No one looked at me.

It seemed Mr Fred and Uncle Warbin had excused themselves. They were probably in the veranda. Shame crept up my neck. I couldn't imagine what Mr Fred must be thinking about my family.

I started walking out the room to look for him and say something apologetic.

Sam's grampappy and Sam's mother walked out too, ahead of me, with Pap trailing behind them. He avoided Uncle Raffie's eyes.

"Junior," Sam's mother called.

No answer.

"Juniyoour!"

Some wood clanked.

"Junior ah callin' fuh you."

"Don't call me Junior!" a voice shouted from the incomplete section of the house.

"Don't shout at your mother," said Sam's grampappy. That was the only thing he'd said all afternoon.

Sam's mother went in the direction of Sam's voice.

Pap followed her quickly and I trailed behind him to see about Sam.

There were no light bulbs in the unfinished part of the house and we tread carefully. Sam must've heard us coming because when we looked in, he was backing away from us. He took a few steps back as his mother stretched out her hand and said, "Come Junior, leh we go home."

He shook his head and stepped back against some rickety pieces of uprights holding up an unbolted beam.

"Don't call me dat!" he shouted and backed into the uprights furiously.

Suddenly everything was swimming. It was the same sensation I had when Lennard pulled me under water at the pool.

Pap moved swiftly between the small crowd but it seemed as if he were under water too.

Something above tilted and the loose beam dislodged.

And then I saw it. The beam. Pummelling down on Sam. Pap leaping forward, covering Sam, twirling his torso with Sam hugged to his chest, pitching himself as far as possible from the path of the falling beam. But Sam's arm was sticking out and the beam came hitting the arm on its way down. Then it went crashing with unbearable permanence onto Pap's shin.

12

Crisp White Collars

The only time we ever saw Mam sob was after we got back from the hospital. She sent us to bed. She didn't tell us to bathe. Didn't tell us to eat. Ivy and I looked at each other, our stomachs grumbling. We'd never not had dinner.

Mam stood by the kitchen table, the one you could see through the crack in the wall. Her palms were pressed on the table, fingers pointing away from her body and she was leaning over. Her head tilted over the table, her back bent, her shoulders hunched almost up to her ears. I stuck my eye closer to the crack. Mam's upper body heaved, and her chignon bun went rising and falling, rising and falling, on the neckline of her dress. The dress was A-lined, pale pink with dozens of tiny cupcakes with cherries on top scattered all over. Some cupcakes were sideways, some upside down, some right side up. I pressed my nose to the wall and followed the path of the cupcakes dancing up and down the sleeves and around the hemline. I couldn't see Mam's tears, but it didn't matter. We heard them across the kitchen and through the wall.

Ivy pushed me aside. She rested her eye to the crack for a long time and when she turned around, her mouth was set in a line and she folded her arms. She faced me squarely like she was looking in a mirror. But the double reflection was deceptive. I didn't have her knowing decisive brain, her grim determined mouth, the balled fists and arms braced with resolve against the sturdy body. I had instead, a mind of old walls with peeling paint, a sour mouth, dangling icy fingers and a non-athletic frame.

"Bakes," Ivy said, her mouth still set for some kind of battle.

"What?"

"Leh we fry bakes for dinner?"

"Shh," I said. The house was silent. Ganee was in bed soaking her head with Limacol and Pappo was outdoors tinkering with the old tractor.

"What we gotta do?" Ivy whispered.

"I dunno. Get some flour."

She brought the flour tin.

"How much?"

"I dunno," I whispered, "Two, three cups?"

She shrugged and dipped and dumped flour wildly into a bowl.

In the end, we had two large trays filled with fried bakes – some burnt, some undercooked and the rest reasonably edible. But Mam didn't even comment on our first independent culinary achievement, not even to say well-what-in-the-world-is-this?

She went to bed late and woke early. I knew she was awake because she moved around behind the flappy curtain strung up with polythene twine that partitioned our half of the room from hers and Pap's. On our side of the curtain, there were shimmery red-orange flowers and a large brown owl with glittery inquiring eyes. Mam and Pap's side had the same print but theirs was the dull side.

"Hoot," I whisper-mouthed to the owl, as I always did.

Mam rummaged in drawers and packed a hospital bag for Pap. I tried to stay awake as long as I could so I could keep her company on the other side of the curtain, even though she wouldn't know. So I tiptoed out of bed and quietly opened the side-window. Our house next door was dark. The Monopoly board must still be lying open on the floor. I couldn't imagine Annie-Lou wanting to take it home with her blood sunk into it. I wondered whether she could breathe same as before with her newly punched nose. I pondered too, about Aunty Melanie and how she had looked like a pot of melon-coloured porridge boiling over. And I worried about Sam's sprained elbow. Pap, I tried not to think about.

That night I dreamt of hundreds of pieces of wood falling from the sky, fracturing everyone, those quarrelling and those silent. And everyone limped around in pain. Corrosive pain in quiet spaces.

Early next morning, we set out for the hospital.

Uncle Warbin was already there.

"Well Warbin," Pap was saying, as he lay outlined against the bleached sheet, "you really is a prophet after all."

Uncle Warbin sucked his teeth and said, "I going to work, yes. Enjoy thee hospital food." He picked up his rucksack and looked at Ivy and me and with a contorted face, flicked his thumb at the breakfast tray.

Pap put on his brightest smile above his fractured tibia and shouted after Uncle Warbin, "The beam did come for me after all boy."

When we didn't laugh, Pap said, "Why y'all sour man, come sit here Ix Pix, Ives Jives," and motioned to both sides of the bed.

I sat on the side furthest from the fractured shin hidden in the cast.

Ivy said, "Pap, you better not call us tings like dat no more."

"Like?"

"Ix Pix and Ives Jives and all that."

"And why not little Miss Muffet?"

"'Cus dat's what break your foot," said my short-sighted twin.

"Dat's not why," I snapped.

"Well, let's hear why then?" Pap said encouragingly and snuggled back into the unreasonably white pillow as if he were about to enjoy a secret.

Ivy said, "Is 'cause Annie-Lou was laughing our names and dat's why Sam box her and dat's why you break your foot."

What a stupid explanation, I thought. That is not at all why.

Pap smiled. "Well," he said, "last I check was a wood dat cause it, not nobody. Besides my whole foot ain't broke you know. Soon I good as new."

Below the bright smile, his leg was throbbing I could tell. He kept grimacing every time he shifted his weight.

"Besides," Ivy was still yapping, "what kinda names y'all give us really? I dunno nobody else name Ivy. Dat's just a vine. And Ixie, she just a normal stiff flower everybody have in they backyard."

Exactly, I thought, mentally agreeing with my twin for the first time in my life on the issue of names. Exactly.

Pap was about to speak when Mam came back from her inquiries with the doctor. I studied the circles under her eyes and the lines at the sides of her mouth. No, I thought, never mind what Pap had said. He wouldn't be as good as new.

When he came out the hospital, his leg in the cast for six weeks, we fussed over him but he didn't want that. He limped around with crutches securing his own eatables. He sunned himself out on the veranda and read the newspaper. We gave him a tiny Christmas bell to ring when he wanted anything. But he rang it only to read us jokes from the joke column.

In those ensuing languid afternoons, Uncle Warbin brought the news from around the village and sat in the veranda and played his harmonica, and Mam didn't even complain about the tunes. Ganee and Pappo too sat out on the veranda, Pappo reading a book about tractors, Ganee keeping quiet. Not sewing, not wrapping parcels for the village children, not saying much, just rocking in her chair. After Uncle Raffie and his family left, Ganee confined to bed with the wet Limacol rag on her head. But sometimes she'd sit on the veranda, where Mam served large cups of tea and Ivy and I helped her spread homemade guava jam on square biscuits, arrange three pairs on each plate and ferry the mismatched plates of varying sizes out on trays.

Often we saw Sam, sometimes with his mother. We called out to him but his mother, her head straight, dragged him up the back street. And when he was alone, he wouldn't come near us either. He looked down the back street, looked at us, looked down the back street again and fled.

I'd sit at the far end of the long veranda, in one of the cushiony rocking chairs, with my feet touching the veranda wall. Pressing gently against the wall, I rocked the chair, savoured my guava jam enclosed between the crisp biscuits and wondered about Sam's father, and Small Spokes and his mother, and Lennard, Annie-Lou, Uncle Raffie and Aunty Melanie. And Miss Pamela. And Suzie and her parents. I wondered where they all were in the world and what kind of jam they were eating between their biscuits, and what they were wearing and if they were thinking of me.

Suzie's house had stood about five years empty now. It didn't seem like she was coming back after all. The cobwebs must've layered thickly over the hair left on her comb and over the jewellery box, the one with her crystal heart inside.

So when the sun went down and the lights flicked on in the houses across the street except in Suzie's – hers melded into the dark – I imagined it was the Miaplambo sending his shadow to do its work above her house, and I sketched what I thought he looked like and wrote a limerick about him. Then I hid the pocket sketchbook under the trapfloor of our doll's house.

"Why won't Sam come play with us?" I asked Mam.

Mam's eyes had more circles under them. As soon as I saw her face, I wished I hadn't asked that question.

"He has an ingrate for a mother is why, a neemakaram," Mam said and slammed the iron down on the collar of a crisp white shirt I'd never seen before.

I lifted the bible off of Mam's dictionary and searched for the word in-grate. Then I searched for the word neemakaram but I couldn't find it. I wasn't sure how to spell it and was afraid to ask.

The next morning Mam was wearing the crisp white shirt with the stiffly ironed collar. The shirt was tucked stiffly into black trousers and her hair was pulled back into a pony tail. Mam looked young, different, severe, sharp, smart, angry, out of place in the kitchen with the onions and garlic and potatoes hanging in yellow nylon mesh bags on nails ponged into the wall. When she left her folder on the table and went for her shoes, I raised the folder's cover, saw the words A Levels and dropped the cover in place when I heard her returning. Then she went out and several hours later came back with a job as a cashier in a pharmacy.

While she told us about the new job, Pap sat on the veranda, shoulders drooping, watching her talk and looking down at his leg.

Except for Sundays, every day Mam rose early and went to work, and every day she returned home when the sun was setting and the Miaplambo, as I'd decidedly taken to identifying it now, was getting ready to cover Suzie's house with the dark shadow. I stood on the long low veranda and looked out for Mam's white shirt bobbing down the street. I'd want to run up and hug her in the street but I wouldn't. She seemed alone encased in the sharp white working shirt and the crisp collar, slimmer, quieter, solitary. And I searched for my old Mam inside the eyes that had the circles beneath them and the lipsticked mouth that had the worry creases at the sides, and it was hard to find her.

Sometimes Pap would let us pull aside the owl curtain so we could see him and whisper conversations while Mam snored.

"Pap when your cast coming off?" Ivy said.

"Shh," Pap said and pointed at Mam. He whispered, "Next week."

Ivy asked, "We can draw on it then?"

"Shh, yes."

When the cast finally came off, Mam was quiet. Every time she looked at Pap walking about the house, she massaged her forehead. Pap's feet were now uneven and he walked with a limp, and still grimaced. And it was hard for him to finish our house next door even though Uncle Warbin still came and helped after work in the evenings. Pap moved very slowly. So Mam worked double shifts and hired two carpenters to finish the house while Pap stood around giving quiet instructions, his shoulders drooping, his arms folded to his chest.

And soon our house was finished.

"By hook or by crook," Ganee said, bustling out of bed and assembling her usual weekly round of food baskets for people that I didn't know, "crook or hook, Laurie make the house finish before y'all high school start. Dat girl!"

13

Proud Harro Harry and Sons – Tailors

We moved into our new house in time for the Christmas school term.

Ganee sniffed as we transported our belongings.

"But Ganee, we goin' right over there. You gon see we every single day," Ivy said when Ganee brought out her sniffly rag.

"Shut up Ivy vine," I snapped.

It was obvious Miss Ivy Lee lacked the capacity to understand that once Ganee Gwenny and Pappo Harro had a full house and now here was the last pair of ducklings filing out down the potholed street, emptying the nest forever. It didn't have to matter where we were going. As long as someone was going somewhere, you just brought out your sniffly rag. It was a simple concept.

Long ago, Pap, Uncle Winnie, Uncle Raffie and their endless line of friends traipsed through the little low house. There were black and white photographs of them. And photos too of Ganee and Pappo, slim with bouffant hair.

"Dis is really you?" I asked, bringing the album close to my eyes.

Ganee laughed.

"And who's all these people?"

Ixora Mara, Sourhouse

"Dat's your Pappo family. Dat old one come on a ship. And those is Pappo brothers. One went to the Interior and Pappo never hear back from he. Dis one is he adopted brother who drowned. And dat one get senile and end up in the Berbice Mad House. Is the only photo dem have together. And these here stooping in front is cousins. He don't know where they all is now."

Pappo's first family. All skinny and small in the square black and white memory. Imagine that.

"And what's dis?"

"Your Pappo with his sewing machine," said Ganee, measuring flour for bread.

"You mean Pappo had a sewing machine?"

"Eh what?" said a voice in the veranda. Old Lady Bargains appeared at the door with a bucket of shrimp. "Child, the whole ah Peaside know 'bout Harro machine and he sour attitude," she said, her hearing evidently sharp today, "Oi Gwenny, how much shrimps yuh want? Price gone up, no lie." She raised her hands to the ceiling, washing them from the price.

"But, he can sew? Where the machine?" I asked.

Then Ganee and Old Lady Bargains, one kneading dough, the other shelling shrimp, excited to retreat into the past, launched into the tale of the machine.

Pappo used to be a tailor. They said he sewed the best pair of men's trousers and jacket in all of Zekerheid – both in Peaside Pasture and Seaside Strip. Even though the tailor over in Seaside Strip had a saloon with employees and space for multiple appointments and walk-in customers, people came to Pappo's, to this same little house on this abandoned side of the former plantation, and they didn't mind how many days or weeks they had to wait for their clothes.

Then the big tailor man up in Seaside Strip took a stroll one afternoon and tried to get Pappo to come work for him.

Pappo refused. After a few weeks, Big Man came again and raised the proposed wages. Again Pappo refused. After some months, the man came again and threatened to send thugs to beat up Pappo and his three boys and wife. They said Pappo just carried on creasing a seam and told the Big Man to just let him know what date and time he planned to send the thugs so that he, Pappo could put it on his schedule, or better yet, could the Big Man take that notebook and pen over there and mark it down for him, because he didn't have the time to write it himself as he was cutting it real close to Mootoo's daughter's wedding. So the Big Man walked out.

Later, Pappo spared some hours and without any measurements sewed the Big Man a crisp suit that afterwards everyone said fit like a glove. Pappo cycled over to Seaside Strip with the starched suit on a hanger over his shoulder, and knocked on the Big Man's house door, not his saloon. They said that Big Man came to the door, surprised.

Pappo said, "Look man, the days of the crown and bossmanning over Tom, Dick and Harry done. Leh we stop this nonsense once for all before somebody get real hurt. Look boy, I sew a suit for you; you sew back one for me, yes? Case close."

They said, the Big Man looked Pappo in the eye like he was going to punch up Pappo's face but he took the suit without saying a word. And when Christmas came, he rolled up in his fancy car outside of Pappo's house and hooked a brand new pinstripe suit on a hanger on Pappo's paling stave gate. Pappo can still fit in it and he wears it to church every Christmas Eve.

Ganee said, Pappo went on sewing in the living room, and dreamed about his own shop when his three boys grew up. That's why he made a makeshift shop in front the house and put up a sign that said Harro, short for Harold – *Harro Harry & Sons: Tailors*. But then he took it down again and made a new sign to tickle the brains and eyeballs of all of Zekerheid. It said *Proud Harry Harry & Sons: Zekerheid Tailors*. Then people loitered about just to talk about the sign and ask Pappo if he was dunce to put up such a thing, that the repetition of Harry made no sense, and why not just put Harry & Sons, or why not leave it as it was. They came in to argue about the sign and left with a receipt for a new suit.

Pappo asked them, "What I must write then? Boring Old Harold Hari and His Three Boys Sew Here?"

That's the real way it was supposed to spell, H-a-r-i, but somebody Anglicised it somewhere in history. Still it didn't matter to Pappo either way since Hari probably wasn't even our real family name since tracing lineage was a luxury in places like British Guiana and Pappo said one family name was as good as the other and besides, sometimes one name had to represent several lineages anyway and a name was just to identify your existence, it wasn't really the whole you from head to toe.

So Pappo told his customers, "I advertise as I feel," and he kept his signboard up and bought a second sewing machine with his savings.

But when Uncle Winnie saw the sign, he got on a ship to St Lucia. Then to Jamaica. Then to Florida. And finally to Canada where he met Aunty Elaine and had Kim and never came back.

Still Pappo kept sewing. He sewed Uncle Raffie's wedding suit and he even sewed a wedding dress for Aunty Melanie. At first, she wanted lace from England or she wanted her family up North to send her a dress. But when she saw the dress Pappo made, her eyeballs boggled and she admitted it fit her better than anything she ever wore, even her first wedding dress from her last wedding. She said it was like she just walked out of a page of a bridal magazine, and she sent her wedding photos to her relatives abroad. But only the photos of herself in the dress flared out in the botanical gardens. Not photos with Uncle Raffie in them.

Pappo probably thought their grand wedding outfits would convince them to join the family business, but Aunty Melanie said she wasn't cut out for pasture culture. So Uncle Raffie stuffed his wedding suit, his two good pants and seven t-shirts in a plastic bag and rented a woodant-ridden house in Georgetown from where Aunty Melanie kept sending dress patterns for Pappo to sew. But Pappo said he wasn't "nobody personal seamstress." And that was that.

Then when my own Pap came home one day and said he was apprenticed to Crabwood Bollo to learn carpentry, Pappo sucked his teeth and shut down the shop.

Ganee said that that Christmas season Pappo quarrelled with her for everything. He said that because Betsy didn't make it – Betsy was Ganee and Pappo's stillborn baby girl – that she Ganee turned the boys into feather heads who cooked and mopped and ran away from duty. On the days when he went to Chin & Sons Dry Goods Store, he came home scowling and wouldn't talk to Ganee for hours. But Ganee said that in life she'd had to deal with much worse than Pappo's old bleeding heart and she told Pappo he could say whatever he wanted but that when he was done he had to apologise. Pappo wasn't much for apologies so he stopped saying things he'd have to apologise for. Then he took a sledge hammer to the tailor shop, used the wood for a tool shed and said his sons were a basket of stale bread. He moved Gooseberry – his beloved old machine, into the kitchen and told Ganee to take it or give it away or bury it in the mud, he didn't care. The second machine, the new one, he chucked in the tool shed, alongside the signboard and never spoke of it again.

I went to the tool shed and looked about for the sign. It was still there behind some junk. Under the thick dust, the lettering was still clear.

Years later I thought more about Ganee's tale. I could imagine Pappo not knowing where his brothers and cousins had gone, and trying hard to unite his own boys under the mysterious and alluring signage – *Proud Harry Harry & Sons: Zekerheid Tailors*.

Proud Harro indeed.

Now here were Ivy and I, ferrying carton boxes next door as Harold, still proud and Gwendoline, still with the sniffly rag watched on. So I got to thinking, whether one crosses a doorway, a street or an ocean, it cannot be uncrossed. And I asked Mam if I could stay with Pappo and Ganee for a few more days, which rolled into a month, even though I didn't want Ivy to start depreciating our new bedroom by herself. But no matter. I took down the owl curtain and enjoyed our whole old room by myself.

After breakfast, Ganee'd go to the back stairway and shout hello to Ivy who'd be hanging about in her nightie next door on our back steps, waiting for Ganee to come out and wave. And one morning Ganee in coaxing tones asked would I like to go next door so she could wave good morning to both Ivy and me. She'd look forward, she said, to seeing us on the platform first thing every morning, rain or shine, and wasn't that a better bargain than even Old Lady Bargains could come up with and I choke-laughed and said it was. Then she helped me pack. She stacked up a heavy basket of goodies, wrapping everything in wax paper as if I were going on a trip through the Amazon jungle, and she waved as I set out on my epic travails.

As I made my journey across the long low veranda and down the path, passing my hibiscus tree, ambling through the gate and onto the bridge where I stood for a few seconds facing Suzie's house, I thought, at least this vertical square abyss wouldn't have to be the first thing I saw every day of my life anymore when I open my window in the mornings. I stepped off the bridge into the potholed street. The broiling sun warmed my scalp through my middle-part as I balanced the motions of my sustenance basket, my old pillow and a pulley cart Pappo lent me to wheel the wooden doll's house to its new destination.

The first Christmas in our new house exploded into a frenzy of pepperpot boiling, vinegary garlic beef frying, fruit cakes baking, fresh paint drying and Pap's new cologne that Mam had bought him, wafting in the air. And on the weekend closest to Christmas day, Mam worked two double shifts so that later in the week she could take a half day off to go greens, grocery and gift shopping. Three G shopping she called it, all the birds with one stone she said. I didn't understand how you could hit three birds with a single stone at the same time. Did the birds have to line up straight to be toppled like a row of dominoes and why would they volunteer to do so, or did you hit one bird at a time and then retrieve the same stone so that you could hit another bird, and even so, why kill the birds at all? But there was no time to discuss it. Everything had to be crammed into a few hours because Mam had to return to work. Ivy didn't mind. She didn't care for the nauseating market, she said. But I minded. I used to like going to market and trailing behind Mam, asking the names of fish and watching the large market ladies deliver produce with one hand and pocket their change with the other. It was mesmerising watching a pair of hands set the weights on the scale, glide across provisions, pull up an eddo, place it in the scale, then another eddo, then another eddo, then whoosh them all into the customer's basket. I used to like to watch the pairs of hands tying and pricing things into bundles and stacking the bundles in high pyramids. Pointer broom pyramids. Callaloo pyramids. Bora pyramids. Tomatoes. I used to like to stick my nose close to the pyramids of tomatoes.

But now, everything had to be rushed. We rushed past the meat and fish stalls. Mam stuffed the newspaper-wrapped meat in the bag that Ivy was half-heartedly holding and she pushed us along. She rushed past a greens stall and priced a bundle of eschallot. I followed feeling flustered and peeved at Sam's father and Sam, and Annie-Lou and her parents for ruining my Christmas – Sam's father for hightailing it out of pasture culture; Annie-Lou for pressing Sam about it because she thought she was the expert on 'going away'; Sam for flaring up at being interrogated about his father and withdrawing into dark unfinished spaces not meant for him, and upsetting the planks and posts there so that my own father had to wind up with a fractured tibia and my own mother had to get a new job and now me, I had to hustle behind her carrying all these bags and sweating in the broiling sun as she hurtled towards Christmas morning like a pelting train.

"Is why dat one face more sour than this lime?" the eschallot vendor laughed, holding up a lime to my face.

Mam handed over a few notes, bagged the eschallot and said, "Please mind your own sour business, thank you very much." Then she hustled us, "Come on, come on."

I gathered up the bags, concentrating on steering the pineapple's crown from poking my knee and I was just dashing behind Ivy, eyes still on the prickly pine head when I stumbled over something and nearly fell. Ivy burst into an uncontrollable guffaw, making everyone stop and stare.

"Man just shut up Ivy," I snapped, wondering if she'd trade bags with me.

Mam would erupt in a frenzy if all the things had gone pitching about. I looked back to see what had almost made me break my neck.

It was Salimanto of course, Zekerheid's Resident beggar, sitting where he always sat, by the orange stand, with his foot outstretched into the path where everyone had to walk. It wasn't the first time I'd tripped over his foot. I scowled at him. He scowled back as if he had the right to stretch his foot there and I was the one who shouldn't be tripping over it.

"Y'all coming or what?" Mam called and I pushed the pineapple down as best I could and hurried along and complained.

"How could Salimanto keep putting his f –"

"Keep up!" Mam, a dozen paces ahead, shouted over her shoulder, hustling to keep Christmas traditions, raise twins – one raucous and one sour, and hold down a tiresome job.

On Christmas Eve, she worked the double shift again so she could be home on Christmas day. But she missed the nativity play and while I said my lines I kept looking up forgetting she wasn't in the pews.

Pappo had constructed my angel wings from a cardboard box and aluminium foil and he bent some wire for a halo. Since Mam wasn't home to tame my hair, my freshly washed curls poofed and frizzed and Ganee said she'd leave them that way and just pop the halo on top. Ivy's hair, Ganee tied back and hid under a headpiece made from a kitchen towel. She looked fine as an innkeeper, with just her face showing out. But I studied my reflection. What an incongruous angel, I thought. I'd hide myself behind someone, I decided, as we climbed up on Sam's grampappy's donkey cart that Pappo had arranged for us to ride on to preserve our costumes.

"What you think under the tree tomorrow?" Ivy whispered when we were in our beds.

"Dunno. Maybe dresses and socks," I said, trying to sleep quickly so that Christmas would come.

But when tomorrow came, there weren't dresses and socks. Instead, Ivy's audacity was rewarded with the Building Set she wanted. I couldn't believe my eyes. I was glad about my books and a small doll I named Pastel, but I wondered whether it would have been alright to ask for something difficult to get too. Still, I didn't want anything else. I wondered if Sam had gotten the model aeroplane and if he'd play with us again as it was Christmas after all. Half the year had gone and his mother still wouldn't let him, even though his arm was in a sling only for two weeks and there was nothing wrong with him after that. Even Sam's grampappy only came to make deliveries and spoke to Pappo in choppy sentences before reluctantly clippity-clopping away with his donkey cart. This Christmas he didn't even come bearing his usual gifts – a crate of yams, ten pounds of plantains and two jumbo bottles of homemade ginger beer. Mam assumed Sam's mother had forbidden even Old man Reid – a grown grandfather with brains of his own, from visiting us and that made Mam all the more, forbid us from visiting Sam.

But it was Christmas after all and I wondered if Mam would let us go to Sam's house this once so we could share our gifts like always, because what about forgiveness and peace and joy to all mankind and all of that. So I went to ask, but Mam was stretched diagonally on the bed, with her mouth wide open snoring.

Maybe, I thought, maybe I'd just run down to the back street to see Sam for one second and run back home. I considered enlisting Ivy's help but it might be a clumsy operation if there were two of us making a racket in the street. Besides, not being skilled at reading the room to keep the peace, Ivy was sure to blurt out where we'd been. No,

I'd have to do it myself. I had to try and scout out whether things could be mended before I went to Mam about it. Yes, that was the most sensible way to operate. For everyone involved.

But when I got there, Sam wasn't in the yard as usual. I couldn't think what to do. I knew where his bedroom was so I threw a few pebbles at his closed board window.

The window opened. His solemn face appeared. Then the window slammed shut.

Sam's mother came out.

I froze, then turned to flee like I was never there.

"He been like dat all day," she called after my back. "Lock away."

"What's the matter with him?" I asked, surprised at myself for managing to get my words out into the tense atmosphere.

A cow mooed somewhere. There in the back street of Peaside Pasture was the connection to the real pasture, acres of land spread out for livestock and plants. A lush healthy green in some spots. But never mind that luscious green, the houses here were smaller than in our street and there were no lights, running water or telephones.

Finally Sam's mother said, "The little aeroplane his daddy was to send him, he didn't send."

"Oh," I said.

"Don't worry," she told me, looking at my downward cast face.

I was studying my toes poking through my old slippers. I didn't know what else to do. Caught between my twin who'd asked and got everything she wanted and my best friend who'd been promised and got nothing he wanted, all I could do was study my toes and bide my time until Sam's mother said I had to go. My eyes strayed from my own feet to her toes. Her nail polish was chipped and worn out around all the corners of her toenails.

"Don't worry," she repeated, using the universal tone of a mother to any child in distress, "my cousin neighbour did ask me if I want a puppy. Tomorrow I gon go for it for Junior. You can come back tomorrow afternoon and he gon let you play with it, you hear?"

"Alright," I said, a little shocked at the ease of which reconciliation could occur. Then in an ambitious burst I added, "He says if we could please call him Sam, not Junior."

"Arite, we gon try call him Sam then," and she smiled for once, revealing the big chip in her front tooth.

Sam's grampappy appeared at the door.

"Wait," he said, hobbling towards me, "kerr dese yams fuh yuh granfadder and these fuh yuh mother."

"Oh," I said terrified that now Mam, if she didn't approve, would now know for sure that I'd been to Sam's. I said, "Well thanks," afraid to decline the yams. I considered dumping both sets off in Ganee's kitchen and sneaking out again, but that would be lying, I thought.

"Where these yams come from?" Mam asked after she woke up and started bustling about getting up the ingredients for baked custard.

Shaking a little, I told her. About how I went to see if Sam got his plane, and how I went to ask her permission but she was sleeping, and about how Sam didn't get his gift and what his mother said about the puppy and finally about his grampappy sending the yams.

When I was done speaking, Mam got up, walked to her bedroom, slammed the door shut and slept for the rest of the day.

I sobbed intermittently under my new sheets. I'd reopened a wound and hurt my tired Mam. I'd spread my sourness like the generous lime keeper that I was. I must be as disappointing to Mam as Pappo's boys were to him, I thought. Then I pulled the cover over my head and pretended

I was in a wintery country vacationing with Suzie and her family who had asked me over for Christmas because I was Suzie's best friend and even though she had moved to somewhere else, she couldn't find a friend as best as me in the whole wide world. I conjured up all my old familiar invisible friends too and talked to them until I fell asleep.

Sam did get a mongrel. Mozart, he named him. He followed Sam everywhere, even on the public bus. And once, Mozart turned up at a wedding, and the bride, Sam's cousin, pointed and shrieked 'out, out' when she saw Mozart muddying up the aisle. So Sam had handed a random person the ring cushion with the rings still on them and stayed in the doorway, holding Mozart at chest level so that Mozart could witness the ceremony.

After that Christmas, until Mozart died, there never was a time anybody could say 'Sam' without following up with 'and Mozart.' Some mornings I'd see Sam and Mozart delivering milk to the neighbours. He'd wave but wouldn't visit because his mother said he had to keep his eye on the ball. "Which ball?" I asked. He shrugged. So, early in the soft mornings I watched him and Mozart delivering the milk and I watched Mam too. Mam hurrying out the gate with her purse on her shoulder, her pony tail pulled back tightly and her crisp white collar almost touching her ears.

And every single morning that I got up and drew my curtains and looked through my glass window facing out onto the street, the first thing I still saw, not directly but obliquely opposite our new house, was Suzie's house, still silent and daunting, sucking me into its souring abyss.

Then I'd go back to bed to postpone eating the cardboard tasting porridge that Pap was pottering about in the kitchen preparing before we arose to attend that new disorienting city school, with the three imposing turrets and its students with the egos to match.

14

The Missing Diamond

Our new moribund sliver of educational practice was twenty miles from home. But it felt like two hundred miles. In the mornings, the wobbling and whizzing of the bus set my stomach lurching. All I could do to keep my breakfast down was mentally recite whatever I'd eaten that morning – bread, tea, sapodilla, boiled egg; bread, jam, porridge, pawpaw; bread.

Mam and Pap had no choice but to let us take the minibus by ourselves into the city. They couldn't accompany us every day because Mam was now in charge of opening the pharmacy before eight in the morning and because Pap had no car, something which we didn't think was anything until we saw that in the city anyone who was someone had a car. After the first two weeks of Pap losing two pounds by hobbling on the bus with us in the mornings, limping back on another bus home, returning for us once more in the afternoons and shuffling back on his fourth bus for the day, Mam put a stop to it and said that we were soon to be little women and had brains and brawn enough to take the minibus by ourselves. I got out the Oxford dictionary and looked up the word brawn. Just as well too, as Pap leaning on a piece of tree branch by the school gate in the afternoons and hobbling after us in his washed out t-shirt was twice as overwhelming as taking the bus by ourselves. Children stared at Pap. Even on graduation day five years later, a girl I'd managed to make friends with giggled at Pap and said, "Where's your tree branch Mr Harry?"

Besides, Mam said it was two of us and that doubled the chances of sensibility and halved the chances of trouble. We were to follow the dozen rules that she made us copy down.

"Eww," said Ivy, to rule number five – 'Hold hands when crossing the road'.

"Just eww," she said and folded the list in the tiniest possible size and put it in the bottommost bottom of her brandless knapsack.

But still, in the first year at high school, we stuck together. If Ivy with her antics and busted head was the star at Zekerheid Primary, she was a Nobody on this new stage. And if I were a Nobody before, here at this school with the three regal turrets – more imposing once on the grounds – and the navy blue interconnecting walls and sprucely maintained games courts, I was a pin. Pins hold swatches of cloth or patterns together or hide modest women's cleavages. That is all.

Being in First Form and every succeeding level was like stumbling through a revolving glass door for five years without getting out. You could see out, but in a blur. And you couldn't get out until you should.

One day I tried smiling at a trio of stylish girls. "Why *are* you always smiling at me?" one asked.

I felt my smile shrivel into my chest and stay there. It was nine in the morning.

Please God, let it be three o'clock, I prayed.

Another day, before Physical Education class, I locked myself in the stall to change into my sports garbs, safe from the sea of cussing wriggling girls modelling their training bras and pleated skirts, when the ringleader of the stylish trio pounded on the door and, interspersed with expletives, said, "Yo! Flower girl! Get out! I gotta change my pad!"

So please God, let it be three o'clock.

After that, the nickname stuck. People called me Flower Girl and I spent all of high school exercising hefty willpower not to hurl furniture at them, apparently while always wearing a facial expression that sealed my character as the Resident Class Sourpuss.

Ivy, though, embraced 'Vine Lady,' her own nickname, and commissioned a boy to draw a cartoon superhero with vines draped over her body. Then she told the class that with the vines shooting out of her body, she could squeeze the air out of them. They believed and to her chagrin, left her alone and dropped the nickname. But I was taunted as Flower Girl until graduation day and long after. And when Ivy became more popular the following year for the same project that we both did, I wondered, *Why* God? What's wrong with me?

"How you two do on dat Spanish test, hmm?" Pap asked from behind a book.

He too was engrossed in studies, reading for a diploma to get a desk job. Every day he sat behind a gloomy hardcover textbook called *Management Principles* and he studied for tests, prepared presentations and typed assignments on an old typewriter, until Mam bought a secondhand desktop computer the following year. Then Pap showed us how to type our assignments on it. And it was one of these assignments that launched Ivy into popularity.

It was in Second Form when the English teacher, the only teacher in the school who bothered to tell Ivy and me apart, assigned poems for analysis. We had to type up our essay in pairs and prepare a complementing dramatic presentation. Ivy and I were assigned 'The Road Not Taken' by Robert Frost. All week, we glued velvet scraps from Ganee's sewing basket on to gigantic mustard yellow cardboard trees, making a backdrop that merged at a fork, or diverged as the poem said. In the end, the teacher awarded us ninety-five per cent for the dramatic piece in which we recited alternating lines, I, starting with, "Two roads diverged in a yellow wood," and Ivy continuing with, "And sorry I could not travel both," a stellar performance which launched Madam Ivy to visibility after the class nincompoops gathered around to touch the stately velvet trees that she declared must've come from unicorn hair to make them so smooth. With this new popularity, by the time we got into Third Form, Miss Ivy Lee's wings grew.

We both knew that we each secretly studied how the city girls wore their hair, slung their bags, walked and talked. City girls didn't have two pig-tail braids, flat shoes or stumpy nails. They got away with four inch heels, polished tapered nails and when it wasn't inspection week, glossy pouts to match.

One morning, as soon as we got on the bus, Ivy yanked her ribbons off, pocketed them and undid her two plaits that Mam had braided at five o'clock that morning.

I said, "Put back your hair how Mam had it."

But for the rest of the term, Ivy unbraided her hair on the bus to school and re-braided it on the homebound bus.

I argued, "Well why you don't ask Mam to just put it in a ponytail then? You only wasting Mam time. Plus what if something happen to us and somebody describe us and say there was one girl with braids and another in a loose ponytail and Mam says, oh no that's not my girls and then nobody come to save us?"

"You *must* shut down that active imagination of yours, you really must," Ivy said, with a slight pseudo-American inflection, sounding like her nine-year-old self performing as a TV villain with an American accent in Suzie's empty house.

That was another new thing she did. As soon as we got on the bus, without words, she let me know that speaking Guyanese Creole, especially Peaside-sounding Creolese was for Peaside Pasture only, not for the bus and certainly not for school. If you wanted to make friends in a turret-shaped school, you couldn't keep speaking like some Peasider.

The next thing Ivy did was to save some of her allowance and buy a bottle of natural nail polish. Then she shared it with other girls, borrowing their glittery lip-gloss in return. They spent every recess bedazzling their lips in the washroom. Often this glittery group of girls was sent to the office for detention slips and to get their nails cut and cleaned and lips wiped. Ivy joined the line of offenders.

But high school exists in an enigmatic reality. There is no disgrace in a line-up with classroom criminals, especially if your crime was to look good. The more Ivy stood in the line-ups, the more her fame increased so I deduced that she set out to get caught. Why else would she walk around school on inspection week with deep burgundy nails, two glittery rings and a bracelet borrowed from Busty Amanda? Busty Amanda – a moniker she adapted for herself – had a make-up bag with an array of shiny rings, bracelets and necklaces. Some were her mother's, and Ivy and the other girls in the clique decked themselves out whenever there was a free period. Sometimes they got caught and once, the head teacher gave Ivy a letter to deliver to Mam and Pap. But Ivy's burgundy nails tore the letter before my eyes and flicked it in the dumpster beside the lemon green mobile canteen.

If only she'd had the guts to accept her pebble of a punishment rather than feed it to the bin then the tonne of rocks that snuffed out my youth would not have tumbled upon us later.

Two weeks later, news spread around the Third Form floor. Busty Amanda had lost one of her mother's rings, the one that cost half a million dollars. People started looking at Amanda's small circle of girlfriends, which included Ivy.

I couldn't imagine what half a million dollars was.

Amanda's bedazzled mother arrived at school, stepping out of her car, buttocks first, hair extensions intact and heels clickety-clacksing on the concrete. We gawked at her heels, high like the high rises in the metropolis from where she, no doubt, had bought them on her vacation last year. Such heels made a woman indispensable. Heels and hands too. Such immaculate hands with shiny pointed orange-tipped nails and numerous sparkling stacked rings, good enough for a hand cream advertisement. The necklaces too, she knew how to model them, layered and glittering resting on a bosom that reminded us of Amanda's – colossal. And the orange-red lips and dark glasses afterwards had me peering in stores at lipsticks and sunglasses whenever Mam took us into town.

The time it took for Amanda's mother's tresses and buttocks, bosoms and shine to sway their way into the head teacher's office was long enough for us rectangular lankety lanky girls to press fuzzball baby hairs behind ears and hide bitten down nails into skirt pockets. Trance-like, we lined the corridor and waited for her to tread there. Amanda's mother made us painfully aware that we were neither women nor girls, and a depressingly long way from both states. A long way from womanhood – you knew this because it was excruciating when your hormones stirred your heart into a racket when a boy-man in class sat in the row beside you and you had to shush the racket down for shame that some evil was sprouting there in the depths of your childish heart. And a long way gone from girlhood – this you knew because you couldn't flatten your irregularly bulging chest or deny the existence of the monthly bleeding or turn cartwheels anymore without people flinching because your dress tumbled over your head and your panties showed out indicating your lack of propriety. Amanda's mother was the kind of sizzle that stirred up panic in a girl-woman's chest. A sizzle that launched the terror that you could never grow into something as lithe and amorous. She came like a towering turret closer to us, kept an impressively impassive face when she walked by us and smelled of silky silver-ish starlight and pillowy planets like Venus.

When she came out of the office, she steered Amanda home and the head teacher summoned Ivy and three other girls. They returned looking startled and exhausted.

But on the bus ride back home, Ivy re-did her braids, added her ribbons at the bottom, patted her matted curls and simply said, "There's no need to raise Mam's blood pressure over such a trite thing, you know." Then she turned her half-contorted face from me and put her head out the window. I thought, well yes, why should I be the bearer of bad news and my sister's keeper? I wasn't the keeper of anyone or anything or anywhere.

And as the minibus sped on, I willed myself into nonchalance about Ivy's predicament. I ought not to be someone's keeper. I've got my own worries. I've got the Chemistry project. The History poster. French test. Biology Report. Geography assignment ... tomorrow and the next day and the day after that ... please God, let this revolving glass school let me out. Besides, I'm nobody's keeper. Nobody's keeper. Nobody's ...

"Where's the woman's ring?" I blurted finally.

"I dunno." Ivy shrugged.

"How y'all dunno?"

"I dunno. I only used to borrow a bracelet and one ring with a red stone and another smaller one with a cat that had two green stones for the eyes."

"And where those?"

"I put them back in Amanda pouch," Ivy said, her eyes watering. "I never wear the diamond one. The one her mother said missing. It too big and ugly. I didn't know anything had real stones. I only used to borrow the one with the red stone and the cat with the green —"

"Who used to wear the diamond one then?" I asked, feeling a bit smug that for the first time in her life, Miss Ivy Lee was finally showing a smidge of remorse for her deeds.

She hesitated.

"One of them other girls."

"Yes, I know, but which one?"

The stupid loyalist shook her head.

"Say who it was and I gon go myself and tell the head teacher tomorrow!" I declared.

Ivy watched the passengers as they got off the bus.

I tried again, "Tell me or I gon tell Mam what trouble you in."

"Don't," Ivy said, tears brimming freely now so that a wave of panic swept over me. I had no recent memory of Ivy crying. "I didn't take it," she gurgled.

"I know, but if you know who take it, then you must say so or else people might say is you," I said, taking care to soften my tone.

"They gon own up by themselves if is they who take it," she said, the stubbornness building. She looked around at the other passengers, lowered her head and whispered. "None of the girls would steal for real. Maybe she didn't know the ring so valuable and she gon bring it back tomorrow. Just 'cause I know who used to wear it, don't mean is she who stole it."

"Well if the ring don't turn up, go to the head teacher and make her believe it wasn't you."

"How?" She was crying again between big gasps of air. Here was Miss Ivy Lee, master of her own destiny, sitting in public transportation, howling. It was high time for my panic to grow.

A market woman in the seat behind us prodded my shoulder with an umbrella. "Why you troubling dat gyurl?" she demanded.

Everyone turned to look at us. I was mortified.

"Me?" I asked, surprised at the clarity of the voice coming out of my own mouth, "Me? I'm not troubling her." I wanted to pelt the woman's umbrella out the window if she prodded me again. I wanted to tell her to just mind her own sour business, please and thank you. But I didn't want to sound like my mother, the way the parroting Annie-Lou used to sound like hers, so I shut up.

To Ivy I whispered, "We gotta tell Mam."

"No," she said stubbornly and sapped her tears with the towel she'd pulled off of her lunch bowl. "It be alright," she said.

But it wasn't.

Suddenly, at the beginning of the August holidays, Ivy was summoned to school, to be accompanied by Mam and Pap.

"But why?" I asked. "And why only you?"

Ivy shrugged.

"I want go too," I said, as Pap stuck his hat on.

"No," snapped Mam, who'd taken time off from work and lost a day's pay, "You wash the wares, hang out those wet clothes and make sure you don't burn the bread."

I did burn the bread.

But when they returned no one spoke of burnt bread. No one spoke at all. Pap hung up his hat, picked up his tree branch and hobbled out again. Mam went into the kitchen without changing out of her road clothes and started making dinner by slamming utensils around.

"What happen?" I whispered to Ivy.

Her face was pale and dry. The sides of her lips had cracked since last I saw her four hours ago. And her eyes were red and puffy.

She slammed the bedroom door, flung herself on her bed and sobbed.

"What happened?" I asked again, sitting on my own bed and looking through the crystal vase on the side table braced on the wall between our beds. It was the same vase that Pap had filled with flowers on our seventh birthday. He'd put it as a permanent fixture in our room and sometimes still filled it with fresh flowers, especially a combination of ixora and ivy, his old special dry joke. I studied the stripes on my bedsheet and waited for her answer.

But Ivy wouldn't stop sobbing.

I went over and threw myself on her and shook her by the shoulders. "What?" I asked, starting to tremble. I, who didn't consider myself lacking in imagination, could not imagine what had possibly happened.

"They expel you?" I tried my best to guess the worst case scenario.

"Worse."

"Worse?"

Downstairs in the kitchen Mam slammed pots and pans. Cladang cladang, cling-ding blam.

"Is Amanda father," said Ivy into the pillow.

"Who?"

"Amanda. Her dad."

"What happen to him?"

"He said we have to pay."

"Pay what?"

"For the ring."

"What r-, oh," I said. "What you mean pay?"

"Pay. Pay. Pay money for it." Ivy sat up cross-legged on the bed, her face a mess.

I inched up, cross-legged too, facing her. "But it wasn't your fault. You didn't tell them?"

"I done tell dem awready. I done tell dem I din wear it, or take it or hide it or loss it."

"Well didn't you tell them which of the girls used to wear it?"

"No."

"Why not? Who you last saw wearing it?"

She sniffed.

"*She* didn't take it either!" Ivy choked.

Then she threw herself on the pillow and started with the sobbing again.

"Well if you know who you last saw wearing it, tell them and let that girl answer the questions or pay for it! Why everybody gotta pay? Ivy why you so stupid?"

"But what if she didn't take it and I point the finger at her and make it worse and she gotta pay it all by herself?" She got up and sat cross-legged again.

"But what if she did?"

"Then she did."

"Ivy Lee, you a lunatic?"

She looked at me.

I studied the plaid pattern of her bed sheet. A taut silence hovered, except for her sniffing and the pots and pans cladanksing downstairs.

"So who has to pay?" I asked finally.

"All of us. Amanda father," Ivy whispered, "he call us nasty little thieves and said we have to split the cost and pay every last cent otherwise he reporting us as juvenile criminals."

The bottoms of my feet started getting cold.

"How much each?" I said fearing I couldn't understand the number she was going to say.

"One hundred and twenty five thousand dollars," she whispered and started gasping for air again.

The cold feeling wound up to my stomach.

"How much is that?" I asked.

"I don't know," she whispered and leaned over for a writing pad and pencil. "How much Mam does make?"

"I dunno."

She wrote some things down and got out a calculator.

It was a very hot day but the chill kept creeping up and was almost to my lungs and still creeping when she said, "Three and a half."

"Three and a half what?" I asked alarmed.

"Three and a half to four years, it might take Mam to pay it back."

We looked at each other.

Then she threw herself on me sob-whimpering, her head on my shoulder, like a small limp puppy without an owner and with a thorn in its paw, and my hard heart broke and my arms rose around the back of her ribs and I vowed to myself that I, Ixora Mara, writer of detective stories, would find the missing diamond and set things right again, no matter how long it took.

I said, "Well! I thought you said Vine Lady could shoot vines outa her body and squeeze people until they behave. Leh we go squeeze Mr Amanda father."

And she laughed her snot onto my t-shirt.

"Ugh. Get it off. Ick. Uck. Awwk," I said, squirming and flailing. "Just eww."

She laughed again.

At last I tried again, hopefully, "Tell me who last wore the ring. Maybe that girl should pay the whole thing."

"But she can't afford. She don't have a Papa and her Mammy sick."

"Who is it?" I persisted.

Quiet tears rolled down her cheeks.

I tried a different tactic. "Well if she got it, she could sell it and pay the whole thing if she don't want to own up and smear her name. Let's call everybody and find out."

The sobbing stopped and the usual determination returned to her mouth. "Alright," she said, "alright."

When the clandanks claddinks of pots downstairs died down, we snuck down to the telephone and called the three girls. I stuck my ear by the receiver and listened.

"N-n-ooo, I d-d-don't have it," Girl Number One, cried into the phone. "D-d-daddy's awready paid my q-quarter, b-but I can't go to Disney this summer he said. I'm punished." She hung up.

We looked at each other. Already paid? I gulped while Ivy dialed the next girl.

"Yes I did wear it a couple a times," Girl Number Two said. "I wear it, yes. And I put it back in Amanda jewellery pouch with thee other things. I put it back in thee afternoon after the bell. Yes, for sure. When Amanda was in thee washroom and the bell went. Yesss, for sure. I not crazy. You think I lying or what? I just went into her bag, zip out the pouch and put it back. I didn't even know it was a million dollars."

"Half," said Ivy.

"What's the difference? I can't 'fford it. My mother sure kill me. She said she jus' taking me outta school to work and pay it back because I'm shame and disgrace just like my daddy and his daddy." She hung up.

Ivy and I looked at each other again. We really weren't going to recover this diamond after all, I thought, feeling like someone was closing the windows in the house and making the room dark.

Girl Number Three was angry and adamant. "Looka dat piece of trash! Accusing me! Who want dat stinking ugly old piece of rat trap compressed carbon? My daddy a lawyer an' he taking that Mr Amanda father to court, just watch."

"To court to say what?" Ivy asked.

"To say he a stinking lying gutter rat," said the girl and hung up.

"Fine friends you have," I said, now beginning to understand the territory I was working with and gradually feeling like everything was getting muffled. Like someone was locking up the last window that let the light in.

"What Amanda and her mother say?" I asked, looking for grace somewhere and trying to press on with my investigation, as the muffling and darkening continued in my head.

"Nothing."

All the windows closed. The last thing I heard was Ivy shouting for Mam before my body swayed forward, collapsing into the carpet as the multitude of peach roses hid themselves in the dark.

15

An Ounce of Justice

"Sorry man," Ivy said, on video call years later as I bemoaned the loss of my youth. The expanse of my August holidays shrank after the demands and threats of Amanda's father. August was the one time a year I could be free from the moribund sliver. But after *The Case of the Missing Diamond* began, my youth was lost to a blur of cycles. School terms blurred into working school breaks that blurred into new school terms, cycling that way for years as Ivy and I completed jobs around Peaside to earn stipends to help pay off the hundred and twenty five thousand dollars. By the end of the second August holidays, Amanda's father was paid in full with our earnings, Pap's small loans and Mam's savings, including the sale of her love knot gold earrings.

Two whole Augusts and more, shrunk down. Where's the justice in that?

"All my youth. Poof. Gone," I repeated, putting my face closer to the laptop camera.

"It wasn't all your youth Sour Fig. Just eight weeks per year, multiplied by two. All the other summers after dat was to help university tuition. Dat don't count."

"Counts yes, 'cus —"

"That's only four months put together, not your whole you –"

"Whole youth, yes. With a cycle of youth loss, you know like hair loss, once it starts –"

"Gotta go, bye," Ivy said and closed her laptop to get rid of me.

"Hmmph."

Poof, all my youth, dwindled, 'unsummered.' I had not exaggerated. If Ivy didn't think that the wiping of medicine shelves and everything else had reduced the August holidays, then that was her own sour business.

Every morning before eight o'clock, we wore gloves that were too big, and swept and mopped the pharmacy till the floor shone. Mam, in her crisp white collar, pretended to ignore us over the counter. The mops and buckets, rakes and yard brooms were large and cumbersome and gave my hands squiggly corns and stubby calluses. Sometimes I couldn't press down hard enough on my mop to shine the floor, and my half of the pharmacy didn't sparkle like Ivy's. "Do it like so," she'd say and press on her mop, her face straight, uncomplaining, even though it was so early that we'd not yet had our breakfast. And on Saturday afternoons, we went and waited for the boss to hand us the stipend. Then we went home, put it in the cookie tin and made a note of what we earned, adding it to last week's amount.

After breakfast every day, we helped Old Lady Bargains with the community garden. She heard about our quest for stipends and suggested we help her get the overgrown garden going again so Peaside could put vegetables in their stomachs without the double dose of fertiliser and pesticides that those bulldozing loudmouths over on Seaside Strip shoved down our gullets. And when the plants started bearing and Peaside people came to buy, Old Lady Bargains gave us the biggest stipends she could afford, after she reclaimed some of her capital.

"What's Old Lady Bargains' real name?" I asked Ganee. But Ganee said that I must have enough fire in my spirit to go and find out things for myself. So I didn't go.

After lunch some days, we shopped groceries and did household chores for Small Spokes' grandmother who still lived alone down the street. On Mondays, we swept and mopped her house. On Tuesdays we washed her clothes and hung them out. Wednesdays came and we folded the clothes washed the day before. She had ginormous underwear and dozens of skirts sent from abroad. Long skirts, so thick and heavy when wet that both of us had to wring them and chuck them up on the clothes line in the yard. On Thursdays, we swept leaves and cared for plants. Fridays came and we shopped for greens and groceries and pushed them on our bicycle that was now too small for us to ride. The cook criticised everything we bought, muttering and cussing, taking her own sweet time delaying the lunch, traipsing in and out of the living room every five minutes to follow the daily soap opera, even though Spokes' grammy'd be getting hungry and cranky. And every day, after Cook left, Ivy volunteered to wash the extra dishes and feed the lazy cat for free.

On Friday afternoons, Spokes' grammy paid us with a little wad of bills. She handed us the bills, brought her palms together to her chest and bowed at us slightly. Ivy accepted the bills, kept them between her palms, brought her own palms together to her chest as if she were praying and bowed deeply in return. Sometimes Ivy widened her eyeballs at me to indicate that I must follow suit. "Show some respect man," she said every time, after we were out of the old lady's earshot. But I always forgot, being too busy watching the little ritual of theirs, with the old lady solemn and grateful and Ivy oddly compliant, her mouth set in the grim determined line and palms with the wages pressed against her sturdy body, bowing.

When we returned home in the afternoons, Mam and Pap'd still be out. Pap now worked as assistant manager in a company that built supermarkets and small stores and long after four in the afternoons, he stayed at the office and calculated things, assessed risks and profits and arranged the team's schedules. Then he had to type the reports because the company was too cheap to hire a secretary, as Mam had politely observed. Pap worked long hours to repay the loan for his diploma and the money that with much swallowing of pride, he'd borrowed from Crabwood Bollo's young nephew to pay the first instalment on Amanda's mother's cursed missing diamond. That day when I fainted into our carpet's peach roses, Pap had been down the street and returned with a small wad of bills, only to find me in bed, my head tied up with a handkerchief soaked in Limacol.

"I'm going to catch the culprit, Pap," I said, touching the Limacol-soaked handkerchief. "I promise."

"Alright there Ixie Pixie, alright there, you do that," Pap pacified me, treating me like I was delirious.

"Y'all don't believe me?" I said, flaring up at his patronising tones.

"Yes, yes," he said, but I knew he didn't.

This was one time he didn't have cratefuls of hope in his eyes. Three times he called Uncle Raffie to ask him to send us a loan but three times he hung up without the guts to ask. Mam watched him and shrugged. "Michael Herbert, it's your prerogative," she said, "Ask or don't ask. Either way, is not the end of the world." Mam had two lists. One that constituted what made the end of the world and another list of things that didn't.

Grown-ups have the oddest ways to solve problems, I thought. They weren't going to fix anything, running round behind loans. It was the truth that needed to be found out.

So I got my notebook from under the trapfloor, wondering what my Inspeck S'mart would do. I imagined putting on Inspeck S'mart's shoes and his belt with the buckle. The first thing he'd do was list the suspects: Girl number One I-can't-go-to Disney, Girl number Two My-mother-is-going-to-kill-me, Girl number Three My-daddy-is-a-lawyer. I thought about each of them, how they dressed, how they spoke and why they'd take the ring. Bam! I'm coming to get you, I said in my head every time I saw them in school. I asked Ivy for a sketch and description of the ring. She sketched a round diamond, flanked on either side by three pronged leaves and handed me the paper. I worked on the case for almost ten years. First with vigour, observing and interrogating the three suspects and others so much that I heard them plotting to tie me up with gym rope and lock me in the toilet. I didn't care. The world doesn't end if one gets locked in a toilet. It ends when there is no ounce of justice. I interrogated Amanda and Ivy too – though she was my own blood, for objectivity and all that. Inspeck S'mart would be thorough, regardless. But I yielded no success. Still, after graduation, I continued cyber stalking and psychoanalyzing the suspects and others in the class, even though everyone including Mam, tried to convince me to "just let the past go Ixie." But it was a good thing I didn't, or the culprit would never have been found.

People were always trying to tell me what to do. As if they know me. As if they know what I've been put on earth to do.

Pap too, tried to convince me to let go the idea of a surgery to fix his tibia.

"Look, it says here, it might work," I said, showing him a page in a big medical book from the school library.

"Aww Ix," was all he said low and slow, like a tiger that lost its stripes.

That's the same kind of exclamation he made when he and Mam would return from work late and see the table that Ivy and I set for dinner.

"Aww Laurs, look." He pointed at the plates of baked chicken, fried rice and corn. He pointed at the utensils rolled up in napkins. At the napkins folded like wrinkled up swans. And at Ganee's warm buns, displayed on rainbow coloured saucers beside the cold lime juice that Ivy made. Such cold awful juice that it made me tingle from shoulders to knees with just one sip.

Such were the cycles of the days, months, years, even if Ivy couldn't see that. For after a while, even on school days, we continued the odd jobs irregularly, both in the mornings and evenings. And all the stipends went into the cookie tin.

Sometimes on our way home from the pharmacy, we met Mr Fred on the street corner opposite the primary school. On occasion, he had a new book to lend me. Ivy'd be bored and continue home.

"She caused this whole thing you know," I complained, holding up the corns on my hands.

"Ripple effect," Mr Fred said. His jaw sagged more these days.

"Ripple?" I studied his jaw.

"Like one drop o' rain in a pothole," he said. The smell of expired cologne was bad.

"Oh," I mused, not forgetting the last time I studied raindrops in a puddle. "We got sports dis term you know," I said, looking at the runner on the cover of the book he'd just handed me.

"You runnin'?"

"Me? Naa."

"But yuh got two good foot."

"But I gonna get last place."

"Neva mind. Somebody must come in last." He laughed. When he laughed, the expired cologne was worse. "Plus," he said, "All body must get at least one dream, small or big."

"One dream? You got one?"

"That I's a rich maharaja with a grateful wife," he said and laughed so loudly that everyone on the street stopped to look. Then he took a sip from his tea flask.

So decided I'd run for sports after all.

And sure enough, it was The Limepicks all over again but worse, with Amanda and her new friends standing by the track, ooing and booing themselves hoarse because I was coming in last. I folded my fist and held my middle finger down to prevent it flying up into their faces, and I said to the grey-haired score keeper writing down the house points, "Well, somebody gotta be last." She grinned and said, "True words."

Richard, a boy one year my senior, was standing beside the score keeper and heard me. He smiled.

Lord help me, what a smile, I thought, and smoothed down my pleats.

The next time I saw Richard, he was in the library, wearing his uniform like a model-student, his marshmallowly hair combed to the right. He looked at me and nodded slightly.

I nodded back.

When I got home, I went to the mirror and recreated the way I thought I'd nodded, trying to see how I must've appeared to Richard. Richard, who played the drums, who played football, volleyball, chess, who sprinted, who threw the javelin, who carted off so many trophies every year on speech day that his parents brought a sizeable toy wagon in which to wheel them home, that Richard. Richard, who spoke three languages, who'd been to the other side of the world more than half a dozen times, who had a penchant for reading poetry in the library. That Richard.

Every day he sat in the library, one desk away from me and nodded hello and I responded with my rehearsed nods. I practised all the things I could say to start a conversation. I recorded my voice and listened to it on repeat, deciding whether I should speak lower, slower or higher, louder, faster. I tried out sentences and exchanged words with synonyms. I made sure I could enunciate. I made sure I would sound cool, chill, not too bookish, but just bookish enough.

Then one day, after our customary nods, Richard to me, and I to him, Busty Amanda and her crew landed right at Richard's desk. By the next day she told everyone that Richard was her boyfriend. And to top it off, Madam Ivy was with them again. What about all the diligent mopping and pious bowing and distancing herself from Amanda, I wondered.

"How you could still be friends with that traitorous tart? Your head bore?" I whispered to Ivy in English class.

She whispered back, "Amanda didn't really do us nothing, you know. Is her father. Plus, she knows lots stuff. Said her father gon send her abroad to study and I can come be her roommate, like in the movies."

"You run behind Amanda, see if I talk to you anymore," I said, trying my hand at emotional blackmail.

"Mademoiselle Harry et Mademoiselle Harry," snapped the French teacher, "shush."

I wished our teachers would stop calling us Miss Harry and Miss Harry. Anyone with sensible eyeballs could see who was who. Instead, the teachers would hold two graded test papers in the air and wait for us to claim the correct one. What was worse though, was when people mixed up our stories. Nobody wants their story mistaken for another's. Nobody wants their story minimised, muddled, interjected, exchanged.

"Who were the ones in the diamond scandal?" a parent in the school yard would say.

"That one over there and that one there, also that one and oh, one of those two," another parent would point out.

Was everything that Ivy did for the rest of her life to follow me around, cover me over, like a Miaplambo shadow, I wondered. So I made good my blackmail and only spoke to her when I had no choice. When she and Amanda and the other prima donnas came into the library throwing their attentions at Richard, Richard with the eco-friendly notebooks, I ignored them.

But one day, in a new development, Richard arrived voluntarily with Amanda and company. It seemed they were no longer happening upon him in the library; instead, he was meeting them elsewhere, whence they made an entrance together as a certified clique.

At once, dozens of sensations flung towards me. Like someone had just broadsided my head with an architectural magazine from the bottom shelf. Like dozens of books were flying off the shelves, hurling themselves at me. Like everyone else was catalogued and checked out and I was an unread book on a shelf. I must get out, I panicked. Out of this library. Out of this moribund sliver. Get on a bus going the opposite direction from here. Ride to the end of the world. Anything. Anything at all but stay here unread, unknown, unseen, a pin, an ant. An ant on a blade of grass bending towards the turrets and the turret-egos.

I watched the clock, and at lunch hour I walked through the school gates.

Students weren't allowed to leave the grounds until the last bell rang for the day. We were allowed only to go through the gates during recess and lunch hour to purchase snacks from the vendors outside, but not to leave the premises. Ever.

I left the premises.

I boarded a bus, a free road stretching before me.

But the thrill of my gall at marching through the gates and boarding the bus soon evaporated. As soon as I got on, I wanted to get off. It felt like I was riding into a town in one of those Western movies that Pappo watched on Sunday evenings, where the rider of the bus was uncertain of where he was headed, and was only moving out because the town wasn't big enough for both of them – whoever they were.

"Uh, stop here please," I told the conductor, deciding I didn't want a ride to the end of the world after all.

I got off and dawdled looking at street signs for somewhere to go. Then in an unusual wave of decisiveness I turned down the street leading to Sam's school, deciding to ferret him out. Startle him with my audacity.

I watched students lining up at the snow cone cart but I couldn't go marching in for Sam. Somebody'd see me in uniform and report me. I braced behind a tree with sweat dripping down my brow. I thought of Pappo and Sam's grandpappy and the stories they told about the sweat dripping down their brows in the canefields in the broiling sun, each one saying it wasn't he but the other who'd fainted in the heat. And I thought of Ganee, Pap and Mam and guilt started burning my stomach. They wouldn't know this girl breaking the rules, riding to the end of the world, peering behind trees.

Just then Sam came out and I swallowed and decided to stick my head out and wave to him. He didn't see at first. But when I withdrew my hand and called his name, I was sure that he and his friends looked in the direction of the tree. When I judged that they had looked away once more, I poked my head out and waved again, hoping to catch Sam's eye. He saw me this time and his eyebrows shot into his scalp.

"What you doin' here?" he whispered, after he joined me behind the tree. "You gone crazy?"

Crazy was better than guts-less, I thought, pleased.

"So?" I said, trying to seem tough, while the marvel and guilt of my daring burned my stomach like bad medicine.

"What you want?" he said, looking around like a madman. "You want us get expel?"

"I've come to pay you a visit. How've you been?" I said airily, like a madwoman in turn.

"Here? Now? You do know where I live right? You do see me delivering milk to your neighbour every morning right? Gwan. Scram!"

It was true. I'd seen him the day before without Mozart and I'd whistled and gestured for Mozart. 'Sick,' Sam had signalled with his hands to his throat and tongue hanging out.

"I ... I ... uh ... I wanted to know if Mozart was feeling better," I said, thinking on my feet. Otherwise, what was I doing here, breaking several school rules – leaving the compound for purposes other than snacks, riding public transport during school hours, fraternising with boys of another school. These were the charges read to me later, as I stood in the deputy head teacher's office. She didn't like me anyway, the deputy. It was easy to tell that she thought I wasn't talented or academic or athletic enough for her precious school with the tall turrets and the even more towering traditions.

"Mozart feeling better," Sam was saying, settling into a warm conversation, assuming that is why I had come after all. "He eating back all his food now and he can run real fast again. And he ..."

"Okay okay, I gotta go," I said, delighted about Mozart but still conscious of my own fate.

"Okay," Sam said and smiled. Then he helped me cross the road and get on a bus. He waved and I waved back. I really could make this a habit, I thought as the guilt subsided. It was freeing. To temporarily escape turret land and have a friend for myself at last. A bird burst out of my chest and soared. I was mistress of my destiny, not any little flower girl. Everyone would see.

The next day, in the presence of my parents, the charges read to me, Mistress-of-my-destiny, were as I said – breaking several rules with intent to do so. Did I deny the charges and what was my defence? The evidence against me was irrefutable. I did leave the grounds with no intention of buying pickled mango or snow cone. I did consciously and of my own free will, hail a bus. I did seek out the attention and conversation of a male student from another school. You couldn't put it any other way.

Mam and Pap were not disappointed. There is little room for disappointment when someone is shocked and scandalised as Mam was. Pap, not so much. He was only sad.

I was punished for a month with extra chores – something to consume my time, Mam said, because it seemed like I had too much of it on my hands, and if I had the time to play a big woman, then I could be one in real life. For forty days, I washed dishes. Swept and mopped the entire house from ceiling to vinyl. Scrubbed mats and hung them on the fence to dry. Washed curtains. Primed and painted all the walls that were still unpainted in the house. Made tea for Pap. Printed his reports. Learned to cook roti on a tawa. Made floral arrangements for both our house and Ganee's. And when it looked like I was taking one idle second to myself, I was sent to Ganee's to help with the chores there, especially to water my own hibiscus bush that I had been neglecting now that I had turned into a big woman.

Everyone steered clear of Mam and me. Nobody interfered with the due process, though Ivy tried to help me with the mopping a few times.

"Get away from me," I said.

Three times Pap tried to talk to me. I could see he was trying to get inside my head to hear me out, to help me out, but I wouldn't let him. I didn't want anybody inside my head.

At the end of my punishment, I was stronger though, more competent, disciplined, more focused than forty days ago. Mam's punishment was fair, but that was my own secret. In fact, when the month was over, I found myself holding on to the habits of rising early, washing dishes, tidying the house and watering my plant and even the rest of Pappo's plants. On the outside though, I willed myself to remain reticent to this unbalanced world.

Just as well too, for in about a year later in Fifth Form, our exam year, Ivy Lee Harry, creator of her own destiny, along with five friends, boarded buses five times that term, in the same reckless manner as I had. They accompanied Busty Amanda who everyone said was spying on her new boyfriend over at the other school for reasons only known to her group. And they were never caught.

All I want is an ounce of justice, I thought, as I watched Ivy propped up against her pillows one evening, perusing random things out of a hodgepodge stack. She was reading a magazine with the cover headline – 'The Roles of the Heir and the Spare', and studying me over the top of the magazine. Then she glanced through a brochure about cruise ships and she examined a university guide of lucrative careers. She ran her finger down the list and stopped at engineering.

"That's the kind of thing I be studying next year. At university," she said, munching on a caramel wafer biscuit and tapping the page twice, "How 'bout you Flower Girl?"

16

Electric Love

As soon as our exam results were out, Ivy was up at the university enrolling in a program like she was some kind of space agency rolling out a blueprint for humanity's discoveries.

Pap said I too had better go. So I went.

In the beginning, I divided my time on campus between classes and the sprawling front lawn where youngsters played cricket and where their cheering or booing spectators sat on long yellow benches under the canopy of trees. There the Biodiversity Majors snapped photos of birds, and Art Majors sketched scenery. It was nice there and I'd sit under the canopy with my friend from high school – the same girl who had laughed at Pap's tree branch, and we'd munch on our lunch. But as the semester went on and the campus grew more populated, the canopy struggled to house everyone. It became loud and hot and when a group of boys with black eyeliner, black nail polish, choker collars and smart phones snapping pictures of chicks – chicks, in air quotes – when these boys started pointing their devices at us, I retreated to the library. My friend though, who reminded me of Suzie or what I remembered of Suzie, enjoyed posing for the boys. Then she became obsessed with their fashion and donned black garbs and accessories.

"You go on, I'll catch up," she'd say, but she never did.

I waited in the library every day but she never came. All she needs now are five bluegreen suitcases, five travel bags and five gravity defying braided knots poking up from the backseat of a lime green mini-bus, and she'd be set, I thought, as the old lime spread into my sinuses. The lime hadn't showed up in my body for a long time and I thought either I'd grown out of it or it had left me alone. But here it was again. Barely perceptible. But there. Still.

Still, I shouldn't have preoccupied myself with these thoughts, for after that, whenever I boarded the bus I saw mutations of Suzie in the back seat of other buses everywhere, especially lime green buses. Sometimes, I even hoped for Suzie's mutation to turn around and wave. And sometimes I sat in the library sketching the back of the bus and Suzie's hair above the seat.

There's something wrong with me, I thought. I'd better get out and eat lunch under the canopy again, like a normal youngster. But the clamouring crowd at the front of the campus made me do an about-turn and plod on to the back of the campus instead.

There at the back was a multi-purpose concrete court, a great shed covering the court, two unpainted wooden benches under the shed and a long lunch table between the benches. The benches were uncomfortable and far from the hub of the front and they overlooked such an uneventful piece of landscape that nobody came there on an average day for average reasons. People only came there to cry or hide. Basketballers came to practise dribbling if they didn't want opponents to see their moves. Couples came to smooch. Cliques came to smoke things beside the No Smoking sign. But they came only at dusk and the landscape lay otherwise uneventful. So as I was akin to uneventful landscapes, I hung about there alone. Sometimes, I even stretched out on one of the benches and cat-napped with a happy breeze in my face.

One day while I was lying there pondering Ivy's condescension at our one university, a young man came to sit on the opposite bench and cry. Until then I'd only seen girls come to cry. But here in broad daylight was a young man sobbing. I didn't know if to startle him by putting my head up from behind the lunch table that was concealing me or to just lie there and let him go on with his crying while I went on with my thinking about this morning's events.

Ivy had accidently taken my bag and I hers and I'd gone peering into her faculty's never-ending row of classrooms. Finally, I heard her voice coming from one of the rooms, "Soon's I done here, ladies and gentlemen, I'm off. Abroad. For a Masters."

Someone said, "Gawd yes. Take me wit you outta dis dump." And the group whistled.

It was the first time I was hearing about this improbable scheme of hers. Abroad was a million miles away. Besides we'd never get all that money for tuition and Mam could never approve letting her set out alone. Just for school. It seemed incredulous and a scoff escaped my lips. The nerve of her expecting me to ferret her out while she sat there spinning yarn.

She came to the door, exchanged the bags without a thank you, and continued talking. "Look, there ain't no Master of Engineering programme here at our one university. That kinda ting requires a woman to stay poor you know." She emphasised condescension on the words one and poor.

Everybody sniggered when she said that.

I didn't have a problem with our *one* university. How many did we need?

So there I was lying on the bench and thinking about all that when the sobbing boy appeared on the opposite bench.

I decided I'd better pop my head over the lunch table.

"What's the matter?" I asked, surprised at my daring to speak.

The sobber sprang out of his bench, pressing where his heart should be. Then he let out a breath. "Oh. You," he said and settled down again, probably relieved it was a human that had popped out.

I studied the teary specimen. His eyebrows were thick and a blob of snot had transferred from his nostril to his right eyebrow. He didn't even have a handkerchief. Just kept transporting the snot around his face.

"Did you fail a test?" I asked, hoping to appear solicitous and also scare him away so I could have my uneventful landscape to myself again.

He opened his mouth but no sound came out.

"Failed a course?" I coaxed. "Lost a game? Got expelled? Went to the doctor, found out you're dying? What?"

I couldn't believe myself. Sitting there saying these bold things to this stranger who seemed familiar.

He smiled slightly. "Worse," he mumbled and transferred the blob of snot to the other eyebrow. I watched the snot and tried to figure out where I might've seen this chap before.

"Everything feels like ... like a bad shock. A hundred volts," said he, softly.

"Oh?" I said, trying to think of something else to say, while the irritation of knowing that I knew him from somewhere gnawed at me.

The air conditioner in the faculty building hummed behind us and the faint cheering travelled from the front of the campus towards our no-man's land and it amused me that on this spot of earth, I had come into existence to at least one person in the world.

"She wants to go away for a while. Abroad. To work," he said, wiping his nose with the back of his hand.

"Who?"

He probably resembles somebody from television. That must be it, I thought.

"Milly. My girl." He flicked a photograph of a girl in gym shorts, posing with dumbells.

"Oh. Well. She might be back soon," I said, putting a little hope in my tone to pacify him. Still, the Robert Frost poem we'd recited in Second Form reeled out in my head – "knowing how way leads on to way,/ I doubted if [she] should ever come back." But I didn't say that aloud.

"Who says?" he said and folded his arms, his long thin fingers resting on his forearms.

"Well maybe you can go to her then," I suggested, thinking his fingers reminded me of a porter gripping valises in a Western movie.

"And what about the shop? And my old man? Anyway, what could I do there? Abroad? Besides, maybe she won't want me to go, I ..." His tears were at it again.

"It's you!" I exclaimed, "I know who you are!"

"How you mean? You didn't know it was me before?" He wiped his eyes with the backs of his hands and I wished he had a handkerchief to clean that awful snot off.

"Well no. You look different now," I said, remembering the long thin fingers wrapping the sweetmeats in wax paper. The decisive hand salvaging Ivy's knapsack. The sturdy arm helping me bear Ivy home with the burgundy gash on her scalp. The dutiful pair of hands towing me to the bus while Mam towed Ivy on her bicycle. And the generous hands again, steering the two bicycles home. I said, "You look different. But it's you."

"You look the same. Only taller. And more serious."

"You sure you don't mean sour?" I said and he laughed a little.

He *was* from Peaside after all, where everyone still said that Ivy was the sunshine and I was the sour. Sunshine and sour. Sour or sunshine. You couldn't be both. In Peaside you had to be one thing. But he didn't live in Peaside anymore. He took care of his grandfather in the next village, he said, and I wondered if his new village had its own Resident Sourpuss. He ran the shop there, he said. And studied Medicine, here at the University.

"Medicine?" I repeated and went into my bag for my spectacles to make sure it was the correct person I thought he was – the young cane cutter I'd cast in a Western movie, as a character called Jack or Bob.

"Well," I said, suddenly feeling the weight of my eroded years spent sourpussing and lying around on benches in quiet landscapes while Jack-Bob there was riding his train through life, taking his pick of occupations, seemingly as good in one profession as he would be in any other. It didn't matter which.

"Well, about your girl ..."

He looked at me hopelessly expectant for a solution.

"Maybe try with the daily email and instant chat," I said.

"Alright then. Every single day, I'll talk to her 'til she comes back."

"Good." I shoved my spectacles back into my bag in a hurry. A manic urge to study fell upon me. "I got to go then. Bye."

I gave a thumbs up and hustled away, resolving to find a profession too.

When my classes ended before Ivy's, I went on home by myself. Many days, I saw Sam getting off his bus too and together we strolled home and talked. We talked about our lecturers. Our grades. The job market and television shows. About poverty and the most beautiful places on earth, though that was mostly Sam. I had no opinion on anywhere except Peaside. Some days I saw Mr Fred too, heading home from Zekerheid Primary.

"Smart," he said one day, pointing at my new square bag.

I looked down at it. He was right, it really was a rather grown up bag to have slung over one's shoulder. Ganee and Pappo had gifted it to me for my birthday.

"How dem journalism classes?" he asked.

I shrugged. "Trying."

His cologne was worse than ever and his collar bone prominent. What a fate I've got, I thought, to have friends without handkerchiefs and poor hygiene. When it wasn't snot, it was red eyes and disinfectant and expired cologne. When would the universe send me someone impeccably dressed and magically scented? Like Suzie.

Mr Fred braced against the telephone pole, saying nothing. Long ago we used to talk about the stories in the books he lent me. These days, I strained to find something to say.

"This is the telephone pole with the phone wire leading to your house?" I asked, inspecting the air like I was interested.

"None phone now."

"What happen to it?"

"Service cut. Na need it. The 'lectric too. Cut."

"But don't you need your 'lectric, um, electricity. Your lights, I mean?"

"Na. For who?"

He looked across the street at the school.

"You don't clip the hedge and bushes into shapes no more?" I asked, following his gaze and trying to see through the school fence.

He shrugged. "Na. Dem pickney na know shapes." He sighed.

The bags under his eyes were spongy. These days he was slow and terse. Didn't even offer to lend me new books. I mean, I was grown now and could get my own books. But still. He's just awfully tired, I thought. I too was tired. I was always tired. I could've been a pair of walking eye-bags with how tired I was. Education tired one's spirit. Especially when the professor didn't turn up for classes and the feeling of waiting and waiting for Miss Pam started creeping up afresh. Once, a professor attended only one of eight lecture sessions during which she spent most of the time lamenting that had she stayed where she completed her doctorate, her salary would be nine times the amount than now. Then she dictated from a textbook two levels below our syllabus, seeming terrifically proud about her dictation.

When I told Ivy, she said, "Exactly. That's why is people rights to work in whichever country they please. Global mobility ma'am. Nine times the amount? Unbelievable!"

That was all she got out of everything I had been saying. Unbelievable indeed.

Then she went out and came back with two cups of tea and a Cadbury bar which she split in half.

"Anyway," I continued, folding my laundry and stacking it on my bed, "you wouldn't believe who I met on campus today. You remember that boy who used to buy –"

"Which boy? You love some boy?"

"Everything is not about love, stupid. That boy who help bring you home when Claude bust up your head."

"Oh yes. That Claude tried to kill m –"

"So he been crying on this bench today. Said his girlfriend gone long distance and so on. I ain't even know was him. Anyway, he studying medicine up there. That mean he know 'bout anatomy. Bones and tings. Listen, I was thinking right, when I see him again I gon ask him an opinion about Pap shin. If it could still fix."

"Oh," was all she said and went out and returned with a tennis roll and cheese, breaking it in half, biting into one half and handing me the other.

But six months later at our campus fair, when I saw the boy again he looked worse than ever so I didn't bother to ask him about delayed tibia restoration. His eyes were glossy and his collar bone protruded. His cologne reminded me of someone's but I couldn't think whose. He was manning the Feed the Clown stall where people were trying to throw balls through the mouth of a large flat face of a wooden clown.

"Hey," I said. The fair music blared and he didn't hear me, so I waved with both arms.

He caught my eye and barely nodded.

"Good game?" I shouted.

He shrugged.

"How much?"

He mumbled something I didn't hear.

"What?" I shouted.

He pointed at a crude sign – 'Three throws for a hundred dollars'. I used to make better signs than that, I thought.

"Gimme three balls then," I said.

He looked at me but didn't hand me anything. I put three fingers in the air and pointed at the sign. Finally, he handed me three balls at the speed of a dying man.

"Well," I shouted, after a patronising but frustrating fifteen balls, "something's wrong with your clown."

He nodded.

"You mean something's really wrong with it?" I shouted into his ear again.

"Mouth too small."

"But it's not fair to use this clown if it's so hard to win."

"Life ain't fair."

And the more his impatient customers built up, the slower he crawled around retrieving the balls behind his stall. So I stepped behind the counter and started scooping up the balls.

"What happened with you and Milly then?" I asked, trying to back away from his strong cologne. But it was cramped behind the stall and there was only so far I could go. I put some bills in the money box and passed three balls to a patron who lost at all three of his attempts and stalked off sucking his teeth.

"Milly? She came and went again. Don't reply much on Messenger now," said the boy.

He braced against some crates and folded his arms as if the stall wasn't his responsibility.

I said, "Maybe you can go visit her for a while then. Spend time. Sort things out."

Talking while repeating the sequence of movements in which I was engaged was harder than it looked – running, bending down, picking up balls, handing them to customers, collecting money, dropping it in the box, making change, running, bending, scooping again, soothing old Jack-Bob there, wishing he would step up and man his stall.

Finally, it seemed like he made up his mind about something. "Yeah," he said finally, "Yeah, I gonna do dat."

Then he regained his rhythm and I picked up my purse to hustle away before he could get into the doldrums and slow up the patrons again.

"I never knew your name," I said.

"Frederick."

"Frederick? As in Fred you mean?"

He nodded.

"I know another Fred," I said. "From Peaside too. He's an old Fred though."

Frederick grinned and finally commanded his stall with the agility of his age.

"Later then," I shouted and was just making a beeline for the pink cotton candy when I spied Sam standing a few yards in front me with a furrow in his brow. He seemed to be studying Frederick and me. I waved and pointed at the Feed the Clown sign. Sam came up and took the tennis balls reluctantly. He handed Frederick a bill while studying him rapidly like Frederick was notes for a pop quiz.

Then with a burst of precise energy, Sam sent each of his three balls flying through the clown's mouth, gave the audience-patrons a slightly arrogant nod and started to walk away.

The crowd went wild.

"Whoa, hold up," Frederick said, holding out a jumbo teddy bear, "First winner! Claim your prize Mister!"

And the crowd oohed and applauded while Sam grabbed up the three and a half foot floppy top-hatted bear and stalked off. Mozart trotted behind him.

I gave Frederick a thumbs up and hurried after Sam.

"Sam! Sam! Saaam!"

He slowed down. Mozart slowed down.

"Wait up Sam."

He sped up. Mozart sped up.

"Lemme see yuh bear," I said.

He shoved the bear in my face. It smelled like wood chips and I coughed.

"You want choke me or what? What's the matter with you? Where you goin'?"

"Home."

"Let's get cones first then," I said and shoved the bear back at him.

Ice cream used to reduce his sullenness when we were children and I knew it still would.

"Alright," he said.

I was about to ask him what flavour he wanted but the music grew louder just then, so I didn't bother to ask.

Besides, I knew he wouldn't be able to make up his mind. When we were little, Sam's mother always held up the line at the ice cream truck much longer than everyone else, demanding that the vendor let Sam have one scoop of chocolate at the bottom and one scoop of vanilla on top. So I bought two cones – one chocolate and one vanilla and held them out to him. He took the vanilla. But before long he was giving my chocolate cone an eyeball.

"Gracious man, what are you? Five years old? Have a taste man." I handed over my cone.

But his hands were filled with his own cone and the lumbering bear, so he leaned in and brought his mouth to my cone, scooping off the entire top swirl.

"Ohh maan," I said forlornly. I really wanted at least a part of the top swirl.

"Here then." He held out his for me and I took a bite, if one can be said to bite ice cream, and I took his top swirl, fair exchange and all that.

"Look, you got some on your nose," I yelled and raised my wrist. He brought his nose to my wrist and rubbed off the ice cream.

And suddenly, stronger than the tizzy of the vibrating music and the whizzing of the rides, I could swear that the nerves in my wrist and in Sam's face burst alight, crackling and sparkling like branches of lightning against a purple-blue sky.

Our eyes locked. Then we continued eating our ice creams, looking in every direction except at each other.

"Who's that person in the stall you been talking to?" he asked.

"Who?"

"The clown guy."

"Oh. Yes! You remember that young cane cutter who used to come to Mam's stall years ago? The one who used to buy all the snacks and wrap them up and take them home? The young one, remember?"

Sam shrugged but seemed relieved.

"That's him," I said.

Sam tried to see Frederick through the crowd.

"The boy who help me bring Ivy home with the busted head."

"Oh?" said Sam, feeding Mozart the cone wafer.

"Wafers ain't good for dogs you know."

"Is just a small piece." He was indignant. Nobody could tell him what to do with Mozart.

Someone turned the music even louder and the earth vibrated.

Sam pointed at the Ferris wheel against the orange evening sky.

Then he held out his hand and I took it. Another jolt of electricity sparked at my fingertips and ran up my arm, straight to my chest and down to the tips of all ten toes. Lord, it's just like in the movies, I thought, as we climbed into the seat. Mozart settled on Sam's lap and the assistant secured the cage.

The top of the Ferris wheel was close to heaven.

"Beautiful," said Sam, gazing devotedly at the fiery sky. Not at me.

A slight sliver of lime squeezed a single drop thereabouts my ribcage.

17

Ixora Mara, Heiress

The Public Relations team announced that the campus fair raised enough funds to repair a major section of the university library, a success which I took as a personal victory. After all, nine times out of ten, I was the first student through the library door in the mornings. The security guard even joked about bequeathing me her duties because I was also often the last one out. She'd say, "What they need me for when they gah you?" One afternoon, she even left her post in a hurry, said she had an emergency and stealthily chucked me the key to the front door. But that's breaking protocol, I tried to tell her. There was no time to write a report and sign off the key, she whispered and waddled off. Here I was, a grown enough woman and still people were always trying to tell me what to do, I thought. But the key was already in my hand and there wasn't much to be done about it. So I hung about and locked the door after everyone left, uneasy that I was locking someone in overnight. Surely the guard didn't think I was going to patrol the stacks and toilets too. Terrified of my illicit responsibility, I tossed in bed, waiting for the sun to rise and before the campus awoke, I dawdled by the library entrance, my eyes glued to my wristwatch, praying for the guard to come and shrivelling up every time I thought someone looked at me suspiciously. Still, a thrill awoke in me. What a marvel to guard in my pocket, the key to an immense cocooning world.

My obsession with libraries had not waned and often I thought of my first library and of Mr Fred and guilt tormented my chest about the distance I'd keep from him while he braced against the telephone pole, his arms folded. These days I waved from the other side of the street and pretended to be in a hurry. I could hardly bear the repugnant disinfectant and cologne now.

Finally, I thought of a way to assuage my guilt. I'd get Mr Fred a birthday gift.

When I got off the bus with the package in my square bag, it was Friday afternoon and I expected him to be leaning against the telephone pole. But he wasn't. So I dallied about, bobbing down and up on the balls of my feet, with my palms sweating into the soft wrapping paper above the box of colourful cotton handkerchiefs and the ocean-scented cologne. After a while, I didn't want to appear silly just bumbling around so I re-crossed the street and went home.

"Mam," I said early Saturday morning after breakfast. "You know where Mr Fred house is? I want go carry dis gift."

She gave me some vague directions and I set off. After more queries from people in the street, I arrived at a plank, not a bridge, and a fence with so few staves left that it wasn't really a fence. And this house that was across the plank, behind the non-fence seemed as if it would blow down with ease if the Miaplambo huffed and puffed at it. I crossed the plank.

"Mr Fred," I called at the gate.

The uneasy sensation that I was back on Miss Pam's bridge calling out for someone to come to me swept over me, and I decided to take some action before the sensation could spread. I was tired of sensations spreading about my body without my approval. Fearing that I would topple into the trench from trying to balance on the single plank much longer, I unhooked the rusted latch and politely stepped into the grass like an ant on a tall blade of grass bending towards the story of the unsteady house before me.

I looked around for a dog.

"Here doggy."

There didn't seem to be one. So I rat-a-tat-tatted on the door.

"Missterr Frredd."

I knocked again.

"Mister Fred? Hello?"

A dog barked in the distance.

"Mister Fred it's me, Ixora Harry."

Knock. Knock.

"Hello in there! Happy Birthday, Mr Fred. Come to the door, will you?"

No one came.

Well, he must've gone away for his birthday. He must be celebrating with his family at a creek picnic somewhere, I cajoled myself into imagining something joyous for him. His wife must've returned for the celebrations and he had gone out, that should be it. And I turned away from the faded peeling door. But just then I spotted a window open a crack. Maybe I could pull the window open a little more, slip my hand in and rest the gift inside. Mr Fred wouldn't mind, I was sure. When he came back he'd be delighted.

Prying the window out, I pulled it towards me until I made a space large enough for my hand to slide through into the house and leave the gift on the table beneath the window. The bottom of the window was rotting and the jagged glass was exposed. So I passed the gift-wrapped box under and extended my arm towards the table, trying not to graze my wrist against the glass.

But when I looked up, quite by accident, because I was concentrating on the gift, what I saw cut my breath and sent unearthly chills flying up my spine.

There he was. Mr Fred. In a chair facing the window. His head hanging back on the chair. Eyes wide open. Staring at me.

I jumped. Dropped the gift inside. Yanked my hand out, and felt the burn where my wrist cut on the glass.

He looked ghastly. He wasn't moving.

The chills circled my stomach.

"Mr Fred?" I whispered.

I yanked the window hard towards me to see if I could climb in.

My arm must have bled all over the window because afterwards there was blood on the sill and in the grass and the police questioned me over and over about it.

I pulled the window out and still looking at Mr Fred, tried to hoist myself up and topple in like a village cat.

"Mr Fred?" my voice shook like a leaf in the wind on an autumn morning in New Jersey, where Mr Fred's wife, his maharani, was.

"Mr Fred?" I said again, after I managed to hoist myself in and run to him. "Mr Fred, wake up." I shook him. My arm bled over his arms and his t-shirt and his rocking chair.

He wouldn't wake up and then I felt myself working up into hysterics. I picked up the telephone but there was no dial tone and my bloody fingerprints were now on the receiver.

It was hard to breathe with the house smelling rank with Mr Fred's cologne. A glob of vomit pushed up my gullet.

"Mr Fred," I said, one last time, hoping he'd hear me and get up and set about clipping the school hedges into funny shapes again.

I climbed out the window. Years later I wondered why I didn't use the door on my way out.

There was a woman in the street. She squinted at me.

"Help," I said, trying to keep my trembling to a minimum. I pointed at Mr Fred's house.

The woman looked at me up and down.

"It's Mr Fred."

"Who?"

"Mr Fred. He ... he's not ... Please help."

"I ain't know none Mr Fred."

A dog sauntered around her, circling her slowly, this way and that. I followed the dog's motions and felt my eyes swaying into my head swaying into my heart.

"I, he lives here," I heard myself speak, distant and muffled.

"Wat yuh bleedin' for?"

"C... cut my hand." I looked down at my arm, at the blood like red crayon scratched all over a page and I almost fainted. "Come. Please," I told the woman.

I started walking back to the house. My vision blurred. I couldn't see where I was going and nearly tripped over the dog that was walking between me and the woman, keeping us company.

When finally the woman reached the window and looked in, she screamed. Then she screamed again. And then again. And then the tall itchy grass, pulled me down into its terror and I was an ant disappearing down, down into the stalks and everything blacked out.

When I woke up there was a crowd around me. Somebody was pouring water down my throat, killing me and I was still in the grass.

"Carry her hospital," someone said.

"Who she be?" someone else asked.

"Wah she doin' hey?" said a third.

"Look like one ah dem twins."

"Well wah she doin' hey?"

"Carry her hospital, she bleedin'."

"Why she lie down here in de grass?"

"She bleedin' bad, take her hospital."

"Fuh wat? If is she kill de old man now? Carry her police station."

"Yuh head bore mister? Yuh sense leak out? Freddo drink heself to the grave, yuh fool. Carry de chile hospital now man."

When finally somebody hoisted me up, I had one last look through the window and it was then that I saw the open bottle beside his chair – XM Rum – Mr Fred's daily cologne.

The familiar scent flew up into my nostrils and everything went black again.

"Hold her up man," somebody shouted, as I slumped.

When I woke up in the cold white hospital, Ivy was peering over me.

"You dead or what?" she said.

I coughed remembering the person pouring the water down my throat.

Mam and Pap stood over me.

"Mr Fr..."

"I know," Mam said softly and stroked my hair.

"He ..."

"Is alright," she said, "His time come."

Then the tears heaved out of my chest and into the universe and wouldn't stop.

My arm felt stiff beneath the bandage, and the scene of Mr Fred, through the window, in the rocking chair, unseeing eyes open, XM Rum keeping him company flashed like a View-Master clicking and clicking the same picture on the whole reel.

Pap gently tapped my shoulder and gestured towards two policemen in the corner.

"These nice men want to clear up a few things quickly," Pap said, his voice gentle.

But they weren't nice men and the interview wasn't quick.

Over and over they asked how I knew Mr Fred, why I went to his house so suddenly having never gone there before, why there was blood on me and in the grass and on the window sill and on the telephone and on the old man, why I hadn't called the authorities, why did I open the window and go in, whether I was a relative or not and since I was a stranger did I know I could and probably should be charged with trespassing. There would be more questioning later, they said. I was not to leave the country, they said.

I laughed hysterically when they said that, Ivy told me later. Then I flung a pillow at one of them, smack in the face, Ivy dramatised and Mam and Pap confirmed it. I didn't remember. I must've been groggy from the sedative.

When I woke up alone in the hospital, Mr Fred's life fell into place. Only now could I see that it wasn't cologne he'd needed in the empty hollow house, across the plank, through the grass, through the window, inside.

Too late. That's when these kinds of realisations come.

When I got out of the hospital on Monday, Mam encouraged me to return to classes.

"Give her more time," Pap whispered.

"Back to routine," Mam argued.

"But Laurs."

But Mam, who grew up in the girls' orphanage and knew about death must have given Pap a cold stare because I heard no more whispered arguments. So even though I didn't want to see school or another library again, I returned to campus because Mam seemed to know what she was talking about.

And when I caught a free period, I went to my campus bench and lay there for a long time, not moving, not wanting the spicy chicken sandwich that Ivy had made for me, not bearing to face my guilt or my old naïveté. I wondered where in the world had Mr Fred's family hopped into lime green buses and gone with bluegreen bags. And then the old familiar lime made its appearance again. It appeared already cut in half and sitting between the pages of a hardcover storybook inside my head. When the story ended, the massive back cover of the book slammed hard, pressing upon the lime, sending the juice soaking into my book-brain, smudging the words on the two pages of the story between which the lime sat, and slowly soaking through to the other pages, scenting up the whole book and sending me gasping for breath.

"What's the matter?"

When I looked up I saw the boy Frederick peering over the lunch table.

I sat up. And for a long time said nothing. Finally in a talk-whisper I said, "You wouldn't believe me if I told you."

"Try me."

And I told him everything. About Old Mr Fred and the cologne. About my repulsed senses and my shame and guilt about it, about how I should have gone to look for him on Friday instead and how maybe if I'd gone to see him earlier ...

"Wouldn't've changed his fate," Frederick said decisively.

I didn't want to waste time arguing about that. So I told young Frederick about how I knew now why his own cologne that I'd smelled at the campus fair smelled exactly like Mr Fred's and that if he didn't stop dousing himself with it, that probably he, Frederick wouldn't change his fate either.

He looked at me tensely while I used the lunch towel with which Ivy'd wrapped the sandwich to sap my rolling tears.

After a long silence, Frederick said, "I'm done with the cologne." He put air quotes around the word cologne. Though he didn't really have to do that. It was so Absurd. Two youths, sitting around on isolated benches, putting air quotes around "secret" words.

"Now what you wanted to ask me about bones?" he changed the subject.

And I told him about Pap's old fracture on the tibia and about how I'd read that sometimes it wasn't too late to have corrective surgery.

"I'll read up," he said looking through a textbook.

"Thanks."

But when I asked Pap again about it, he told me to let the tibia be and that I should shower and rest my head since I kept getting headaches. For when I got off the bus that day, and for all the days to come, there was no one leaning against the telephone pole waving and the book in my head with the lime squished between the pages still had juice seeping through the whole story and sogging up all the neurons in my brain.

After the funeral, the son who had read a dry eulogy came up to me.

"You the Harry girl, Zora Moira?"

I nodded, not bothering to correct him, wanting him to go away.

"The old man named you in the will."

What now? I said in my head.

"Tomorrow. Round 'bout four clock is a chill time to collect your inheritance. Come then."

"But what he leave for you?" Ivy speculated all evening. "You gon split any money you got fifty-fifty right? I be the other half of you, you know? You mustn't forget I made you a sandwich and everything. And, and, I put a lil kit-kat in your lunch pack too. But if you didn't bother eat it, you best gimme back."

She knew quite well that Mr Fred had no money, that's why Mrs Fred, maharani, Needer-of-more-money, went away to begin with.

"Fifty-fifty," Ivy said and winked.

But even I couldn't think of what Mr Fred might have left me.

The next day, I stood in Mr Fred's house, now empty of him. The smell of rum had faded into the floors and walls, now masked by lavender Mistolin. Mr Fred's son had got somebody to come in and home-up the empty house. Everything was now tidy and airy. Human. Dirty dishes were cleared from around the rocking chair, windows were opened and wiped. Clutter was cleared. The gift I'd dropped through the window was probably disposed of and the sill was wiped of my blood. Even the bridge was now a bridge, not a plank, and the grass had been cut.

Across the bridge, through the lawn, between the curtain gaps – now a homey empty house, I thought. Society is a well-dressed hypocrite, is what it is.

"There," the young man pointed into a small room, "the old man left you those."

I wish he'd stop calling his own father 'the old man.'

I tiptoed to the cramped room. It had one chair, a small round desk and some shelves.

And the shelves, they were lined with books.

There were hundreds of books, maybe close to a thousand – very old ones, newer ones, large ones, arranged in some sort of size order. Titles I'd never heard of. Some I'd already borrowed, unaware of the collection from which they had come. Books crammed closely together. Like a real library. Just small.

"I ... how'd he ..."

"Bought one with all the extra money he ever had since he was 'bout ten or eleven years old I heard," the youth explained.

"I –"

"I know," he laughed, "the old man was a strange one. 'specially since he couldn't read."

"Couldn't read?"

"Naww."

"But if he couldn't read why –"

"That was just the old man."

"Don't you ever call him dad?" I said, letting my irritation show.

"Naww, he just never said I was to."

"What?"

"Took me in when I was liddle. Bedder any day than my own old drunken Paps who threatened to leave me in the orphanage. Freddo took me in you know, even though was a daughter he wanted. And he said I could call him Ole Man Freddo. He buy me books. Call me sonny. Him and his ole lady sen' me school. Feed me. Bettah any day than my own peeps." His voice shook a little. His Creolese was coming back now and melding with his current accent. He turned around and brushed at his eyes. "Sorry," he said, "old memories." Then he pretended to cough. "Oh," he said, "the shelves and table and chair's all yours too, the old man decreed."

"But, how do you know all this is for me? If he couldn't write, I mean –"

"Went to his lawyer cousin in Georgetown. Look." He rolled out a paper and showed me.

The paper said: I hereby bequeath my entire book collection and library furniture to Miss Ixora Mara Harry of Zekerheid Village, County of Demerara, Guyana, it said.

I'd never seen my name spelled out with such confident validity on an official looking document, except my birth certificate. I touched the letters of my name and address. He must've asked one of the teachers to write my name down for him.

I felt like my skull was cracking open from the massive book with its liminal story pressing against my brain and I braced against one of the bookshelves to steady myself.

A black and white photo of an impossibly young Mr Fred in a dhoti and a turban, standing beside a slim narrow-faced girl was propped up on the bookshelf. She didn't even come to send him off into The Great Beyond. Just as well, I thought, they have a tendency for burning down libraries.

"Here maan," said the adopted son, when he was done mopping his eyes, "my contact info. Call me up if you ever in Miami, ya? Don't hesitate, I mean it, no kidding." He wiped his drippy nose with the palm of his hand and handed me a business card with the same hand. I cringed at all the germs that must be on the card.

I gave the card to Ivy. She was always taking a wide interest in the emigrated, inserting herself into their narratives – receiving trinkets they brought back for her, communicating with them while they were away, tacking postcards up in our bedroom, developing a list of contacts she barely even knew. "Ooo, thanks, this gon come in handy some day, fuh sure."

I didn't answer. Just continued taping down the carton boxes with my inheritance. And shoving the boxes far under the indoor stairs cupboard, a reasonable substitute for a trapfloor. I wasn't going to have anything to do with this inheritance!

The nerve of people thinking they could just go their own way into the elements of the universe and bequeath me with things. The limey nerve!

18

Thou Shalt Not Swap Thy Shoes

Every day after graduation, I bought newspapers with the allowance Mam gave us and I scoured the pages for a job. Since her promotion to the pharmacy's headquarters in the city, Mam doled out generous allowances to Ivy and me. And I bought newspapers with mine.

On the morning of my first interview, I vomited up my breakfast.

"Maam, come see Ixie puking her guts out 'cause she scared of the interview," Ivy yelled as she dashed down the stairs to her own job.

My interview didn't last two minutes.

"Look towards that camera and read the passage on the monitor behind it," said the interviewer, contemplating which corner of his sandwich to bite.

I read the passage.

"Why do you want this job?" he asked, picking out a piece of tomato and tossing it in his mouth.

"Umm, I ... well, I ..." I began. Hundreds of words bounced around on springs inside my head and jostled each other to find their right sequences. But they didn't make it through my voice box.

Forty-five seconds later I emerged from the boardroom. Doomed, I thought, I'm doomed.

"We'll call you," said the secretary in an automated voice.

They won't, I thought, call me.

But two weeks later, Pap left a note next to the phone: Phone call from The Daily News channel for Ms Ixora M. Harry. Report to work on Monday at 8:00am sharp.

But on Monday morning sharp, I didn't take a shine to the lights, the camera, the newsroom or Natasha, who called herself 'Hair and Make-up.'

"That's what you're wearing? On camera?" she asked at least three times in one week. "Your hair is impossible," she'd shriek, "It is not camera-ready!" Every week she ranted, "Your complexion is blotchy, dull here, shiny there! It is not camera-ready! Use sunscreen! That jacket is lopsided! It leans to the left. It's impossible! Who sewed it? Your grandma?"

"Yes," I said, wishing it was Pappo who'd sewn it instead.

One day Natasha called me into the screen room where five separate monitors were set up and she played the foreign news on all of them, at once.

"Get in here girl," she said. "Look at these news anchors. Look at their clothes! Look at their hair! Look at how they round their lips! Listen to their in-toe-naation!"

I looked and looked and listened.

That weekend when Ganee showed me some navy blue cloth, I grew irritated. I was just feeling content with two large warm slices of cassava pone in my stomach and studying the painting hanging over the pot spoons when she brought out the cloth.

"Where you get dat painting from Ganee?" I pointed to *Keeper of the House* by I.M.G.

"People say is my grandmother who paint it but I dunno."

"Your grandmother?"

"So people say."

"Oh?" I wondered if it was true. The women who came on ships didn't really paint. I savoured the last bite of cassava pone.

"Look I buy you dis to make a skirt suit," Ganee said, rolling out the bolt of cloth on the dining table.

I wanted to turn on the news and say to her, "Look at their clothes! Look at their hair!"

I said nothing and pretended to smile. But pins and needles prickled inside me. I was already impossible and here was Ganee not understanding how the world worked. I wanted to burst out of my impossible body and disappear down the street.

"Thanks Ganee," I said half-heartedly, hurrying out, going wherever my speedy feet went.

I found myself outside Sam's yard. He and Mozart were weeding the grass by the side fence. Whack whack went the cutlass into the brush. Mozart ran up to me and Sam looked up.

"There, take a cutlass and weed if you standin' there doing nothing," he said. He was always preoccupied with time and who was wasting it.

I took up a cutlass and whacked around wildly, pausing to see what old Mr Reid was doing on the roof.

"What your grampappy doing?"

"Pasting it with bitumen tape. It leaking. Look, you better stop whacking so crazy-like before you break yuh elbow and gotta read de news in a cast," he said, going indoors to fetch tall glasses of cherry juice. I wondered what Natasha would say about me wearing a broken elbow on her news and I laid the cutlass down.

We sat side-by-side on the low stairs, shoulders grazing, sipping the juice. He watched Mozart roll about in the cut grass and I watched the crimson pink sky. Sam smelled of the mild sweat of lightly busy evenings and freshly washed burlap sacks and I thought if only Time and Space would press the slow-motion button on their two-step waltz, Sam and I could sit here like this much longer while tomorrow took its own dear time to come.

The next day, I went into the city and bought two tailor-made dark suits and detangling and frizz-busting hair products. And later, I tucked the navy blue skirt suit that Ganee'd made into the back of my wardrobe. Whenever I looked at it a pang shot up in my chest.

Ivy, for her job, only needed jeans, t-shirts and her robust water proof Timberland work-boots that she had saved and spent a fortune on. Her job, in the Ministry of Infrastructure, required a lot of field work she explained importantly to Ganee, and there was no way she could get by in skirts and high-heels.

"Lemme try on your heels," she begged one day when it was a national holiday and we were in our room sharing plantain chips in a ginormous bowl, "Iz been forever since I got into a good pair of heels."

And she modelled them up and down the room and turned around in front the mirror, admiring her calves.

"What do your Timbs feel like?" I asked.

"See for yourself, I can't get a moment's prettiness in them." She kicked them towards me.

Inside the flat robust work-boots, I felt sturdy, not as if I were teetering on unnatural heights trying my best to be Possible.

"You know what?" said my twin.

"Ohh no."

I knew that look coming over her, her eyes darting like a chameleon, thinking up some scheme like when we were little. Like the time when the Sunday School teacher didn't know the difference between us to begin with, and we swapped places because Ivy wanted to be Joseph, not some baa-ing sheep. And not even Mam could tell us apart under the costumes, though when we long thought that the time for peril had passed and we confessed two years later about the swap, Mam still made us write twenty-five times – I must always be myself. When the line-writing was over, Ivy said it was a stupid punishment and of course we would always be ourselves because who else would we be? This was the plotting look I saw on her face now.

"Let's swap," she said.

"Noo," I groaned, "Too old fuh dat."

"Look how long we didn't play swap?"

"Nuh-uh."

"I show up to your workplace tomorrow. You show up to mine." She was rolling around her bed, cracking up now.

"Absolutely not. Besides we don't look dat much alike anymore. Plus I won't even know how to –"

"I gon tell you everything you gotta do."

"Give up."

But I knew I couldn't resist a chance to keep these sturdy Timbs on my feet and to meet the world in them – and just for one day even, to shed my gutslessness and embrace an open canvas uninhibited. In the end I knew Ivy would wear my resistance down as always.

"Look these reports I gotta submit. I done do dem awready. And dis week my team goin' out to look at the sea defence in a low lying village dat getting flood out every time is high tide."

"What? No. I ain't doin' dat. How I gon know what to –"

"Jus' agree with everyting Audrey say and pop in a suggestion now and then. Just –"

"Who's Audrey?"

Ivy sat up and whispered, mischief sparkling in her eyeballs, "The boss. Her desk right next to mine and," she said, "twice a week she bringing beef stew for lunch you know and eating some for breakfast in the office too." Then she rambled at length about what I could do to make my act believable. Finally she said, "Now tell me again 'bout everybody at The Daily News."

I wondered what Ivy would make of Natasha and what Natasha would make of her and what it would be like to see my own face, or something like it, reading the news at me, on live TV. So I laid out my duties for her to memorise and she shrieked and jumped up in my heels, almost breaking them.

"But remember, if we get in trouble, this was your idea Vine Lady," I said, "And please keep my heels in working condition, thank you very much."

Before I could finish my sentence, Ivy was in my closet, wiggling into my skirt. She was an inch or two wider than me around the waist.

"Well you gotta starve yourself of dinner and breakfast and run all night if you really want to play the part," I said, hoping to dissuade her one last time.

"Gladly!" she said and pulled on some other item of my clothing.

But she ate a hearty dinner and breakfast and I worried about the state of my expensive seams and buttons.

"Don't grind down my heels," I whispered for the hundredth time.

"Shush, Mam gon hear you. Sit flat lemme fix yuh hair."

And she rolled the sides of my hair and tucked the boisterous curls into a low chignon.

"Wear a helmet when you got to," she said.

"What? When? You didn't say I was goin' somewhere that required helmets."

"You won't. I just saying, if you bust your head, Mam says we gon send her to an early grave. Remember wen—"

"Yes, yes –"

"Now go," she said, "Just put on this cap to cover your face and walk sideways by the kitchen and shout to Mam that you leaving, but don't turn 'round. Then grab your, ahem, my lunch quick off the table and walk out fast. I gon hide here till she leave for the office. Go. Go!"

If I'd gotten any closer to Mam, she would've heard my heart making a racket. I grabbed Ivy's lunch off the table and sped out the gate. But the shoes that felt commanding the day before were now ambivalent. I wasn't sure I could walk in them. As I plodded along I thought about how heavy Ivy's feet must feel every day. The t-shirt and jeans clung to my sweat.

The outside of Ivy's workplace sucked me into its dull tones and lowered my pluck. No, I couldn't manage this. I'd better turn around, I panicked. But Ivy was probably already at the news station. I couldn't show up there. Besides, if I abandoned her post here, she would lose her day's wages and choke me.

Deep breaths, Ixora, deep breaths. What was I thinking to get Ivy to talk me into this unnecessary jam? Jam, I thought, jam on Ganee's table. Guava jam in bottles. Warm guava jam, I thought and walked into the dull building.

Ivy had given me a diagram with instructions and I followed the directions to her desk. Go straight, turn right, one flight of stairs on the right, turn left, walk straight, enter room with several desks, count three rows down, count four desks from the middle of the fourth row. How exhausting, I thought, and was just trying to work out where the middle of the row was when I spied a woman at her desk with her lunch bowl spread out. I inched forward. She smelled like beef stew and like pomegranate and peppermint, like fresh bold ideas against old robust ones.

"Audrey?" I said involuntarily.

She narrowed her eyes and said, "What pranks y'all pulling on me today?"

I jumped. Did she know it wasn't Ivy?

"Just tryin' to see if you bring beef stew again, so I could tell everyone," I managed to say, bewildered at my smooth save and the nonchalance in my body language.

She rolled her head, precariously rocking her wooden leaf-shaped earrings. Then she slammed her bowl shut and said, "We ready to roll. Everybody march."

A few young men sprang up and straightened their clothes. One headed for the toilet. Somebody said, "The pick-up leaving now. You mean is now Squado gon see to go bust a leak when he could'a go all the time? He always."

The man called Squado came out of the washroom and I decided to walk behind him and see where I ... Ivy was meant to go. Squado went out of the building and hopped into an open-backed vehicle. Was I supposed to get into that? Oh no, no, no, I said in my head and climbed in like a sloth.

Somebody said, "Vine Lady, like yuh develop arthritis this morning or what?"

I texted Ivy: U didn't tell me I had to climb in some open out tram wit sun roasting me like bird.

Ivy replied: Stupid skirt cutting my breath. U didn't tell me I had to edit every single report. What the crabs is a dangling modifier? U suppose to jus be reading the news, not writin it.

I ignored her. I had my own real problems.

The sun beat down. The pick-up sped along. Trees and cars whizzed past. Once, the vehicle stopped so abruptly for a herd of goats that I flung forward and hit my head on the glass partition between the front of the vehicle and the open tray where we sat.

The group roared.

Audrey watched me closely but didn't join the laughter.

"What wrong witchoo today, Ivy?" somebody asked.

"I think I'm getting a headache," I said truthfully, hanging on to the side as we started swaying about again. I wanted to vomit. I was going to choke Ivy when I got home.

The vehicle pulled over at our destination.

When the seawall was built on Guyana's coastland in the 1800s, it did a solid job of making this swatch of earth go unthreatened by the Atlantic waves. But that was a long time ago and every now and then one needs to upgrade one's house to accommodate the new challenges. That's what Audrey and the team were attempting. And even a pick-up-truck-tumbling-around-non-engineer like me could appreciate that. The ocean had taken over more land than when Mam and Pap were my age. They had shown us where the water used to stop years ago. And now, here they were, these waves, almost at our toes and we'd done few renovations to a house that needed to withstand the beating of many more waves, wet ones and dry ones. Besides, people said that the Atlantic Ocean was getting wider.

"And wat y'all tink 'bout dat?" Audrey asked, but nobody answered.

She was measuring and explaining something from behind a survey tripod, her feet planted firmly in her camel-coloured Timberlands, her white t-shirt tucked into her denim skirt, her braids swaying, her wooden braid beads clacking music about her waist. She adjusted her sunglasses and looked out at the ocean, mouth determined. I imagined her riding a sea chariot pulled by seahorses out into the deep, setting out to hold a consultation with the waves and bargain for more flood-free years here on our low coastal plain.

I was standing closest to her, so she said quietly, "Hold this tape Ixora, watchoo tink?"

I didn't know what to say, "Um ... let's ask Squado. Squado, any opinions?"

"Na, is a reasonable idea. The additional few feet gon work for now," Squado was squinting and trying to imagine it, whatever the 'it' was.

Later, back at the office was too hot, Ivy's lunch was too much and the staff too loud, and when I stumbled out at the end of the day, Audrey stood in the doorway, arms akimbo, giving me an eye and smirking slightly.

On the news that evening, Ivy made a mistake, fumbling over the syllables of a word and when the camera returned from a commercial break she was caught yawning. I was horrified.

"Couldn't you just look at the prompter and read everything correctly?" I asked and I shook her till her head bobbed around like a bobble head.

"Shush man. I goin' sleep. I be tired and hungry you know. And dat Natasha is a piece o' work."

"What she say?"

"Say how I impossible. And ask was I drunk today because I left subject-verb errors and dangling modifiers in the reports. And she be hollering how I defying the rule of parallel structure. So then I ask her if dat's like when you put two pillars and line them up. And she said if the university was giving out free degrees now," Ivy said and thumped the pillow over her head.

"And?" I tapped my knee wildly against the bed frame.

"And she told me come off de caffeine and move to de city sos I could get some polish. How I should travel more to develop a global air about me. And how news anchors can't be slow an' countrified. How more and more I dragging the station down. How today was the worst of all. Besides, when did I get this extra crust on my skin like overbaked whole wheat bread, soo not camera ready, she said."

My horror increased by the second. I really should have thought this through. Should have known that Natasha and Ivy's personalities would clash.

"What did you say to her?" I asked, afraid to hear the answer.

"Nothin'. Isn't that what you usually say to her?"

"Oh," I said, a bit hurt at being told so bluntly that I had no courage to say anything to Natasha, or anyone for that matter.

Ivy yawned. "Oh," she mumbled, drifting off in sleep, "after the news she said that I, or you, whoever she meant, was a piece of work."

I gulped. "And?"

"And I heard myself say, 'No Natasha, *you* are the piece of work'."

A spit ball stuck in my throat.

Ivy continued, "But then I realise I only said it in my head and not aloud and I manage a fake smile and walk off. How you could live with that pest? Geez."

I didn't know the answer.

I lay awake half the night, half-relieved and half-disappointed that Ivy hadn't told Natasha aloud that she was a piece of work. When I finally dropped off to sleep I dreamed of a television floating in the sea and my face was on it, or Ivy's, I couldn't tell which. The sun was glinting on the screen, glinting at our face on the screen, our face trying too hard to read the news. Suddenly I bolted up in bed. Audrey. Oh my gosh! Audrey, when she handed me the measuring tape had called me Ixora! I sprang out of bed and shook Ivy.

"She knows, she knows. Ms Audrey Barney knows," I said in a whisper-shout. "But how? How she know about me? You think she gon to report us?"

Ivy groaned, turned over and went back to sleep.

"Barney be a dinosaur on TV," she mumbled, and buried her head under the pillow.

I could barely sleep the rest of the night. All sorts of things came cracking and tumbling inside my head. There was a price to pay for wearing another's shoes, even if they fit, I heard Mam's voice bubbling. I *must always be myself* – twenty-five lines. I could hear Ivy's voice defending her scheme – but Mam we are the same, what's the difference, people barely noticed and that's enough proof. Pap's face floated along, tired and amused and Ganee and Pappo's neutral faces peered from a long low veranda that was shaped like a bird. And Sam glued to a kite, was flying away and calling down to us saying that it was just like we were eight years old again, doubling up, doubling against the world and getting the best of everyone. It was me and Ivy, Ivy and me against the world. Ivy and Mam and Sam's voices kept rising in uneven cadences and soon my own voice was pulled down through my voice box and into my chest and the alarm was ringing and Ivy was sticking an ice cube down the back of my pyjama shirt.

"Ahh. Go away!" I screamed and threw the ice cube after her.

And she did. In more ways than one.

That evening two letters came that changed our house.

The first was a letter for me from the News Station, stating that my services were no longer needed and that I was given three weeks' notice. I showed it to Ivy and she scowled and wanted to march downstairs and tell Pap. She was going in to the News Station tomorrow and explain that it was her fault I'd been fired.

"It wasn't," I said. But I wasn't sure that it wasn't. "Leave it alone. Besides, we'd get into more trouble than we can resolve."

The second letter was for Ivy. At dinner, she had the letter in her hand which she handed to Pap and Mam. She'd been accepted at a university in the United States to do a Master's degree in Engineering. She qualified for a partial scholarship from the local Ministry and the rest she was going to pay for from her savings and part-time student jobs she could get near the campus.

As if I were inside a TV show, preferably a cartoon, all I could think about, as I watched Ivy stirring her tea, was that the Miaplambo's long arms really were going to tap the shoulders of every last one of us in Peaside, some way or the other.

In three months Pap and Mam had saved up to add to Ivy's fund. Ganee and Pappo also brought a contribution. And I too handed her an envelope with most of my savings, placing it in her palm with some ambivalence.

"I can't take this Ix," she said, handing me back the packet, "not after I got you sacked." She seemed teary for two seconds.

"I'll get more soon when I find a new job. Take it. For text books," I said, with a measure of warmth springing up in my chest.

"Alright," she said, "alright." And then the un-cry-able Ivy Lee seemed teary again for two more seconds.

I spent those three months, in which Ivy was preparing to leave, in a flowing fountain of denial. It was a fountain flowing in and out of me long after she left and even after she started talking to us through computer screens across the ever widening Atlantic.

At the airport, Mam and Ganee cried into sniffly rags. Pappo was mellow. Only Pap was pretending to be his usual self. Sam was there too, standing around uselessly.

"I gon come visit you some time for sure," Sam told her.

I jumped a little at that but tried not to look at him.

"Ivy Jivey don't forget dis bag here with your snacks. You don't want starve on the plane," Pap said.

Ivy grinned, grabbed the bag and kissed Pap. "G'bye Papsy. G'bye Pappo. G'bye Ganee. G'bye Mammy. G'bye Sam. G'bye twin," she said and that startled me a little.

We embraced stiffly and I tried to think of something to say, other than the fact that I was splitting in two, right down the middle, starting at the old middle part on my scalp.

"You never tell me what Audrey say 'bout us swapping for the day," I said, my heart unsure if to soften or neutralise or harden. I couldn't see the way forward.

"All she said was, 'Your appetite came back between yesterday and today Missy' and she be bobbing round her head and wagging her finger at me."

"That's all?"

"Yea," said Ivy and looked at me for a full two seconds, then wheeled her suitcase away.

Beyond the barriers of the airport, I could not see.

Then the old lime returned, in its first ever spot, spinning and splitting like on its first day, but this time flinging about like a large tempest in my whole torso, like a storm swirling tumultuously, rattling everything on the inside and lashing outwards to the tips of my fingers and to the tip of every strand of hair. And this time it seemed the lime had come to stay. Only my legs remained sturdy and free of it. I'd have to try and keep my lime storm in my upper body and save my legs I vowed in desperation, or else, or else I might become exactly what Ivy'd long predicted – Peaside's Resident Sourpuss.

19

Bougainvillea spectabilis

When we returned home from the airport and Pap turned the key, inside was hollow.

The crystal vase lay on the bedroom floor. Broken in two. I super-glued the pieces. It worked fine, but the cracks still showed and sometimes water seeped out.

At dinner, the three of us sat around the dining table that Pap had built with his own hands, though what was the point of that, building a table with your own hands.

Mam sat opposite Pap.

The empty chair sat opposite me.

We ate stewed snapper and rice.

Pap tried conversation. But Mam and I were not conversationalists. So the silent dinners went on for days, months.

The symmetry of my bedroom was Absurd.

When I came home from my new part-time job at the City Library, I flung my bags on Ivy's bed. Eventually I started using it, the bed, as a laundry basket for dirty clothes, because there was no point in not using an empty bed as a laundry basket for dirty clothes. It was athletic to throw clothes from one side of the room to the next. Psshaaow! I was a basketball player and people in the stands cheered for me when I dunked. Psshaaow!

Mam bought me a large laundry basket and added it to my old one. Then she brought Ivy's old one and lined it up beside my two. Now I had three and there was no excuse she said for throwing my dirty clothes around the room.

The lime concoction was as persistent as ever and thrusting through my body these days. One cannot be bothered about propriety when that type of thing is happening in one's body. So I took to using Ivy's bed as a bookshelf. I cleared my bookshelf, stacked all my books on her bed and put useless paraphernalia on my bookshelf.

Any old body could see that that was a useful thing to do.

Mam made me put the books back on the bookshelf.

So I started chewing gum and sticking it under Ivy's bookshelf. Gook gook.

I imagined people coming around and peeping under the shelf and saying 'Oh my goodness, just terrible.' I would just go right on chewing and I'd stick gum in the backs of their heads, I thought. Gum in the backs of their heads would suit them, the pryers, the judgers, the chewing gum peepers. Gook gook.

In the next few months I came right out and told myself that the symmetry of the room was stifling me, because what would I lie about it for, the stifling. The vertical blue and yellow and red stripes on both sides of the room converged and constricted my lungs. So I tried looking out the window every time I wanted to breathe and what was the use of that? When I looked out the window, Suzie's stupid square house, standing there empty for over a decade and a half, menaced me still. The next time you menace me, I threatened the house, I shall load my bags and hop on a plane. Then I tried to slam my window shut. But a bougainvillea branch kept growing into the window's space, and every morning and every night I had to push the branch back so that the window could open and close. Pappo with the approval of Ivy had planted that bougainvillea tree so close to our new house the year we moved in, knowing how uncontrollable it would eventually grow. They could've predicted that it would humbug the above window, which turned out to be mine. But clearly they hadn't thought about anything else other than what their tunnel vision could afford. So there it grew, the bougainvillea spectabilis, climbing the side of the wall. So after a while I stopped opening that window and had to kneel on my bed and look through the side window instead, where occasionally I saw Sam hurrying down the street at dawn. Sometimes I blew an old toy whistle at him and he'd grin and wave. Then I'd tumble back into bed and study the cracks on the wall.

Once, at two o'clock in the morning, I got out of bed, turned on the light and started pulling things out of their deceitful alignment – Ivy's bed, her vanity. I pulled them out. I yanked her books off her shelf. Yanked. And I took a steel ruler and started scraping the mural off the wall. I scraped at the red flowers and the golden coconuts and the horrible stripes running all around the room and at Sam's aeroplane. Samuel Reid, Mister-never-walk-onto-a-runway-without-being-cleared-to-do-so. I scraped hard on the plane's nose.

Scrape scrape.

I heard footsteps coming and I froze.

Somebody knocked.

"Yes?" I said, with a great measure of dignity.

"What happen Ix?"

"Nothing Pap, I cleaning."

He paused.

"Now?"

"Yes."

"Lemme in."

I paused.

"Door blocked," I said and tiptoed quickly to a chair and braced it against the door.

"What happenin'?" came Mam's voice.

We all paused.

"She cleaning," Pap said softly.

"Now?"

Everything fell still. I could tell that they were looking at each other outside the door and deciding what to do.

"Open dis door lemme see what you doing."

"Door blocked," I said, knowing I couldn't get away with that for much longer, not with Mam.

"Clear it," she said, fiddling with the knob. The door swung in knocking over the chair.

Around me, my room was falling about, my hair was dishevelled, my pyjama shirt was falling off my shoulder, and the nose of the plane was unsuccessfully scraped when the parents peered into the scene like they were watching a bad movie.

They pretended composure. I give them credit for that.

"Come over to our room for the night," Pap said softly, calmly in a radio announcer's steady tone, "tomorrow you can continue cleaning." Then he firmly said, "You *must* sleep." When I was little and afraid of the Miaplambo under the bed and Ivy was already snoring, I used to imagine Pap as a radio announcer, his voice carrying over the airwaves bearing me to tranquillity.

"Come," he said now, kind of radio-announcer-ish, "bring that pillow."

Then he closed the door to the Absurdly symmetrical room.

The next day neither he nor Mam said anything about my nocturnal dismantlings. All Pap said was that he was going to the shop and did I need anything, anything at all.

He paused for a long time, braced against the door frame waiting as if willing me to want something.

"White paint," I said at last.

He bought me two gallons and I repainted my bedroom walls. Then he moved some of Ivy's things to the store room where we kept groceries and brooms. He asked me if I wanted her bed dismantled until she came home again and I said yes. Mam stood at the doorway and watched disapprovingly as Ivy's bed came apart. She opened her mouth to say something but Pap coughed loudly and cleared his throat and hobbled around busily rearranging things.

"We'll bring it back when Ivy Jivey back," he said, and that was that.

As soon as I rolled the white paint on the walls, a manageable room opened up inside me, or so I thought. So I emptied my faded pink piggy bank to buy a pair of sneakers and started jogging beside the canefields every afternoon when I came home from the library. At first, I inched along, nursing my chest. But after two weeks I could run fifteen minutes without perishing. And by the end of the month, thirty minutes.

Sometimes after my run, sweating and finally feeling functional, I went and surveyed my inheritance under the stairs. I peeled the tape off the carton boxes and I studied the book covers. Mr Fred must've made his selections based solely on the covers, like the old musty *Robinson Crusoe*, for instance. Something about the cover art of lone Robbie in his rice hat, back turned to the reader, looking out at sea must've appealed to Mr Fred when he bought it, knowing that opening the cover could not, for him, open the world inside.

Lone Robbie. Disinfectant. Rice hat.

A surge of lime juice circulated with a passionate swirl through my brain and I shoved my inheritance back under the trap-stairs, dashed into bed and pulled the sheet over my head. One never really knew what went on across planks, behind fences, through doors, behind walls. Even through glass windows through which someone shone a light out at you, you could still never know. There was nothing you could ever know, I thought.

On the bus to and from work, I studied houses and wondered what went on behind their walls. And when I got off the bus, I tried imagining the stories in the houses in Peaside. I imagined Small Spokes' grammy, across her bridge, through her walls, probably still shouting at Cook. I studied all the houses – including old Mr Crapaud's – that had become empty in the last several years, imagining the cobweb patterns and the scrap mats and moth eaten sofas inside them. I thought about Ganee and Pappo alone in their low house. Did Ganee use her walking stick everywhere inside like she did outside. When she woke to go to the toilet at nights when I wasn't there, did she hold on to furniture in the dark and go slowly because of her arthritis, or did she use the stick and go faster. And what of our own house, with that mad Bougainvillea spectabilis growing up the front wall, shouting its way up to my window sill? Did people know that across my bridge, inside my room, the freshly painted wooden walls wobbled like white jello jiggling into my head? Or that my night times were dark cyclonic gravity pools from which I forced a brazen dive up into workdays at the City Library, where rows of books blurred into long lines stretching away from me. Could they imagine that Pap brought me vitamins and made me steaming vegetable soup and coaxed me away from the wobbles and pools?

"Come sit in the sun," Pap said one day, after I'd courageously employed my limbs to hold up the soup bowl and slurp away the noodle and broth.

So I willed my legs to cooperate, got out of bed and joined Pap. He was hand-planing a rocking chair someone had ordered. These days, since getting his desk job, he hardly built things. I sat out in the sun and watched the bougainvillea tree, that airily querulous riotous free pink, imposing itself above Pap's head, like branches growing out of his scalp. I looked further up and saw the branch that lodged against my bedroom window. Robust branches sprang here and there, growing out and into spaces in which they shouldn't be. Meandering into this path and that. By the gate, where people had to stoop instead of walk upright. Into the side passageway, where people couldn't be thorn-free. Hanging over everyone's heads everywhere.

Maybe, I thought, if I could get the garden shears and pare off the branches, a little bit of walking could be possible. So I pared down the low hanging bracts, sorry to see the pink from its vine, falling. I thought of scooping up the blossoms and putting them in a bucket for someone. But I let them be. You don't have to do something with everything, I said inside my head. Trying to make something of everything is exhausting, souring. And I let the sheared pink fall.

When the branches became too sturdy for the shears, I borrowed Pappo's cutlass, and with half-closed eyes to guard against the flying thorns, I hacked the excess hangings with a mad wilfulness that matched the mad wilful branches. That was the first day I learned how to train something massive. A strong branch chopped just once didn't come down. It had to be chopped in the same place again and again, notched away at an angle until green splices appeared beneath the old bold brown before it even considered to bend. Notch, and no noticeable progress. Notch, notch, no visible outcome. Notch, notch, notch, falling pink, clearer spaces.

So I hacked and notched, swinging and flourishing, a free mad woman. And my arms grew wild and emotional, dangerous, commanding. I hadn't known that feeling before.

So I went back for more. In the air I flung the heavy cutlass, notching, hacking, taming as the pink fell around me.

Eventually, the pink at an arm's length above my head was tamed. Still, there were more insatiable branches high in the sky, including the one pressing against my window. So though my wrist hurt and my body had heated up in rapid alarm in the sun, these new counter-sour motions were crystallising in my body and I knew that there was one more thing to do.

I trod indoors with the cutlass at my side and ascended the stairs. I pushed my bedroom window out and pulled the branch towards me. And with three mighty notches, I felled the burdening branch. Notch and breathe. That is all one had to do to tame a large thing and survive, notch and breathe.

The window could now open freely into the visual path of Suzie's deteriorating house and her untameable parapet. I contemplated the parapet and the blade of my cutlass. Then I dashed downstairs and across the street and hacked at the unsightly bush in front of Suzie's fence. But her bush was denser than I imagined and I notched and chopped in perpetual cycles until the bush was flat and Suzie's paling stave fence could be seen again. I wondered what her new fence looked like now, wherever she was in the world. And the lime juice manic, riled up in my torso and swirled a mad cyclone in me. And I thought I was done for.

But when I opened my window the next morning, Suzie's house and parapet looked less menacing and my lime juice retracted its fury and settled down.

One day while jogging, I bumped into Sam on his way home from work.

"You jogging alone?" He seemed surprised, protective. "I coming. Wait." And off he went to change clothes and get Mozart.

"Race you to that Hymac," he sang when they returned, he and Mozart, sprinting past me, running in zigzags like two synchronised comedians.

When I caught up to him, he was skipping stones on the canal.

"Going for a swim," he said, hauling off his t-shirt and diving in.

Then he and Mozart swam the width of the canal and climbed up on the sugarcane beds where he stood barechested amidst the stalks.

"Come over," he shouted.

"You crazy, boy?"

"Come on." He beckoned, as if I was still eight years old and he could tell me what to do.

"How I gon reach there?"

"Just jump in and come."

"Absolutely not," I shouted airily, pretending I didn't want to sink into the rippling canal too and disappear between the cane stalks, into another realm.

"Scaredy weirdy," he said and he and Mozart went into the cane.

When they emerged, Sam had a short stalk of cane. He held it above his head and waved. Then he and Mozart dived into the canal and swam back, zigzagging across. When I saw them zigging and zagging I couldn't help releasing some hearty laughter that went gliding along the canal channels and echoing between the beds of cane, preserving itself there in the land.

Sam climbed out, wet boxer shorts sticking to his legs, afternoon sun glistening on his marble sculpted chest. I tried not to look.

"Stop being an idiot and put your stupid shirt on," I said tossing the shirt at him and for five seconds I looked.

"Look," he said pulling the shirt on. The shirt stuck to his skin. "Look what I got." He waved the stump of cane in the sunlight. Then grabbing up his shoes and socks, with the stalk of cane still raised to the air, he zigzagged down the road squealing at Mozart while Mozart followed zigzagging and squealing back.

What a pair of synchronised comedians, I thought, as I sped after them, with Mozart barking and Sam and I laughing into the universe.

We continued that way for weeks.

One day as we jogged, I said, "I think I ..."

A flock of birds went by. The sun was setting on the canal. Yellow-orange. I paused to watch everything.

"Think faster," said Sam, counting his push-ups, his nose one inch from the dust.

There was a newspaper clipping in my pocket. I unfolded it.

"I think maybe I should do this. But I dunno if I can," I said.

"Cross-country racing?" said he softly, coming closer and looking at me longer than usual, and not just at my face, but the top of my head and around my collarbone. Probably to see if I was serious about the race, I told myself, and swallowed. He smelled like freshly cut grass, Dettol soap and some kind of smouldering campfire cologne.

"Oi Mozart, look at this." He tilted the clipping at Mozart and Mozart looked.

I was about to get offended and say never mind. After all, I, Ixora Mara, Loser of the Limepicks, did not expect to be taken seriously about this.

"You can do it," he said at last, determination and faith flowing into his nostrils. "And I run with you too. Me and Mozart. We better start training today."

An extraordinary charge surged through my body and lit up my neurons, ligaments and bones. I couldn't believe that there was once a time that I, Ixora Mara, had an absurd corrosive lime taking over my veins. When now, here I was, being believed in. And I surged like a hundred houses on an evening street, all lighting up at exactly the same time.

Sam timed my paces. Eventually, he, Mozart and I could jog for an hour, side-by-side, carrying on a full conversation without panting and puffing.

"That dog really got his wits about him," I said.

"Of course," Sam said "Dunno what I'd do without 'im."

And I dunno what I'd do without you Samuel A. Reid, Junior, I said, but only in my head, because I couldn't get it out through my voice box, just yet.

Two weeks later, I decided to put on my training shoes early and seek out Sam to complain about how Ivy'd called and how maddening she was being, expecting everyone to line up and report all of Peaside's business to her. I made my way down the back street, preparing to whine. I'd tell Sam how all Ivy did was ask about what we had for lunch and dinner and whether the sun was shining and if the breadfruit tree was bearing. He'd have to agree that she was being maddening. Never once asking about me, she never even –

But when I saw Sam, I couldn't finish my thought.

He was sitting in the street, his back braced to his fence. His face was turned towards the heavens and his mouth open as if he were letting out a terrifying howl. But no sound came out.

He clutched a limp Mozart.

I ran to Sam and tumbled at his feet.

We held eyes. And our universe swayed and shifted.

Then he was sobbing and shaking and couldn't breathe. I knew a thing or two about not being able to breathe. About things constricting your chest. About your lime rising up like a corrosive fountain inside you and always, you had to keep your lime water from flowing down to your toes. Always you had to make sure that no one knew about it. Or that would be the end of you, I knew. I knew about these things and I crawled closer to Sam.

He wouldn't let go of Mozart.

And I wouldn't let go of him.

After his sobs settled into silence, I found a shovel and tried to help him dig a hole in his backyard. But he yanked the shovel from me. I was afraid that with tears obscuring his vision that he would jam the shovel into his foot so I tried to take it back. But he pulled it back from me, and dug and dug until it was enough.

After that, Sam either underdid or overdid his part as if he were some performer's understudy and it was not his own life he was living.

On Saturday mornings he towed his mother to market on a bicycle, robotically pedalling up the street and robotically pedalling back down. On Sundays he borrowed his cousin No-Jo's car and sped up and down the streets like a man on steroids. On weekdays I saw him run-walking as he left for his day job at six in the morning and though I'd stay awake looking through my window for the single dull beam of his torchlight dancing on the street, often I fell asleep and didn't get to see him coming home from his night job. Whenever I managed to see him, he barely spoke. I garnered that in the evenings he hauled boxes and stacked produce at a supermarket in the city and in the mornings he worked as a solicitor's clerk.

One Saturday when Mam was still at work, I decided to take the market list and get our vegetables and fish and some things for Old Lady Bargains because she had the flu and Ganee'd asked if I could help. Old Lady Bargains said she wanted a good many oranges because she believed in vitamin C.

I'd just got the good many oranges when I tripped and stumbled. And there, without fail, after all these years, beside the orange stand, with his foot outstretched was Salimanto. I scowled at him and he scowled right back at me, as always. Never before had there been a long-term homeless beggar with such an air of entitlement about his feet as Salimanto.

"Arrrgh," I said and was about to continue my old row with him when I caught sight of Sam's mother and stopped myself.

She was more haggard than the last time.

"Y'all must talk to Junior," she said.

"What happened?"

"He working too hard. He getting fine fine. He don't talk talk," she explained.

You're telling me, I thought, and helped fetch her bags.

How was I to talk to somebody if I couldn't even get to see him five feet in front of me? It was too early in the mornings to disturb the neighbourhood with my toy whistle through the window, but I tried it thrice and every time Sam barely nodded. He didn't come jogging in the afternoons anymore. And I didn't know if that meant he would no longer run the cross-country race with me and if at all I had the spirit or the limbs to run it on my own.

Finally I set a hare-brained scheme in motion.

One Sunday when Sam was out in the streets recklessly driving No-Jo's car, I stood smack in the middle of his path with my arms akimbo. A fast cold sweat broke out around my forehead as the car flew at me. Omigosh, I thought, I'm going to die by car. My parents were going to live out their lives with one half of a twin, I thought. Oh God, oh God.

Screech!

The car halted ten inches from my body. It was ten seconds before I could unfreeze and keep going with my plan.

Shaking a little, I ran to the passenger's side, yanked the door open and jumped in before Sam could wise up to my plan and drive away without me.

"Drive," I said.

He glared at me but not before I noticed how sunken his eyes were, how sharp his cheekbones had gotten and how thin his face was now, but still remarkably magnetic.

"Well if you won't drive," I said, "teach me."

He looked at me, unwilling to talk.

"Teach me," I said.

"You don't have a provisional driver's licence," his voice sounded husky and brusque and sly as if he knew he'd catch me out and have an excuse to bring the conversation to an end.

"I do too. Look," I pulled a small booklet from my pocket.

His brows showed a flicker of surprise. He snatched the licence, examined it and turned down his lips.

"When you get this?"

"I'm not as entirely lacking in guts as some seem to think you know," I said, pleased at my poise and the voice coming out of my mouth.

He turned his lips down again. I could see that he was trying hard to think of a way to get me out of the car.

"This isn't my car you know," he said at last.

"I know."

"Well my cousin might not be happy 'bout me teaching somebody to drive in it."

"Oh I talked to No-Jo about it already," I said, waving my hand as if brushing away a marabunta. I had anticipated this conversation and I really had run into the street the previous Sunday and flagged No-Jo down. He was a little doubtful at first, but when I explained about Sam's sullenness and how Sam's mother had asked us to try to talk to Sam, No-Jo said it was alright then, as long as I didn't drive his car into a tree or a trench because he was still paying for it. And I'd promised I'd try my best not to and he looked at me with his brows coming together and smiled. When No-Jo smiled he resembled Sam and I thought about how things might've been with Sam if he'd had a brother or a father in the house.

"You did what?" Sam asked, "I don't believe you."

"Well call him and ask him yourself." I folded my arms and sat back.

"Miss Harry, I can't remember the last time you told a lie," Sam said, taking out his new cellphone. It was one of those brick-sized cell phones which youths today call dinosaurs.

"I not lying," I said, delighted that he was finally talking, arguing even, "besides, why don't you answer my text messages?"

"Jo?" Sam said, "You told Ixora she could use your car?"

A pause followed and Sam's mouth turned down.

"I see," he said and hung up.

He got out of the car and walked around to the passenger's side and opened the door.

"Well," he said gruffly.

Delighted, I crawled over into the driver's seat.

"Adjust the seat, adjust the mirrors and buckle up," he said.

I fumbled at all three tasks.

"One hundred years later," he said, impatiently.

I was trembling slightly

"Hands at a ten to two position," he barked.

"What's that?"

"You can't tell time? Like so, ten minutes to two o'clock. Put your foot on the brake."

"What's the brake?"

He gave me a look.

"Now put the car in Drive, like so. Now step off the brake. Easy."

"How's the jobs?" I snuck a sentence in.

"Fine. Focus on the street. Now step on the gas. Gently."

"Where's the —"

"Pedal on the right. Gently. Gently! You deaf?"

"You working too hard. Your mammy worried about you."

"Look the street corner coming up, brakes up. Brakes up! You got to stop at corners and look woman."

"Stop shouting Samuel," I said and stepped on the gas hard. The car shot forward and I delighted in my ability to operate a machine. "It's a beautiful thing, a car," I said, "look at how it moves."

I could feel Sam turning his head looking somewhat surprised and a little intrigued at me. I, myself, couldn't believe the words coming out of my mouth.

"Yes," he said calming down, "especially this one. It's smooth."

"Yea," I said, and jammed down too hard on the brake at a street corner. Sam pitched forward and almost hit his head on the dashboard. I saw him opening his mouth and I steeled myself for the shouting to start up again, but laughter broke out in the car and when I looked around, I saw that it was coming from him.

Well! I thought.

For several Sunday afternoons after church, Sam continued the lessons we'd started. We marvelled at automobiles and Sam showed me car magazines. His tones were still muted but he had improved in temperament about twenty-five per cent since my first driving lesson. And twenty-five is better than zero.

"Here's one of planes," he said, one afternoon flattening down a magazine on the dashboard, "Isn't this one smooth?"

"Oh," I said, I didn't know much about planes. I thought of the one I had tried to scrape off in my bedroom and had eventually painted over in white. I wasn't going to tell him about that, that I'd painted over his plane. He didn't have to know. He didn't have to know either that I wasn't sure about how much I liked planes. They were the machines that stood behind airport barriers, whose vibrations shook your house.

I was sorry that I'd tried scraping the plane and flowers off the wall and painted everything over. But I supposed it wouldn't have mattered to him or to Ivy, for later, when she came home during 'summer,' she walked into our room and didn't even flinch. She never asked for her stuff or about why the mural had disappeared. And I felt my heart building turrets and erecting surge barriers to slow the lime river from creeping lower into my already sour guts.

What did I expect from Ivy League? A confrontation, a demand for an explanation, an exchange of feeling? Why? She now had a whole world with tallest towers of brick and steel and marble in backgrounds, a world of husky hunks in photos, of higher graduate degrees and cool weather, art galleries and universities – plural, a world of bold brave friends who did not vomit at their own shadows. She had four dimensional people now. She had the side of the world that tipped, no weighed down the scale against the side with the erased childish mural, the rickety vanity, the tattered outdated books borrowed from the other side, and one half of a passive Self. Why would she want them back?

"I'm saving up to go to flying school you know?" Sam said suddenly.

My heart sank. I fiddled with the radio.

"Oh," I said, "Abroad?"

"No. The one right here." He tuned into the radio station and a top twenty hit rang out. His hand brushed against mine and a little electrical surge flowed and crackled in my fingertips.

"Oh," I said, relieved.

"Then maybe later, I can learn more abroad. My father been saying I must come."

"Oh," I said and turned off the radio and came out the car, "Thanks for the lesson."

The trees started wobbling at me like green and brown jello, though I'd never seen brown jello. All these weeks, Sam had said nothing about how he was feeling about Mozart or about his mother worrying about him. He had said nothing about his jobs or anything else that I'd coaxed him into sharing. Or about whether he was still going to run the cross-country race with me. Or when we could start training again. And I had listened, winding myself around his every word about cars and planes and his father, as if my attentions could keep him, keep us, secure, steady. He had reeled me in like a kite and here he was reeling me out again, maybe even one day letting go of the twine.

He nodded and drove off with his aeroplane magazine in the passenger's seat.

My lime rose, spinning in riot under my rib-cage.

But I thought, let go of the twine then if you want, Samuel Reid, the Second. I am Ixora Mara and I'm going to enter that cross-country race by myself.

20

Song of the Metropolis

When I landed back home everything be stellar vibes yes. But when I scrammed to my bedroom to catch up on a nap, the first thing I thought was oh geesh, is the wrong door I come through. But nope; 'twas the right door. Well excuse me. The blank-slate paint and the sparse décor jarred my engines a bit, I got to admit. My room been doing its own thing without me. Well fine, what could I say. Still, when I put my bags down, my elbows wobbled. But what could I say. I didn't expect my elbows to shake here of all places. Odd to find unease going from the elbows to the rest of the body everywhere. In organs and muscle. Blood and veins. Spirit and soul and all that. Here in my own room. I looked at my twin. But the Ixie standing in this room was not the same as the Ixie standing at the airport to pick me up an hour ago. It got to be this new minimalist paint job in the room that be chiselling out her cheeks. What else? But I kinda accustomed to these things now. Accustomed to walking into everywhere for the first time where things just be new and odd. The first time I walked out the airport in New York, the cold whipped my face and chest and went straight to my bones and never came out again. No lie. Not the triple layers of clothes or sticking my head in Mam's freezer for ten minutes, though it was fun, prepared me for that cold. It took me just about ten seconds to see how pathetic my preparations had been. Boy was I ashamed. I hoped nobody could see my knock-knees shivering. I stood in the airport doorway steeling myself and feigning competence in my knees 'til cousin Lennard – he was going by Len now, started wheeling my suitcase in the direction of his car. Then he noncommittally dropped me off outside what seemed to be the campus dorms. See you round he said and zoomed off into the night. In the first twenty-four hours I absorbed the city. By the second day, I'd absorbed so much of it so quickly, boy I got a bad case of city indigestion. It wasn't long before one of those embarrassing feely-thinky moods caught up with me. And my mind just be rejecting the metropolis glut and I vomited for three days in a row. Me, vomiting. Like I was the wrong half of the twin. Every day I longed for the warm Guyana sun. 'Til one day, I had to stop longing for it. The longing for that deep hot sun could kill you boy. Seven days in a row I went and bought a pair of fuzzy socks. Like some crazy flamboyant ones, yes. Every day, I went to the same store and bought the socks 'cause I didn't know my way to other stores yet. Besides, it was a dollar store. So I could 'fford it. It was chill to just be walking down the street and turning right and then down again towards a row of businesses. I'd just be marvelling I could go anywhere and do anything as I pleased without Mam yelling that I must hold my sister hand. But no matter what I pleased, all I ended up doing in those first days was buying socks. What a clutz. Standing in the sock store, I never felt so foolish and proud at the same time. When spring came, some of the girls in my dorm planned a road trip through some open country. They said it was fantastic weather for the outdoors and I was loads ashamed to say I was still shivering, so I put on a whole set of vests underneath and went. They had boyfriends and the boyfriends came too. I discovered that everyone in my circle was getting it on with their boyfriend, except a girl named Morgan. Nobody wanted her because she had braces. So she told me. One night, a young man came and knocked on my door. His eyes prowled 'round to see if I was alone. Hello there, Ivy League, he joked. They always be calling me Ivy League and yapping how my parents had to gimme that name to make sure I was destined for an Ivy League school, otherwise I'd be picking peas down in a hot third world country somewhere off the map. What a bunch of jerks! At least my father took the time to give me and Ixie names from the flora of our land, so we would know we had the same blooming qualities like the beautiful things around us. Hello there Ivy League, the idiot said. He had an accent from somewhere else, not my new metropolis. He said, I've brought some wine from the pawhty next door. I've got a bit of a headache luv. They're getting a bit loud and I'm longing for a spot o' peace and quiet. You look like a spot of peace and quiet, hot cakes. No, I don't, I said to myself. He just be getting into the flirts with me. No, I heard myself say abruptly, I was just on my way out. Then I jammed my feet into some flip-flops and grabbed my door keys. Nancy's cabinet might have some aspirin for your headache young man, I said, not wanting to fully offend the crack-pot, in case he decided to chase after me and break the wine bottle on my head. Look, I had to care my skull, yes. Mam said I wasn't to bust it up again. In case I got Parkinson's. Still, I slammed the door in his face and vamoosed. I found myself standing outside the sock store, in public, in pyjamas, in my flip-flops, feet feeling like big ice blocks that Uncle Warbin used to pound up with the ice pick when we had luncheons. I never felt so stupid in my life, standing there. People just be pushing you out of your chill man, showing up at your door, as if. This boy was nothing like Samuel with whom a girl was free and safe. So many things in the new land that can kinda shock your system. In group photographs it seemed like I always faded into the walls of the university. In fast food joints with the circle of girls, after the first six weeks of thrill at pizzas, burgers, fries and things, my stomach just be shrivelling up. Boy I thought of Mam's mango achar with hot dhal and rice and callaloo and Ganee's buns for dessert and Pappo's passion fruit drink. I discovered a West Indian Store and took the subway and searched around for powdered milk, Demerara Gold sugar, plantains and yams. It was like I was always hungry. I cornered a boy named Paul in the university library. Paul was from my university in Guyana and he'd been here before me. Paul, I said, how do you do it, eh boy? How you make it stop, the cold and the rumbling in your tummy? Paul said it buried itself and he didn't bother with it no more and it didn't bother with him. Oh, I'd said. I didn't bother asking him about coping with the foreignness of one's tongue in one's own mouth. He already sounded like he was born and raised in this metropolis, except his English Grammar was sometimes wrong. I don't know what I mean by except. I don't know anymore. If I go about interrogating every word and concept I used since landing here, I could even have trouble with baby functions like talking and thinking. I couldn't switch my accent so easy like Paul. I couldn't stop from adapting either. I wanted to adapt so bad. I knew it in my guts. I didn't want to stand in a line buying a sandwich or fries and not be understood. Can I get-the-chili-cheese-sauce, I heard myself running all the words together, halting and dragging syllables as necessary to not be stared at, and I was super thrilled and horrified at the sounds flying through my pearly whites. Just like I was thrilled at the chill air. Fall was magical, like in the movies, and the winter ground was jiving, just like the Christmas cards Aunty Melanie used to force Len and Ann to send us in Guyana. If the crisp cold was just right, it could sting and bring you alive and excited about being alive for real. In Guyana, the sun was too hot and baked you down and aged your skin. Over here it's, let me see how to say everything all melodramatic like Ixie would say it – it's like the energy and all the brilliance that converged in the metropolis struck a chord in you as if your heart were a harp and as if you were playing music to the history woven into the towering powerful architecture of the land. My, what a land! Buildings so tall you could look up and break your neck. Churches with so many details in the ceilings and windows and columns and doors, so that you couldn't help but feel you were a part of something. Bridges too. Imposing brick university campuses, plural, decided your course of life – grand and forward-paced, audibly intelligent. Fast. Highways. Many roads, many side streets, opportunities endless. Endlessness. Signs everywhere. Automobiles. Hundreds of them. Going somewhere. Always. Productive. The output – immense. How slow I was. How limited. There was so much to catch up with since I had been born and living in a country behind a curtain. A curtain that hadn't been pulled and tied back. A country in labour to acknowledge its characters and write its script. One wants to be on the stage before one is dead. Here in this metropolis all you had to do was exist and you were already on the stage. Here where even when the trees were dead they were still alive. I was not wrong to come here, I told my stomach and at some point I think it shut up or shut down. I showed the old stomik that this land here was teeming with brains and drive. No lie. Movie theatres, block busters, mega-sized billboards with superheroes on them. Here this land is grand and delightful. Bustling skyline, beautiful parks, calming spaces, lovely gardens. Pappo's garden was pretty chill too. I remember seeing it from the other side of the street, when me, Ixie and Junior used to have a ball of a time in the empty house. I saw Pappo's garden and Ixie's red hibiscus blooming in the yard. I wish Ixie would come with me, could see this land. She'd barely speak to me on the phone. Always disappearing from me. I be wanting to ask her had Ganee and Pappo got more wrinkles. Did Mam and Pap split the chores in three now I was gone so that she, Ix didn't have to do all of my share. But maybe she didn't want to lose her breath on mundane things. I'd lose my breath on things though. I'd lose my breath underground. It be dark in the tunnels outside those hurtling trains man. Life disappeared. My body disappeared under my layers of clothing, teaching itself new stability, especially when things that were supposed to stay stable slid about – like stairs. In the metropolis, stairs moved everywhere. You had to look hard for some stairs to ground you. Ground. Ground. My old country is ground. The landscape from overhead is fertile, rugged like, strong. At the airport, I felt myself rushing to Ixie, Mam, Pap, Ganee, Pappo, even clinky-dinky old Peaside. The warmth inside burst my heart with feely-thinkies boy. My ground was all around me, embracing me, birthing me back into being. I got to admit, that moment at the airport when everybody came to get me was grand as the tallest building in New York. No boy, grander. But standing here now though, in a room that was once and supposedly still is mine, my elbows shake. My ground has been shaken boy. Where *is* my ground. Where was my ground. My own tongue feels foreign. I try to work it back into its old Guyanese accent but it's gone all wonky-doodles. What is wrong with my tongue for crab's sake. What's with the temperature in these parts and why don't Pap install air conditioner. Twelve sessions of black out popped in since I arrived. Twelve. The internet is a snail. I be trying to get on to my friends 'round the globe and the webpage says loading. Plus it's hard to go anywhere without a car. There's nothing to do here once you've seen the couple of people and said hello and once Old Lady Bargains has invited you over for food. You can't starve here boy. Every morning Pappo be putting fruits for me in a basket that Ganee made with her own hands. And Ixie and I and even Sam went back to our old ways. Sam and I talked for hours and played cards. I told him we gotta go back in the empty house across the street, the one where we used to imagine all manner of things. The Imagine House. But we didn't go. Sam arranged for trips 'round the country. The old Harbour Bridge is not as long and bold as I remember. Ixie came with us and said nothing when I talked to Sam about the design of the bridge and suggested improvements. She just don't be sayin' much. I can't imagine what there is for her to keep being all preoccupied and sullen about. She didn't have to deal with two whole years of fitting in with a new world and getting some respect in it and then to top it off, coming home and finding your own room busted up. She's just been on the same spot of ground, doing the same old thing since she was born, always sweet-soaped, always coddled – oh little one, never mind the writing on the wall boo-hoo-hoo, oh doudou dumpling you're not an egg boo-hoo – so why won't she try more. Leaving her newspaper clipping lying around – *Zekerheid Resident Shines at Cross-country Race*. What's so hard not to shine about here among Old Lady Bargains and Salimanto in this backwater for goodness' sake. Besides, you only needed to exist to shine once you're the heir. The spare always has to outdo herself. The second of a twin is kinda like the extra cheese and toppings on a pizza, 'cus what you gonna do with toppings without a crust. Listen, I go, I compete with crème de la crème to move everything along for everyone. It's like she can't see I'm to be the lever. She knows how levers work, Pappo showed us. Yet, she tries to unnerve me by calling me Ivy League. Nobody calls me that on this side of the world, in that condescending tone. She, in the comfort of her spaces tries to dislodge me from mine. Why mustn't I have a space there *and* here? Absence of presence isn't absence of essence. This is my space Miss Ixora Mara, Sourpuss of Peaside Pasture – and doing a grand job at it too since old dour dope Mr Crapaud handed you his baton. This is my space too. So get off it. I ain't 'The Spare.' Even Sam is more accommodating. I've fallen out of sync with everyone's routines. Pap wakes me too early on Sunday mornings for church. At church their music is out of time and their singing is flat. I am embarrassed to admit that I once sang in this choir. Lord! Here nothing ever happens except the same thing. In Peaside, something just be happening to it; it doesn't happen to anything. I long for the hum of the plane and the endless spaces stretching before me again. I am wanderlust. Mam and Ganee are crying at the airport again. I never forget Mam crying when Pap's shin got busted. That is why I must go. When you're poor the world looks different. Somebody gotta make sure we not always poor. Pappo waves goodbye. Pap is a little more solemn this time around. And Ixie be bustling about with my bags and helping me carry them. She don't look me in the eye like the last time. I try to catch them, her eyeballs, and even when I do for one second, I see some kind of barrier, a wall behind her eyes and then another wall behind that wall. I stand on the threshold, turn around and look back. I'm not sure I want to leave. I feel like I must be breaking up some kind of crystal vase situation or something. I can't stand these faces lined up behind the glass looking at me. Pulling me back. Come with me then. Come. Look at me. Look at me Ixora Mara. Twin. Stop fiddling with your wristwatch. The old one. Not the new one I bought you. She's the only one not looking at me. I am the arm pulling the curtain and tying it back. Look out onto the world through the tied back curtain, everyone. Look at me as I tie it back for you all. And then I'm to be the lever. That is what I gotta go and do. That is what. In the air, the coastland looks flat and quiet. I vomit thrice on the journey. When I land in the Big Apple, amorous city, smutty beautiful, I spend an hour in line waiting for a taxi, 'cause ain't nobody picking you up on this side of the water. I can't hear myself feel outside in this mighty exciting prolific metropolis. But when I get to my dorm room, the peach walls close in. The stomach cramps start. Headaches come back. I want to go back. I want to go home. Ah wan go home.

21

In the Empty House Again

After Ivy left, her bed and vanity remained in our room. This time I would leave them there, I thought. After all, surely she couldn't stay across that ocean forever. Besides, since it was her first time back home, I'd expended my last ounce of energy to haul her things in again and raise everything to the impeccable standard to which she must now be accustomed.

I had crawled under all the crawlable furniture and swept every centimetre of dust. I mopped our bedroom three times. I polished our vanities. I tucked in our bedsheets, unbudging and crisp, five-star hotel style. I filled the crystal vase with water; arranged ivy leaves and ixora flowers with an amateur florist's sensibility; rewashed Ivy's old clothes with lavender-smelling detergent; folded and arranged them by hue in her drawers; ironed and hung up new curtains that Mam and I bought in the city; wore out my arm stirring batter; decorated the cake and wrote Welcome Home Ivy. But I mis-averaged the letter sizes and the y from Ivy fell off to the side of the festive red and green icing.

"Oh ho ho," she said, as soon as she walked through the door, "Is like I be toppling right over into Chrismass when is only summer. Bring a knife and plate Ix." And she cut into HOME straight down the middle.

She settled in and after two days asked, "What's for fun around here?"

"Nothing," I said, worried she would find out the shenanigans I was up to and rat me out without meaning to do harm.

After my part-time job at the City Library, I tutored a seven year old boy and his two sisters who lived down the street. People called him Cappy. The dirty red cap perpetually perched atop his scalp might have had something to do with it. The girls were called Onesy and Twosy. When I first saw them bounding silently over the street towards me, I imagined Cappy as the captain and the girls as his first and second mates. If I stood on our veranda and leaned far enough I could see their ten foot by ten foot zinc house that their father nailed up when they moved to Peaside a few months ago. Cappy's mammy'd just had a baby and Peaside said she spent all day on the crocus bags – they didn't have a bed – bawling while the baby bawled. Market women said that Cappy's father drank, cussed, slept all day and hit his family with a belt; they said even the baby's wrist he'd smacked to make it stop bawling. When I asked Cappy about that, he said it was true. He said too that his father told him to go look for a job because he was old enough to. But how I ever got dragged into Cappy's family affairs was a whole surreal situation.

The shenanigans started the day Cappy's mammy showed up at my house, her potato sack dress trembling. She said she'd heard from someone who heard from someone that I knew how to read real good, that I used to read the news on TV and that I was an athlete who won a big prize for Peaside, that I worked at the library and was bright.

"I'm not bright," I said, embarrassed at my Impossible stint on the news. "And I'm not an athlete. It was just for survival."

When I said that, she looked at me like I was some entitled numskull, then trembling in the sun she begged me to teach her children some of their school lessons.

"But I'm not a teacher," I said. "What happened to their real school?"

She looked down the street as if she expected Cappy's father to come wielding a stick.

"Yes, but dem, especially Cap, miss nuff nuff days at school. He pappy don't want he go school but I still send he some days when he pappy not 'round, but he still miss nuff days and he do bad in school. Bad bad. Dem girls too. Help dem out nuh. Me beg yuh. If dem don't larn school, dem go turn out jus' like dem pappy and me. Please Miss, me beg yuh."

I followed the pathway of her vision and looked down the street too, half-expecting this man, Cappy's pappy, to appear with a stick and threaten us. I whispered, though afterwards I wondered why I was whispering out in the open air in the broiling sun. I was a grown woman in front of my own abode and nobody had the right to come wielding some stupid stick at me. Still, I found myself whispering, "But I dunno how to teach."

"Anything nuh. Teach dem anyting till dem know someting. Ow me beg yuh. But don't tell nobody, you hear? Swear. Don't tell nobody or he guh choke me dead dead and bury meh and meh done. Nobody. Yuh hear? Swear."

"I can't swear that. What do you mean choke y–"

Then she looked down the street and darted off. I'd never before seen a woman run barefoot, potato sack dress flying, running from an invisible man by running towards the real man.

It was an odd experience and I didn't believe anything would come of it until one morning when the boy called Cappy who apparently had been hiding behind a bush waiting for me, appeared.

When I woke on a Saturday morning, a little later than usual, pulled back my curtain and looked at Suzie's persistently existing house, that shadowy universe across the rotting purpleheart bridge, and I looked too at the newly emptied house beside Suzie's, I saw a small head, wearing a red cap turned backwards, appear from behind a bush. I choked on my spit. It was Cappy, notebook and pencil in hand. He looked at me, made sure I saw him, then crouched back behind the bush.

"What in the –" I said to myself.

Still in my pyjamas, I ran down to our gate and beckoned Cappy over. He shot across the street towards me. Two more balls in little brown potato sack dresses bounded behind him. Then they came through our gate and Cappy looked for a bush and proceeded to hide behind it.

"Hello boy," I whispered, crawling behind the bush, dusting up my pyjama knees. "Hello you boy and you two, what you doing?"

"Shh," he said. "Mammy says you can show me the work." He opened his book and pointed at red exes everywhere.

"But –"

"You have to show me this page fast before my pappy wake up."

"But –"

"Look, what's dis answer?" Business-like he pointed at something I did not remember. Long division, it seemed.

"I, I don't remember how to –"

"My mammy said you know." He looked at me like I was stupid.

"No I don't remember this stuff. I'm not a real teacher."

"You dunno nothing?" He snatched his book back. "You dunce then?" He crawled backwards, setting up to leave.

"What? No, I'm not dunce, you little tyke!"

His two sisters peered into my face and one of them lightly touched the collar of my pyjamas.

"Just let me see that book," I said bewildered at my defensiveness towards this rude little human and at the surreal indignity of crawling around behind bushes in pyjamas and demanding primary school notebooks with long division in them.

"Come back tomorrow," I said.

He chucked the book over, shrugged like he had no faith in me, crawled backwards, turned the visor of his cap in front and sneaked out. The two balls of potato sack dresses tiptoe-ran behind him.

All day long I worked out the sums, creating a worksheet and including answers on the back, and the next morning when Cappy came and hid behind the bush in front of Suzie's house as the sun was rising, I ran down in my pyjamas again and beckoned. He shot across, holding on to his cap and crawled behind the bush. One of the little balls in the brown dress crawled behind the bush too.

Good gracious, I thought, crawling in disbelief behind the bush again in a clean pair of pyjamas. "Look here," I said, "This is how it works."

And Cappy watched and listened and shook his head. Then he snatched the worksheet and sneaked away like a cat.

"Wait, where's the other one?" I asked the girl who was hurrying to get up and sneak out behind her brother.

She put her palms together, rested her cheek against the back of her left hand and closed her eyes.

"Asleep?"

She nodded and scampered off like a smaller cat.

I remained behind the bush trying to catch my bearings, until I heard Mam calling up the stairs for me to come down for breakfast. I crawled from behind the bush and appeared at the front door with the dust on my pyjama knees.

"You? Outside? At this hour? In pyjamas? Look Mikey," Mam said, pointing at me and turning to Pap who was hobbling around getting out the coffee.

Pap laughed. "What you up to outdoors Ix Pix?"

"I, uh, um, er, well –"

Pap laughed. He still hobbled and limped but he laughed and joked a lot these days since getting a promotion at work and paying off his student loans. He and Mam made enough money now so that they were home together on weekends and could take several weeks off per year with leave benefits. And when they were at home, it was trickier for me to go out to Cappy, Onesy and Twosy and explain the lessons behind what we started calling The School Bush which was a massively untidy hedge that Pap was always wrestling and pruning.

Then one evening, of all the bushes to chop, Pap chopped down The School Bush and said he was replacing it with a less unruly species of hedge.

A panic wave took hold of me and I even wondered whether I should tell Pap and Mam about the trio so they could invite them inside to do their lessons. But that might turn Pap and Mam into accomplices, and if Cappy's father knew about it, he could show up with a stick and threaten them. I had to think fast. Tomorrow morning was upon me and Cappy, Onesy and Twosy would be waiting behind Suzie's bush.

And then, an idea floated in to me through the window, like ideas used to do a long time ago when my brain would receive them.

I would sneak into Suzie's house and have the lessons there. Yes, that is what I'd do.

I set my alarm and tossed all night. Next morning, before the sun rose, I snuck outdoors, secured a cutlass, pelted across the street and hacked a little path through the bush. I climbed the stairs, stepping carefully so as not to fall through the rotting steps and pushed the door open. It was the same way Ivy, Sam and I had left it about twenty years ago, with the piece of wood lodged between the old hasp and staple, only it had rot to pulp and disintegrated at my touch. Inside smelled of wood ants. Vines grew down and up the walls. It was a mausoleum, the thick eerie cobwebs working hard. My brain, slow in catching up, felt like I was in a parallel universe – existing both in the space and time of Suzie's house and in my own house across the street. Or like I was in another universe and in the usual one, I had ceased to exist.

I was just looking through Suzie's bedroom window and deciding to abandon my plan because the old lime concoction had started doing its routine work, when the three little figures arrived and sat behind the bush waiting for my signal. They cut such a pathetic figure sitting there together waiting in the dark dawn behind a bush to scrape an education from a random dunce lady down the street that I burst into a ten second sob.

"Psst," I called down, when my silent bawling subsided, "psst."

They jumped.

"Psst, it's me." I signalled them to come up.

Cappy, cat-like as always, was up. Before I could come out to the steps, he was already through the door. The two brown dress balls scampered up too.

"Whatchoo doin here?" he said, looking around.

"Shh. My Pap chop down The School Bush. But listen, you could stay in my yard and do the lessons or come inside my house, my mother and father won't mind."

But Cappy started shaking his head, eyes darting left and right. Onesy and Twosy bit their nails.

So I continued quickly, "But if we stay there in my yard, your father might come and quarrel with my Pap. I already saw your father try to chop a man in the street you know?"

Cappy nodded, unashamed of his father's behaviour. The sisters nodded.

I went on, "And my Pap can't fight back 'cus his leg ain't good. And your mammy made me swear nobody would know. Because what if he tries to fight her too if the secret comes out? So is best we borrow this house sometimes, but real quick, okay?" I sorted the worksheets into three sets.

"What 'appen to it mek he can't fight back?" Cappy asked, taking the worksheets.

"To what?"

"He leg."

"Whose leg?"

"Your pappy," he said.

"Oh, the bone fractured long ago and never healed back right. He has lots of pains in it still. In his hip too. It kinda rotated inwards, the leg." I became more bewildered at myself, standing in this hollow dying house, talking about my Pap's leg to someone's odd little boy and the two additional pairs of ears beside him. I said, "Anyway, he won't try and fix the leg, and if he fights your father, he won't win. Anyway, read those instructions to start off."

"Answer the following questions," he struggled to read, as we stood among the cobwebs and rotted floorboards and vines, I with the light of a torch reading the passage aloud for him, racing against the rising sun and he nodding his red cap at a rate fit to beat the dawn

"And you two, look, trace these letters. Trace, look, like this see? Trace."

The pair nodded.

"Bye," I said, shoving the worksheets over, "I gotta go before people see me coming out dis house. That's trespassing you know."

"What's trespassing?" Cappy asked, turning the visor of his cap forward.

"Look it up I said," but I'd forgotten that they probably hadn't a dictionary.

I ran down the stairs almost plummeting through a rotten step. I hung on to the shaking banister, saved myself and pelted across to my yard, heart racketing about inside my chest. Such were the shenanigans that tested and strained my nerves several mornings every week. Then I'd sneak back into bed until it was time to wake up for the second time that day and go to work at the city library.

So when Ivy returned home for the first time since she left and slept in her own bed again and Mam and Pap stayed home on leave for eight weeks so we could all bond or whatever, my fears of being caught trespassing multiplied. I couldn't sneak over to Suzie's house anymore because I was afraid Ivy would see me leaving, so I put some worksheets with what I thought were clear explanations under a flat rock outside our gate. Cappy collected and returned them and I put ticks where he got things right. But there were many things he got wrong. It seemed that explaining something for five or ten minutes in Suzie's rotting house made a difference after all. Still, the chance couldn't be taken. I couldn't involve anyone else. I'd seen Cappy's father too many times brandishing a cutlass or a stick or an axe, smoking and cussing. He didn't seem like he could be reasoned with and I didn't want him on our bridge with sharp implements. I didn't know what made Cappy's mammy think she could just tell me to do something and I would heed, as if I didn't have a brain and a life of my own. The nerve of people, I thought, pulling you into their messy dramas, guilting you into participating in the fabric of life. Nevertheless, for many weeks, I put the lessons under the rock to keep everyone in one piece. I wanted to tell Ivy about Cappy and ask her what to do, but I didn't know that she'd grasp the gravity of it all. She didn't really know Cappy's father. Still, it was hard to keep the secret. But I knew that once the door to one's chest was open for a crack, it wouldn't just be one little secret shared, everything else could come flying out – the good, the bad and the imaginary. And I had to be cautious or I could dismantle just from opening my mouth. So I safeguarded the locks on the trapfloor of my chest. Besides, Ivy'd soon be gone again and couldn't help me. No, whatever had to be done on this side of the Atlantic, I had to do it alone.

And she, Ivy, when she was not working at the ministry to return service hours as per the contract of her partial scholarship, wanted to do everything at once. We did each other's nails. She helped me and Pappo water plants. We ferreted out an old kite, repaired it and went to the National Park to fly it. Sam came but remained under a tree reading a textbook called *Avionics 101* and didn't get up to help raise the kite. What an idiot, Ivy and I said behind his back, and giggled like old times. Nothing had changed.

Except Sam. Ivy. And me.

Sam suggested trips around the country. It would do Ivy good, he said, to tour a little of her homeland. It would be a shame if someone from her university asked her about the great Kaieteur for instance, and she hadn't seen it.

Ivy agreed. She said, "Great idea guys. Let's live it up this summer!"

That summer, as Ivy referred to it, not the August holidays anymore, that summer, I started hearing defined exclamations circulating in my head. At first it was about semantic trifles and I could distinguish the words as a sequence arising from a small part of my brain and not from the rest of me. Whatever the string of words was, it rang out, in spite of me, on occasion even sounding like Putty. Like when Ivy spoke about summer, my brain said – Summer? Squawk, say Aug-ust break. Say, August break. Squawk. Not summer, not summer.

Ivy chatted with Sam on all the trips we went. He chatted back. She wanted to do outdoorsy, summery things, she said.

"Take pictures of me here next to it," she said, handing me her sleek camera phone and posing next to the bougainvillea tree that was pushing its fuchsia bracts and branches into breathing spaces and against my window again. Always it had to be tamed, trained.

And she always wanted to climb trees.

"Ivy League get down before you fall outta there and break your head," I tried to command her.

She laughed and went higher. "Get up here," she said. "Look Pappo through the window. He combing whatever hair he got left. And wot you calling me Ivy League for, Miss Sourdough?" She scowled.

"Get down!"

"You come up!"

"Down."

"Up."

She tried to settle herself in a crook of a tamarind tree and almost fell out. I got impatient. What if she had fallen out and broken something, or worse? She wanted to relive the past. But we were not seven or eight and everything was not the same. Just about anyone with cataracts could see that. Cat-are-acts, I heard the voice say in my head. She wanted to romanticise and nostalgia-ise everything. Cataracts, romanticise, nostalgee-ise. And she pleaded with me to get my transcripts and apply to a university and get a student visa. "Come na man Ix. It be fun. What you doin' here really? Come with me."

Before she left, she and Sam exchanged gifts. She had bought him a sleek silver pen in a box and he gave her one of those tourist shop key rings in the shape of the Guyana map. Well, with an exclamation mark, I heard my brain exclaim, when have you ever given me a present Samuel Reid. The last thing you gave me was a colouring book when I was seven and your mammy made you bring it. And even then it was only one book for Ivy and me. That was all. That and that stinking wood-chippy old bear from the fair. From the fair. On a luck and chance. Not even meant for me, Samuel Reid, Junior. Junior, which is a part of your name, by the way. I *can* call you Junior if I want. It *is* your name after all, you old hypocrite. I heard all of this clearly in my head and I sat there feeling small and terrible as if on a blade of grass, bending towards all these unmanageable feelings, hating myself and my sour, wanting to be better. To be transparent and proactive like Ivy and oblivious and ambitious like Sam. I didn't want to be the lime bearer, my only quality – sour.

Ivy had brought presents for the rest of us too. Several large ones for everyone – like a jumbo box of chocolates, pot holders, a wad of cash for Pappo and Ganee. She'd wrapped everything carefully, thoughtfully and my heart warmed a little. She handed me a gold toned oval-faced watch with multi-coloured stones around the face. I studied the colours of the stones as they appeared in sequence— turquoise, scarlet, dandelion, lime green, lavender; turquoise, scarlet, dandelion ...

I replaced the pretty watch in its box and left it on my vanity. Sour doesn't deserve pretty.

It rained on the way back from the airport. When the bus turned into our old street in Peaside, all the trees and houses sagged. The whole scene was outdated and poor. Nobody would pay a cent for it even on a postcard. It started choking me all at once, the scene with all the potholes in the road. The potholes that if you were kind enough you drove around slowly to avoid splashing pedestrians or cyclists. And I wished with all the blood in my heart that I was on the plane too. That I was Ivy or with Ivy and going, to a contemporary place on the map, with a metropolis and a breathing dream, where the rain would not be damp and archival like here but fresh and crisp and thriving. Where the pulse of things wouldn't be so slow.

The first thing I saw when I walked into my bedroom was the crystal vase, broken into three pieces this time. I super-glued the pieces together. Then I skipped dinner, went to bed and pulled the sheet over my head.

All night rain hammered on our aluminium roof.

In the middle of the night the phone rang me awake. Pap went downstairs and answered. I stood by the stairs craning my neck.

"Yes Ives, you reach in? Everything go okay. Good, yes. Rest up now. Talk tomorrow."

I tiptoed back to bed. Hid my head under the pillow.

Pap knocked softly.

"Ivy reach," he said through the door.

"Hmm," I groaned, feigning sleep and nonchalance, holding my chest, struggling to keep the raging lime storm in one spot.

22

Tell me Telmond, Should I Go?

At the city library during my breaks, I started obsessing over a book series. It's nice to have someone to talk to from books, I thought. I whispered to the three exploring brothers in the *Safari Series* and the *Amazon Series* by J.M. Greniff, and I went with them on their adventures inside the books. At nights, I stayed awake for hours walking about my room, crossing rivers and savannah with Telmond, the eldest Safari boy, calling him Tel and sometimes pretending to be in love. I imagined all sorts of scraps and scrapes that he'd gotten himself into and each time I saved him, Tel. I walked around my room, grabbing at posts and walls, telling him I'd got him and that he would be fine, bandaging his jungle wounds while we discovered new birds and recorded them in a journal. I'd hit upon an immutable friendship with that Tel. School doesn't teach you how to make friends from books. It's a secret they keep to themselves, the school people. But I discovered the secret at the same time that I discovered real friendships and other things were not really real.

Once Tel and I leapt from the top of a tall waterfall and plunged into the clearest freshest pool. When I surfaced, the idiot was not to be seen. Frantically I scanned the water while the waterfall droned on behind me. Tel? He must've hit his head on a rock somewhere in the plunge basin, I imagined. I imagined that underneath the water was clean, that the shapes distorted but there was no fear. When I surfaced, I spotted some motion in the water. Tel was kicking limply and trying to stay afloat. I swam up to him, dragged him to the rocks. That evening under the stars, Tel, looking up at me said, 'Thank God you came when you did, I swear my life was flashing before me.' 'Yeah,' I said, 'I dunno what I'd do without you.'

(Ivy emailed to say she was almost done with her degree but wanted to get on an exchange program and finish her last semester at another university to experience a new environment. Pap spent hours on the phone discussing options with her. Mam asked when she was coming home again.

But never mind that.)

Tel used to convince me to climb skyscraper hotels, fifteen floors up to retrieve an emerald that was stolen and return it to its rightful owner. 'You couldn't get me to go up there, strapped in or not,' I told him. 'Sure I could,' he said, that Tel. Three times I lived in that scene. The first time we climbed I was competent, swinging on my rope like a Jamie Ann Bond and way ahead of Tel I was, so that I could look down and smile at him. The second time Tel lost his footing and I lowered myself quickly to scramble him up. I was good at things like that, you see. The third time I spiralled down rapidly, my rope tightening too much and squeezing my chest. Tel saved me. 'I swear my life was flashing before me,' I said to him. 'Yeah,' he said, 'I dunno what I'd do without you.'

(Ivy said she was going to yet another state with her friends for a short break. Pap quizzed her about the details before agreeing that she could go.

But, whatever.)

By now Tel was going to travel with the circus for four months – one third of the year. He was going to walk the tightrope. 'Say you'll come with me,' he said, his eyes twinkling in his head. Today he had wavy shoulder length dark brown hair. 'And what do you want me to come and do?' I asked. 'Do anything you please.' 'I do not please,' I said and he cajoled, 'You do, oh say you do. You can sell popcorn or be the circus photographer.' 'Ahh, I don't know,' I said, pretending I didn't want to go, and thinking how marvellously visible I was to Tel. 'Come with me,' he insisted, 'you must.' In the end, I went. We performed in three countries in four months, doing shows every night for weeks at a time. It was the most magnificent time of my whole life.

(One day Sam said that his father was encouraging him to come live with him.)

When I heard that I went to sit in the hammock under the trees in Ole Pap's yard and Telmond and I went off to sing in a choir. Tel said we'd go on a tour of Europe. We sang in the most echoing of halls, with the best acoustics flattering our voices as they made a mark on the old spaces of the old world. Sometimes on the tour, Tel would sneak a violin out from the instruments' trailer and play tunes for me in parks in the city under the stars. Fantastic fellow.

(Ganee Gwenny came outside with a letter in her hand. She sat with me in the hammock, where she didn't know that Tel was sitting too, so he got up. What a good sport that Tel is. Ganee sat with me. Did I know that several years ago Uncle Winnie had asked her and Pappo to come live with them? Did I know that they had said no but uncle still filed the papers so they could come? "Nobody ever told me," I said, my heart plummeting to a universal hole as I looked around for Telmond to hold on to. "Well," Ganee said, "we still not going live there. We born and grow here. But we thinking to go see Winnie, Elaine and Kim. We never see her you know. And imagine she's we grandchild too. We not gon take long. Soon we come back." Of all the people in the world who I thought would never let me out of their sight, not even for a second, were my own Ganee Gwenny and Pappo Harro. Ganee, who I'd stayed all those extra days with, after Ivy, Pap and Mam had filed over to our new house so unceremoniously. Ganee whose arthritis immobilised her so often that I volunteered to be her hands and feet whenever she needed. And Pappo who, I helped every single day to water his plants because they were so many for him to keep up now. Pappo who, when I found his old sewing machine in the tool shed and asked him about it, went outdoors and tinkered with the old tractor, so that I followed and kept him company until he was done pouring his feelings out into the old stalled engine. Yes, these two too – Ganee and Pappo, packed their bags and went. They spent five and a half months. That's almost a whole year, I thought. Kim didn't want them to come back. She was thrilled at the prospect of ready-made grandparents. During that time, Sam's grampappy watched over Pappo's garden. He picked the tomatoes, peppers and ochro. When he came to deliver them, he spoke to Pappo on the phone about the garden. Pappo and Ganee weren't even back for Christmas and old Mr. Reid had to gift just three of us all the yams instead. We had yam balls, yam pies, yam bakes, yam cakes.

But never mind that.)

Tel used to bring me flowers every day for all of the five and a half months. Great guy! 'Let's go climb the ladder that leads into the clouds,' he said. 'Let's go sit on that fluffy cloud yonder. Oh and let's take a sandwich too.' 'Marvellous,' I said, 'we can just pop these tomato slices in.'

(For his Practical exams, Sam kept leaving to fly to different islands. One day, after being in and out of the country for twelve weeks straight, I saw him coming through the gate with a package in his hand. So I snuck through the back door, glided along the backyard and hid behind the ixora hedge that Pappo and I had grown and trimmed over the years.

"She just been here," Mam was saying, "Ixora?"

I remained motionless behind my hedge.

When I came in Mam said where was I, that Sam was just here and brought me a package of souvenirs from several Caribbean islands.)

I told Telmond, 'Stand over there and pretend to be Sam. I want to say some things to him.' Telmond changed his hair and the colour of his eyes and skin and stood in front of me. 'Make your brows a little thicker, I said. Good, that's it. Then I reeled out my monologue. 'It would have been nice to tell me Sam where and when you were going all these weeks gone by, and it would've been nice to send me, Sam photos of when you got there. It might even have been nice to pretend to ask me along to one of your trips, Samuel Reid, Jr. even though we both know you'd be working and it wouldn't be practical or ethical, but still just to ask would've counted, or for you to say perhaps you wished that I could come would've done it Sam.' Telmond giggled. 'That Sam sure deserved it,' he said, and changed himself again.

(Ivy drove to Canada to meet Ganee and Pappo at Uncle Winnie's and she met Aunty Elaine and Kim for the first time. They journeyed about a lot and sent us photos on email. "What is she like, cousin Kim?" I asked Ivy. "Oh she be such a chill pill, nicer than her photos and all," Ivy said, "Says she wants to meet you. Says she'll visit Guyana sometime, experience the country of her heritage. You know, family tree and blood and all that." Aloud I said, "Oh wow!" Inside I said, and what good can come from that? And I hated my resentment and hated myself. Hated the old lime.)

Telmond said, 'Shake it off old girl, you can be quite beastly when you want to you know?' I told him, 'Go away Mister Small Talk, I'm getting real tired of you.' And he went.

(Just before Christmas, Sam came with his grand news. Sam, who, I thought for sure would be my own kindred spirit, always at the back street in old man Reid's old wood house, never going on something as luxurious as a vacation – that same Sam, he came and said he was going to visit his father for a few weeks and would be visiting Ivy too and did we have anything to send for her. Also he was carrying her share of the souvenirs he'd brought for her from the islands. I jumped when he said that, and hoped nobody noticed. I thought, how fair and just of you to get us both the same souvenirs Sam. There really is no difference between Ivy and me after all. None whatsoever. I handed him a wooden jewellery box I'd bought Ivy.

"I've been keeping this for her," I said in my carefully modulated external voice, "Would you carry it please?"

To Ivy, I wrote in a carefully modulated hand on a sticky note, To Ivy – Happy Christmas. With twinship and love, Ixie.

"No problem," he said.

And left.)

Before the school term ended, Cappy, with Onesy and Twosy who on a haphazard schedule had still been sneaking into Suzie's house and learning some of the lessons that I'd half-heartedly leave there for them, came to me with a plan. Cappy said that I must come to his school and teach because then I could make the school threaten his pappy if they were absent from class. He heard on the radio that if parents didn't send their children to school, they could get in some kind of trouble. He couldn't sneak off before dawn anymore because now they had cows and his father collared him if he didn't take the cows to graze.

"Me? Teach? At Zekerheid Primary? No way," I said.

"Look." He held up a test paper that said fifty per cent.

Telmond appeared with an attaché case and a tie and said, 'Teaching sounds like a splendid adventure.' I turned to him in my head and said, 'Shut up Telmond, You're not my advisor. You're turning me into a real basket case.'

(Sam returned with a good many elaborate gifts from Ivy for us and handed them out as she'd directed. His digital camera was filled with pictures which he showed to Mam and Pap and most certainly to his grampappy and mother and all his friends at the hangar.

"Come see Ixie," Pap called.)

I snuck out and hung around my ixora hedge with Tel for an hour, then returned indoors.

Somebody had left the digital camera on the table. Finally, I picked it up, swallowed and pressed the power button. Tel came up beside me. 'Let's have a look see,' he said. My hands trembled. It's nothing really, I said to myself. It's everything, I changed my mind. 'Hurry up let's have a look,' Tel said. There were pictures of Sam and his mother on the day that he left, with Sam's forearm titling awkwardly into the frame as he held the camera. More photos of Sam alone in the plane, in front of skyscrapers, beside fast food joints. Several photos of Sam and a man to whom Sam bore a sharp resemblance and who I vaguely remembered criticising pasture culture. Many photos of Sam and some youngsters, probably his new-found siblings and their friends, some startlingly pretty friends with cat eye make-up and chandelier earrings with their grubby little arms around Sam. Then came the first photo of Sam and Ivy standing in front of a restaurant, with Ivy doing bunny ears behind Sam's head and grinning. It felt like a cricket ball hit a limey hole smack through my stomach and flew right out my back. A string of photos of Sam and Ivy followed.

Sam and Ivy in winter hats and scarves, Sam and Ivy in sweaters and coats, in Rockefeller Center, in a buggy ride, beside tall Christmas trees with giant balls the size of their heads. Making new memories in a glamorous square, with enough distance between them and this emptying backwater. I shut the camera off. 'Going for a walk then?' Tel said from behind my shoulders. 'Why not?' I answered, without moving my lips. I replaced the camera. 'Tell me Telmond,' I said, 'should I go?' 'Of course,' he said, 'if you must. Survival and all that, old girl.'

Here I was, Ixora Mara – a Sourhouse, marking time in this brown-water land, behind this grey old seawall, marking time in a new world country that had outlived its sweet usefulness to the world. Marking time all my life, a part of something so small it would never be known, and when it *was* known it was only because something in it had imploded upon something else in itself. A country so unusually unbalanced you could see from the air a narrow strip of lights like a strand of fairy bulbs, where people lived, set against the immeasurable rainforest, Ivy'd said. Here where I would have to spend my life on a board of inertia, a plank that had fallen off the platform of the world stage. Marking time, with nobody but my own self to blame.

'That's settled then,' Telmond sneaked up behind me and said, 'Quick march.' I said, 'Boy, I thought I told you to go away.' 'Righto then,' he said and vanished.

(Ivy's email said she was graduating and would we like to come. I thought, maybe if I really wanted to go, I could stop marking time in the brown waters, on this loose floor board, and just go and see what could happen, as "way leads on to way," you know, Robert Frost and all that. So together we went as a family to apply for visitors' visas to attend Ivy's graduation. Two days later, Pap and Mam came home with their visas. I didn't get one. I didn't want to go anyway,

I willed myself to think. Pap said that Mam could go and he would stay with me.

"Why?" Ivy asked, "The old Ixoranous Rex be alright for a week or two, gee, she can eat over by Ganee if she too lazy to cook. Geesh Pap come on man."

"Sure, go on. It's only two weeks. Is no time," I heard my outside voice manage to say. But it was. It was a lot of time.

Pap told me to go and stay over by Ganee and Pappo.

"Delighted," I said and packed my bag for my epic return next door.

Pap furrowed his brow at me.)

I moved back in my old room that Ganee was now using to store onions, flour and rice. Replaceable with a bag of onions, I thought, well!

During the time that Pap and Mam were away, our house would've stood empty if I hadn't decided to let Cappy, Onesy and Twosy sneak in and study there. I planned two weeks' worth of work and left it on the dining table, with coloured pencils and paper and I left the door unlocked, so they could go in as they pleased. Onesy and Twosy enjoyed drawing and colouring. Cappy's work improved and I couldn't tell if I was more impressed with his ability to learn or my own surprising ability to teach. He left one of his marked test papers from school for me to see. Seventy-five per cent, it said.

One evening Pappo, with the latest wrinkle growing on his face, brought out a game of Monopoly.

"Pappo, where you get this?" It looked like the game with Annie-Lou's drop of blood.

"Find it in a bag o' ole tings," he said, peeping out because the gate had slammed.

Sam was dropping off a bag of coal from his grampappy.

"Junior boy, come play dis game," Pappo told him.

"What's dat?" Sam stuck his head in the door.

I kept my head down sorting the paper money into the tray.

"Alright," Sam said.

Ganee came too, sitting painfully with her arthritic knees, putting on her thick round-rimmed bifocals, and the four of us sat around the living room playing. I couldn't take my eyes off the spot where Annie-Lou's blood had never really come off. Annie-Lou, who had spoken to me once on the phone in the past decade, to say "Whaz goin' down Iggs? Jus' call me Ann."

When the game was over and Sam had won, I packed the pieces back in the box and went out on the long low veranda. Suzie's house was in shadow, same as it was on my seventh birthday. The house beside Suzie's was also in shadow. My own house on the left, as well as other houses down the street were in shadow. Small Spokes' grammy's house was dark because she went to bed early and Cappy's family's house was dark because they had no electricity. Peaside had grown into a land of shadows. Miaplambo, shadow monster, must be pleased with himself, I thought.

"Goin' Ixu," said Sam, coming up beside me and looking at the stars. It was the first time he had called me anything like Ixu. Ixu sounded like a beautiful alternate person that I could get used to being if he wanted me to. A fairy queen. His arm brushed against my shoulder and a crackling electric jolt came like at the fair a long time ago.

"I like flyin' in the stars," he said.

"Why?"

"'Cus...the air nice, the whole sky just like a wide house you know?"

"Oh."

His cologne floated through the breeze under the stars.

"Why you always do that?" he asked.

"What?"

"Tilt your head and press your ear like that?"

"To get the sour out."

"Get what?"

"Never mind."

We stood for a few more seconds, shoulder to arm before his arm wrenched away from mine as Ganee came out and asked him to carry two breadfruits for his grampappy and mother.

"Thanks," Sam said, "G'nite then."

"Yea," I said clutching my arm, feeling the glow of the bold stars in my chest subdue, like fairy bulbs when they're coming round to the slow dim part of the cycle.

(The next day Sam departed to co-pilot another series of interior and Caribbean flights transporting local and regional produce. He'd bring Ganee guava jam from somewhere else for her to try, he said. Whatever, Samuel Reid, Junior, whatever! Nobody wants your stupid jam.)

"Know anything more about your ancestor, the woman who painted that?" I asked Ganee, pointing at *Keeper of the House* while I sat at the old kitchen table eating sponge cake.

"Naa, nobody remember her name. All dem remember is she used to know to draw and paint."

She was making food parcels to send to the community centre for children.

"Tie these up on yuh bike and drop them off for me eh? And help me take these to dem three small children up the street," she said, meaning Cappy and sisters.

I collected the packages and went up to the painting. It had unusual brush strokes, not refined and well thought-out but not scared either, just deliberate.

Ganee pushed her spectacles up her nose, pulled out a bench and climbed, puffing and grunting.

"Ganee, what you climbin' up there for?!" I shouted, with my heart rocking, as her bench tilted and I couldn't reach out to steady it because of the parcels piled in my hands.

"Here," she said, and wincing from knee pains, climbed down and stuck the painting under my armpit.

(When Mam and Pap returned they told us about their trip. Showed us pictures of Ivy's graduation and the places they went. I couldn't believe it was my Mam and Pap with their faces peering out from pictures of the metropolis. They looked out of place and stranger still for seeming at home there. When I asked when Ivy was coming back home, they said that she wasn't for now, that she had gotten a work visa and would stay on for some time. That was when I knew for sure that she was lost or found, depending on where you were standing in the world's mind. She even looked a little like Kim in her pictures, her tight bushy curls flat-ironed and flowing out silky from beneath her graduation cap. And she had Mam's jade green butterfly pendant pinned to her gown. Mam's wooden jewellery box was empty now. She'd given Ivy the butterfly and me, the emerald turtle. Why should I have had to get the turtle, I wondered. Ancient and slow.

"Come with us Ixoranous Rex," said Ivy on the phone, calling me by my latest given title, "We renting a new apartment and working downtown. You could go to school right here. Get a job near us too and rent with us."

"Us who?"

"Me and Amanda."

"Which Amanda?"

"From high school."

I hung up the phone.)

'Telmond, how about you just come back.'

23

A Hundred Empty Houses

I went for afternoon strolls alone. Though sometimes Telmond appeared in waistcoat, pocket watch and walking cane. We'd pass the community garden and spot the tomatoes under Old Lady Bargains' green thumb. 'Let's courage-up and ask for her real name,' Telmond said. I nodded at Old Lady Bargains. 'Not now with the shenanigans Telmond. I can manage alright today. I just want to have a good think in my head.' So Telmond boarded a soap bubble and floated off into the afternoon sky.

On my walks, I'd counted a hundred empty houses in Peaside. But I was certain my count had been wrong, so lifting the trapfloor of the doll's house, I ferreted out the old pocket-sized notebook that had my sketches of the Miaplambo and I counted afresh, beginning with Suzie's house, because where else would I start. One. The one next to Suzie's, two. The one obliquely opposite the one next to Suzie's, three. My own, four. Ganee and Pappo's, five. I drew up a tally. Then I stopped, erased that tally and started again, this time categorising the empty houses into three kinds. Those truly empty like Suzie's. Those partially empty, in which someone had gone and left an empty space but in which people still lived – like mine and Ganee's. And those temporarily empty, their occupants away on vacation or work. I drew up three columns and continued down the street, counting.

When people saw me with the notepad and pencil, they bolted the opposite way. The gossipy neighbour who'd let loose a discussion thread that I was a loony turning into an old maid without chick, child or man, hustled inside and wrapped some wire around her gate to keep it shut. People get their feelers out if they think they're going to see themselves reflected on paper. I smirked. Maybe I should go away to university and become a social scientist so I could walk around with writing equipment making people nervous. After all, I needed to start doing something quantifiable with my life, not just float about Peaside, wrestling with its rhyme and rhythm.

My recount yielded the same results. There were a hundred empty houses in Peaside. The deeper I pondered this, the more I felt the hollowness of the empty houses transferring to me, like a sour seeping under my skin and I tried to imagine whether wheeling my bags out of Peaside would release me from the sour. It must, I thought. After all, didn't the old lime belong in and to Peaside in the first place?

I passed the house that once belonged to puffy-cheeked sour-faced Mr Crapaud – the man that Ivy'd teased was my predecessor. I remember him as a walking breathing permanent scowl. He was sour about everything from azaleas to children, candy to crab vendors, carburettors to zooplankton. Then one day, Mr Crapaud boarded a plane and left Peaside for good without a goodbye. Beyond that, I'd refused to think of him. Why should I have thought of him? I was not his successor. There was no such thing as a successor of some old lime. And even if there was, it wasn't me. I hoped everyone knew that by now, I thought, as I passed Cappy's shack.

And then I decided.

I'd apply for a job at Zekerheid Primary after all. Teaching paid more than the City Library and I could save enough to start my journey across the ocean. And the whole world would soon see, that I wasn't going to be in Peaside perpetually, that I was Somebody, not some old lime.

I stood my old doll Pastel outside of the doll's house and turned her to face North. The only thing was, I'd have to tell Ivy I wasn't keen on living under the same roof as Amanda. The same Amanda who'd made my youth waste away. I wondered where the other three girls in the old ring affair were. I had not forgotten their names or faces. It still nagged at me that I hadn't made good on my promise to Pap to find the culprit. I remembered Richard too.

And then in a fresh burst of Inspeck S'marting, I was pulling up social media websites, searching for the three old suspects.

I scrolled through the profile of Girl Number One, the one whose daddy had paid up and punished her from going to Disney; she'd migrated. She seemed to be a model, with her pouty glossy lips, current Parisian fashion and nails of all shapes, designs and lengths. I mused about the day Ivy and I had called each girl. This was a flustered girl, upset she couldn't go to Disney, a girl coddled by her parents. It didn't seem likely she had taken the ring. Surely, she would want something prettier, more suited to her dainty hands. Besides she could get anything she wanted and going to the trouble of scooping up somebody's chunky rock would've been too much of a hassle for Miss I-can't-go-to-Disney. It couldn't have been her, I thought.

I looked up Girl Number Two, the one who'd said that her mammy would kill her. Well here she was, still alive and working somewhere sharp it seemed. There were a few scattered photos of her in suits, smiling, her hair combed back, not a flyaway strand. Here was a girl who knew her mother's sacrifices, who understood the need to work hard and not become like her daddy as she had said. She didn't seem to be one who would risk taking someone else's property without fear of consequences. It couldn't have been her.

Maybe I should apply for a job in the investigative services, I thought, my heart kicking up its old detective thrills.

So I searched for the third girl, the one I always referred to as Miss My-daddy-a-lawyer. It seemed that she too had become a lawyer. I scrolled through the feed of her endless graduation reel, with her gown and cap and her parents and siblings gathered around her. Here was a girl who by high school was already treading a path her father had cleared and who understood the value of making good choices and the workings of justice. Unless she was conducting some sort of social experiment on the consequences of thievery, being branded a thief didn't seem high on her list of priorities.

Over and over I scrolled up and down the profiles of the three suspects and the more I thought about it, just as Ivy had felt, the less likely it seemed that either of them had stolen Amanda's mother's diamond ring. I sent them friend requests.

But before logging out, I couldn't resist searching for Richard. There were many Richards but at last I hit upon a profile of a dashing man, and a girl with long eyelashes beside him, standing in front of the Eiffel Tower. Oh well, I thought, as an odd feeling crept up on me. And before I knew it I couldn't shut down the laptop. I was searching for everyone I could remember. I found Frederick, his timeline loaded with photos of himself and a tiny baby and someone who obviously was his wife, but not the same girl for whom he was pining and dying in his youth on campus. He had posted wedding pictures too. Good for you, Frederick old boy, beating that XM cologne. I searched for Suzie too and looked through many Suzies. I tried Suzannah, but there were too many Suzannahs and I didn't know what Suzie looked like now so I gave up. After that, I felt like a deflated balloon. Everyone was out there, doing a magnificent two-step waltz with life while I sat around Peaside, deflating. And never even having solved the mystery I'd vowed I would.

I wondered who else in our class could have taken the ring. I wondered after Amanda's mother and whether she still glided and swayed. I looked up Amanda. Ivy was in some of Amanda's photos in their apartment. I contemplated whether this was an apartment in which I could live comfortably. It seemed so. But I'd get rattled within three feet of that Amanda. I continued scrolling down her profile, making quick work of the photos of her with her boobs in the camera and very close close-ups of her butt in tights, shorts, bikinis. She looked a little like her mother did when she came to our school years ago. Here was an enabled entitled girl, I thought. She had never made a fuss about the ring. It was her father who did. Her mother too had remained quiet. Amanda herself had never accused any of the girls in her circle. Or anyone in the class. She never looked worried or panicked to have lost it. She never seemed regretful for all Ivy and I and the other girls had to go through. She always kept a straight face when the ring was mentioned. And she never seemed to search for it. Not even when I was going about the class Inspeck S'marting around. Here she was now, posing with her neck and ears and hands laden with jewellery which I couldn't tell was artificial or real. Amanda was the one always with the real penchant for jewellery, not the other girls. I studied how she covered her neck in layers of necklaces. There was a certain flow about Amanda and the way she wore her accessories, a world-wiseness, a notion of economic shrewdness, a knowledge of the momentum of the West. I suppose that is the area of grown-up finesse that drew Ivy to her company in high school. And that was when I saw it. At first I thought I was imagining it, as I was prone to imagining things. But when I zoomed in on the photo of Amanda with the layers of necklaces and rings I saw it with my real eyeballs. No, that couldn't be it, I thought, pulling up the trapfloor of the doll's house and locating a yellowing scrunched up paper, the one on which Ivy had sketched the ring. I zoomed in on one of the rings on Amanda's finger. It was a round diamond set between two sets of three pronged leaves. The sketch and the photo matched.

I dialled Ivy at once.

"You better talk to Amanda about it," I said.

But Ivy never got back to the topic. She left the past in the past, put her head down and studied and worked. She started sending money for Ganee and Pappo to hire someone to do the large load of monthly washing because Ganee's arthritis was flaring up daily. She kept asking if we needed anything, if we had everything. She sent gadgets and appliances for Mam and Pap. Mam enjoyed her electric chopper. Pap played games on his iPad and googled things.

Then out of the blue, Ivy came home for a week, slept the first two days and looked about for exciting ventures. She brought me brochures from several universities and circled programs.

"And Amanda?" I pressed, "I told you a hundred times to ask her about it."

"Yes," Ivy said, "Said she had the ring all the time."

"All the – how – how could she?"

She shrugged. "Dunno. Said she was gonna sell it and buy a video game for her boyfriend, but didn't bother once everyone got in trouble."

"Didn't bother? Didn't both–"

"How you get dat painting?" Ivy pointed at *Keeper of the House*.

"Ganee gimme it. But we gotta tell her parents, Amanda's. So they can pay the girls back. And us too."

"Her mother knew. Eventually."

"Her moth– What the –"

She shrugged and pointed to a University. "This one expensive. But you gon like it. I got some savings could help with first semester tuition. Then you could get a job at –"

"But we gotta tell her father. We gotta tell the other girls and their parents. We gotta tell Mam and Pap and get everybody money back. Or at least tell everybody the truth. Speak up na man. And why you still room-mating with her? You dunno nobody else in the whole world?"

"Because Miss Mara, in the great wide world outside itty bitty incy wincy Peaside, it be better to keep company with a marabunta whose sting you know than a crab whose claws ya can't imagine. But okay, when you come we gon go get our own apartment. I done tell her."

"Alright. But –"

"I going and get a tennis roll man. We don't get them fresh up there." She went her way.

At the airport, everyone was sullen again but this time I felt full and warm.

"See you soon," Ivy said, bumping my shoulder and wheeling her little bag.

"Yeah," I said, thinking to buy a little bluegreen bag for my own journey.

The next day my elbow bumped the crystal vase. This time it re-cracked in the same three places as before and into a fourth new piece. It might not be able to hold water for the flowers and vines again. But I super-glued the four pieces together and carried on applying for the teaching job at Zekerheid Primary so I could earn some cash while waiting on my applications abroad, and also so I could ease my conscience by keeping an eye on Cappy's progress without having to worry about spraining my ankle sneaking up Suzie's stairs and standing stupidly in her musty dismantling house before the crack of dawn. Or worry about Cappy's father, who one day I spied in the distance bull-charging at me.

Cappy, breathless and worried like a little old man, had given me the heads-up that his pap had a hint I'd been teaching them. So when I spied the man bulldozing towards me, I dodged down a side street and took the longer route home. This taking the long way home to avoid a bully felt all too familiar and I was just burning in shame at being grown and still being gutsless when I saw the man puffing towards me again. Peaside had many intersecting streets, long and short. You could weave up and down any which way and eventually find yourself in front your gate. So there was the man bulldozing towards me and I doing about-turns, cutting down short cross-streets and walking back up short cuts in circles. When I was sure the man couldn't see me, I started running – not believing this was my own life – until I met my front gate. Me, a terrified woman, running from a human bull. But that wasn't everything that rattled me about my precious village. This bull wasn't the only one after me for no good reason. By the end of my first week on the new job, my life had descended into an even more bewildering battle.

On Monday morning, I arrived at Zekerheid Primary to a locked gate. If Mr Fred were here the gate would already be open, I thought. The sensation of a bad cologne rose to my nostrils and I gripped the chain link fence and pressed the sensation back into a dark deep trapfloor somewhere. I peered through the chain link fence, trying to identify where Ivy and I used to stand in the sun during assembly.

After a while, an enormous man appeared, fiddled with some keys, flung the gates wide, not even bothering to open them at right angles. He went up to the doors; the scuff marks from his shoes were visible at the bottoms of the doors where he must've kicked them in every day. Mr Fred never kicked in doors. I followed the man into the large upper flat where he was flinging windows half open and I looked out.

Downstairs, little people in umber tunics or pants were arriving. They looked like ants, crawling in. And before the day was over I saw a little girl I thought looked like Ivy, a boy, who from a distance resembled Sam when we still called him Junior and others who I could swear looked exactly like my old classmates. It was a déjà vu, only that's not the precise word. It was like a palimpsestic chalkboard. A layering. Or a double consciousness. No, a repetitiveness. A cycle. A continuity. A clarity. A madness? And amidst all that, I couldn't find my place in the grand scheme of things. I thought of quitting on the first day, wondering how Miss Pam used to simply appear in front a chalkboard with such command and finesse. I was nothing like her – my teacher-suits fit chunky, my body grew flustered and sweaty, my words crawled at a snail's pace from my brain through my lips, and my only prominent make-up was my regular sour scowl. I was not who I wanted to be when I grew up. It seemed that I had as hard a time accepting myself, as did everyone else, I thought, as I spied Miss March bulldozing towards me.

I remembered her from when I was a student. She had the same grating voice and high nose. She was older now but not so old as to be ancient. She must have been younger than my current age when she started teaching, when we had thought her old. Is this how my students would see me now? Gracious, I wasn't even thirty and my primary school memories were still alive in my head.

"Madam, madam," she snapped, hitting at the desk with a ruler and making me jump, "Get your class to stop acting like mad coots."

"Oh Ms March! It's me Ixora Harry, from long ago. You might not remember me. Do you? I'm happy to be back," I half-truthed, extending my hand for a hearty shake.

"That makes one of us," she said, ignoring my hand and launching the first cannonball of her gratuitous siege against me.

24

The Ghosts of the Empty Houses

Routine rolled round in Peaside. On weekdays, my pupils and I drew maps and studied the solar system, observed plants and made dioramas, recited poetry and broke words into syllables. On the weekends, I went to market and church and ironed my clothes for Mondays again. And every day, the empty and emptying houses in the street trained their eyes on me luring, daring, scaring me. At first, I tried training my eyes back on them. But I couldn't lure, dare, scare them back. And I only ended up feeling like an ant on a blade of grass, bending with an uneasy consciousness towards their vast haunting universe. So I kept my head straight and pressed on with my routine.

One day in the market, as per routine, I tripped over Salimanto's foot. For over fifteen years he'd extended his feet in the path by the orange stand, and for fifteen years I'd tripped over them.

"Please fah ah lil help," he said and put out his hand.

"You nearly made me fall on my face again." I was surprised to hear my voice come out so coarsely and strong, so accusing, defensive, bold. It must be because I was soon going away, I thought. That is what must be giving me this new energy, this power.

"Is hey I live. Where you want me put me foot?" said he, attitude of entitlement intact.

I handed out a twenty dollar note between my thumb and forefinger, trying not to touch his germy hand. Beggars, no matter how carefully you try to hand them a note, always manage to brush their germy little hands on yours when they grab the money. Not Salimanto though. He was always mindful of using his thumb and forefinger to collect his bill, as if he knew you scorned his estate, and he wanted to let you know that he was mindful of your feelings about him and also because he didn't want to trouble you with his germs. And most importantly, probably because he didn't want *your* germs. I handed him his note. He picked it off with his thumb and forefinger and I went my way.

Thirty seconds later, I retraced my steps.

"Listen," I said, lowering my voice conspiratorially. He looked up, puzzled, unused to conspiratorial tones. The sun was getting in his eyes. It was about five in the afternoon when the sun was sharp and got into your eyes just before dipping right down.

"Look, listen here," I said again.

He didn't say anything, just listened, didn't even give me an acknowledgement to go on. I could see that I would have to do everything on my own.

"You don't have to live out here all the time. I know somewhere you could sleep at nights but listen, you can't say nothin' to nobody 'bout it," I crouched down and whispered.

"Aaay?"

"You hearin' me? I know somewhere you could go when the night time come. But you just have to come quiet and don't tell nobody."

"Aaay? Wey?"

"Look, you can jus' follow me at a good distance, and when I reach the place, I gon stand up and yawn and stretch out my hand toward it, like so, look." I brought my palms together, fingers interlaced, then turned outwards towards the world. "You see?"

Salimanto didn't look like he was going to co-operate.

"Listen, I not trapping you or nothing. Is just I know a place dat nobody don't use for a hundred years now and you can use it in secret in the nights so you can have a kinda house."

He squinted at me and rolled his twenty dollar notes slowly. Then he put a rubber band on them and got up.

"Well just follow me then," I said.

And turning around one last time I said, "But you have to promise not to tell nobody, or is trouble for me and you. You hear?"

"Yea," he said, shaking his head now and warming up to the conspiracy.

When I reached my house, I walked a few paces down the street and facing the opposite side, yawned and flipped my interlaced palms out towards Suzie's old house. Then, in case the gossipy neighbour was watching, I yawned and stretched towards the sky, dawdled, then walked the few paces back home.

I came out on our veranda and looked about for Salimanto but he was sitting behind some bushes, probably waiting for darkness to fall. I kept watch until I saw a shadow hurrying up the rotten stair boards and disappearing into the shadowy square.

Next morning, I rose early to see how Salimanto had fared in the empty house but there was no sign of him. Like an expert co-conspirator, he must've risen early and slipped out.

The conspiracy was so exhilarating that I bobbed and whistled and smiled so much at work that Ms March came over to let me know that I worked in an educational institution, not a rum shop and that I must cut the whistling out at once.

Days and nights passed without me catching sight of Salimanto in the empty house. I would still see him in the market propped up beside the fruit stand but he didn't ask me for twenty dollars anymore, just pulled his feet in, nodded and busied himself with his earnings. And so we went on for many weeks, Salimanto sneaking into Suzie's house to get a roof over his head at nights and sneaking out before dawn, unseen, even by me. And every time I thought of our conspiracy, a little ball of sunshine lit up in my brain. In fact, when I looked into the mirror in the mornings, I thought my skin around my cheeks and under my eyes looked clear and fresh and I was astounded at the level of attractive energy my average face could attain.

Soon a rumour started in Peaside about a house down south being haunted. It took me a while to realise which was the ghost house everyone was talking about. One morning when I was locked out of the school and sitting on a stone waiting because the gatekeeper had forgotten the key as usual, I finally figured it out. It was Suzie's house from which people must have seen a shadow going and coming. I chuckled and snorted, thoroughly amused and was just feeling thrilled at myself for single-handedly stirring Peaside to consciousness, when Cappy came up.

"My pap tear up the school book, look." He held up a mangled text book.

"How could he —"

"Every time he ketch me reading, he say I wasting time and choke me or tear my books."

"He can't do that. I'm going straight to him today."

But Cap pulled the red visor lower over his forehead and started whimpering.

"My mammy say Pappy want me end up just like him, hitting, cussin' my own shadow, minding cow, shovelling and talking sh–"

"I'm going to talk to him."

"He sure kill me and mammy if you go." He shook a bit.

"Alright. Alright. I won't go."

The gateman was coming back. I had to think quickly.

"Look here, listen," I said. I heard the low conspiratorial tones coming on again. "I know somewhere better you could take your books and go study before school and on weekends but you can't tell nobody 'bout it."

"Where?" He raised the visor and looked at me so hopefully that I thought I was in danger of breaking out into the old sudden sobs I'd kept at bay for a long time.

"You know the house next to that house we borrowed to study in last year?"

The cap nodded.

"Well the house next to it is empty. But it newer and must be cleaner. Not so rotten and smelly. You could sneak in there but you can't let nobody see or hear you. You and Onesy and Twosy could put your books there and read. But then you gotta sneak out back quiet and go home."

He bobbed his head at every word.

"Wat you think? That could help?"

The cap bobbing continued.

"Saturday when Pappy go out betting on horse race, I go," he said and then shut up because the gateman was near.

On Saturday, I kept watch from my window. When the street was clear, I saw a small figure make a beeline from behind a bush towards the old gate of the house next to Suzie's. My heart summersaulted.

Cappy pulled the gate but it wouldn't budge.

A donkey cart was rolling and clippity-clopping towards us.

Cappy pushed the gate but it held fast.

The donkey cart came closer.

"Psst Cappy, run."

But one hard push and the gate swung in just as the donkey cart rounded the corner. And I breathed out at last. Cap would get along just fine, I thought, smug at my machinations.

But as I settled down with a book, a "Psst" came through my window.

"Who's there?"

A branch of the mango tree by the side window shook.

"What the —"

Cappy was camouflaged in the tree.

"What you —"

"Shh," he gestured and pointed down.

Below the tree Pap was picking up mangoes. I swallowed and waited. I signalled with open palms to ask Cappy what was wrong. He folded his fingers into a fist and made a clockwise turning motion. I opened my palms again to show I didn't understand. He made the same twisting motion and mouthed something.

"What?" I whispered.

He mouthed again.

It looked like he was saying Roodiver?

"Roodiver?" I mouthed. "What in the world is a roodiv—"

He started spelling, making letters with his hands. S-c-r-e-w-d-r-i ...

"Screwdriver?" I mouthed, puzzled.

He nodded like a bobble head.

I gave a thumbs up and went to get one.

"What you goin' to make there Ix Pix?" Pap said.

"Err ..." I couldn't remember the last time I told Pap a lie. Deceit is a hard thing to master. "Eee ..."

"Full steam ahead then," said Pap, and grinned, not bothering to wait for an answer.

When I came around to the mango tree Cappy was gone.

A glint, a reflection off a mirror slanted at me. Following it, I saw a hand beckoning from the empty yard next to Suzie's. I wondered what my life was coming to, tucked the screwdriver under my shirt, checked the street, checked the window blinds of the gossipy neighbour and sneaked into the empty yard.

"Cappy, what you –"

"House door lock, but we could screw the hinge offa dat garden shed and –"

"Oh come quick then before Pap come round the front of my house and see us," I whispered like a madwoman, echoes of my childhood of standing infront Suzie's empty yard and Pap ponging and Junior holding the staves open and Ivy saying, 'he gon ketch us if you stand up there asking if he gon ketch us' coming back to me all at once. I couldn't believe what I, a grown-up was facilitating. Trespassing. This must be so very wrong or it wouldn't warrant whispers and trembling. Cappy turned his cap backwards and pointed to the hinge that needed unhinging. Lord, I thought, I am becoming unhinged myself. I'm becoming a criminal. My hands shook. I couldn't get the screwdriver to steady. Cappy grabbed it and soon the hinge was off and he was pulling the door out. It was too heavy for him. So I helped drag it and he squeezed through.

"Thanks," he whispered, "Bye."

I tried to see inside the shed but Cappy, in high stealth mode, shooed me away. Then I waited until the street was clear and made a beeline for my front gate, a cycle of relief following.

But later that afternoon, Pap who was making a pantry for our kitchen looked about for his screwdriver.

"Ixo, you finish wit my screwdriver?"

I jumped and clapped my hand to my mouth.

Lord, help me, I had left it beside the garden shed of the empty house next to Suzie's.

"Er ... yes."

"Where it?"

"Uh ..."

I looked outside but people were liming in the street. It would be a while before dusk fell and they dispersed.

"Ermm ..." I disappeared into my room and hid for a while pretending to look.

"Ixie?" Pap called from downstairs.

I swallowed and looked out the window. What to do, what to do. I braced against my door and swallowed. Praying.

"Ixora?"

"Erm ... in a bit Pap."

I dawdled by my window and waited until everyone'd left the street, then I tiptoed out the house. My heart beat in my eardrums. I shot across the street, pushed the gate, sped to the shed and felt around in the grass, wondering if there was a night creature behind the shed, just like when we were little and I'd think the Miaplambo was under the bed and wake Ivy to follow me to pee pee. Yes, it was the same feeling. And I wished she were here now, guarding the gate while my heart racketed about as I felt in the grass for the screwdriver. I found it, snatched it and ran.

But on my way to the gate, I heard whispers coming from inside the empty house and my heart nearly gave out. Could Cappy have found a way inside the house after all and was he up there talking to himself? I decided to run up the stairs and investigate. A stair creaked under my foot.

Ixora Mara, Sourhouse

I paused and listened to see if the person inside had heard me sneak up.

But there were no sounds coming from inside this second empty house.

There were whispers though. And they were coming from Suzie's house!

Salimanto must be talking to himself. How could he be so loud? If I could hear him, other people might too.

The fence between the empty house and Suzie's was chain links and it was torn in many places. I needed to get through and tell Salimanto to whisper softly for goodness sake. No wonder people were saying this house was haunted.

My cheekbones warmed at that, and at myself crawling between chain link fences of empty houses under the stars and having adventures on my own. Ivy and Sam, even Small Spokes, should see me now, I thought. How's this for guts.

On my most precarious of tiptoes, fearing I would plummet in the dark to the end of my life, I made my way up Suzie's rotting stairs, while Salimanto talked to himself. But when I reached the top of the platform, it sounded like two voices. Was Salimanto preparing for an acting career, changing up his voices, doing lines? I couldn't make out the words but the textures of the voices were distinct. Good, gosh, he is good, I thought, giving himself voice lessons and all. Still, if he wanted to keep his empty house, he had to reduce his volume. People would hear him.

I pushed the door, half-terrified that maybe Salimanto was one of those people who I'd seen on TV, those people who had several personalities. What if one of the personalities that didn't know me lunged at me?

My eyes grew accustomed to the outline of Suzie's old, now sagging sofa and the two shoulders and two heads facing away from the door and towards the windows into the street. My eyes flew out of their sockets.

One shadow, the one who appeared to be Salimanto had his arm along the back and around the shoulder of the other and the other person had their head resting on Salimanto's shoulder.

Oh crabs and sardines, I thought, Salimanto has gone and brought a woman into Suzie's empty house!

I stood for a few seconds, embarrassed, trying to decide how to exit this very private family scene. These two may have very well been Suzie's parents and Suzie might have gone to bed. That is exactly what it looked like. There was something intrusive about being there, so I carefully backed away. Salimanto clearly had more dreams and dignity than the streets could afford him. And now that he was housed, his dignity and dreams had started to align.

And he would've been left in peace. Except how could I have known that he had spent some of his beggar's lot on a mop and a broom and an aluminium pail and that these were leaning against the wall? I backed into them. Cladanks!

Salimanto and his lady leapt up.

She shrieked and he said, "Hiiya," and lunged at me like a cat.

"Shh, shh, it's me Ixora," I whisper-talked, trying to untangle my foot from the pointer broom. "It's me."

"Who?"

"Ixora. Harry. From over there. Me. From the market."

"Oh," he said, so caught up with his woman that he had forgotten my name or perhaps he never even knew it at all.

Then he shrunk down a little, probably ashamed about the woman, and uncertain what to do now.

We stood staring at each other, if people could stare at each other in the dark.

"I go now," I said, "I just heard voices, I thought to tell you dat you a bit loud."

"Ya."

Next morning the rumours of hauntings took centre stage and performed.

"Yes, I hear a screaming and ah ain't lyin'," someone said.

"Yuh lie," the other person said.

"Ah swear to gawd I hear it," the first woman said.

"Fuh true?"

"True true story. Ah wake up fuh pee middle night an' den ah hear it plain plain. A scream come out from one ah dem house down back suh." I imagined she was pointing in the direction of Suzie's house.

"Lawd gaawd!" the second voice shrieked and when I turned stealthily to see who it was, the woman was surrendering her palms to the heavens.

"Lil gurl, you na frighten?" the first voice asked and about ten seconds went before I realised it was addressing me.

"Huh?"

"Yuh live right deh, you ain't hear nutting, you ain't frighten?" the gossipy neighbour asked.

"You live right deh?" said someone else, peering at me closely now as if she could learn something about the jumbie just by looking at my face. "Yuh hear anyting?"

"Uh ..." I said, struggling to think of a truth that wasn't too much of a lie, and feeling riotously sour that the empty house was only now haunting Peaside when it had haunted me from its first empty second. "I, uh, I'm not afraid, no," I mumbled, avoiding the question of whether I'd heard anything.

"Oh lawwd, dis chile na frighten," the woman said. "Chile yuh lie."

I shook my head and hurried away before they could think of more questions to ask me, me being so physically close to the action and all. Still, they couldn't dream of how close. Nobody could.

What the sentence was for aiding and abetting trespassing is what I should have looked up before aiding and abetting trespassing. I wished Ivy were here. She would know what to do about Salimanto's new underground family life that I'd facilitated in Suzie's empty house. I did lie to the woman in the street, it seems. I was scared after all. Would Salimanto when caught, give me away? Or would I have to tell him that he couldn't stay anymore, and then might he blackmail me and give me away still? Could I be charged for this? If anyone had told me twenty years ago that it was me who'd bring shame and disgrace to the family, not Ivy, I would've bet them a push-point pencil no. But I would have lost my precious pencil. *I* was the menace machinating the bodily ghosts, as revenge to Peaside and its empty houses for having haunted and soured only me.

25

The Neighbourhood Hero

Now that he had an evening house, Salimanto seemed out of place propped up beside the orange stand. Here was a man with a mop, a broom, an aluminium pail, a roof over his head and a common-law wife. Evening-Salimanto and Broad-daylight-Salimanto were different persons. Why should I tell him that he had to leave his evening house? For twenty years its emptiness taunted me. Wasn't the house itself telling me I should invite Salimanto in? If that house didn't belong to my psyche and *I* couldn't avail it, then what was real in this world? It was my house. It existed in my central vision and took up such expansive space in *my* psyche that there was hardly room for anything else. I was the true keeper of that house, not Suzie, wherever she was, whoever she even was. And if houses were not for living in, then excuse me, what were they for? But I knew that all this was rationalising and that I had no legal right. If Ivy were here she'd know what to do now about this moral descent I'd begun.

By weekend, the hullabaloo about the ghosts had lulled and on Saturday I kept watch to see if Cappy and the sisters would sneak into the yard beside Suzie's. Eventually I saw him and another boy standing by a tree. When he saw me, he looked left and right and beckoned.

"Hear," Cappy panted, "dis is Willy. He ain't got nowhey to study either. Bring he too?"

"What? You can't just bring random pe—"

"He say he wouldn't tell nobody. He gon help me wit Reading. I help he wit Maths. His father can't buy he no books so he could use the ones you lend me. Plus he know how to pick the door lock so we could get in."

"No you can't pick the —"

But Cappy was off. He grabbed his friend's shirt, dragged him out the gate and pushed him across the street. They disappeared behind the dilapidated fence of the empty house beside Suzie's. Onesy and Twosy emerged from a bush and bounded after the boys.

"Cappy you come back here! This is getting outta hand," I whisper-shouted. "Cappy!"

He'll go and bring half a dozen more little brats if I let him keep this up, I thought. And then what? Please, I said in my head, please come home Ivy and tell me what I've done. That house over there was not my house. I was not its keeper. I was nobody. I was a pin. What were they coming to me for to give them permission to trespass on private property?

My sleeping troubles started again, and I wished Mam would stop blending things so loudly and Pap would stop experimenting with that electric saw. My shenanigans would have to boil over soon somehow. Nothing lasts forever. Still we carried on in our routines. At market, Salimanto and I pretended we didn't know each other. On weekends, I snuck into the empty house beside Suzie's and left books, writing supplies and snacks for the trio and their friend.

Suddenly one morning two men showed up and barged into Suzie's house for an inspection. I watched from behind my curtain and saw them come out with Salimanto's mop and broom and what looked like some empty sardine cans. I couldn't tell what else they'd retrieved and I didn't want to step away to get my spectacles. The glove-handed inspectors went into the house beside Suzie's and came out with some books. My heart dipped. How could Cappy not properly hide the books? Those must be the City Library's textbooks. And was there a book there too with my name written on the inside, I couldn't remember. I thought my heart dropped into my shoes, but when I looked down I wasn't wearing any shoes.

The whole of Peaside went out to see the items displayed by the inspectors. They went crowding around, excited, puzzled, terrified of jumbie.

"Ixie, did you see?" Pap asked, after the inspectors bagged the evidence and drove off.

"See what?" I stalled. My heart was making a racket. Our house felt stuffy and dark like someone was closing the windows. I steadied myself. I must not faint, I must not faint.

"Things they found in the empty houses. People musta been living in dem and we didn't even know. You see anybody strange lurking lately?"

"I ... uh, strange? Strange, no."

"Imagine dat. And we didn't even see nothing neither."

On the news that evening they said that the books belonging to the City Library were being kept in evidence and that they were following up on who had borrowed them. They were going to track the borrower down and get to the bottom of this ghastly business, reported Natasha's 'Possible' news anchor. All perpetrators who knowingly and unknowingly had invaded the personal property of our law abiding citizens from the diaspora and who had engaged in trespassing and vile destruction – the anchor stressed these last four words – of private property, would be charged to the fullest extent of the law. I breathed out a little, relieved I had some time before I was discovered. As a past staff member of the library I was allowed to sign out on a special check out sheet, just the number of books borrowed, not their titles.

Vile destruction? I said in my head.

"Harsh penalty for some ole bruk down houses though," Pap said. "I never see the day boy." He looked like he was enjoying everything.

"Well if you do wrong, you pay the consequences, what else you want them say?" Mam asked. "Ah wonder who it is though."

Lord help me.

The Lord did help me, it seemed. For after I told them about the inspectors and the news and the trouble we were in, Salimanto and the pupils, loyal true friends of mine as it turned out, bowed their heads and never went back into the houses, and the inspectors closed the investigation for lack of leads and returned the books to the library. People concluded that maybe the occupants of the home had left the books behind in the second house and maybe some vagrant had trespassed in the first house and had moved on.

But when the uproar turned into quiet ripples, I hit upon a thought. How did the two inspectors know exactly where to come and into which houses to go at once? Did someone in Peaside rat us out? Soon enough the answer floated in to me, through my front door.

I spied a ruddy smiley-faced tall young man with thick hair, sunglasses, enormous shoulders and generous about the waist, walking up and down the street in flip flops, ferrying baskets with food supplies encased in transparent plastic tied up with large bows. He called at every gate of every occupied house and handed out the hampers and he kept going back into Small Spokes' grammy's yard and bringing out more hampers. He looked like someone from the Peace Corps or some kind of Corps bestowing hand-outs to the locals. I hoped to goodness he wasn't coming on our bridge.

"Mam? Mam! Come out here," I whispered, as I watched Mister Tall Ruddy Smiley hoisting baskets.

Mam came out with a pencil behind her ear.

"Mam, what that youngster doing?"

Mam put on her glasses, then let out a rare echoing laugh.

As if the youngster could hear, I whispered "Who is that?"

"That ain't no youngster," she said, amused. "Dat's Small Spokes."

I squinted. Small Spokes?

Mam said, "He here to visit his grammy. You didn't know?"

"Oh? No. But how he could be so big? And what he doing sharing out things?"

"Doing charity and goodwill na gurl." Mam laughed again and went back to her accounts.

She had the liberty of working from home some days, and soon with a loan for which she'd applied and the small change that Ivy had been sending, Mam was almost ready to open a small store of her own.

"Mam! Come back out! He coming here."

Small Spokes, still as smiley-faced as I remembered, but quite stretched out and grown, stood on our bridge with a generous hamper.

"Hi there," he said and waved.

"Hi."

"I'm from around here but from a long time ago," he said.

"I know."

"My Gram lives over there." He yanked his thumb sideways.

"Ai know."

"You know me?"

I nodded.

"Wow! Everybody knows me." He seemed so proud of his popular existence.

Mam came out on the veranda and waved. Then she went down and hugged Small or Large Spokes, as he had become. She received the hamper and invited him in. He came in, larger-than-life, beaming to be welcomed and sat at the kitchen table downing three glasses of lime juice and he talked much, in his same toddler chatter, just deeper. He was excited about his visit back home after so many years. He didn't remember much he said. He kept glancing at me.

"Wasn't there two of you?" he asked, "and another boy yaah?"

I raised my eyebrows. Mam saw that my mouth wasn't opening and she explained about Ivy and Sam and tried to help bring his memories back.

"I, I, I remember the street a little yaah, but not too well."

Pap spoke of the houses down the street and asked which he remembered. Then he told Spokes the joke about the ghosts of the empty houses.

"Oh yaah, yaah. I called the cops," said the Spokes and took another glug of swank.

We stared at him.

"Yaaa. Was on Gram's veranda thee other night, late out, trying to remember this place and tawt I saw someone lurking round by dah two houses. But I was too far to see, so I called the cops to save the neighbourhood. I said it had to be burglars and vandals, that type-a thing."

Mam looked amused. Pap was cracking up and saying, "Well boy, it took Small Spokes to come back and save Peaside."

As The Spokes drank his swank and chewed up all his ice cubes from the bottom of his pink glass, I watched his maiwiri pepper-shaped face, and imagined him as Columbus, while my own swank stirred hard in my body.

After he left, Mam unpacked the hamper and spread all the things on the table saying, "Oww, a sweet gesture from a sweet boy."

"More salty than sweet," I said, highlighting in yellow the amount of sodium recorded on the label of a tin of corned beef from the hamper.

Then I put my doll Pastel back into the doll's house and went to write a tune to help my pupils learn about photosynthesis.

26

Suzie

"Abominable," Miss March said, "this singing, it's abominable. Your class, always it has to be disturbing the rest of us civilised people."

"Sorry," I said and signalled my pupils to sing softer.

Then she scuttled to the headmaster to complain about my teaching methods and J.A.J. Lee, now head teacher, summoned me.

"Complaints have been received that you have been disrupting the school," sighed J.A.J. He sounded like a dehydrated whole-wheat crust atop a loaf of bread.

"My pupils were just singing about photosynthesis sir. It goes like this," I whistled the key and started singing, "Green leaves, green leaves have chloroph–"

"No no, don't need to hear it." He raised his right palm.

"Yes, well I wasn't disrupting the whole school sir."

"Keep it down please," he said and waved me out.

Again the next day, as my pupils shrieked at the baking soda erupting from our model volcano, Battlefoot March, as I'd started calling her in my head, appeared.

"Madam, you run your class like a circus," she said.

"Then I take that as a compliment," I replied, scraping my chair back and standing up to my full height that was shorter than she. "Circuses are, after all, the epitome of kinaesthetic art."

She looked down on me.

"I'm filing a report of insubordination," she said and stormed off.

J.A.J. summoned me. Again.

"Miss Harry, with three complaints I'll have to write you up officially. That's in the rule book. This is strike two. Please."

"But I didn't do anything wrong."

"March says you've been insubordinate," said J.A.J., tired, old, uninspired.

"I was not!"

"You're raising your voice Miss."

"She said I ran my class like a cir–"

"She says you aren't following the curriculum guide."

"But we were doing the volcanoes bit."

He took up the guide and showed me where March had circled 'Students must draw and label a cross-section of a volcano.'

"Yes, well, I did draw and label a volcano on the board. And then we did a demonstr–"

"Did each student draw and label a volcano in their book?"

"Well no but –"

"Well then, I trust you shall remedy that immediately."

"Fair enough," I said and walked off.

"And Miss Harry?"

I sighed.

"Yes sir."

"I must not see you in here with another complaint under your belt."

"No sir. But it's unbelievable. What could she possibly have against me? I never did anything to her. I nev–"

"She read your CV. Says you're a green pea and never seemed to hold down a job for long. Says she had enough of young alumni waltzing in every six months and creating a ruckus, then waltzing out again," admitted J.A.J.

Battlefoot watched me over the top of her glasses while her students traced diagrams from textbooks.

That weekend I studied the primary school syllabi from cover to cover. It was the same things Ivy and I had been taught two decades ago, in the very same way. So I took a pencil and started amending the learning objectives, editing old ones, keeping some as they were, combining some, adding new ones. It was four or five on Saturday morning when I tumbled into bed and it was long past time for breakfast when finally I awoke, my stomach rumbling.

I rambled around in my pyjamas feeling heavy-headed, and as always, first thing in the morning flung my window out and looked at Suzie's house as if looking in a mirror. This morning, a green Suzuki Rav4 was parked in front of Suzie's house, where two men and two women stood around pointing. The two men and one of the women were probably in their fifties but one, she was younger. Maybe they were a family come to buy Suzie's house. My heart started with its ridiculous racket. I fumbled for my glasses and shoved them up my nose bridge.

The girl was about my age. I pushed the glasses as close to my eyes as possible. It looked like her hair was pressed out and had extensions too. And she had the slimmest waist and lithest curves. She was tall and balanced well on stilettos. She wore her fringe bottom jeans well, snug but not too snug. She stared at the house, arms akimbo, lithe long arms. When she turned sideways to point at something in the yard I could see her pale yellow armless blouse tucked in against her flat athletic stomach, and her bracelet glinting in the sunlight brought me déjà vu. But I couldn't work it out just then. What could they want with Suzie's house, I wondered.

No one in their senses would want to rent that house. It needed many repairs, too much refurbishing. Maybe they were purchasing the whole property to have it rebuilt, but these people didn't look like they would be living here. They looked foreign. They looked ... Oh dear Lord, I said in my head. My heart pumped fast. My head reeled. The group walked away from the bridge and pointed around in the street. Now they were crossing the street. They were on Pappo Harro's bridge. He was out there shaking hands, smiling, pointing at my house. I ran from the window, leaped into bed. My heart was killing me now. Soon the people were on my bridge. They were calling. Pap was at the gate. Greetings were exchanged. Billowy laughter followed. They were in the house. Someone was coming up the stairs. I pulled the sheet over my head, lay motionless. But my heart racketed about in my chest. It wouldn't behave.

"Ixie," Pap said. "Ix Pix?"

I didn't move.

"Ixie? Wake up. Come see who here." He shook me.

"Hmm?"

"Come downstairs. You won't believe who here to see you."

"Tell them come back another day."

"No no, you have to come now."

"Why?"

"'Cus they jus' passin' through and leavin' in a few minutes. I going tell them you coming," he said and left.

The chattering resounded downstairs. Ice cubes clinked around in glasses.

With my heart, limbs and brain uncooperative, I stumbled out of bed and looked at myself in the mirror. Sweat had broken out under my thin light moustache that you could see if you came right up to my face. There was nothing remarkable about it, my face, or my purple penguin pyjamas. The penguins looked juvenile, as did my frizzy head, the dark circles under my eyes and the little extra weight around my tummy from sitting around and growing old writing lesson plans.

"Ixora!" Mam called up the stairs.

I didn't answer.

I went and sat on the toilet and took a very long time at urinating and thinking what to do. At least I'd better brush my teeth, I thought.

Mam called through the bathroom door. "Come see who come to see you."

"Comin'," I said making a big pretence of hurrying to brush my teeth and talking through the toothpaste suds.

I walked back to my room and stood in front of the mirror, studying the middle part in my hair and wondering if I had time to change into something decent. Why try, I thought, and went downstairs looking my worst.

She rose from the couch and floated towards me when she saw me coming down. Up close, she was more of a vision than she had been through my window and across the street. She was like the glamour girls on internet make-up tutorials – eyeliner, eye shadow, eyelashes, mascara, lipstick, foundation it seemed, and rouge. She came towards me still smelling of lemony cream biscuits, her irises still bright and pulsing.

"Suzie," I said simply.

"Oh mai gash, oh mai gash, it's been like what? A hundred years. Oh mai gash, it's so-ho good to see you. You haven't changed a bit. Oh gawwd, you still look the same." She squeezed me into her chest and stepped back. She was about a foot taller than me. "Oh mai gash," she kept saying.

She sat down again.

"You look the same, only grew a liddle, but that's all, you look the same, oh mai gash it's been how many years?"

"Twenty-two," I said.

"Naa," she said.

"Almost," I said. "It'll be twenty-two years in two weeks."

"Noo waay."

"That's right," said Suzie's mom, "only the other day I was counting and I said to myself ..." She kept talking to whoever was listening.

"Oh yes that's so true ..." Mam said, about whatever they were talking about.

The adults kept talking.

"So whad are you doing now?" Suzie asked me. "You look jus' the same."

"I, uh, teach."

"Oh yes? Where?"

"Primary school, where we used to g..."

"Go, yes," she finished my sentence. "Oh gash, why there?" she laughed and as I watched her, each 'ha' of her laugh felt like a droplet of lime drizzle plunking itself on me, and growing into a steady rain.

"What do you do?" I asked, brushing off her last comment, and imagining myself opening an umbrella.

"I work in pharmaceudicals."

"Which has nothing to do with her Master's degree," her dad said. "Suzannah wasted good money to go study something she won't do." He clicked his tongue on the top of his palate.

"What did –" I began.

But everyone started chattering again and my voice went under.

The visit went on forever while the adults chattered and Suzie and I kept glancing at and saying polite things to each other.

"You wish another pine tart?" I asked.

"Oh no, no thanks, thanks. I'm trying to cut back on the sugar."

"Oh, that's good."

"Yea."

"I haven't had a pine tart in years."

"Oh?"

"Yaa."

The adults talked on, with Suzie's parents trying to sample all the topics at once, sipping Guyana through a straw, like a burning ice cold drink with a slice of pineapple on top. Politics, economics, the value of a United States dollar to Guyana dollars, education, progress, this –ism, that –ism, the weather, the nostalgia from the little country.

Little? I thought, raising my eyebrows.

"Oh gawd, sometimes I can't bear the cold even though it's been so many years and still I ..." Suzie's mother was carrying on.

"It's quite hot here," Suzie said to me. Her hypnotising hoop earrings dangled between her loose flowing extensions, and I wished she'd put her hair back in the five braided knots at the top of her head.

"Let me bring you a fan," I said.

"Oh no no. That's alright."

"I'll get it."

While I unplugged the fan from the socket in my bedroom, I looked out of the window at Suzie's house where she didn't live. My stomach was growling. It was almost midday and I hadn't had any breakfast.

I took the fan downstairs and plugged it in.

"Oh thank you deary, that's so much bedda," Suzie's mom said.

"Thanks," Suzie said. "Where's your twin?"

"Uh, in the U.S."

"Oh really! Where?"

Mam and Suzie's mom picked up the conversation. The men droned on about politics and poverty. Suzie listened as Mam told them about Ivy. And I sat on the arm of the chair while my stomach rumbled. I was starting to get dizzy from hunger. My pyjamas stuck to my body with sweat. The edited syllabi were still swimming in my brain. I smiled politely when Suzie looked at me and said, "Oh mai gash, why don't you come live there too, with your sister? Or just to study maan. Or just for vacay? And look me up. And we can hang out. Like the good ole times."

Her mother was saying something to Mam.

Suzie turned to me and said, "Really? You never been? Unbelievable. From where I live to Ivy's place, we just gotta take two trains but it'll be worth it. It's not that far." To Mam she said, "Give Ivy my contact info and she can come over. Gawwd knows it'll be awesome to have somebody from home to hang out with, Lord."

She smoothed back her hair and fanned herself with the tips of her fingers.

"Well, it was so nice catching up with the old village," said Suzie's mother, getting up and picking up her magenta sequined purse.

Old?

Suzie squeezed me to her chest again and I patted her back a little.

We all walked out into the street together.

"You remember we used to play hopscotch there? It's soo awesome to see that spot, oh mai gash." Suzie pointed at a spot on the street, so gosh darn proud of her romanticised memories.

I said, "Yea" and force-flashed a lighted up smile on my face.

"What a quaint past," she said.

Past?

That's when my lime juice – that had been a steady rain all morning – poured down hard and raged inside and out, like a storm upon the rattling zinc roof of an empty house, like a wild swinging tempest crashing through old wooden windows barely hanging on to hinges, swirling through the hollow torso of the house, soaking, crashing in its path all the desperately framed memories, the gently preserved hopes in jewellery boxes and the carefully replaced drawings of old truths. My old delayed lime storm went wracking about, and rushing towards my toes.

Please don't let it reach my toes. Please God, please. That will be the end of me.

"You guys must come up for Suzie's wedding, yaa? We'll send an invite to the other twin too," Suzie's mom said.

The other half *of*, I thought.

"When is it?" Mam asked.

"Next spring."

I had thought the bulging stone on Suzie's left ring finger couldn't be anything more than something from her costume jewellery collection. It was too pronounced to be real. But it was real alright.

Suzie in her stilettos now, squeezed me again, this time to her ribcage, and I came face-to-face with a red heart pendant dangling over her blouse. I jumped. Did she find the pendant after all, from where I was saving it for her in the ballerina box, I wondered, my heart warming. But, no it wasn't the same crystal heart. This one was flat and bordered by a larger silver heart. Suzie had two hearts after all, I thought.

"Oh mai gaassh, itz so good to see you," she said, completing the hug, and she got into the green Rav4 in which their driver was waiting. The vehicle drove straight to the end of the street and turned around. Suzie winded down the window and waved when they passed by.

Ixora Mara, Sourhouse

I raised my hand politely.

The vehicle ambled on through the potholes and Suzie's flat shiny head kept getting smaller and smaller. She turned around and waved endlessly.

And my lime storm retracted up my calves, pulling itself back a little, defying gravity, and I waved back.

The sun was burning down on my sweaty pyjamas. It was long past lunch. Mam had already gone indoors. Pap said "oh maai gassh," grinned, hugged my right shoulder and we walked in, him hobbling and me walking slowly, pressed under his armpit.

"Shut up Pap-Pap."

"Want some swank?" he asked.

"No thanks." My insides felt hollowed out, despite the dissipating sourness.

Later I asked Pap what Suzie's family was going to do about their house.

"Nothing," he said, "Suzie father said they leaving it be. He don't able think 'bout it."

"They never fixing it up? Or renting? Or selling? Nothing?"

From behind his newspaper, Pap shook his head, no.

I went to my room and looked out the window at Suzie's very haunting house.

If I stayed here, marking time on this fallen plank, I would have to keep opening my window and looking out into the street, looking into the mirror of Suzie's house, seeing my reflection there, every day of my life until I died. So I made up my mind once and for all.

Again I moved Pastel. Put her to stand far away from the doll's house. Good thing too because on Monday, Battlefoot March tried to yank my suspenders again and it was freeing to think that I didn't have to see her ever again.

I was walking around the section that used to be my old library. It hadn't been rebuilt. Somebody just put a blank wall where the fire stopped. The ruins were still ruins. Nothing had changed. Nothing was going to change. I was going to live and die in this eternity of inertia, in which people left and returned in cycles all progressive-like, and referring to this spot of earth as quaint and little and old and past. That was what I was living in, what I was becoming. Quaint, little, old, past.

I was walking around watching the ruins and thinking all this, with my sour flaring up when Cappy and others came up.

"Miss Ixie, we have to write a 'ssignment on a animal. What it look like, what it eat and where it live and so."

"Yes, yes, I know," I said, some impatience escaping, "The investigation into the animal kingdom."

"Miss, he say ants is not a animal," Cappy said, jerking his thumb at his classmate.

"Yes, ants are animals," I said, thinking of an ant on a blade of grass bending north.

"You see?" Cappy said to his friend. "We *could* write 'bout ants, yes."

Then some girls asked me what they could write about butterflies.

"Why don't we go outside and see if we can find ants and butterflies and observe them," I said, strolling out and getting excited myself and changing my mind again about whether to go or stay. We didn't have to be inert here in Peaside. There was too much to be in this beating young land.

And before I knew it, like ducklings, half of Cappy's class and all of my own class had waddled behind me to the back of the school yard.

"Look ants," said a boy and got on his knees and peered.

"Look a orange butterfly," somebody said and ran to it.

"Shh shh," said another, "don't run, you scare it."

I was just standing on tiptoe, shielding my eyes from the sun, surveying the landscape for where Mr Fred's hedges used to be and looking up at the window from which I had looked down and seen The Nephew writing my name on the wall, when I saw Battlefoot March, her eyes blazing brimstone down upon us. And by the time I made my way back into the building, J.A.J. was summoning me. Again.

J.A.J., swingy worn scholar, last century, looked at me and said, "I don't want to write you up."

"Then don't," I said, surprised that the voice coming out of my head was mine.

"She says you've got the pupils, and hers too, outside of the classroom in the yard when they should be doing their lessons."

"And where is she when they have all these questions *about* the lesson?"

"Don't raise your voice, young lady."

"They *were* doing the lesson on the animal kingdom."

"She says they needed to divide and classify the animals."

"Yes, that *is* the lesson they *were* doing."

"Young lady, please, I asked you not to shou –"

"Look, look at this syllabus," I spread the book on the desk, "Look at this lesson. Why does it only have to say list and memorise the –"

"What did you *do* to the syllabus?" he said, shouting now.

"Please don't raise *your* voice, Sir."

He blinked half a dozen times like he was going into anaphylactic shock.

"Look I'm sorry," I said, "but you and I, we can edit, rewrite these syllabi. Or at least you can. People said you wrote books and policies. You're a real scholar. People will listen to you about curriculum reform and things like that. I've thought about it all weekend." I watched him. "You know?" I added, when he said nothing.

"Things are not that simple young lady," he said, seeming a little pleased and a little offended.

"So you'd rather waste your last years on earth writing me up? Or updating syllabi?"

His face got red. I had taken it too far, it appeared

"Miss Harry, please leave at once. I have to write you up. It is the rule."

"Cover-to-cover," I muttered.

"Beg your pardon?"

"Nothing," I said and slammed the door hard.

Keep your plank, I said in my head, I'm going to the world stage. You'll see. All of Zekerheid Primary will see. All of Peaside and the whole world, will see.

And then something happened that hastened my preparations for departure.

27

Cousin Kim Kisses Local Soil

Cousin Kim arrived in Guyana, poised and vanilla chocolatey sweet. Not sour. She landed at Timehri with a cream scarf draped over her shoulders, all Grecian goddess-like, with eternal hair and luxurious skin, more magical than her pictures on Ganee's wall. Her eyes sparkled the colour of her mother's ancestry, whatever it was, and her everything-else-ancestry that was ours that had come to this soil on different ships from many places around the world and had fused into cells and everything else. When I saw the hundred thousand root-to-tip silky strands floating down the plane's stairs in the distance and her ivory boot hitting the ground, when I saw her gliding onto the tarmac, I knew that no such sweetly balanced poise or poised balance had ever come to Peaside before. Or since.

"I wanted to kiss the ground when I stepped off the plane, oh my. Wait, lemme do it now," she said, bringing her lips to the soil. "It's so marvelously good to finally be home," she said, when she walked into Ganee and Pappo's small last-century house.

Home? I thought.

She wanted to see everything at once.

"Oh cousin!" she said and hooked her arm through mine, "I've never had cousins before you and Ivy. Show me everything!"

Everything? I wondered. The streets without electricity and the zinc shacks without water, education or breakfast? Or the schools with toxic toilets and without teachers? Or the – I stopped, and pushed my sourness far down. If I cared to summon Telmond, he'd tell me I was being beastly.

I took Kim through our grandparents' old house and our new house next door. I showed her the great outdoors. I walked her around Peaside in the afternoons. I took her to visit Sam and he was extremely well-mannered, unscowling and accommodating, something he never was with me. I took her swimming in the canal by the canefields even though I was still afraid of putting my head under, but she wanted to go swimming in there for authenticity and everything, so I said I'd go with her, in case there were piranhas. And I took a cricket bat so I could shoo them away if they came.

"I want to climb that mango tree," Kim said one day, sinking her freshly strip-whitened teeth into her fifth mango.

I rolled my inner eyes. What was she trying to do? Belong? Outwardly, I set up a bench on top of a barrel for her to hoist herself, and I held the bench steady.

"It's a marvellous feeling up here. An absolutely fantastic spread!" she said, reaching for another mango. "Take pictures of me up here Ixie. Lots. I have to post them online. I want everyone to know about this place!"

Why, is it the lost city of El Dorado?

When she was not in the great outdoors trying to cram it into her deoxyribonucleic acid, she was indoors documenting all of my Ganee Gwenny's recipes or talking to my Pappo Harro about her exploits and accomplishments or showing Pap and Mam photos of everything back home – her two poodles named Posh and Noble, her goldfish called Margery

Merfilia Morale and her delightfully comfortable home-away-from-home dorm room where she was pursuing graduate studies. She also had endless photos of a string of friends, each one as chummy and marvellous as the next, and she had over a dozen digital albums of her trips abroad from when she had grown tired of the old red maple leaf land that she'd already seen much of. "So cold," she said. "So terribly cold sometimes, but otherwise exquisitely comfortable. But it helps to take a break from it sometimes, like coming here. And then it all balances out again – the boiling heat, the calculating cold – the collective beauty of the whole world. An immaculate balance when you've tasted it all. Like a smorgasbord of delights," said the one man symphony laughing and fitting Peaside Pasture, the smallest piece of her thousand piece puzzle, into its place next to the nine hundred and ninety nine pieces of her madly beautiful global collective.

I ground down hard on my jaw, as the old lime in the guise of a tiny globe this time, readied itself and broke out into its latest performance.

"I want to go watch Samuel milk the cow and take a video," she said, "so that I could show my friends."

Happy to be of service, I thought in the sourest notes of sarcasm, as it grew harder by the second to smile while fresh bursts of lime juice exploded on my taste buds and shocked the nerves in my teeth, and as my legs grew heavier and heavier to lead the saccharine Kim around, while the laden juice made its way through my thighs and past my knees.

When she called her parents, Kim turned on the video camera on her iPhone and hugged Pappo to her side and shoved his face into the camera. Pappo didn't even flinch. Just stood there and allowed himself to be hugged.

I chugged glasses of water to neutralise the rapid work of the lime globe.

"Look mom," Kim said, "Granddad and I have the same high arch in the left eyebrow. Itz unbelievable. Look, look." She pointed at Pappo's brow. It didn't seem that high to me.

Uncle Winnie, who had never come back to Guyana, said, "Didn't I tell you so, sweet pea. Are you enjoying my old room?"

His old room?

I went outdoors to help set the table. Kim wanted a spread outside, she said. She wanted to use the large dining table that Pappo had made with his own hands years ago, that we hardly used. So immensely crafty, she said. She would love outdoor family dinner in the cool afternoon around the big family table before she left. She loved saying the word family. She went out of her way to say it like it was melted chocolate on her tongue.

Everyone sat around the table. Pappo opposite Ganee who was sitting next to me, Mam opposite Pap who was sitting next to me, and Kim in the middle of Pappo and Mam and opposite me. Kim had arranged the placements.

We joined hands and Pappo said he thought the guest of honour should say grace.

Kim fumbled over the Lord's Prayer and said Amen.

"Well the table looks so pretty Kim," Mam said.

"Yes," agreed Ganee.

"Oh thank you. I'm definitely going to be a party planner in another life," Kim said. "But right now, I totally have to stay in school and languish in the liberating field of law," she kept talking, rolling her privileged eyes.

Languishing in the liberating field of law, I said in my head, stressing on the alliterative words, so that I didn't know when my own mouth opened and my voice flew out and said, "Entitled to dreams of another life ay? Some people can't afford dreams in their one life, you know?"

Pap who was speed-feeding himself mashed potatoes and Pappo who was biting into a cob of corn stopped and looked at me. Mam and Ganee looked at me. Kim looked at me, a combination of surprise, embarrassment and innocence in her forehead creases.

As soon as I saw her face, I was sorry. The little lime globe had squeezed its juice strong and had taken over almost all of my body now. It was running cold down the veins in my calves. Only my feet were left to be claimed. Everything else was corroded and the juice was spilling from my tongue. But I was sorry.

"I mean, you know what I mean," Kim said and stuck her fork in a wedge of tomato, thoughtfully.

A kiskadee chirped on the phone wire above.

"Well," Kim continued after a moment, trying to remain upbeat, "when I get home, I can't wait to upload all my videos of Guyana and make them public for everyone to enjoy."

"Like Cappy and Onesy and Twosy's quaint little shack?" I asked, as gravity pulled the juice to my feet.

"Ohhh, definitely," replied the innocent tone-deaf travel blogger.

"And you going to monetise these videos?" I couldn't stop myself now.

"Oh no no no. I don't. Soon's I get back, my study group and I are going to Mumbai, so I'll need to put up my Guyana videos in a hurry."

Kim's globe expanded with every sentence she spoke, as my own globe squeezed, shrunk and shrivelled me up. I wanted to bolt from this last supper, but Ganee and Pap were sitting on either side of my bench and I couldn't fling myself around as fast as I wanted.

"Oh and Grandma and Grandddad, you both must come again to see me figure skate in December, I'm —"

"Who says they want to come see you figure skate?" I said, my brain and mouth unfortunately finally marching in sour sync, after their many torturous years of dissonance.

Pappo Harro stood up and banged on the table. The one he had built with his own hands.

"Ixora Harry apologise," he said softly.

Crickets croaked around us.

Pappo did not take his eyes from mine.

I felt my lips tremble. Then the tears started. First one, then another, then dozens.

I looked at Pap for affirmation but he didn't come to my aid.

Kim had her delicate arms around herself, like a Hershey's kiss embraced in a silvery wrapper, and she was crying quietly. I ground down hard on my teeth. Pappo still had eyes locked on me and he was still standing. Never in my life had he come out like a tiger to growl at anything, except now. And for what? Kimberly, princess, pixie, blossom. Why didn't Pappo tell her to stop crying for everything, that she wasn't an egg?

Ganee held her spoon mid-air.

I looked over at the disappointment in Mam's eyes and her apparent irritation at this scene. Wasn't she going to defend me? Wasn't she going to say, "Don't tell my daughter what to do?" like you saw in movies. Like Aunty Melanie would've done for Annie-Lou.

"Ix, that wasn't very nice," Pap tapped my elbow and said softly.

And that was when I deflated. Like the balloons I had blown for my seventh birthday, back when I thought I was still somebody and that Suzie would come. My own father, like Abraham was giving me up on a sacrificial altar, when there was no lamb lurking behind the bushes to take my place. I had no one or nothing left to defend me.

"I'm sorry," I said, without looking at Kim.

"Sorry for the trouble I caused," Kim said and pushed her chair back and left the table, her baigan choka untouched. Later, I saw that Ganee had saved it for her in a little pink plastic bowl. I was glad. Just because my sour repelled Kim's sweet didn't mean I wanted her to starve.

I turned around, jumped over the backless bench and left the table. I didn't know what else to say or do, or where to go or who I was.

I went behind my ixora hedge and lay face down on the grass and sobbed into the earth. My limey sensation had finally spread to the tops of my feet and I tried to brush them off, one on top the other. Just the bottoms of my feet were left to corrode now and I would be finished. So I just lay there my heart beating into the ground in the grass, Ixora behind her ixora hedge, waiting for the earth to swallow her.

Someone came up behind me. I didn't care which of those traitors it was.

The person knelt beside me.

I kept my head turned the opposite side and looked at an ant on a blade of grass. The grass was bending north. I didn't want to see who had come up to me. I needed to get as far away from Peaside as possible. Ivy had been right all along.

The person bent down on the ground some more. Maybe it was Pap, come to coax me back to the table. Get me to behave and stop acting juvenile. Pap's coaxing was really getting dated, I thought. He'd better try some other craft if he wanted to get back in my good books. How did he expect to get my respect sitting around tables commanding me to make apologies? I closed my eyes and pretended not to care.

The human body lay side to side with me now. So curiosity, the cat and all that, and I opened my eyes and turned my head.

Vanilla Hershey Kim, innocent, unblemished, kind, with her Chanel Paris perfume wafting in the gentle breeze, had her head on the grass too, but her face was turned towards, not away from mine.

Me and Kim; Kim and me. Family. Lying face-to-face, mirrored. In our parallel universes, but mirrored; in the same universe but on different, equal sides. Lying on the floor of the earth's house. So flat that blades of grass could grow up into our nostrils. So close, a blade of grass could not get between us. Same tears but different persons; different tears but the same.

And then, I saw it.

Kim wasn't the enemy. Kim was her own beautiful free sweet person.

I was my own enemy, my own sour person. Me. Not Kim or her parents. Not Pap or Mam, Ganee or Pappo. Or Ivy Lee Harry, freedom lady, economic brain, adventurer, twin. Neither was Sam or his father. Or Lennard or Annie-Lou or their parents. Or Mr Fred's wife. Or Miss Pamela. Or The Nephew. Or Small Spokes. Or Suzie. And there probably was no Miaplambo with his long arms reaching over them all so that I had to grow sour and fight him. Just every man for himself.

That's when I knew it, the lime acid hadn't taken over all of me yet. There was still a chance for me to grow sweet like Kim. There were still my uncorroded free foot bottoms left. And I could plant them firmly on the ground and walk about. I could walk to the ends of the earth to be me.

There was nothing stopping me, but myself.

28

The Disappearance of the BN Trislander and Samuel A. Reid, Jr.

I was almost packed and practically in the frame of my new life. Already Ivy was windmilling about the things she wanted us to do, wanted me to see.

"It gon be like old times, only new," she said. "Look at these road trip maps. And watch this, next year if we save enough we can go Europe. You know how to speak Italian?"

She had moved out of Amanda's apartment and settled in a new one, waiting for me.

My acceptance letter, student visa and a humble but sufficient wad of cash were in hand. I adhesive-taped my boxes of inheritance, piled them high in my bedroom and covered them with a tarpaulin. I looked at *Keeper of the House* by I.M.G. and touched the rough angry bold brush strokes. The fluffy hair of the figure in the shadows with her back to the viewer resembled my own. I pressed the large orange handle on her door, wondering whether hers was an empty house too and which category of empty. Then I wrapped the painting with newspaper.

"Pap-Pap," I whispered one night when Mam was snoring, "I got someting to tell you."

Then my confession rolled out – about the houses and Salimanto and his woman, about Cappy, Onesy and Twosy and Cappy's mother, father and crying baby sibling, about the library books the inspectors had found. Soon more spilled out. How I felt about Small Spokes showing up and interfering. About the plank off the world stage and Battlefoot March. About J.A.J. Lee sweet-soaping Miss March and ignoring me about the curriculum. And I let a tear fall.

"Well the Lord's Prayer does ask, 'Forgive us our trespasses'," Pap said smirking and stressing on 'trespasses.'

There I was, baring my soul and there was Pap doing humour. When I left him fluffing cushions and hobbling around the living room, I thought I saw pride beaming from his cheekbones, but it must've just been the light and shadows, for how could he be pleased about all I'd confessed? And when together, Pap and I told Mam about everything, and I ended with "Maybe is the right thing to do to go away, start fresh," and I added, "like Ivy," all Mam said was, "Ixora Mara, whether you go or stay, we love you. Everything else is to decide for yourself, from who you are inside. Nobody gon know that for you." Then she put on a pot of soup, and Pap and I looked at each other. Philosophising was unusual for Mam. Things were usually either yes or no. So what was she doing philosophising?

I poked around in Pappo's tool shed for the old suitcase someone had once filled with used clothes and given Ganee to distribute to Peaside's children. I tested the zipper and pondered. Surely, if I too didn't leave like Ivy, that would be the end of me, the end of any impact I could make on the world. The longer I stayed on this side of the ocean, the more obscure I became for a hundred empty reasons. It was stupid to remain obscure, just waiting for the old lime to take whatever form it fancied on any given day. Marking time only. Flinging open windows as a morning routine and looking into houses like mirrors. Looking to see *what*, goodness knows. Side-stepping rotted planks on the stairs of empty houses. Whacking bushes in front of empty houses, like a madwoman. Studying the decaying pillars of emptying houses, wondering when the pillars collapsed how I could take their place, hold the houses up. Alone. Dawdling on verandas at sunset, waiting for lights to glow on in the houses across the street, staring down the darkness in others' empty houses. And staring down the abyss in my own liminal house and waiting, waiting for light. That was all one did here. Round and round like a dog chasing its tail. There on the other side, opportunities stretched before them like an elastic road. Marching only. *There* was from where, when people returned their Somebodyness elevated. Incrementally. Sometimes unstoppably. All I ever wanted was to be Somebody. Not a pin that held swatches of cloth together and put her head down, invisibly. I wanted to be somebody, with whom somebody else wanted to be a friend. And for whom someone would stay. Yes, it would be best to go. Go to become somebody for whom someone would stay.

I had already steeled myself to say goodbye to Ganee and Pappo, Mam and Pap. Even Sam, but he was up in the air more than he was on the ground, so he didn't count. Besides, he could visit me up North. After all, the world was smaller now. There's air travel and there's wireless fidelity. It's not as if I were taking a boat to the other side, having to send telegrams, mail letters at a post office, wonder what everyone back home was doing or what they looked like, and it's not as if I would never return. All I was doing was saying I didn't want life on a plank that had fallen off the stage, the stage that everyone else had gone to. That was all.

I went down the street and sought out Uncle Warbin; perhaps I expected a prophecy. He and Putty were swinging in a hammock, uncomplaining these days. I looked through his Polaroid collection and studied the photo with Ivy in the pink polka dot dress and her eight friends on one side and me on the other side, alone, in my pants and t-shirt and wet hair parted down the middle.

"Uncle Warbin, ah finally getting on dat plane you know?"

"Well planes come down and planes go up," said he, flinging a rambutan in the air and catching it in his mouth. He tossed me one.

I ate it and thought about how it seemed his steam for stories and prophesying had run out. Or probably I'd grown out of his stories, as I had grown out of Peaside.

Still, Uncle Warbin's prophecy came through. A plane came down and one went up. And I marvelled at how he knew these things.

A few weeks before I boarded the plane, Mam had some salted fish sizzling in a skillet, saying she was fattening me with good breakfasts because where I was going breakfasts were not the same, and Pap was snickering behind his newspaper, when Sam's mother dashed in our yard in hysterics.

"Dem cyant fin' he. Dem cyant fin' he."

"Who?" said Mam abandoning the good breakfast, rushing out and holding up Sam's mother who'd tumbled to the grass.

"De plane, de plane. Junior plane. Dem say it gone down somewhere. Dem caan't hear from inside de plane," she sobbed and shook, shook and sobbed.

Pap sprinted out. Then he and Mam led Sam's mother indoors. Ganee and Pappo hobbled over. "Wah happen?" they said together. They looked so wrinkled and similar.

I turned off the stove and studied the crispy golden brown salted fish and the fried tomatoes tossed between. Then I covered the skillet, feeling my world detaching itself from me. I was standing on a weightless platform floating in navy blue outer space with dotted stars, like I was making a courteous cameo in somebody's music video. Maybe when I went abroad I could act in music videos. Except, who abroad would want a girl with dry coconut husk hair who was only half of a twin, whose voice kept getting stuck and exploding in her cerebrum and who officially now – because of this disappearing act of Samuel A. Reid, the Second, probably officially had no friends left in the world? I felt a bonging limey headache coming on, as if the lime had appeared like a cricket ball in my brain and someone were playing cricket inside my head, batting the ball about. But as no one was fielding the ball, it kept flying about, hitting the insides of my skull.

Sam's mother repeated her story, until it became trapped, enfolded in my head. That Sam's BN Trislander had probably gone down somewhere in Guyana's hearty jungle.

Outside, a crane and his friends flew homeward.

The afternoons grew more silent. Stiller, slower. Birds flew slowly, clouds moved slowly.

A day, two, three days passed.

Samuel didn't come home.

Sam's grampappy went to sleep and drifted on to the other side, clutching Sam's old teddy bear.

"He treat me like he own daughter for thirty years. Even after Senior go 'way," Sam's mother sobbed, and Mam and Ganee held on to her and they sniffed in a trio.

Pappo Harro's shoulders crumpled and the wrinkles on his face multiplied. He bowed his head and touched the name on the coffin, Mr Akono Reid.

Pap leaned against the fence, unsuccessfully controlling his facial muscles.

Afterwards, Uncle Warbin came around with a large pot of cook-up rice into which he had mixed ground provisions and herbs. Mam dished out some for herself, gulping it down. "Thanks Warbs," she said, "You is a true chef."

I looked at Uncle Warbs for some sort of prediction about Sam. Knowing what I needed, he obliged, "He gon come back. Watch and see."

I scanned the news for stories about Sam, but there was nothing. I wondered if there could be a clue to his whereabouts lying around his room. So I visited Sam's mother with soup, hoping she'd let me prowl about. She lay in bed, said I was welcome to stay.

I entered the world of Sam's room, the world of unpainted walls, without posters or murals, the world with a wood ant tunnel trailing from floor to roof to the outdoors through the gap between the wall and the rusting zinc roof. I had never been inside Sam's room. He'd usually come to us. And I had expected, with major measure of entitlement, for him to keep coming – to see my hibiscus tree, to marvel at our new room, attend our parties, accompany us on trips, to make his face amicable, to be gallant and responsive. I sat on his bed and looked around, at the cracks in the wall through which glints of sunlight came. I looked at the bare floor, no mats, no linoleum; looked at the holes in the mosquito net and the thin bed sheet, no cover sheets; looked at the carton boxes with his clothes in them, no chest of drawers; at a yam crate turned into table to hold his text books on aviation and famous musicians, his bible and crucifix. I sat on the bed proud, proud of Sam for flying out of this room and prouder of him for always returning to it. I thought, I'm proud of you Samuel Reid, the Second, even if you are dead somewhere. And I searched in Sam's mother's kitchen for a needle and thread and sewed up the holes on the mosquito net, rolled the net and tucked it in the top. Then I spread Sam's bed and fluffed his flat pillow that smelled like Dettol, pondering on how little I knew about love, how little one could know about another, even though you'd broken bread with him – or at the very least, exchanged the top swirls of ice cream cones. Sam had a right to choose whether he belonged to the earth or the air. I shouldn't have expected him to orbit my routine. Maybe he had run away from us all. From Peaside. From this back street with no electricity or phones or running water. Only cows and grass and land and sky, and people. Waiting for him to orbit them. There was a divide in Sam's world and mine that I had not known about. Here we were, one street, just paces away from each other, not even as far as Seaside was from Peaside, and still we were as far as an ocean between. It is not oceans that create divides. Divides exist only where they remain unbridged.

So yes, I should get on the plane and go. An ocean would be nothing after all.

He did come home at the end of the week – Sam, making me jump out of my ribs. He walked right through our gate and simply stood there saying hi, while I was patting some manure down around my neglected hibiscus tree.

"Well, where you been?"

He grinned.

The next day the newspapers carried the news of Sam's plane giving trouble, about the crash-landing on water, about him and the pilot swimming to shore and walking through the jungle for two days and staying exhausted in a village without phone service for three days where they were nursed back to robustness. From there they travelled to a small town and made the call to the airline that then sent a flight down and picked them up, and here they were back home. Such a tidy adventure with a neat ending, like a proper little story, not like real life.

That was Sam, elusive like aeroplanes, unreachable like the sky he loved. Sam, down on the ground one minute, up in the air the next. Disappearing last week, appearing this week. Probably dead days ago, alive today. Grinning now, scowling tomorrow. Always to one extreme, a man easy to love, a man hard to be in love with. And why should love be hard, I thought. I thought, I need someone who would love with the constant passion of an epic poem that could bring the world to its knees. Goodbye Sam, I said in my head after I looked up, saw him grinning, got up and hugged him. "Sorry 'bout your grampappy," I said aloud. Sam wrapped his arms around his chest and nodded. In my head I said, Goodbye Junior's grampappy; whether it was you or Pappo who had fainted in the canefields, whether it was your story or his doesn't matter; our life here is in the same story; we are as different as we are same. The comings on ships, the goings on planes, the cutting of canes, the same, goodbye. Fruit trees on the land, the soil in our hand, multitudes of trips, goodbye. I silently titled my musings 'Ode to Junior's Grampappy and the Land,' while Sam rattled on, probably about his ordeal or adventure, depending on the viewpoint from which one listened. If one was even listening.

29

Boarding the Boeing 737

I stood in front of Cappy's house with several books that I'd taken out of my inheritance.

"These are for you," I said. "And you two."

Cappy, Onesy and Twosy collected their books in silence.

"I won't be home anymore," I said, not knowing if to add 'for a while.'

"Well where you gon be?" Cappy asked.

Onesy and Twosy stopped looking at their books and listened.

"I'm going away to university abroad. To live with my twin sister."

"When you be back?"

"I dunno. Maybe in two years. Maybe more. I don't really know." 'Way leads on to way,' I thought. "Oh no, don't be angry," I said to Cappy. His nostrils flared. "Don't cry," I told the girls. "I'll send you toys. Please don't cry. I'll send books and anything you need." I sounded like a vending machine, I thought, a tear for a toy.

Cappy lifted his dirty red cap, scratched his head and put the cap back on.

"Well bye," he said, a sourness creeping into the creases near his eyes.

Well then, I thought, I had successfully bequeathed him my books *and* my lime. The role of Resident Sourpuss really could be handed down after all. Cappy retreated to his house and shut the zinc door on me. Onesy and Twosy went up to the zinc door, turned around and looked at me. They didn't wave.

"Don't come with me to the airport," I insisted to everyone at home. "Please, I gon jus take a taxi. Y'all mustn't come."

I got in the taxi just as the clouds started bunching themselves into incredulous shapes and greying Peaside.

I wouldn't be hugging or waving, I had warned them. I'd just be going, that's all. Don't wave either, I'd said. I looked out the car window where Mam, Pap, Ganee and Pappo lined the street and I nodded business-like, cleared my throat and fixed my eyes ahead on a cloud.

The taxi ambled past Cappy's house. I wondered how his education would fare. And about Onesy and Twosy and the belt brands on their calves. I wondered why they never spoke and when their voices would grow out into the atmosphere. I thought about Pappo Harro's plants and the tailor's signboard in the shed and about Ganee Gwenny's arthritis. Maybe I'd better tell the driver to turn back now since we were still in Peaside. I did have to hug everyone after all, before I set foot on the plane. Mam and Pap's meals would be a giant silent ball now, unless they ran the TV in the background, I thought. Still, these were such meagre worryings, such small hurdles to step over in the grand scheme of things. Everything would take on its own life and evolve into what it would be. Whether I was there or not wouldn't matter. I'd thought about that a long time. Maybe it would matter one per cent or ten, yes. But in the grand design, life would roll on exactly as always and nothing would he shifted exceptionally. The taxi whizzed past my old school. Goodbye turrets, I said, and all the fuzzballs who used to be plotting to tie me up with gym rope. I am going to be a Somebody today. Not a pin or a Resident Sourpuss. Goodbye.

I kept my gaze on the overcast sky. One particular cloud seemed intent on chasing me, its fluffy head and long arms trailing across the sky seemed about to lunge vertically at me. It resembled my drawing of the Miaplambo. Well then, I thought, you've come for me at last.

The driver hit on the brake and I pitched forward.

"You aright back deh gyrl?"

"Yea."

"You sick?"

"Bit."

"You want come out and vomit?"

"No."

"We almost reach de airport."

I didn't answer. A drizzle was starting up.

I got out and wheeled my suitcase. Glass barriers enclosed me inside the airport. I had visual contact with the society behind it, but no aural, no tactile contact. The strangers behind the glass were swimming in a silent film, far away from me. Straighten up, I said to myself, don't look back through that glass. It's a dangerous glass. Then I laid my passport on the counter.

Only a few more hours and this will be behind me, I thought, taking off my shoes, emptying my pockets, walking through the scanner, floating along in the line. I must ignore these cramps in my limbs. Coax my body to cooperate. What kind of body does not want to cooperate?

I thought of my grand new university, and oh my word, the massively massive library there! I thought of Ivy's road trips and vacationing in Europe, and my, all the libraries in Europe. To think what Mr Fred would say if he could know.

I put one foot in front the other. Hadn't felt so decisive in all my life. A wave of heat warmed up in me. I felt bold. Unstoppable. Finally, the lime juice was evaporating from my body. I could feel the sourness leaving and invincibility pouring in.

And then, then the Boeing 737, its wings outspread, drawing me to a boundless me. This is how Ivy must've felt on her first journey. If she and the wide legacy of embarkers could do it, so must I. What coward couldn't put one foot in front the other and get on a plane? What coward? If my ancestors had come in ships from all over the world to land here, with nothing and all was alright now, I too could go anywhere by choice and it would be alright too.

I would go.

I could come back as I pleased.

I had the power of mobility, the power of decisiveness. The opportunity of a lifetime, two lifetimes. Two worlds. Two whole worlds. I would bridge them, the sunny and the wintery, the first world and the third, the visible and the invisible and all those polar opposites and clashes and mixes and things. Already I could see all those things Kim had said about the world being big and beautiful, even as she herself was being marvellously beautiful in the world somewhere. For sure I could. I was Ixora Mara, not an egg, and no writing on the wall could stop me.

Goodbye, goodbye, my shoes lifted off the soil and on to the plane stairs.

My heart wrenched. But I held my chest in place. Paused. Continued on.

I settled into my window seat and looked out at the rain starting to patter on the tarmac, while the flight attendant jammed people's bags above.

I knew. I knew that the curtain was coming down behind me. Tomorrow I would be on a new stage. My heart kicked up a racket. What an unruly heart. The wildest of wilds. Wouldn't settle down. An embarrassment, really. Listen old heart, I soothed, you could tie the curtain back just a little. If that would be more agreeable to you and to the people on the other side.

To the people. On the other side?

The racketing in my heart stopped.

I stood up.

Stepping over an elderly gentleman's feet, I excused myself.

I made my way down the long aisle, out of the Boeing 737 and on to the wet runway.

The flight attendant was frantically calling after me.

30

Bloom

They all watch me now.

Not Mam, Pap, Ganee or Pappo, of course. Not them. After a round of questions and instructions to change out of my wet clothes and to come sip hot tea, they rallied around me and unpacked my bags. Then Mam gave me a ten second hug, seven seconds more than usual and my heart started beating right again and we carried on with our lives.

But the others down the street in Peaside Pasture and even Seaside Strip, they watch me. Acquaintances from my old primary school, people from work, anyone really, even Ivy's friends from abroad who'd come to hear about it, scrutinise me. They study my face over or under their spectacles, with a left side-eye or right side-eye. They inspect me without saying anything. Watching my flat sandals, my unpolished toes, my clean feet that no longer feel dusty, my writing hands, my unbrushed head as if there's a maniac let loose inside my skull and running off from planes in there and on to deadly runways. They search for the old sour in my face. Sometimes it still appears. And so what? Your sour wasn't the end of you. Besides, everyone's got some sour in their heads or hearts or little toes.

Ixora Mara, Sourhouse

I returned Pastel to her house, thinking in soft whispers, just plant Ixora, plant. Grow Ixora, bloom. Let them watch. Or not watch. No matter. Plant. Grow. Bloom.

Early one morning before people flitted about, I knocked on the office door and said, "Dr Lee, Sir, in less than a hundred years I shall be dead and so will you." He dead-stared me. I kept going, "What does it matter that we die? But curriculum reform, Sir, imagine what it can do, for hundreds of pupils," like one rain drop making ripples in a puddle, I said in my head. The twitch in J.A.J's jaw was barely perceptible, but I caught it and prepared to continue, "And since we –" but before I could finish, the old dormant brilliant volcano erupted from his chair. With his atrophied muscles and wrinkles, he heaved a stocky greenheart desk against the windows.

"You'll have to bring your own chair," he said, gesturing at the desk. "And no talking in here before eight in the morning. Talking thinkers grate my nerves."

He opened a cobweb-draped box and yanked out an old desktop monitor from last century. I couldn't even remember how to use one of those. He thumped it on my new old desk. "Update that system. Type the new syllabi proposal. And hurry up before I retire."

"I –"

"What did I tell you about the talking before eight?"

"It's eight oh one sir."

"Humph." He scribbled something. It was my Recommendation of Reinstatement.

"One more thing," I said, "we've got to see social services about parents like Cappy's father. That man even traumatises me. It must not go on."

J.A.J. sighed like a pressure pot letting out steam. I wasn't the pre-retirement plan he had anticipated.

With my job back, I rode the bus to the City Bank one morning to inquire about a loan.

"Collateral?" asked the young teller, bright eyed and bushy tailed.

How does one get collateral in order to get something if one has nothing to begin with, I mulled.

"We have the following loan plans," the teller explained, gesturing at a brochure.

"Thanks. I'll be back soon. Remain a stellar teller."

He raised a brow and bowed a little.

When I got home, I dialled Suzie's number. "Suzie," I said. "Sell me your old house across the street."

"Who's this?"

"What other old house do you have in the world that's across the street from someone you know?" Use your brain Suzie, ohmaigassh, I said in my head.

Silence.

"Ixie?"

"Tell your parents to sell me the house and land at the absolutely lowest price, plus a discount. Call me back in an hour."

"But I dunno about –"

"Suzie," I said simply. "You owe me a promise you know."

Let's not pretend we haven't had several conversations like this in the deep recesses of our consciousnesses Suzannah, I thought. You know and I know. Where we stand. On opposite ends of a liminal horizontal totem pole, meeting and anguishing, meeting and growing, meeting and perishing and living again in the deep recesses of our souls. Totem pole.

She was sniffling on her end of the pole like she was perishing and living.

And her tears distilled the old lime juice in my chest.

"I owe you too Suzie. Your chequers and ice cream."

She laughed, sobbed, sniffled and laughed again.

Ixora Mara, Sourhouse

"Ohh maii gasssh you do."

"Well you can have them in a way. I want to fix up your house as a free learning centre for children in the village. That can be your yellow marbles and ice cream, sort of."

Before she hung up she said, "You know, I thought we were going to come back in time for your birthday. I didn't know ..."

She stopped talking, while we cried on either ends of the diasporic totem pole.

And my tears didn't have the taste of lime.

So I bought Suzie's house.

We repaired and repainted it, Pappo and Ganee, Pap and Mam and I. Cappy and his friend Willy, and Onesy and Twosy helped too. Even Old Lady Bargains appeared and donated a pointer broom, she'd made.

"Psst," I said to Onesy and Twosy, "go ask that lady her real name and tell her thanks for the broom."

They came back giggling.

We fitted bookshelves, desks and storage cabinets into the corners, maximising the right angles of the very square house. I untaped my inheritance and unpacked the books, running my hands over them, opening them, smelling them.

I brushed off the cover of a purple encyclopaedia. I'd seen this book before. The cover was scarred but it was hardcover and thick and though the edges of some pages were burnt round, the book was not burnt through. Mr Fred had rescued our primary school's encyclopaedia of birds! I opened it. Out fell my half-finished story and drawing of my Inspeck S'mart. He with the jumbo shoes and prominent belt! A trickle of lime juice sprang forth from a crack somewhere in my chest, like a fountain under a trapfloor, pushing up. And I let it. I let it do its work, bursting through the trapfloor and flowing over this way and that, distilling itself and refreshing anywhere it pleased.

Above the doorway of the Reading Centre, I hung *Keeper of the House* by I.M.G.

An inspector showed up under the painting one morning when we were categorising the books, library-style.

"Where's your permit?" he demanded.

"Processing," I said.

"Ma'am you're not allowed to operate on the premises until the permit for public use is processed."

"But it's my property."

"We're not operating. We're preparing it," Pap said, getting ruffled.

"You're prohibited," said the man.

"Who says so? That's not in the laws," argued Pap, peaceful all his life until today.

"You're prohibited."

"Who sent you?" Pap raised his voice.

"I'm not at liberty to say."

"No problem," I said, amused at Pap's unusual burst of irritation. "We'll comply."

I called Cappy and the others and with exaggerated flourishes, I told them what the inspector'd said. By now they were accustomed to my conspiratorial tones, so the cheeky little tykes filed out with their books and sat in the potholed street in the broiling sun.

I took a photo of them sitting there and posted it on social media with the caption, 'Local Children vs. Academic Oppression & Other −sions, −isms and −isations.' Then I sent the photo to the press. After that some people liked me and some didn't. They, my own people, including the gossipy neighbour said things like: "Mike Harry twin daughter was a shame and disgrace who couldn't even find a good man to marry her and settle her down." They said: "Dat mad girl gallivanting all over the school and village stirring up ruckus," and "She really insubordinate and unpleasant," a statement, no doubt Miss March had circulated, since insubordinate wasn't in Peaside's vocabulary on an average day, and since she was the one who had sent the inspector to our Reading Centre, as some teachers from Zekerheid Primary had found out. People even said: "At least the other one," referring to Ivy, "gone 'way and deh good but this one like something wrong with she or she papers dem must be wrong up mek dem send she back at the airport." I heard that remark with my own ears the day that I was wheeling home a twenty pound pumpkin on my bicycle and I had the urge to hurl the pumpkin at the vendor who'd said it. And I didn't even feel guilt about my sudden eruption of sour. I was Ixora Mara, Mistress of My Sour.

But when Ivy, who had easily peasily forgiven me for abandoning her and moved back in with Amanda so that rent would be cheaper, video-called us from a homely park where she was practicing yoga, and I saw the falling leaves and the cool sedative skyline of the vibrant elastic metropolis, I handed Mam the phone and went to bed. I pulled the cover sheet over my head and weighed the hurling pumpkin against the falling pumpkin leaves.

Plant Ixora Mara, I thought. Never mind the weighing, just keep planting.

Cappy and his cohorts, he had several more now, helped me secure a fluffy brown puppy with a white part down the front of its head.

Sam saw me coming with it and folded his arms.

"Here," I said.

"Wot I supposed to do wit dat?"

"Yours."

"No thanks."

The puppy wriggled from my grip and whimpered at Sam.

"Yes thanks," I said and handed it over.

"And wot I supposed to do wit him when I leave for work?"

"Your mother'll watch him. Besides she needs some company when you gone, which is always and forever."

"I don't —"

"You do."

"You didn't even know wot I was gonna say."

The puppy licked Sam's face, and the old stony statue broke into a smile.

What cheekbones, I thought, as I backed out and walked away. Quickly.

"Hey," he called.

I felt an old fluttering in my rib cage but kept walking. He ran up behind me.

"Thanks," he said, "for Ludwig."

"Ludwig?"

"I'm calling him Ludwig," Sam said.

He was panting a little from the short sprint, sculpted marble chest heaving and all that. Lead us not into temptation, I said in my head.

"Come to the centre sometimes and teach the youngsters the things you got in that brain of yours, Samuel Reid, Junior," I said.

He laughed.

"Alright," he said, "Ludwig too."

I rolled my eyes and walked on.

I passed four empty houses, two in the back street that weren't in my original count and two up the side street that I already knew about. Over a hundred empty houses, a hundred empty houses, a hundred empty houses I repeated, until I reached my bridge.

Two days later I was in front of Audrey's gate, by invitation. This was Audrey, Ivy's old boss from the Department of Housing and Public Engineering.

"Audrey," I got straight to the point, "Remember me?"

"Who could forget you two pranksters?"

"Could you help me with something?"

"Come inside," she said, gesturing at an outdoors table with a snazzy umbrella. "I got swank in the fridge." Her german shepherd ran up and put his nose to my hand. "He don't bite you if you don't bite him," said Audrey.

"Advise me on something," I said when my glass was drained to the lees and the ice chewed up. The dog was sitting beside me. And I felt invincible, like I was soaring sensibly, protected by an umbrella, buoyed up by chewed ice, sitting beside a trained dog, conversing with a bolder older woman who knew how to get technical things done.

She looked at me. "You could only be thinkin' to stir up trouble eh?"

"How could we turn empty houses into low income homes for people, like maybe vagrants? Through some sort of leasing partly sponsored by someone with funds, until they can pay something? I dunno. Some kind of –"

"Just like that? Out of the blue?"

"I mean, I got this friend, Salimanto. Fifteen, twenty, thirty years he on the road sitting there, tripping me over –"

"Let him look for a job."

Audrey and I argued and haggled and brainstormed. She resisted everything I said. Said I was impractical. Called me nuts three times. Said she couldn't help me, nobody would.

"But you worked there," I said. "You know the ins and outs. You know how to do things. You can draft the proposal and ask the right people," I pleaded.

"You a little green nut," she said as she closed the gate behind me and shook her head.

Oh well, I thought, if that's not going to work out, then on to the next order of business.

"May I have your nephew's email address?" I said to J.A.J.

"Who?"

"How many nephews you got?"

I was getting used to my own sass.

"What do you need it for?"

"I need it."

Dear The Nephew, I wrote and back-spaced it. Dear Claude, I wrote. You and I went to school together in Guyana for a little while. I work at that same school now where your uncle is the head teacher. You probably don't remember me. I stopped, backspaced everything and shut down the browser.

I woke a little after midnight and got out a writing pad and paper.

Dear The Nephew aka Pollard-stealer, I wrote. You probably don't remember me, the one half of the twin from primary school, because any memory of me would be a constant reminder of the hell you deserve for all your past deeds, not merely that little dunking in the puddle I gave you. So please send donations to cover the cost of a brand new state-of-the art library here if you know what's good for you or I will drop an anonymous tip that will see you being investigated for arson, even though you were a little victim boy and nobody cares about petty criminals or things that happened ages ago. And don't take your time about it. You have twenty-four hours or else ...

Then I sobbed at the fresh images of the burning library, smoke billowing, the list on the school wall with my name at the bottom, the ashes settling on my toes and I tore the letter and pulled the sheet over my head. How long was it going to take me to become a grown woman who had a healthy, less sour relationship with her past?

Dear Claude, I wrote the next day. You probably don't remember me but you and I went to primary school together in Guyana for a little while. I work at that same school now where your uncle is the head teacher. I was wondering how interested you'd be in supporting the rebuilding of our school library and becoming a permanent sponsor of said library. I'm in the process of confirming alumni, local and in the diaspora, who may be willing to contribute to such a venture. Sincerely, Ixora Mara Harry, I signed.

Half an hour later, The Nephew replied in two lines.

He said that he remembered my sister and me and he named such a hefty sum he would be wiring to the school immediately that I needed thirty whole minutes to recover. I sat with my jaw hanging open imagining how the whole library could be built, furnished and sourced with books again for such a sum. And not with discarded stamped books from somebody else's old library either.

"Wonders!" I thought.

Two days later Audrey called.

"Listen young lady, I been thinkin' 'bout it," she said. "Sorry I say you nuts, but you nuts girl. Still your idea good but it hard to get done. Things not so easy, you gotta understand. You young. You bright. You got energy. You think the world got energy too and care. You wrong. You sulking young lady? Look I got five daughters too, and sulking don't work on me."

I didn't know what to say to Audrey. Some days were like bricks holding me down in bed. It was an old feeling coming on more lately. Some days I thought I knew what I was doing and some days I didn't.

"Look, listen, I gon try talk to somebody down at Housing," said Audrey. "Cheer up little penguin. Everything is not just black or white." She hung up.

It didn't matter what directive she gave. Today I was flying real low, with sea salt bothering my Icarus wings. I went to bed and pulled the sheet over my head.

In the morning, I opened my window to the Reading Centre's open windows with its chequered curtains fluttering. Cappy and sisters stood by my gate waiting for me.

"Miss Ixie," he shouted up, "I boil a egg for you." He held up a transparent little bowl. Some people had come and spoken to his pappy and his pappy worked some days now and had given his mammy money to buy hens, he explained, and he'd boiled eggs for himself and sisters for breakfast and one for me too.

I went downstairs and crouched beside the bougainvillea that was growing cantankerously beautiful again and I accepted my boiled egg in the little transparent bowl. I studied the little battered bowl and burst out crying. Cappy seemed terrified that he had done something offensive.

"Miss Ixie, I so sorry miss. You did want a slice of bread wit it?"

I laughed so loudly that the man passing with a donkey cart stopped the donkey just to watch me laugh.

"No this is just enough, thanks Cap."

It was a breakfast unmatched anywhere in the world.

I freed the yellow marbles, the frayed skipping rope with the broken handle, the handwritten stories, Miss Pam's Molly Mumpkins and everything else from under the trapfloor and transported the wooden doll's house to the Reading Centre for Onesy and Twosy who'd started blooming. They painted the doll's house with an array of colours. They invited me to their school concert to hear them sing. They made kites and asked could I come kite-flying. I remembered Sam's father's condescension about kites and pasture culture. Well, if pasture culture is kites calling to heaven, Mr Reid, Senior, then let me have it.

I'll have that and I'll have Mam – the robust entrepreneur with her new business and her brand new gold earrings she's bought herself – giving advice. I'll have Pap with his sleek newly imported cane, quietly hanging a kaleidoscopic birthday banner for me in the Reading Centre and whispering, "For a low-stimulus birthday Ix Pix." I'll have Uncle Warbin, volunteering to weed and garden at the centre where his Miaplambo stories send the children shrieking and jumping and holding on to their caps. And I'll have Ganee Gwenny, confined to bed some days, but on other days, packing parcels for neighbours and baking buns with red cherries on top. And I'll have Cappy and his classmates watering Pappo Harro's plants, and Pappo rolling out Gooseberry and the other machine and teaching the pupils to sew. I'll have this pasture culture – with the snazziest soaring star point kite that I can make with my own two hands, and with a drink of cold lime juice please.

While they advise and decorate, read and weed, while they write and bake, sew and grow, while they water the plants, I walk the length of the loving land.

My own hibiscus tree is large and bright and blooming. I water that one myself.